NEVADA

A TREATY HAD BEEN BROKEN . . . A CHIEF'S
HONOR BETRAYED . . . BUT RED CLOUD
WOULD HAVE HIS VENGEANCE . . .

General Connor pushed himself flat against the
rock to wait, hoping he was out of sight of the brave.

"Grimes! Help! Henley! Help!" he shouted one
last time.

No answer. Connor felt flushed and icy at the
same time. Sweat poured off him, as cold as rain. He
didn't want to shoot himself. That was a coward's
way out. The bone butt of his gun felt cold and slippery in his hand.

A sudden, ear-piercing shriek split the air.

The general rose from his knees and swung the
pistol around, but it was already too late. The Indian
threw himself forward, knocking the gun away from
Connor's numb fingers. With savage energy Connor
pushed his opponent back.

It was only then he recognized him—Red Cloud,
the man who had forged all the Sioux tribes into a
single fighting weapon.

The chief had a knife in his hand. As the blade
plunged toward him, Connor grabbed the Indian's arm,
struggling to hold back the deadly blade. Relentlessly,
a fraction of an inch at a time, the blade moved down.

Everything seemed to slow then. Connor saw the
corded muscles in Red Cloud's neck and the sun glistening on the blade, felt the ground slip under him
as they strained against each other, heard his own
harsh breathing. . . .

SIOUX ARROWS

DONALD PORTER

A Dell/Banbury Book

Published by
Banbury Books, Inc.
37 West Avenue
Wayne, Pennsylvania 19087

Dell ® TM 681510, Dell Publishing Co., Inc.

ISBN: 0-440-07914-4

Printed in the United States of America

First printing—December 1982

Chapter 1

White clouds drifted lazily across a Wyoming sky almost too blue to be real. It was the morning of June 13, 1866. Below, spread out across the dusty parade ground of Fort Laramie, sat the chiefs, head warriors and braves of the Sioux, Cheyenne and Arapaho. Facing them from behind a plain oak table on a wooden dais were two white men: John Richards, an Indian trader, and Nathaniel Taylor, the government's latest peace emissary to the Plains Indians.

"What Man-Afraid-of-His-Horses wants to know," translated Richards, "is whether you think you're buying their lands or what with this here treaty?" He nodded at the handsome old Sioux.

The wind had shifted and Taylor had all he could do not to betray the sudden lurch of his stomach. The foul stench of unwashed bodies and uncured skins clung to these men, who dressed in hides and lived cheek by jowl with their dogs and horses.

"No, a thousand times no," he answered, swallowing against nausea. He remembered to smile his most Christian smile as he rose to answer his red brothers.

How he wished they would sometimes smile back, particularly the contingent off to his left, where Man-Afraid-of-His-Horses now waited for an answer. These were the Oglala Sioux, who Richards said were the most hostile in the crowd.

"I haven't come here to take your land," said Taylor. "I admit that in the past white men have treated the Indian badly. But now the Great Council in Washington has sent me to make sure that you are treated fairly. It was a mistake for the military to attack you last year. No, all the Great Council wants is permission for our people to travel the roads through your country to their homes and mines in Montana. Translate that, please, Mr. Richards."

The fat trader slid his chair back and shuffled to his feet. Out of the broad-lipped mouth in the flabby Anglo-Saxon face the Sioux flowed incongruously.

Taylor sat back while Richards spoke. He was in general well satisfied with his progress in Wyoming. Ever since the whites had arrived in America, they had treated the other races badly. Only last year, the Union had ended one of the bloodiest wars in history, fought in good part over wrongs to blacks. He hoped to prevent similar bloodshed between the whites and the Indians.

But could a tenderfoot Episcopal churchman from Manhattan bring peace to the Great Plains? He had, he thought, a real chance at it. He was proud to be the one to put into effect the new peace policy. Hundreds of his fellow churchmen had convinced President Andrew Johnson and Congress that it was due the Indians. On this splendid June day, with the heat roasting him in his black broadcloth suit, Taylor believed he would shortly have his treaty. He would show the nation that to come to terms with the red man you need only a decent measure of Christian forebearance and kindness, not the muskets and sabers of swaggering frontier soldiers.

Fort Laramie, Wyoming! How romantic the picture conjured up by the name when he persuaded the peace commission to send him here, and how dreary the reality. Not even a fort, actually. There were no walls, no stockade, just a couple of dozen low wooden buildings and this vast dusty parade ground plus roads leading in half a dozen directions into scrubby wilderness.

Man-Afraid-of-His-Horses was answering Trader Richards in the singsong language of the Sioux.

Richards turned to Taylor. "Man Afraid wants to know what roads you're talking about."

"Roads?"

"You said 'roads.' "

"That's what the treaty says. The Department drew it up in Washington. What's the matter with it?"

Richards' exasperated sigh always irritated Taylor. Like the old frontiersman he was, John Richards believed anybody who hadn't spent ten years in the wilderness couldn't understand anything about the Indian. Well, maybe Taylor understood something about decency and respect for others; the frontiersmen surely didn't.

"Do you mean just the Bozeman Trail, or other trails, or what?" asked Richards.

"Well, we mean the Bozeman Trail," Taylor acknowledged. "That's the essence of this agreement. But I suppose the government would like to build another if it needs it."

"They don't like 'roads,' Mr. Taylor," said Richards. "They don't even like 'road.'"

"Please don't argue with me in front of them," hissed Taylor. He struggled simultaneously to smile. "I think it's important to show unity of purpose."

"I think you'd better make it 'road' if you want Red Cloud and Man Afraid to sign this thing."

"I can't change the terms, Mr. Richards," Taylor objected. "We've been all over this. I was sent to get *this* treaty signed."

"They ain't going to sign shit then—pardon my French, sir."

Taylor stood, taking a deep breath and telling himself not to get angry at Richards. Too long in the woods and a man forgot what it was to be a Christian. He looked around at the assembled Indians and smiled again. Lord, did they *never* smile back?

"My friends," he began, "I've come a long way to be with you, some two thousand miles from the Great Council back East. I've listened to your complaints. I've heard them all and will carry them back to the Great Chief in Washington. I've come with many presents of guns, ammunition, cloth, blankets and rations, which I will give you when we have signed the treaty. I pledge my solemn word that from this day forward, white men who travel across your lands will not disturb the game. All we want is safe passage along the Bozeman Trail. It will be a condition that travelers not take so much as a rabbit or a squirrel. Translate that, Mr. Richards."

Taylor sat down again, but Richards didn't rise. "How the hell are you going to do that?" he demanded.

"Mr. Richards, will you *please* translate?"

When Richards had reluctantly complied, Man-

Afraid-of-His-Horses stood to reply. As the chief spoke, Taylor thought how sullen and sly he looked, like all the wild Oglala, how savage. Man Afraid wore deerskin leggings and moccasins embroidered with quills and beads and a loincloth that Richards said had been made from the worn buffalo skin of a tepee. A strip of embroidered deerskin almost a foot wide trailed from the loincloth and dragged behind him like some fancy tail. In his right hand he held an ornamented bag that Richards said contained his clay pipe, an object sacred to his crude religion. Taylor reflected on what children these people really were and how much the Christian culture had to give them.

"Now Man-Afraid-of-His-Horses is asking the Cheyenne and Arapaho interpreters to translate his words," Richards murmured.

"What a curious name," Taylor observed. "How can a man who's afraid of horses be such an important chief?"

Richards suppressed a laugh. "Man Afraid ain't easy to translate into English. It means everybody who meets him in battle is so scared of him they're even scared of his horses."

"Ah, the proud primitive warrior," Taylor smiled. "What is he saying now?"

Just then his glance fell on a warrior seated slightly to the right and rear of Man Afraid. The face, like the other Oglalas', was expressionless, but the eyes that met Taylor's were filled with mocking scorn.

For two weeks now Red Cloud had sat and listened with growing frustration and anger while Trader Richards translated Yellow Hair Taylor's lying speeches. He was not taken in by the cunning promises. This

5

man hoped to buy the birthright of the Sioux with a few guns, some ammunition and a thousand tricks and false words.

Red Cloud longed to challenge Yellow Hair, but it wasn't his place. He was only war captain of one Oglala band, the Bad Faces, and treaties were argued by tribal chiefs and generals. He didn't dare overstep the council of Big Bellies, so Red Cloud held his tongue day after day while Yellow Hair Taylor waved the treaty, read from it and urged the chiefs to touch the pen and live in peace.

But each night he argued against signing the document with everyone who came to his tepee. "They have only one purpose, these whites," he warned, "to slaughter the Sioux, chase away the buffalo with their iron horses and pull from the ground the yellow rock they worship."

There were members of the council who believed as he did and could speak. One of them, Old-Man-Afraid-of-His-Horses, was arguing right now that it made no sense for the Sioux and their friends the Arapaho and Cheyenne to allow the whites to use the Bozeman Trail.

But Red Cloud knew most of them weren't listening. The white man's presents had stopped their ears. Besides, what did Spotted Tail and Big Mouth care about the Bozeman Trail? Big Mouth and his people, the Laramie loafers, the ones who lived around the fort, would let the whites do whatever they liked. Spotted Tail's Brulé Sioux lived south of the Platte. The Bozeman Trail didn't pass through their hunting grounds.

"When John Bozeman came through here four years ago, we saw scarcely a dozen wagons a month,"

6

Man Afraid was saying. "Now, no sooner does one train leave us than over the hill comes another. Today there is no place on this long road where you cannot see a covered wagon! White men ride out from these wagons and shoot our deer, bear and buffalo. This trail has become an empty riverbed running through our hunting ground, a foul path that has turned away the buffalo herds."

He raised his arms and held them out. "Black Twin, Big Mouth, Spotted Tail, this road does not go through your camp or your hunting ground, but doesn't the fate of the buffalo concern you too? Haven't we Sioux been put here by Wakan-Takan, the great mystery, to care for the buffalo? Isn't this our duty? Have you forgotten the pleasures of the hunt? That we are Sioux? That we live with the buffalo as brothers, and he with us? What will Wakan-Takan say if we allow the buffalo to die?"

A stir ran through the crowd of chiefs and warriors. Man Afraid was as powerful a chief as Spotted Tail, and his argument moved the Sioux. Red Cloud felt his spirits rise. They might refuse to sign after all, except Big Mouth and his Laramie loafers.

Several of Spotted Tail's subchiefs rose now to agree with Man Afraid. Red Cloud saw that Spotted Tail too was moved. While Spotted Tail was perhaps the most respected Sioux chief present, in order to govern he needed the entire council behind him. If Man Afraid swayed the rest to his side, Spotted Tail would have to come along.

Red Cloud suppressed the urge to laugh at what was happening at the oak table. Trader Richards was translating and Yellow Hair couldn't hide his dismay. Red Cloud glanced up at the midday sun. Shortly Yel-

7

low Hair would want to stop to eat. Red Cloud and Man Afraid could use the time to consolidate the morning's work. If they got Spotted Tail on their side, they would have the combined might of the Brulé and the Oglala. No white soldiers could oppose such an alliance.

Taylor rose to speak; Red Cloud expected him to announce a recess. "I didn't come here empty-handed." Richards spoke for Taylor. "In addition to the fine presents I've brought, my government has decided to give the Sioux who sign this treaty seventy thousand dollars a year for twenty years. The Cheyenne and Arapaho who sign will receive fifteen thousand dollars yearly for the same period. We'll stop now for something to eat and meet again in two hours to sign the treaty."

From the excited stir around him, Red Cloud knew that the work Man Afraid had done this morning was wasted. So much money! Could it be true? Or was it another white man's lie? But while the money might be attractive to Sioux like Big Mouth, what besides guns could it buy wilderness tribes? And the white soldiers wouldn't let Richards sell guns to the Oglala Sioux unless they were certain that the Oglala had gone as tame as the Laramie loafers.

In 1866, a dollar bought ten to twelve times what it does today. Richards' mind reeled at the opportunities eighty-five thousand represented. He had made his living for twenty years trading with the Sioux. In his biggest year he had taken in maybe fifteen thousand dollars' worth of furs and buffalo robes. Such a windfall to the Indians! He too might get rich. He had to make sure Colonel Many Deer didn't go handing out too many trading permits. Indeed, he realized, he needed one himself, remembering sourly that essentially he had been out of business for the last two years because of the Indian trouble.

At lunch that day, Richards remarked to Taylor, who looked to him less and less like a pious ninny, "You never told me you had all that money! That's going to make a whale of a difference."

"I supposed it might," Taylor smirked. He turned to smile at their host, the commander of Fort Laramie, Colonel Henry Maynadier, whom the Indians called Many Deer. "I didn't want it to leak out, Colonel. I wanted to present the offer at just the right time." He turned back to Richards. "Perhaps this afternoon we'll get their signatures; don't you agree?"

"Yes, sir." Now was the time, while there was all this good feeling about how the negotiations were going, to call in some favors. "And then, with your permission, Colonel, I'd like to go back to trading."

Tall, slim, unruffled, Henry Maynadier had spent the Civil War in Indian country. Like the colonel's men and the Sioux, Richards found him hard to push around. Henry Maynadier knew he was often wrong about the Sioux, but he made a real effort to do right by all concerned.

Richards figured that without the colonel at Laramie, the trouble would have been a lot worse. Many Deer and old Spotted Tail were practically blood brothers if the scuttlebutt was right. Certainly Spotted Tail hadn't raised nearly the fuss about the Bozeman Trail you might have expected.

"No guns," insisted Maynadier.

"Come on!" complained Richards. "You got to let them hunt."

"No guns," repeated the colonel.

"But he's going to *give* them guns." Richards pointed a loaded fork at Taylor, who gave him a benign smile. Richards felt the old juices rise in him at the sight of it. What the hell did people need preachers for anyway?

"Presents from Congress," said Maynadier sourly. "I've got no control over Congress."

"Damnit, Colonel," said Richards, "if I can't sell them guns, what are they going to spend their money on?"

"Not on whiskey and rum either, friend," Maynadier chuckled. "But don't worry; I'm sure you'll find something to sell them."

That afternoon Red Cloud came back to the conference reluctantly. He had agreed to come to Laramie in the first place only because runners sent by the whites had promised that on signing, his Bad Faces would get the supplies, rations, guns and ammunition that were long overdue according to the treaty of 1855. The white chiefs sat before and above the seated Indians as if they ruled his people, Red Cloud thought. On the wooden table he saw a brass inkpot and a tankard holding the quills with which the chiefs were expected to make their marks on the paper.

Red Cloud had said nothing during lunch, waiting for the excitement of the offer of so much money to die down. His heart had ached to see how these white devils made proud warriors jabber like silly birds. Sioux were being bought, and bought cheaply. Somehow he had to make them see that if they were to survive as a people, they must resist these white devils.

10

Spotted Tail announced that he wanted to reply to Yellow Hair's offer. For a few moments the dignified Brulé chief stood and looked at the seated tribesmen. Spotted Tail knew how to get the attention of the chiefs. Red Cloud didn't like his closeness with the whites, but he had to admire the Brulé's dignity.

Years before, Spotted Tail had been sent to Fort Leavenworth to be executed for taking part in a murderous raid on a mail coach. Instead he had spent two pleasant years of scout duty there and learned the white man's language and ways. Unfortunately, living with the whites had given Spotted Tail a feeling of superiority. In council he sometimes acted as if he had a wisdom the other Sioux didn't have, lecturing on how the whites thought and on how powerful their weapons and numbers were. Warriors like Man Afraid, his son Young Man Afraid and Red Cloud didn't quite trust him.

"You've spoken well, Commissioner Taylor," Spotted Tail began now.

Red Cloud groaned inwardly. Why snuggle up to these white ghosts? Here was a man who had enormous influence over every warrior and chief there, and what did he do with it? He behaved like a well-trained wife in her husband's lodge.

"This is like a dream to me," Spotted Tail was saying. "For three months I've stayed here by the fort. I've eaten your rations and I've talked to Colonel Many Deer, who helped me bury my daughter in the military cemetery next to Old Smoke. I thought of all the years of hardship I spent before I came here—four years! Am I now dreaming? Will I wake to find I'm dying in a snowbank somewhere? Or am I really standing here at Laramie on a beautiful day? The air is calm to remind me that I came because you offer peace. We have been much wronged. So many roads through our country drive off our buffalo and game and plunge our hearts into grief. But now the Great Father has sent Commissioner Taylor, and he has made our hearts happy. Commissioner Taylor offers justice to fill the great hole of injustice that his people dug across the face of our land. I wish to accept the offer."

Red Cloud felt ashamed for Spotted Tail. What a way for a warrior to talk to an enemy! Yellow Hair, he saw, was flushed with pleasure as he rose to answer. Red Cloud hardened his heart, for he knew what was coming now. Big Mouth, Spotted Tail, Many Deer and Yellow Hair would fill every ear with honey.

From behind him suddenly came a loud clatter. Red Cloud and the warriors turned and saw a long column of bluecoats spilling in at the far side of the parade ground.

"Prepare to dismount!" shouted their officer. "Dismount!" A great clatter of boots and sabers rattled across the parade ground.

Alarmed, the Indians rose to their feet. Many reached for guns and cocked them. Those without guns drew bows.

"Who the hell is that?" Richards demanded of Maynadier. "I ain't never seen them soldiers before."

Taylor rose up on tiptoe and peered across the parade ground. "Isn't that a colonel on that white horse? I suspect it's Carrington."

"Carrington?" repeated Richards. "Ain't no Carrington stationed here."

"No," Taylor agreed. "Send over and ask him to join us."

"Better quiet the Indians first, Richards," Maynadier advised. To Taylor: "They get jumpy when a troop marches up next to them."

Richards snorted. "So would you if you had bluecoats chasing and killing you from here to hell and back."

Colonel Henry B. Carrington, a short, rather handsome Ohioan, was delighted to join the peace commission at the table on the wooden dais.

His gloves in his hands, occasionally slapping them nervously against his trousers, Carrington sat at the table in front of the Indians. They made him feel exposed, the way they stared at him. He fingered the little mustache he had grown to make him look older. What luck finding the Indians here, he thought. And what luck that a peace treaty was actually going to be signed! Trained as a lawyer and an engineer, Carrington had been an administrator and organizer for the Union during the Civil War. The last thing he wanted to have to do was fight an Indian war.

"Mr. Richards, tell the chiefs that Colonel Carrington has not come to harm them," Taylor suggested.

"I already did," the potbellied trader snorted. "But what's he come for? Some of them think he's going up into Powder River country."

"Yes, that's true," Carrington smiled. He sat up straighter to emphasize his military bearing. He knew he had a pretty blond face that often made other men think they could take advantage of him. Now he sought to dispel that notion before it got started. "General Cooke has sent me out to make the Bozeman Trail safe for emigrant wagons and freight travel."

"You ain't planning to stay up there?" Richards demanded.

13

"I certainly am," answered Carrington. He was amused by the man's incredulity.

"Translate Mr. Carrington's intentions for the Indians, will you, Mr. Richards?" requested Taylor.

But Richards ignored him. "They don't want the road protected," he said, eyes on Carrington. "They want it abandoned."

"Translate, will you, Mr. Richards?" insisted Taylor in a hard unchristian tone. "You have to fight with him to get your least statement spoken," he told Carrington. "Having you here is really a stroke of luck. They'll doubtless have some questions about what you're doing, but if you just assure them you have no intention of chasing them around, I feel sure we'll have their marks on paper by nightfall, and you'll have a much easier time over the next couple of years."

Carrington found himself liking the reedy churchman with the big teeth and long, thin, pale hair. He smiled and bowed slightly from the waist. "Most happy to, Mr. Taylor. You seem to be doing a commendable job here."

Taylor flushed with pleasure. "Thank you, Colonel. And I wish you success."

"Ah, I'll need more than wishes."

No sooner had Richards finished translating than a hawk-nosed member of Man Afraid's party got to his feet.

"Oh ho," said Maynadier softly. "The angry fallen angel finally rises to speak. That's Red Cloud," he told Carrington, "war chief of the Bad Faces."

"Bad Faces!" exclaimed Carrington. "How did they get—?"

"Hush up," hissed Richards. "This is important.

14

I told them you came out to add to the troops here at Laramie."

"But that's not true, Mr. Richards," Carrington protested.

He looked at Red Cloud. He saw a thin Sioux of forty or so with long straight black hair framing a stoic face. His dark eyes swept the scene with a hard gaze, making the face look as sharp and dangerous as an axe.

Red Cloud spoke. The rush of noise meant nothing to Carrington, who turned to Richards for an explanation.

"He says that a couple of days ago you, Colonel Carrington, told Chief Standing Bear of the Brulé that you were going to build forts up on the Powder River. You didn't say that, did you?"

Carrington felt naked under Richards' hard stare. "Yes, that's what I'm here to do."

Richards looked at him then as if he were an imp of the devil. "You people can't be that crazy!" the trader exclaimed. "You can't be!"

Carrington laughed nervously and looked around at Maynadier, Taylor and Richards. "But General Cooke was most specific. I have detailed plans for forts—"

"But you promised just this morning, Mr. Taylor." Richards turned to the peace commissioner. "Nobody's going to molest their game. You only want to use the road and only with their permission."

"Colonel Maynadier," Taylor said stiffly, "do you have another interpreter? I find this man insufferable."

To Carrington's relief, Richards backed down and agreed to act strictly as a translator. Through him this dialogue passed between Colonel Carrington and Red Cloud.

Red Cloud opened, "Are you going to march up into the Powder River country?"

"Yes, I am."

"You will build forts there?"

"Yes."

Red Cloud grunted. "Then you will attack our villages and kill our women and children."

"No!" Carrington was shocked. "I'm here strictly on a protective mission. My orders are very clear. I'm to protect travelers, not make war. I'm to protect your people too, Chief Red Cloud. If white people molest the Sioux, I will put a speedy stop to it."

"How many bluecoats will go into the Powder River country?" Red Cloud asked.

"Seven hundred." Carrington hitched forward. "To show you that we mean peace, my officers and I have brought our wives and children. Why, we even have a forty-piece marching band, a preacher and Christmas tree ornaments."

Carrington hoped his try at humor would ease the tension between himself and the Oglala war chief. But Red Cloud strode through the crowd to the drillmaster's platform on the side of the assembly. He leaped lightly up onto it and turned to address the company of Indians.

"I don't want Yellow Hair's presents! I don't want his money. These people come here and treat us like children who can be bribed with a bit of honey."

Like everyone else present, Carrington stared transfixed at the lithe figure on the platform. By his side, Richards translated in a low mutter. Carrington

16

felt uneasy and vaguely menaced by the ranting chief. He glanced over at his officers, who stood off to one side looking jumpy.

"We're like rabbits baited into a trap. Yellow Hair pretends to negotiate with us, promises to pay us for our road, while this other one with all the bluecoat soldiers admits he has come to steal the very road Yellow Hair is buying. Soon there will be more wagons on our hunting lands. More whites will come. We are made fools of by trick after trick. They want to take from us what Wakan-Takan has given us, take from us that without which we cannot live—our land! Think of the Pawnee." Red Cloud spat. "Traitors to their own people." He paused. "Think of the Crow." He spat again. "Driven off their land and starved to death. Living off the whites, weak as women, like those who hang around this fort and who lie when they call themselves Sioux!"

From the way the fat Indians on the right swayed in anger, Carrington gathered that these were the ones who hung around the fort. He had to admit that they didn't look so formidable as their relatives from the wilderness.

"Time was, we Lakota could hunt to the south," Red Cloud went on. "My father could ride for days and find buffalo covering the ground. Can I now? No, where the iron road crosses the plain the buffalo have fled. Except for the Oglala country north of the Platte, where can we hunt? So little is left! And this man—" he pointed a long finger at Carrington "—this man has come to steal even this little from us!"

Every head turned to look at Carrington, who felt more naked still. General Cooke had said nothing about negotiations with hundreds of angry Indians. If this treaty wasn't signed, would he be able to fulfill the mission he was charged with?

Several young braves among the Brulé Sioux now stood and peered menacingly toward Carrington and his officers. Carrington wished he had worn his pistol. He was acutely aware that the four white men at the table could be crushed by an Indian rush before his officers and men could stop it. He breathed deeply, trying to calm his pounding heart.

"Will the Lakota allow their homes to be taken?" Red Cloud shouted. He paused to let that thought sink in. "Will the Lakota allow their women and children to be starved to death? Will the Lakota allow their buffalo to be driven from where Wakan-Takan has placed them? Will they then still be Sioux warriors?" Red Cloud's voice rose. "For my part, I prefer to die fighting than to be starved to death!"

As Red Cloud spoke these last words, the young Brulé warriors who had stood made their way through the crowd to the drillmaster's platform. Here they turned to face the other Indians in obvious support of Red Cloud and in defiance of Spotted Tail's talk of peace. Half a dozen young Oglala and Arapaho braves rose. Then five Cheyenne moved in a tight group to join the little band with Red Cloud.

Throwing his head back, Red Cloud shouted, "Better to die on the battlefield than to die old! If we fight together, we can drive these pale devils out and keep our homes and our way of life. Yes, it will be hard, but isn't it better to die with a bow in your hand than with a begging bowl? We are defending our last hunting grounds! We must win!"

My God, thought Carrington, he's asking for war!

Chapter 2

When Red Cloud strode off the parade ground, it astonished him to see a third of the five hundred warriors and chiefs rise and follow him. Exultant over his audacity, jubilant at his success, he marched the three miles back to his camp.

That afternoon and evening he sat in his tepee and received the congratulations of the young men while his wife Pretty Owl passed out bowls of buffalo stew. They would ride with him, they swore, against this White Eagle Chief. They would send these bluecoat soldiers running, just as last year they had sent the soldiers of the Star Chiefs scurrying back to Laramie.

Though grateful for their support, Red Cloud still didn't know the full effects of his rashness. Of course these young men would cheer a fighting speech, but what would the Big Bellies say? What would they do? Red Cloud had been banished from the tribe before. For his impulsive speech to the white ghosts the elders might brand him an outlaw and drive him from Sioux gatherings. After all, he was only a warrior chief of one band. While he was important among the Bad Faces, he had almost no influence with the other Sioux.

Red Cloud sighed as he looked around the tepee crowded with excited young men. It wasn't wise to stir up these braves without the Big Bellies' permission.

He heard voices outside and then Young-Man-Afraid-of-His-Horses, Man Afraid's son, entered the tepee. Red Cloud made a place for his best friend. Pretty Owl quickly brought the old chief's son a bowl of stew in which floated choice pieces of buffalo hump.

"Well said, Red Cloud." Young Man Afraid's face was flushed with excitement. "You can count on me to ride with you!"

Red Cloud felt better with his friend's support. "There is nobody I'd rather have. How is your father?"

Red Cloud was asking what Old Man Afraid had thought of his speech. Both knew that without the old chief's support, Red Cloud wasn't likely to gain the approval of the Big Bellies. Without it he wouldn't have enough warriors to drive out Carrington.

"Ah, you know my father," Young Man Afraid laughed. "You shouldn't worry about him. It was the same when we used to go out after Crow and Pawnee horses. Remember? He would tell me over and over again I couldn't go, tell me he wouldn't talk to me again if I did. But after we'd sneak off and come back with the horses and a few scalps, he'd brag about what a brave warrior he had for a son."

Red Cloud and the other warriors laughed.

"My father's going to come over here tonight," Young Man Afraid said softly as the laughter stopped.

"Here?" Red Cloud exclaimed. "That wouldn't be right. I'll go to him."

"Too late. He went over to see Spotted Tail."

Red Cloud's heart sank. The old man probably had gone to assure Spotted Tail that their bargaining strategy remained the same. Tomorrow the Oglala and the Brulé would speak as one. They might even decide that Red Cloud should take back the words he had flung at Yellow Hair, but he wouldn't. Never. He didn't want to defy the elders, but couldn't they see? Wasn't it plain? After the whites took over the land, after they built their walled forts, after they set up the big guns that shot once on the ground and again in the air, it was too late to stop them. With such fortifications it became almost impossible to drive them out. The only reason they had been able to whip them last year was that the bluecoats hadn't established a garrison yet. If they attacked this new White Eagle at once, they could drive him back too.

But for this task Red Cloud needed the support of the council of elders. If he continued to cross them, he would never be invited to sit with the Big Bellies as an equal, no matter how many coups he accumulated. He would get a reputation as an adventurer and be forever left out of the most important deliberations. He would have no influence over his people's welfare.

Red Cloud asked if someone would run to Spotted Tail's camp and ask Old Man Afraid to wait there for him. He wanted to talk to both chiefs.

One of young Crazy Horse's admirers, a boy named Dog Leg who was always trying to make himself useful to the warriors, volunteered. The men jeered at his boyish eagerness.

"I can go and come back before any of these bags of wind could get there in the first place," in-

21

sisted Dog Leg, and indeed he was back in an hour. Man Afraid would wait for Red Cloud, he reported, and Spotted Tail would be happy to meet with him.

Trailing forty men and boys, Red Cloud set out. It was almost midnight when they reached Spotted Tail's camp. It was crowded with excited Brulé Sioux, as if the events of the day allowed no sleep. Red Cloud recognized Cheyenne paint on some of the braves. The escort that led his party to Spotted Tail's tepee had to push its way through more than a hundred men surrounding it.

Inside, as custom dictated, Red Cloud went to the right. Spotted Tail indicated where he should sit. The walls of the tepee had been rolled up, and Red Cloud realized that the men around the tepee had been watching and listening to the deliberations of the Big Bellies within. All the major chiefs at the Laramie conference were there, including Man Afraid of the Oglala, Standing Elk and Swift Bear of the Corn Band Brulé and Black Horse and Dull Knife of the Cheyenne. Behind them stood Red Leaf of the Brulé; Red Cloud returned this friend's nod.

As befitted a Sioux chief, Red Cloud kept his face expressionless, but his heart pounded. He was seated in the first row with the most important Big Bellies, an honor he had never before received.

Spotted Tail chanted his "We're here together" song as he made a ceremony of mixing sweet grass, sage and cedar leaves, then sprinkled on a little buffalo-chip powder. At the chief's side, the Brulé shaman lit a little incense of sweet grass and chanted. Red Cloud felt good that such care was being taken. It meant that what was to come was important and that his presence was being taken seriously.

Spotted Tail took the pipe in his left hand, holding the bowl so the stem did not point away from himself. Slowly he filled the bowl, carefully tamping the mixture with the first finger of his right hand. Around him everyone watched to see from the way he handled the pipe ceremony how it was with him. Spotted Tail finally lit the pipe with a coal, for as everybody knew, the spirit of the fire was in the coal, not in the blaze.

Spotted Tail astonished Red Cloud by pointing the stem of the pipe at him. This meant the smoke was made as an offering to him. Then the pipe was passed around, each chief taking just a puff or two. The finished pipe was passed back to Spotted Tail, who cleared a little spot in the earth and deposited the ashes there so that no one would step on them.

Red Cloud began to feel more at ease. Perhaps he was wrong to separate himself from his people the way he had this afternoon. A coal could not burn without a fire; it went out. Neither could a Lakota exist without his people.

For some little while no one spoke. Outside chatter drifted in. Dogs barked. Children wailed. A woman sang a lullaby. Then the wind shifted and a fetid odor wafted in under the rolled-up tepee walls. This wasn't a Bad Face camp; Red Cloud's nose told him that. Ugh, how these Brulé stank!

Man Afraid began at last. "One here spoke today without the blessing of the council. Tonight I came to talk to Spotted Tail about it."

Oh, no! Sitting here wasn't to be any honor, after all. "I had to speak what was in my heart," Red Cloud acknowledged.

"These people learned last year that they cannot kick Sioux," said Spotted Tail. "Besides, this is a

23

new commissioner. He's offering us money and guns. Red Cloud, they're even willing to sign a pledge not to hunt our game."

"They've lied before," Red Cloud argued. "I don't trust them. I trust my gun, my bow and my lance."

The Big Bellies stirred restlessly. "I know the ways of these people," Spotted Tail insisted. "I lived at Fort Leavenworth for two years. We Indians only fight in the summer. We must stop to hunt in the fall or we will starve. The whites don't have to hunt and can fight all year long. We always have our women and children with us and must feed and protect them. They leave theirs in the East."

Red Cloud nodded toward the Cheyenne chiefs. "Two years ago Black Kettle of your tribe had nothing but friendly families in his camp," he said. "They invited him to camp near Fort Lyon and peace was certain, wasn't it?"

They felt so full of shame no Cheyenne could answer him. Two years ago Colonel John M. Chivington of the Colorado volunteers had been determined to strike a blow at the Indians, and he hadn't cared whether that blow fell on friendly tribesmen or hostiles. The colonel concentrated a large force near Denver, mostly rough miners from the Colorado mining camps. Making a swift and secret march, Chivington reached Fort Lyon and threw a screen of pickets about the post to keep any friendly white from slipping through to warn his intended victims. At dawn on November 29, 1864, his men rode into Black Kettle's camp, taking the village by surprise and shooting down men, women and children as they ran out of the lodges.

The Cheyenne fled to a dry creek bed, where whooping miners surrounded them and butchered them all, the women and children as well as the warriors. The survivors, dozens out of hundreds, fled to a Cheyenne camp at Smoky Hill Fork, where they arrived nearly naked with frozen hands and feet. Many of the wounded later died. Others lost toes or feet.

"These people aren't Chivington," Spotted Tail objected. "They've explained that their leaders in the East now want peace with us."

"That's what they told Black Kettle," Red Cloud grunted.

The mention of Black Kettle saddened every chief present. For a moment there was silence again. Then Spotted Tail broke it. "The council has decided that it's wisest to bargain for all we can get, particularly for guns and ammunition. Now that so much money has been offered, we are tempted to allow the whites to pass on the road as they want and buy the guns we need from Trader Richards."

"So much money buys many guns," Dull Knife grinned. "For twenty years! Many guns!"

"If they'll sell them to you," Red Cloud put in. "Have you been able to buy guns in the past three years?"

Red Cloud saw the others stir uneasily and heard muttering from the watchers outside the tepee. None there liked being so dependent on the whites for guns and ammunition, but no Sioux or Cheyenne could make guns or powder. And since the disappearance of the huge herds of buffalo, they needed guns.

"We've talked among ourselves, Red Cloud," Spotted Tail announced. "We don't want to go to war against these whites."

"They can be beaten," insisted Red Cloud. "We made a start last year with the troops they sent against

25

us. Trader Richards says they have a big war with themselves at the edge of the water. They're weak now."

"No." Spotted Tail shook his head. "That war was settled last year."

"Settled?" Red Cloud repeated.

"Many Deer told me the bluecoats won. They will be free to come here and fight us if we oppose them."

This news stopped Red Cloud. As usual, Spotted Tail knew things—or said he did—about the whites that tipped the balance toward what he wanted the tribes to do. But perhaps he was right. The Big Bellies were shrewd. They had led their people for years both in battle and in such deliberations as this.

"What is this road, anyway?" asked Standing Elk of the Corn Band Brulé. "Let them march on it. Let them pay us for the game they shoot. Let them march through and vanish out the other side of our hunting land. As long as they don't stay, what does it matter?"

"It's just the beginning," argued Red Cloud. "You see Big Mouth, Big Ribs and Blue Horse?" These were the leading Laramie loafers, who sickened every real Sioux. "That is what we will all become if we take the white men's handouts. In time we'll obey them the way a dog obeys us."

"My Oglala brother speaks well," Man Afraid agreed. "Many of us want to fight the whites. After all, this road doesn't go through your country, Spotted Tail. We Oglala must live with these white ghosts in our midst, and the more I'm around these people, the more they make me sick."

The old man shuddered. Red Cloud felt a wave

of hope. Man Afraid wasn't so powerful as Spotted Tail, but he still had influence. Maybe together they could sway this council yet.

Red Leaf spoke now. "I agree with Red Cloud. We fight them as men—as Lakota—or live as women. Better to die fighting than grow old."

Dull Knife and Black Horse said this wasn't a Cheyenne fight. Red Cloud wondered if Chivington had beaten the Cheyenne so badly they would never fight again. Seeing no reason to fight, Standing Elk and Swift Bear both sided with Spotted Tail.

"Join us," Spotted Tail urged Red Cloud. "Put your hatred of whites in the bag. There are good whites and bad ones, as there are good and bad Indians. We have no choice. We must get along with them."

"Fight with us," urged Red Cloud, "or the Lakota will lose the way of Lakota."

"Eventually they'll shoot us down if we don't learn to live with them," Spotted Tail warned. "I've lived with them. I know."

Spotted Tail's conviction made Red Cloud hesitate a moment. Was the Brulé chief right? Was Red Cloud about to bring down the wrath of a Chivington or a Harney, who had massacred the Brulé at the Blue Water in Nebraska?

"We'll go up on the Powder River tomorrow," said Old Man Afraid in his reedy voice. They all looked at him. "We'll have a Sun Dance. We'll ask Wakan-Takan what to do." He paused for the statement to sink in. "We'll listen to the answer." The elderly Lakota looked around the tepee, his glance taking in all the chiefs and warriors. "Come with us.

Red Cloud will submit to the dance. He'll ask Wakan-Takan if we should fight these whites. You Cheyenne too, come dance with us."

Red Cloud's heart leaped and fell almost at the same instant. Yes, he would dance the Sun Dance. The idea of letting go, of submitting to a higher power to guide him, was a relief. He saw at once that he had been guilty of the old sin Man Afraid had long struggled to help him overcome: trying to make life turn out his way. Still, to submit to the last day of the Sun Dance! He shrank even from the thought of the ordeal. On the last day the guide or shaman who led the dancers pierced each dancer's chest with skewers and tied those skewers to long rawhide thongs. These were tied to the top of the pole in the center of the Sun Dance circle. The dancers pulled against the skewers stuck under their skin and struggled to pull them clear of the flesh. That struggle could take hours. The skin, elastic there, might stretch out as far as a man's elbow or wrist before the skewers ripped through. Normally only young men seeking a vision to guide them through adult life endured the pain. Red Cloud had taken part twice before, the last time when he was in his twenties. Now he was over forty. It would go hard, but Man Afraid was right. It was the one way to make sure that his anger toward the whites was not sent by bad *wakan*.

For another hour the chiefs considered Man Afraid's proposal. The entire Sioux nation, the separate tribes of Oglala, Sans Arcs, Brulé, Hunkpapa, Minneconjou, Two Kettles and Blackfoot, gathered every July to dance the Sun Dance together. The tribes joined each year only for these three weeks, as the land could not support such a large number of ponies and people for long. But Red Cloud saw how uneasy the invitation had made Dull Knife of the Cheyenne and Spotted Tail and Standing Elk. He knew why. If they or their warriors got a vision from Wakan-Takan that told them to fight, fight they must. Maybe they would fight and die, part of a wakan order they didn't completely understand.

"Red Cloud and Man Afraid have spoken well," said Red Leaf. "My people will be with them at this Sun Dance. And we will stay here to listen to what Yellow Hair has to offer."

The others murmured agreement and a time was chosen for the dance. Spotted Tail's clay pipe was re-filled with tobacco, sage and sweet grass and he passed it around. Everybody took the ritual four pulls.

When Man Afraid and Red Cloud rose to go, it was almost dawn. It cheered Red Cloud to see that the crowd outside Spotted Tail's tepee had grown during the long night. As they passed through it, Red Cloud heard many murmurs:

"I'll ride where you ride, Red Cloud."

"Better to die fighting than to starve."

The words encouraged him. He might not have the support of the Big Bellies, but he definitely had the young braves on his side. Enough of them and he wouldn't need the Big Bellies to send the Little White Chief running back to Laramie.

Chapter 3

On June 15, 1866, Colonel Henry Carrington had the following order posted on his command's bulletin board at Fort Laramie:

> The pending treaty between the United States and the Sioux Indians at Fort Laramie renders it the duty of every soldier to treat all Indians with kindness. Every Indian who is wronged will visit his vengeance upon any white man he may meet. As soldiers are sent to preserve the peace of the border and to prevent warfare as much as to fight well when warfare becomes indispensable, it will be considered a very gross offense to wrong or insult an Indian.

"That's the stupidest thing I've ever seen," said Captain Fred Brown, one of Carrington's officers. "Colonel Schoolmarm thinks you can tame a bear by sticking out your hand with honey on it, but old Grizzly's just going to bite it off."

Lieutenant George Grummond laughed. "Maybe

it'll work. I don't want to get shot full of arrows up there."

"Work!" jeered Brown. A small dark man from upstate New York, Brown had been through the Civil War in a regiment that conducted only mop-up and patrol operations, and he was ashamed that he had missed "real" combat. "I learned in the Conflict that you had to push a bayonet if you wanted peace. Them Indians! Why, just look at them!"

He peered around at the vast parade ground of Fort Laramie. At nine in the morning, some Sioux and Cheyenne were already seated on their buffalo robes. The two officers knew that by ten o'clock the grounds would be aswarm with Indians dressed in all the skins, feathers and fur that the Big Horn region could provide.

"They smell like hogs that been rolling in their own shit—no, worse than that." Brown hawked and spat.

His companion laughed. George Grummond had been married not four weeks before, and it took a great deal to upset his sunny disposition these days. His Frances was with him, and he was young and delighted to be alive. This rugged country, so different from his home state of Vermont, staggered him with its abundant game and vast spaces. The lieutenant hadn't fought in the Conflict, as his new friend called it, but he wished he had.

"That business with the ugly chief yesterday," Grummond said, "doesn't seem to have made much difference. The Indians are all coming back for the conference just like nothing happened."

"Shit, I don't like this duty. I'm not an engineer," Brown whined.

"You don't need to be. Colonel Carrington is."

"That's just it. I'm a soldier. I fight. The only way to handle these savages is to go out there and whip their tails, then talk."

Grummond shook his head and grinned. "Come on. We can get some coffee at the BOQ."

The bachelor officers' quarters at Fort Laramie were called New Bedlam. Here the garrison's unmarried officers, hundreds of miles from civilized pleasures, manufactured their own. Their whiskey was rawer, their parties louder and their women wilder than back East, being black laundresses and whores from Squaw Town, the nearby Sioux camp.

In the almost deserted sitting room of the BOQ, Carrington's two officers found coffee and conversation as well. Captain Robert Jeffers, a large red-nosed officer from Philadelphia, seemed eager to chat.

"I'm glad I ain't going up there with you," Jeffers admitted. "Your colonel let you shoot game?"

"No," Brown grunted, "and we hear you ain't allowed either."

"We're allowed to stick them with our sabers." Jeffers winked broadly.

"Sabers!" exclaimed Grummond. "What can you kill with a saber?"

"Antelope. Deer. Buffalo." Jeffers grinned wickedly and then looked pious.

"That's impossible."

The captain's red nose seemed to shine at them. "They say the Laramie sabers are lethal at forty yards."

"Oh, he's pulling our leg," Brown shrugged.

Jeffers went on, "You got to take care of yourself out here, boys, 'cause ain't nobody else going to take care of you. Have some more coffee. Where you're going you ain't going to have much coffee or anything else. Did you bring your bear overcoats? I hope they're warm. You ain't never seen snow and the great northern wind like you get up here."

"You've never been to Vermont then," Grummond cheerfully observed.

"You ain't never been out here in the winter, either, friend." Jeffers' hard little eyes narrowed. "If I was you, I'd trot me over to the sutler's and lay me down as many kegs of whiskey as my pocketbook could stand."

"Why's that?" Brown asked.

Jeffers gave them another wink. "The paymaster don't get out here but twice a year, and I'll bet there'll be times when the sutler runs out of supplies, if you get what I mean. The man with a few extra kegs of rum—why, he can swap them for just about anything he wants. If it gets as lonely on the Powder River as it does here, why, I'd take me all the comfort I could get my hands on."

Brown and Grummond looked at each other, not sure their legs weren't being pulled again.

"Course, the best cure for the lonelies is having a few redskins to chase," Jeffers laughed.

"Our commander loves the noble red man," Brown remarked.

"That's a pity." Jeffers looked thoughtful. "But you can change that right fast."

"How?"

"Why, just shoot at the first two or three Indians you see."

"Shoot?" Grummond was puzzled. "Shoot if they do what? Suppose they're not doing anything?"

"Don't worry. They'll be doing something or they

33

wouldn't be Indians. After you get their attention with a couple of broadsides, your commander will see enough action to make sure you do some hard riding and shooting. Best hunting in the world, Indians."

At that moment, Trader John Richards stepped inside to see if he couldn't find a cup of coffee at the BOQ. As he crossed the sitting room with its usual squalid catchall of officers' tunics, belts, dirty dishes and worn boots, the three officers stopped talking and looked up at him.

"Morning, boys. Unless anybody objects, I aim to warm myself up with some of this hot coffee."

He recognized Jeffers and reckoned the two younger men were with Carrington's outfit. Maybe if he was clever about it he could get some more information out of them.

"Help yourself. Just put your penny in the jug, Trader," invited Jeffers.

"Aren't you the translator for the conference?" one of the young officers asked.

"That I am, me boys." Richards surveyed the three at the table.

He knew the impression he made, a confident man in his fifties who must know all there was to know about life on the frontier. He also knew he had something of the manner of a tough sergeant major, which meant these young officers would tend to trust him. He poured a cup of coffee and spilled some into his saucer to cool.

"I ain't seen you young squirts around here." Richards had decided to push them a bit. "You part of Carrington's overland circus?"

Brown and Grummond laughed. "That's a good name for it," Grummond said.

34

He and Brown introduced themselves as Jeffers got up to go drill some recruits.

"You really got a forty-piece band with you?" Richards asked.

"Hell, yes," Brown snorted. "We don't have more than forty rounds for each man, but we got us a band."

Richards shook his head and slurped up his saucer of coffee, then carefully poured out another. "Y'all got more guns and soldiers on the way though."

Brown glanced at Grummond, who seemed fascinated by the trader's coffee-pouring act. "That's something of a military secret," the captain drawled.

Richards peered over the saucer. "I hope somebody in your command knows the answer, young sir."

"Why?" Brown demanded, stung.

"Because your boss didn't make much of a friend of Red Cloud yesterday."

Grummond tore his eyes off the saucer of coffee and spoke. "The chief who made that speech? We talked to the peace commissioner last night in the officers' mess. He's about to sign a treaty."

"Not with Red Cloud, he ain't," denied Richards.

"So what?" Brown sneered.

"So Red Cloud will fight you boys. Better tie your hair tight on your head."

"He'll fight? Even if others sign the treaty?" Grummond was shocked.

"Sure."

"You mean he's an outlaw?" Brown looked avid.

"Yes and no."

"What does that mean?" The captain glared at him.

"Years ago Red Cloud had a run-in with Bull

35

Bear of the Brulé and killed him. He became something of an outlaw then; took his family and moved
away. But lately he's been trying to come back into
the big Sioux flock. And he's got two hundred and
fifty lodges with him."

"Lodges?" repeated Grummond. "You mean tepees?"

"Yeah. That's five hundred warriors. I know what
Taylor thinks—that if he gets Spotted Tail, Standing
Elk and Swift Bear to sign his treaty, he's got the
Sioux. But if you ask me, five hundred warriors is
some outlaw band."

"Almost an army," Grummond agreed.

"How do you know so much about the Sioux?"
Brown asked.

"I married one of them," Richards told them.
"All my sons and daughters are half Oglala."

"Half what?" asked the lieutenant.

"The local tribe," Richards explained, "of which
Red Cloud has one band, the Bad Faces. I've hunted
and horsed around with them more'n any other white
man."

"Bad Faces," Brown sneered. "They'll have an
even worse face when they catch sight of our guns."

"Lakota?" Richards laughed at the suggestion.

"What's Lakota?" Lieutenant Grummond was beginning to lose patience.

"That's what the Sioux call themselves. Means
'the men,' and for damn good reason."

"Horseshit," Brown snapped.

Richards shook his head. "That attitude is what
got Cole and Walker into all that trouble last year.
They went hunting Sioux, found them and got bottled

36

up. Wound up eating their own horses raw before they was rescued."

He leaned forward. "The Sioux love to take chances in battle; it's what proves them a man. Ain't a man in this world more loyal to his lodge brothers than a Sioux brave. He'll gladly, proudly, lay down his life as he sings what a brave warrior he is. He'll trick and cheat anyone from outside his tribe. That's how they advance in rank, with bravery and cunning. How do you think they've managed to survive?" He paused.

"And Sioux don't just kill their enemies; they mutilate them. Woman cheats on a Sioux brave, he cuts off her nose and ears. A boy has to endure pain almost from the day he's born or they make him into a woman. There ain't a white man or another Indian on the whole continent could stand the pain of hanging from skewers stuck in him for half a day like they do in the Sun Dance. But every year Sioux braves by the dozen do it. Yup, you think about your scalps before you go running around up there on the Powder like that ass Jeffers told you to do."

From the nervous way the two young officers glanced at each other, Richards knew he had hit his mark. He walked over to freshen his coffee. "How many men you got with you?"

"Enough," Brown grunted.

"Look, lad, I can go out there and count them," Richards pointed out.

Brown eyed him coldly. "Colonel Maynadier said you were almost an Indian. Whose side are you on?"

Richards smiled broadly. "Ain't my skin white?"

"Yeah, but being you're married to a Sioux and all, maybe you've changed sides."

"I'm a trader, that's all. I buy their furs and hides and I sell them supplies. Been doing it for—oh, more'n twenty years now. I got me a house up on the Platte. All you might say is that I'm an honorary Sioux. I'm still a white man. I don't want no war up there on the Powder River. It's terrible for business."

All three were silent again. Then Richards went on in a more reflective tone. "Last year, Cole and Walker had three thousand cavalry between them." He looked at them. "Three thousand! You didn't come marching in here yesterday with no three thousand cavalry, more like eight hundred or a thousand."

"Seven hundred," Brown admitted.

"And they looked pretty green to me, not that I'm any expert on the U. S. Army."

"I don't think most of those kids were ever on a horse up until a month ago," Grummond agreed. "They're recruits, not cavalry."

"And ain't they carrying muskets?" asked Richards. "I didn't think the army even issued them any more."

"But we're signing a treaty!" protested Grummond. "We've been sent up here for—well, it's almost picket duty."

"I wouldn't be so sure what it's going to be," Richards warned them. "Red Cloud and Old Man Afraid don't want you to build those forts."

"Well, they may wish they'd signed this treaty while they had the chance," Brown maintained. "A musket ball travels a lot farther than an arrow."

"Yeah, that's true," Richards conceded. "On the other hand, a thousand warriors can shoot about five thousand arrows while seven hundred soldiers reload their old-fashioned muskets."

* * *

The next morning Taylor discussed an entirely different approach to the Indian problem with two more members of Carrington's party. These were Reverend and Mrs. Clarence Darcy Simmons, lately of the South Commons Episcopal Church in Boston, a brother church to Taylor's Manhattan pulpit.

"I envy you," said Taylor to Cynthia Simmons, who was so striking that most men, ministers or not, had a hard time not addressing her instead of her pudgy husband. "I must wend my way back to civilization, but you two have the opportunity of a lifetime, to take the word of our Savior to heathens, just as He did. To found an entirely new church out here!"

"It *is* exciting." The Reverend Simmons, a moonfaced man with a modest paunch, answered for his wife. The thirty-six-year-old Simmons had risen rapidly in the church, having had eight increasingly important parishes in the last sixteen years. While his sermons were sometimes hard to follow, he was a patient counselor and a genius at raising money from his parishioners. The latter talent excused his faults to every board of alderman he had ever worked for.

But at this stage in his career, Simmons had needed something more than just another rich parish. To be considered for a bishopric he needed a different kind of challenge. Because he felt guilty about not serving as a chaplain in the Civil War, he determined to go to the western frontier and bring Christ to the savages. It would "leather him," as he liked to term it.

"I think these savages will be ready for Christ," Taylor intoned. He gave them a thin smile, as if he saw more than they did. "I've dealt with them now for a couple of months. You learn. Of course, I don't think more than one white man out of forty has treated the Indian right since the pilgrims landed."

"Very true." Simmons and his wife murmured agreement. Her bright, long-lashed eyes focused politely on Taylor's face.

"That's part of what you and I are doing here," the commissioner went on. "When I get down on my knees every day, I thank God we finally stopped the army before it killed every Indian."

Simmons shook his head sadly. "Sometimes a Christian soldier seems a contradiction in terms."

"I know, but they did free the slaves. We won that one."

Simmons nodded and sighed in bewilderment over the mysterious ways of the Divine Shaper.

"This Colonel Carrington you're with," Taylor probed. "He seems like a decent man."

"We've found him to be a Christian commander." Simmons took his wife's hand. Cynthia gave him a quick smile and covered his hand with her free one, then pulled both away. She was three years younger than her husband; they had been married for seven years. Back home in Boston it had been thought a splendid match. Clarence Simmons obviously wasn't going to be one of those mousy churchmen whose only answer to adversity was prayer. Cynthia had been eager to support him in the work of the Lord and to bear him and the world half a dozen more of Christ's standard-bearers. The trouble was, the Lord didn't seem to want any more Simmons standard-bearers and over the years they had become more and more depressed with the growing realization that Cynthia would never conceive. Clarence knew his duty; he was too wise, too kind, too forbearing to reproach her for this disappointment, but Cynthia sensed that she had let him down and that he could never forgive her.

"Colonel Carrington doesn't travel on Sundays like some commanders," Cynthia added. "I don't know if you saw the orders he posted two days ago, but he works hard to keep his men restrained to a civilized code."

"I like to think that I've had some little influence with Colonel Carrington," murmured Simmons.

"Thank God some of us have come out here." Taylor's expression was grim. "One of my most important tasks when I get back home will be to persuade more people who believe in the peace policy to come out here to influence others."

"We've made a point of getting to know the junior officers," Cynthia said. Clarence smiled at her, but she was looking at Taylor. "We invite them over in the evenings, a practice I shall continue when we're on the Powder River, and try to teach them that the Indian has a soul just as they do."

"Ah, but you know youth," put in Simmons. This time his fond glance caught her eye. "They like to kick up their heels. Unfortunately, that sometimes involves doing harm to someone else."

"Well, I can't tell you how much I think of your work," Taylor smiled. "It will save lives. Not that I think a capable commander like Colonel Carrington needs reminding of his duties, but if we had people like you spread out across the West—if we had had them for the past fifty years—we wouldn't have spilled the blood of thousands of red souls. That stain will never be bleached from the fabric of America."

For a few moments the three were so moved they could hardly speak.

41

Simmons finally broke the silence. "When you go back to New York and Washington, there is something you can do for us."

"My dear boy, anything! What is it?"

"Colonel Carrington has brought seven hundred men to keep the peace on the Bozeman Trail. Our supporters have convinced Congress and the generals that he should not have more."

"I dread to think of what adventures too many troops and too many arms would spark," Taylor agreed, shuddering.

"Precisely," replied Simmons. "Repeating rifles, for instance. Soldiers must try new toys, but with muskets they won't be quite so bold. If you can convince them to continue to hold back men, arms and ammunition, I think it will give your treaty enough time to take hold. Don't you agree?"

"Yes, yes, I do!" Taylor gazed off into the middle distance as he examined the future. "If we can show here that the peace policy can work, that more men and arms are not the answer to the Indian problem, then we can duplicate this work across the country."

"Yes, but without such lobbying, I don't think our policy will have time to work." Simmons shook his head.

"My dear boy, what courage!" Taylor seized the young clergyman's hand and gave him a fervent look. "My boy, you have my word that I will not let you down. While you and your brave lady are saving heathen souls, leading them to Christ, I shall work to make certain the army doesn't undermine your efforts. My God, it's the very least I can do!"

Chapter 4

On June 17, the day Colonel Carrington was to march his "overland circus" up into Powder River country to choose sites for the forts, Maynadier entertained Carrington and his second in command, Captain Tenodor Ten Eyke, at breakfast in his quarters.

"By God, Tenodor, enjoy this," said Carrington as they downed eggs, fried hash, biscuits, coffee, home-made jam and country butter. "I suspect it's going to be months before we feast like this again."

"Possibly years, sir," Ten Eyke sighed. Tall, blond, muscular, Tenodor Ten Eyke was a "galvanized Yankee," a former Confederate officer who had been captured in the Civil War, grown increasingly discouraged and hungry and signed up with the Union army for service on the frontier to get out of his Yankee prison camp. His Southern speech and manners separated him from Carrington and the other officers on this expedition. Carrington, however, had insisted that he be his second because of his lengthy and distinguished combat record. The colonel figured the former Rebel would unbend once they were out in the wilderness.

Maynadier opened a humidor and offered them long, thin cigars. "I'll give you thirty of these to take with you, Henry. Damn few good cigars where you two're going."

Carrington and Ten Eyke each took one and Maynadier lit them. The Fort Laramie commander looked fresh and relaxed this morning; he told them the reason for his good mood.

"That business with Red Cloud—well, that worried all of us who've been out here for any time, but I think it's blown over. I've sat in on a lot of these talks, but this time Spotted Tail, Standing Elk, Swift Bear and even the Cheyenne, Dull Knife and Black Horse, sound like they're finally ready to sign. They're sick of fighting and they want supplies."

"Will you send me word about what happens?" requested Carrington.

"Of course. If Captain Ten Eyke will work with my people, I think we should set up a regular series of pony runs for mail."

"Sir," asked Ten Eyke, "how much of a problem do you think we'll have with the Indians?"

Maynadier considered. He had commanded Fort Laramie for five years. What he had to say was not simple. "Captain, the Indian is a funny creature. I know him and I don't know him. The longer I'm around him, the more I realize I don't know about him. I don't mean to speak in riddles, but that's what it's like."

Carrington and Ten Eyke exchanged glances. "What do you mean?" Carrington asked.

Maynadier sighed. "If I had to make a prediction, I'd say you should have easy duty up there. You get a couple of good, solid forts built before winter, lay up plenty of firewood, and I think you'll make it fine. You're going to have to act like policemen, patrol the Bozeman Trail, settle disputes between wagon masters and emigrants, lend a hand with things like wagon repair. Charge them for such services. I wouldn't let regulations get in my way too much." Maynadier winked at them.

Ten Eyke asked, "But what about attacks? How good is this treaty?"

"Hang the treaty," Carrington put in. "I mean the Indian no harm. He'll soon get to know me. I'm sure there will be some sticky moments, but in the long run everything will be fine. I'm not a hothead like Harney or Chivington or Connor, chasing him around the countryside to tame him. Let him live his life and me mine. I'll make sure our men don't abuse him. We've baited these poor people unmercifully. I'll keep the wagon trains from molesting their game, which seems to be the most important thing to them. Once things settle down, why, I'm sure we'll get along fine."

"I get along with them," said Maynadier. "Of course, the Sioux have always had a fondness for Laramie."

"Why's that?" asked Ten Eyke.

"They started traveling here fifty, sixty years ago. No, I think if you have any problems, it'll be with Red Cloud and Man Afraid and maybe Man Afraid's son. They're still full of themselves for the licking they gave Cole and Walker last year. Of course our policy was different last year. Then it was whip them into being peaceful. Now it's supposed to be cheaper to buy them off."

"And all those Indians are still up there?" That hadn't occurred to Ten Eyke before.

"They're all still up there," Maynadier nodded. "Now, some of them will sign this treaty, but some won't."

"But Spotted Tail will, and I thought he was the head Sioux," Carrington sounded plaintive.

"The first thing you have to learn is how independent these people are, Colonel. Spotted Tail's only got his two thousand Brulé under loose control, and Red Cloud is still full of piss and vinegar."

"How many warriors does Red Cloud have?" asked Ten Eyke.

"That's the good part," Maynadier grinned. "Most of his life, Red Cloud's been something of an outcast. He's not really a chief as I understand these things. Oh, he'll gather a few hotheads, but if you show him that he can't push you around, I don't think you'll have much of a problem."

"You sound pretty sure." Ten Eyke cocked an eyebrow. "I'll be going out on patrol, and I'd like to know if he's going to attack me or not."

"There'll be attacks," Maynadier assured him. "The wagon trains have had some if the word I get back from Bozeman City is right, but nothing you can't handle." He grinned again. "You're the army. They're afraid of soldiers and guns. Just your presence up there is going to make them think twice. That's what General Cooke's sending you for.

"Another thing. You've got howitzers. If there's one thing the Indian is terrified of, it's a howitzer.

Fire it over their heads and normally they run away. And there's something else that may reduce the chance of conflict."

"What's that?" asked Carrington.

"I'm going to push Taylor not to give out all the presents to Spotted Tail and his gang right away," said Maynadier. "I want to hold some back as an enticement to Red Cloud and Man Afraid. Come this winter, if it's as bad as last year's, the Bad Face Oglala are going to be hungry. If you can get in touch with them, let them know we've got provisions for them, they might come in and sign the treaty."

"Will they be likely to keep their word if they do sign, sir?" asked Ten Eyke.

"Not particularly," Maynadier admitted. "But they'll remember where they got their grub. An Indian isn't any dumber than a private, Captain. He can remember where to find the hand that feeds him, and he knows it ain't the better part of wisdom to bite it."

Carrington and Ten Eyke smiled. "We'll do all we can to open up communications with them," Carrington said.

"You'll likely get a couple of traders up there," Maynadier added. "John Richards you've met and there's a chap called Joe Bissonnette. You'll have to watch them."

"What for?" Carrington thought traders should be harmless enough.

"Contraband. Search their wagons for rifles, ammunition and whiskey. The War Department doesn't want the Indians to have them. Too much fighting and general mayhem when the braves get drunk. The chiefs can't control them. The guns—they'll just turn around and shoot you with them."

Carrington and Ten Eyke nodded soberly. The captain asked, "And what other problems will we have?"

"You'll have nothing but problems, young man. You're going into the wilderness to hack out civilization, something this country resists like all the furies of hell."

"Yes, but specifically what else?"

Maynadier shook his head as if listing them all was hopeless. "Morale. I'd work the men's fannies off so they don't have time to think about what they're missing back home. Let them fall into bed exhausted every night. Fresh food. You won't have any fresh vegetables till you get a garden going next year. Get your men to eat wild onions and those awful vegetable bricks you're packing, or you're bound to have a few cases of scurvy. How are you going to amuse these fellows?"

"We've got a band. Our Reverend Simmons will preach. And of course the officers' wives will give entertainments and socials," Carrington beamed.

Maynadier looked sour. "A band? That's fine for Sunday morning after church, but what about the men's Saturday night needs?"

"Saturday night needs?"

Maynadier looked from Carrington to Ten Eyke. Was he dealing with two dummies or just one?

Ten Eyke answered. "Well, sir, I don't know the particulars, but I understand a couple of the Negro laundresses have been willing."

"My God," Carrington exclaimed, catching on. "I won't allow that!"

Maynadier burst out laughing. "Good Lord, Carrington, why not? You can't stop it, anyway."

"We're going out there to civilize the country, Colonel. I hardly think my men's using the laundresses—Negresses at that—is going to set the right kind of example for the Indians."

Maynadier rolled his eyes. "Colonel Carrington, have you ever commanded a fort before?"

Carrington reddened slightly. This was a sore subject with him. "I've commanded a regiment at Fort Carson."

"But you weren't camp commander?"

"No. What of it?"

"I wouldn't fight it, Colonel," Maynadier advised. "The Supreme Commander gave men that rod between their legs because he meant it to be used. You can't stop them without creating a serious morale problem."

His face hardening with disapproval, Carrington stood and slapped his gloves into his left hand.

"I think we've quite taken up our fair share of Colonel Maynadier's hospitality, Captain," he told Ten Eyke, who quickly got to his feet.

Maynadier stood too. He gave his fellow commander a knowing look. "Colonel, Colonel, I've been out here a long time. I'm on your side."

"You've given us a lot to think about, Colonel," Carrington said stiffly. He didn't look Maynadier in the eye. "On behalf of my officers and the men, I thank you."

As his guests turned to go, Maynadier said softly, "If you find later on that you need a couple of my laundresses, Colonel, just send word. You might find them just the thing for the restlessness your boys will be feeling up there. I won't hold it against you. Goodbye."

Carrington didn't offer his hand or look at him. Without another word he led the way out. The next time he spoke it was to order Ten Eyke to get the men ready to hit the trail.

By midmorning the parade ground at Fort Laramie was full of wagons and shouting men racing around struggling with horses and mules. Officers yelled at noncoms and privates to get into column formation. Everybody seemed to have forgotten to pack something or to have to buy one last item from the sutler before the train pulled out. All were acutely aware that Fort Laramie was the place where civilization ceased.

All this confusion made it look as if the company would never be ready to leave. But Carrington had learned just to order Ten Eyke to pull out and trust the stragglers to catch up.

"Move out, Captain!" he shouted to Ten Eyke. The captain relayed the order to the head of the line. Captain William Powell led the column out, twenty of their best cavalrymen armed with loaded muskets forming the advance guard.

Behind them came the first of the eighty wagons, giant canvas-topped land ships filled with all the goods they would need to hack a new civilization out of the backwoods. There were axes, saws, hammers and lengths of chain. There were four hundred muskets, twelve thousand ounces of powder, a thousand pounds of lead shot and hundreds of pounds of spare musket parts. In one wagon were five iron stoves, ten forty-gallon kettles and forty five-gallon bowls for the kitchen. Another contained twenty bolts of blue wool for uniforms, seven hundred fifty bone and brass buttons, four hundred spools of thread and five hundred needles, plus nine sets of architect's drawings for the three forts, ten thousand sheets of paper, fifty bottles of ink and three hundred unsharpened quill pens. Two wagons carried the marching band's equipment, including seven trumpets, a bass drum, five snares and twenty pairs of drumsticks.

The Reverend and Mrs. Simmons had their own wagon, which had been fitted out by the excited ladies of their home diocese and was driven by a cheerful ex-slave named Hank. The wagon contained everything the ladies thought a small cabin in the wilderness would need. There were a complete set of parlor furniture covered with damask and silk, a full kitchen down to its last colander and quarter-teaspoon measure, and a bedroom suite. There were also four black suits for the reverend, half a dozen dresses for Cynthia, three sets of double sheets and eight pincushions in assorted colors and sizes, gifts from ladies who wanted something of theirs to go along with Cynthia on her trek into the unknown.

Hank drove with Cynthia beside him, a sunbonnet shading her face. Clarence liked to ride at the point to show the men that not only soldiers could be brave. That was where he was that June morning as the wagon train pulled out.

Captain Ten Eyke, riding his black gelding, pulled up alongside the Simmons wagon. Studiously avoiding looking at Cynthia as he trotted beside her, he shouted, "How's it going, Hank?" as if all he cared about was how the team was pulling and the wagon rolling.

"Going just fine, Captain," the lanky black man

shouted back. "I think Nelly's foot's all right now."

They all three peered down at the horse; indeed, the powerful animal was stepping out smartly.

"Keep an eye on it, Hank. I'll put one of those boys on foot and hook his horse up to you if you need it."

"Thank you, Captain," said Cynthia. Her voice shivered right through him. "Everybody get off all right?"

"I think so." As Ten Eyke's horse fell into step on her side of the wagon, he forced himself to look at her, trying to pretend she was just another traveler he was entrusted to safeguard, but her loveliness moved him too much. He hated Clarence Simmons for owning this creature with her glossy black hair, lively black eyes, smooth cheeks and quick smiles.

"The carpenters and blacksmiths have been busy since we stopped," Ten Eyke told her. "I think we're in better repair than we've been for two weeks."

"Were you one of those who made sure New Bedlam was appropriately named last night?" Cynthia asked, her eyes dancing. "Hank tells me the guards had to help someone down off the flagpole early this morning."

Hank chuckled. "Somebody tied one of them Chicago boys to the pole and drug him up almost to the top."

Ten Eyke grinned. "Whiskey's work, I'm afraid, Hank. Let it be a lesson to you." They all laughed; Hank guffawed and slapped his knee.

Ten Eyke continued riding alongside the minister's wagon, knowing he should move on but unable to. He struggled to find something else to talk about, some legitimate concern. It shamed him that he felt like such a schoolboy around Cynthia Simmons. Her heart-shaped face, her sweetness, her merry glances, the saucy way she tossed her head sometimes—it was wasted, all of it wasted on the minister, who surely couldn't appreciate it. Ten Eyke sighed and smiled at her, still trying to find something to talk about.

Cynthia helped him out. "How far will we travel today, Captain?"

"Oh, maybe twenty miles."

"When will we reach Fort Reno?"

"Not for several days, maybe a week."

"It will be a relief finally to get where we'll build the fort," she sighed. "This traveling is harder than I realized it would be."

"I know." The march to Fort Laramie had shown them all how hard such travel was on the ladies. The heat, the dust, the hours of bouncing that stretched into grim days, the lack of water, the unappetizing camp food, none of it fresh, all of it greasy and boiled or fried, plus the constant packing and unpacking wore down man and woman alike.

For the half a dozen ladies in the column there were added problems. Several times a day Colonel Carrington stopped the wagons for rest and relief. The ladies, accompanied by an armed guard, went off into the bushes on the right of the trail while the men went to the left. Of course, to spare the women embarrassment, the guard positioned himself some yards away, but he couldn't go too far, or what was the sense of his being there? Reaching Fort Laramie had been a relief itself. At least at the fort the ladies had had the privacy of real bedrooms and proper outhouses.

"Well, I better see how things are going at the rear." But Ten Eyke still did not turn away.

Cynthia gave him a warm smile, as if she knew the trouble he was having and felt sorry for him. "Why don't you come by our fire for supper tonight, Captain? We'll have enough, won't we, Hank?"

"Oh, yes, ma'am, all you wants. Glad to have the captain." He peered around uneasily at the grasslands they were moving through. "Just in case some Injun decides to get hisself a nigger's scalp!"

When the column pulled out of Fort Laramie, Trader John Richards and his oldest boy, John Jr., rode with it. The older Richards figured he would go along with the caravan and see how his Deer Creek homestead was doing as well as try and find out more about Carrington's crazy mission.

The dispatching of the colonel and his troopers to build forts on the Powder River had shocked and dismayed John Richards almost as much as it had Red Cloud and the other Oglala. Richards saw it as deviousness on the part of Maynadier and Taylor. He still believed they must have known that General Cooke was sending Carrington out here. For the last couple of days he had kept his mouth shut, being of the firm opinion that this was the smartest course in dealing with both red and white, while he struggled to figure out what he could do to save his business.

He had arrived in the land of the Oglala Sioux some thirty years before and had begun to play the same game he had already played down in Mexico and Texas. He swapped guns and whiskey to the Sioux for furs and hides. Life in Wyoming and the Dakotas with the Sioux suited him so much that Richards not only stayed, he married White Deer, back then a pretty Oglala maiden of twenty. They had five sons and two daughters. Around Fort Laramie all the sons had the reputation of being bold as hawks, especially John Jr., who belonged to one of the lesser Sioux war societies, which meant among other things that every Sioux tribe had to welcome both father and son. Often John Jr. went on horse raids against the Pawnee and Crow. Twice he had brought back Indian scalps, which had made his father shiver. But the older Indians had congratulated him and called him Lakota.

Richards had to do something soon. He owed Tully, the Fort Laramie sutler, more than two thousand dollars, and he had no idea how to pay it back without losing everything he owned. Tully was already chuckling at the prospect of taking over the Deer Creek homestead with its six outbuildings, Indian trading post, emigrant store and the toll bridge that every emigrant and government wagon train to Bozeman City had to use.

When Richards could freely trade with the Sioux, he felt rich, but these new troopers could mean war with the Oglala, and war meant Maynadier wouldn't allow him to trade whiskey or guns. In that case no Sioux would want to trade with him, which meant Richards would go broke—or rather, broker than he already was. This skirmishing had been going on now for over a year.

War also meant that no emigrants would come through to trade with him. It meant he would collect no tolls from the Deer Creek bridge; what wagon train would choose to cross a battlefield? It meant Tully would foreclose on all his property in a few months.

With John Jr. following, Richards rode up to Jim Bridger, who as the finest scout in the West had been selected by General Cooke to guide Carrington.

Hunched over in his saddle, Bridger rode at the head of the train's twenty-man advance guard.

"There he is!" shouted John Jr., greeting the old scout. "Got any more shit to splatter on us this morning?"

Bridger grinned as if in pain. Lean and sinewy, somewhere in his sixties, he had a face that looked as if it had been carved from tree bark. "You young pups got to age some before you know what to believe and what to throw away. I told you nothin' but the truth last night."

"Aw, shit! You was drinking too much whiskey to tell the truth, wasn't he, Pa?"

Richards peered into Bridger's craggy face. The man had one hell of a reputation. In fact, John Richards had never heard any scout spoken of more highly, although after last night he wondered. Drunk and egged on by the officers in the caravan who had heard his tales before, Bridger had told them of his trips farther west and the wonders he had seen there: springs that boiled so hot they gushed up into the air, dancing bears, white buffalo, flying Indians, hot mud, mountains so high they reached into the clouds and disappeared, trees so large you could build a house inside them, a lake as salty as the sea.

"How do you feel this morning?" Richards asked.

Bridger looked sheepish. "I don't know what gets into me. I get a glass of whiskey in my hand and it leads to another. 'Fore I know it, I'm having one hell of a time. I'd sure like to swap this head for another this morning, though."

Richards grinned. "Let's go look for some Sioux, Jim."

John Jr. looked up in surprise. He opened his

mouth to say there were no Sioux around here, but his father shook his head and silenced him.

Bridger looked around. "Where the heck would they hide?"

On all sides of them stretched endless prairie, the sky like a great bowl inverted on the flatness. Hardly a tree stuck up against the horizon. The sun blazed down and there was no place to find relief from it. The grass was short and sparse, and many of the brooks and streams had dried up. Occasionally they passed eruptions of sand and limestone broken into confused masses that looked like the ruins of the world.

The two older men spurred their horses, Richards talking as they rode.

"A Sioux scout could be behind that rock, Jim. A warrior could hide just over the lip of that ravine. But I don't think there's been an Indian up here for the past week."

"What'd you want to talk about?" the old scout asked.

"I can't get any of these blue wonders to listen to me."

"About what?"

Now a mile in front of the long line of soldiers and wagons, the two trotted along the dim trail. To their left flowed the Platte, shrunken and weakened by the furnace of the sun.

"What are they really doing out here?" Richards wondered.

"Come out to guard that goddamn road," Bridger supposed.

"What for?"

"So folks can take the short way to Montana, to Bozeman City."

Richards pushed him a bit. "The chiefs tell me Red Cloud and Old Man Afraid don't like it."

"Enough of them to make a difference?"

"Red Cloud's the war chief for the Bad Faces."

"And Man Afraid?"

"Well, there's his son, Young Man Afraid," said Richards. "Him and Red Cloud is real big buddies. Between them, they can give a man a lot of trouble."

Bridger looked at him sharply. "What're you trying to tell me?"

"I don't think Carrington ought to go up there. The man looks more like he ought to be teaching school somewhere than leading a bunch of troopers."

Bridger released a long sigh. "Shit, you know the army. Some generals got burned up and started looking at a map, after they heard the reports that the redskins had lifted a few too many scalps. They sent the fellow up here."

"These ain't Cheyenne or Crow or Pawnee or Arapaho," Richards pointed out.

"Whoever said they was? All of them'll scalp you just as bald."

"No, sir," Richards argued. "The Sioux will scalp you slickest of all and take your ears and nose to make sure you understand them. I married into the wildest bunch of all, the Oglala. Red Cloud, Red Leaf, Crazy Horse, Hump, both Man Afraids—I know them real good, and I'm here to tell you they're going to push back."

"Aw, John, you can't scare off a column like this. What are you after?"

"Huh?"

Bridger grinned knowingly. "You want to trade, don't you?"

"Hell, yes, that's how I buy my rations. If I don't trade, I don't eat."

"You tell your relatives, you tell Red Cloud and Man Afraid to let this man guard the road. Let things settle down. You work to settle things down."

Richards saw he wasn't getting anywhere and it depressed him. None of these people would listen to him. He had a mind to pack up and leave this country, but where would he go? The Sioux were family. Besides, he loved it here. Anyway, how could you pack up a homestead? "I got to be careful what I say, Jim. I can't have Red Cloud think I've turned against him."

"Then you're going to have to do without trading till things settle down," Bridger recommended. "This ain't Cole and Walker running around chasing tribes. This is the U. S. Army building a fort. No Indian is going to stop that."

"It ain't going to be so simple as the army figures." Richards shook his head.

"The Sioux's day is close to over," Bridger shrugged. "You ought to be telling your relatives that, instead of encouraging them to think the old days is coming back."

Richards snorted in disgust. "Red Cloud don't need encouraging."

"I'm sure he don't. But somebody like you ought to tell him who he's messing with. After all, he's going up against the same outfit that beat the Confederacy. How much trouble does he think it's going to be to beat one tribe of redskins?"

Richards sighed, not knowing how to get across to the old scout what he knew so well in his bones. Red Cloud felt his back against the wall, believed he would have damn little trouble getting young braves to fight with him, was sure the army wasn't going to stop Red Cloud from carrying out his kind of war, which damn sure wasn't the same kind the Union had fought against the Confederacy.

Chapter 5

Red Cloud did little hunting on his return to the village. As he waited out the weeks before the Sun Dance, a cold hollow feeling began to form in the pit of his stomach. It wasn't fear so much as an expectation of something unusual about to happen. Once he had placed himself in the palm of Wakan-Takan and all the power that Old Hump the medicine man could call up, his fate would be like that of a hailstone in a gale.

He sat in front of his tepee and watched the activity of the camp with new eyes, as if the coming ordeal had already cast a wakan shadow over him. Before him men gambled and threw stones. Children played at hunting and chased each other and the dogs. Angry quarrels sprang up and were resolved. Women worked at their sewing, quilling and tanning, gossiping all the while. Life in the village had a circular quality. Every activity began, arrived at a middle and continued to a conclusion, to begin all over again with different players. Red Cloud found himself fascinated by the way the drama played and replayed itself. He wondered if it was some sort of old man's vision.

His first wife, Pretty Owl, his two daughters and his niece Black Buffalo Woman, who lived with them, worked in the June sun preparing buffalo hides. Now and then Pretty Owl glanced at him anxiously, puzzled by his uncharacteristic behavior.

It took strength, skill and patience to remove the flesh and gristle from the staked-out buffalo hide. It had to be scraped out with a bone chisel. Once the hide was worked on one side, it was turned over and the hair removed with the scraper. At this point the hide was stiff and hard. Pretty Owl must soak it in water for two days to make it pliable before the final curing.

"Why are you so interested in what I'm doing?" she asked one afternoon. "Do you want to help?" She was teasing him. No warrior would stoop to doing woman's work.

"You have a helper." Red Cloud glanced at Black Buffalo Woman, who was pulling on the hide with her.

"Ha! I don't know if this one is ever going to make herself a tepee or if she's going to spend her life being courted," said Pretty Owl in mock disgust, for not thirty feet away sat three of the girl's suitors, blowing wispy little tunes on their love flutes.

Red Cloud chuckled. He knew that Buffalo Woman would marry in good time, if not as soon as some of her friends. She might well marry that daredevil Crazy Horse if he could be induced to go courting properly. Of course Crazy Horse might live to regret it, for a pretty woman wasn't always willing to work as hard as a plain one; but that was something a young man rarely considered when he was courting.

Pretty Owl had never been a beauty, but she made a good tepee, Red Cloud reflected as he looked up at their lodge. Fashioned of fifteen buffalo skins with four painted medallions depicting the four seasons, it was as large and handsome as any in the village, as befitted Red Cloud's status among the Bad Faces. In addition, everything was in its proper place. A water bag hung from a forked stick to the left of the door. Firewood was stacked just outside the tepee flaps. From the lodge poles drooped Red Cloud's painted bonnet case and his wakan pouch. His war shield hung from a forked pole at the rear. Topping the tepee like a flag were a red deerskin streamer and a Pawnee scalp Red Cloud had taken five years before.

The lodge was as handsome inside as out, and peaceful. The thick skin kept out harsh daylight; the tepee was filled with a translucent glow. Inside hung rows of pendants painted with multicolored symbols of power animals: beaver, fox, deer, antelope, eagle, bear, wolf and buffalo. A dew cloth embroidered with horizontal stripes of quilling served as a handsome background for a dozen painted willow-rod backrests Pretty Owl had made for guests; it also showed off leather storage bags filled with food, tools and clothing. On the floor dark buffalo rugs softened the bright-colored walls and gave the interior a feeling of comfort and spaciousness.

The tepee was Pretty Owl's, her property as well as her responsibility. Even the names of the parts of the lodge were female. The opening flaps, for instance, were called "woman's arms." Red Cloud smiled thinking of the coarse jokes on the name.

Puffing on his pipe, he found himself looking again at Black Buffalo Woman. He and Pretty Owl had taken her to raise as a daughter eighteen years ago, after his brother died in a fight with the Cheyenne.

What a pity that Black Buffalo Woman was his niece, for sometimes he had thoughts about her that no uncle should have. It would be nice to be able to marry her, though Pretty Owl would raise a fuss the way she had over his second and third wives. For the past year the path in front of the lodge had been crowded with Buffalo Woman's suitors. It amused Red Cloud to watch them. They did the same silly things he had done when he had gone courting, things that his father and his father's father had done before him. They played flutes made by some wakan man, brought the girl carvings of little animals, followed her when she went for water and when Pretty Owl escorted her out to pick berries. When the young men weren't out hunting, and even when they should have been, as many as eight sat in front of Red Cloud's lodge blowing their flutes, each hoping that Black Buffalo Woman might be induced to sit under the blanket with him so he could whisper endearments into her ear.

No one in the village could remember a young woman who matched Black Buffalo Woman for beauty and bearing. She was about average height and slender, but she carried herself with a dignity and poise equal to her uncle's. Her narrow almond-shaped eyes shone. Her lovely mouth laughed derisively at any youth who wasn't so quick-witted as she was. She played the field of suitors so skillfully that each man thought he was winning.

In truth, Buffalo Woman had let the game run on longer than a maiden normally did. As the niece of Red Cloud and a great beauty, she could get away with it though, and it did bring her more and richer suitors.

Chief among them was No Water, the brother of Black Twin, who was high up in the councils of the Brulé Sioux. Black Twin, though still a young man, had been on eight Pawnee raids and had a personal fortune of fifty horses. Red Cloud could do much worse in a son-in-law, particularly when he needed influence with the Brulé.

Until No Water appeared outside Red Cloud's lodge, everybody thought Crazy Horse, or Young Curly, as many in the village still called him for his hair, would be Buffalo Woman's choice. After all they had grown up together, and except for Red Cloud himself, no young Oglala warrior had ever ridden and fought so well. But as good as Crazy Horse was in battle and on the hunt, he was terrible at courting Black Buffalo Woman.

It was traditional among Sioux men to brag about their exploits. Such bragging, the Lakota believed, encouraged the younger braves to try harder, to attempt even more daring exploits that they in turn could boast about.

Crazy Horse had never bragged about such things. As a boy he had wandered off one summer afternoon and was missing for days. His father and Old Hump searched the hills for him. On the fourth day they found him, weak and barely conscious, in a ravine in the hills above the Bad Face summer camp. Old Crazy Horse started to scold the boy, but Hump stopped him. Somehow the medicine man knew at once that something extraordinary had taken place.

Every young male Sioux hoped for a personal vision, a sign sent to him by White Buffalo Woman or Wakan-Takan to tell him how his life would go. Would he kill many enemies and live long or would he soon die? And what animal would be the one to give him his strength in battle? But such visions came to young men of seventeen or eighteen, and after arduous preparation by the medicine man. They did not come to eleven-year-old boys.

Old Hump got Young Curly to talk. The boy had seen a man on a horse in the sky with a hawk flying around him. A streak of lightning was painted on the horse's chest and there was a blue stone behind the man's ear. This Lakota had ridden among hundreds of enemies and struck them down with his lance.

Young Curly had no idea what it was all about. He was feverish when his father and Old Hump found him and had to stay in bed for ten days. For two months afterward he wasn't interested in playing with the other boys. Old Hump knew then that it was a true vision, that the hawk was Young Curly's power animal, the lightning flash his boldness as a warrior and the blue stone his bravery. The boy's father was so impressed that he renamed Young Curly after himself, for Old Hump said he would likely surpass Old Crazy Horse's exploits.

Young Crazy Horse didn't tell the other boys about his vision. Word of it got out slowly through his father and Old Hump. By the time he was fourteen, he was accompanying the men on raids. He carried their firewood and took care of their horses while the men raided the Crow and Pawnee for horses. Even then the warriors found him dependable and valuable. Told to keep the horses, he kept them. He didn't sneak away to the top of a hill to watch the battle, or twist Red Cloud's instructions to get in on some skirmish. He knew from the beginning that watching the horses so the raiding party could make its getaway was no less important than taking out the guards or leading the attack.

He was this way with everything. As a young warrior first riding into battle, he never broke formation and attacked the enemy before the order was given, as almost all young braves did on occasion. The leader of a raid knew Crazy Horse would always stand and obey.

The four cardinal virtues of the Lakota were bravery, fortitude, generosity and wisdom. Of these, bravery came first. This virtue reached fullest flower in counting coups, the practice of riding among the enemy and touching them with coup-sticks instead of shooting them from a safe distance. No one counted more coups than Crazy Horse.

Fortitude? No one could bear pain or show reserve during periods of stress better than Crazy Horse. In sweat baths he endured the steam longer than the other young men of his age. In battle and on the hunt he suffered minor wounds without complaint. He could fast for a week without mentioning hunger.

Generosity? Crazy Horse kept himself poor by giving away everything he killed on the hunt except what he required for his immediate needs.

The fourth virtue of the Lakota, wisdom, Crazy Horse had received from his connection with the supernatural. Even his name showed it. The unfortunate English interpretation, "crazy," came from a Sioux word meaning enchanted or magic. More accurately his name should have been translated as "Enchanted

Horse." Wisdom, for Crazy Horse, meant using his supernatural power to inspire others to fight more bravely.

In all the Lakota skills except bragging Crazy Horse had no equal. And while his un-Siouxlike reserve was no deterrent in battle or on a hunt, it was no help in the courtship of Black Buffalo Woman. Crazy Horse went through the required motions with undisguised reluctance. No lover had ever played the flute with less feeling, as if a turtle were blowing it, the men of the village joked. They hoped Black Buffalo Woman wouldn't judge him by his flute-playing.

Some of the women, gossiping about the courtship, remarked that it was No Water's high-class Brulé style that had attracted Buffalo Woman away from her childhood sweetheart. But others maintained that she was just using No Water and all the others to make Crazy Horse jealous.

One July evening, after sharing a meal with a few other Bad Face chiefs, Red Cloud leaned back against a buffalo robe to smoke tobacco and sweet grass and discuss the approaching Sun Dance. Black Buffalo Woman had helped Pretty Owl and Red Cloud's second wife serve the meal. Now she and Pretty Owl prepared to go down to the stream for water.

No sooner did Buffalo Woman step outside the tepee than a half dozen suitors' flute-playing rose to fever pitch. Red Cloud and the other men laughed, but then a furious argument began. The chiefs heard Pretty Owl cry, "Stop it, now! This isn't getting me any water!"

Red Cloud and the others laughed even harder. Young Man Afraid said, "I bet they're arguing over who's going to carry Buffalo Woman's water bag."

They waited for the ruckus to die, but if anything the noise increased:

"I saw her first!"

"Why don't you hit me? Then I'll hit you and we'll see!"

Red Cloud stood grinning. "They're eager now to carry her water bag, but one month after they're married, none of them would be caught dead with a water bag in their hands."

The other chiefs were still laughing as Red Cloud put on a stern face and stepped out of the tepee.

"You boys!" he shouted at the group of young braves, insulting them. "No man in here can speak without your squabbling stopping his ears."

"I saw her first!" shouted No Water. "I should carry her water bag."

An enormous youth, well-muscled and with a large thick chest, stood defiantly before Red Cloud. No Water was wearing his honor shirt. Because he was still young, it didn't have many scalp-locks woven into it, but it was remarkable that at his age he had an honor shirt at all.

Red Cloud was no longer amused. Something was happening here that he didn't like to see in his camp. No Water looked all puffed up, as a man did before battle, ready to use that big knife that the whites had given him at the last gift-giving. Around him stood six more of Black Buffalo Woman's suitors, five Oglala and one Minneconjou. Behind them all stood Crazy Horse, blowing lightly on his flute as if nothing were going on. The squabbling youths had completely blocked the path. Pretty Owl and her niece couldn't get by.

Looking at them, Red Cloud recalled his own stupid youthful frustrations and how quickly frustration could turn into blind rage. That was what had killed Bull Bear.

"Hai!" shouted Red Cloud. "You may all carry her water bag, each one part of the way. No fighting. Pretty Owl will decide when your turn has come. You! Curly! You go too," he shouted at Crazy Horse. He hoped that calling him Curly would remind him to act more like a warrior and less like a moon-crazed coyote.

He watched them go, musing about Crazy Horse. Why was he so unmanly at times? He was as fine a young warrior as Red Cloud could put into the field. But when he had to talk, in council or around a campfire or outside a girl's tepee, he held back. And all he had to do was walk to the head of the line and none of the others, except maybe No Water, would dare cross him.

Either he was a bit childlike, touched in the head, or else he was wakan, as Old Hump claimed. With an impatient sigh, Red Cloud turned to go back to his guests. Such un-Lakotalike behavior irritated him.

For an hour the six chiefs in Red Cloud's tepee went over the arrangements for the Sun Dance. In the weeks since the meeting at Fort Laramie, many eager youths but few chiefs of the other tribes had come to Red Cloud and Old-Man-Afraid-of-His-Horses to volunteer to oppose the whites on the Powder River. This meant that while Red Cloud would have some braves, perhaps even several hundred, the full strength of the tribes was denied him. Armed and brave warriors were certainly important in battle, but just as important were chiefs, subchiefs, medicine men, boys and women.

Today the last of the messengers had returned from the neighboring tribes. The answer from Spotted Tail of the Brulé was typical: Yes, they would come to the Sun Dance sponsored by Red Cloud, but they would not fight the Little White Chief.

"Well, we drove out many cavalry from this country just last year," said Young Man Afraid. "We'll drive out these whites too."

"We don't want to drive them off completely," Limping Bear objected.

"Why not?"

"Because we want to trade at Laramie with Richards," Red Cloud answered for him. "We need their guns and powder, not to speak of their knives, cloth and salt."

"Let's attack the Little White Chief now, before they can build a fort," said Young Man Afraid.

Red Cloud shook his head. "It's time for the Sun Dance."

"But once they build the fort, we'll never drive them out."

They had been arguing this point in typical Sioux fashion, which meant that they had spent days and might spend weeks or months debating the issue until it no longer mattered. Half the chiefs were in favor of a sudden attack on Carrington's force now. The others considered that the Sioux needed a Sun Dance more. Once July was gone, the time for a good Sun Dance would have passed, and the Sioux didn't feel so strong without one. To miss it this year of all years seemed stupid.

The meeting broke up well after midnight; nothing was decided. The others left and Young Man Afraid asked Red Cloud if he might stay awhile longer.

When they were alone, Young Man Afraid came straight to the point. "Who's going to marry your niece?"

Red Cloud grunted and glanced over at the sleeping women. "I don't know."

"Come walk down to the end of the village."

Outside everything was quiet. Three diehard suitors were curled up sound asleep in their blankets on the path.

When they were far enough from the tepee, Young Man Afraid said, "We have had no voice in the councils of the Brulé since we became the Bad Faces all those years ago."

"So?"

"So wouldn't it be helpful if your niece married that Brulé lout who keeps hanging around your tepee?"

Red Cloud grinned. "I have thought of it. But she has a mind of her own. Besides, I suspect all this is a game she's playing to get Crazy Horse to speak up more loudly."

"Perhaps you should ask her about No Water for a husband."

"I did. She says he's thick-headed."

Man Afraid laughed. "Women! There'll be something wrong with every one of them, you'll see."

Red Cloud had to agree. But Black Buffalo Woman was his favorite even though she wasn't his own daughter, and he hated the idea of asking her to marry someone who wasn't her own choice.

"If we're going to get the support of other tribes, we'll need the support of the Brulé. It would be extremely useful to have the support of a son-in-law whose brother is so well thought of in Brulé councils."

Red Cloud sighed. "She thinks well of me and certainly of Pretty Owl, but I don't know if I can convince her to marry No Water."

"Convince her? Order her!"

Red Cloud shook his head. "Black Buffalo Woman isn't the kind of woman you order around."

"If she were in my lodge she would be."

"No, not in anybody's lodge."

The two men were silent then as they walked back through the silent village.

What Young Man Afraid said made a good deal of sense, Red Cloud reflected. Since the Oglala had left the Brulé they had done well, but only as a splinter group. Though Red Cloud had a voice in the deliberations of the Oglala, he had no influence in the all-important council of the Brulé. As long as the Oglala were just skirmishing with the Pawnee and the Crow, it didn't matter. But if they lost the Powder River to these white soldiers, where could they go? No one knew of a better hunting ground, and to go elsewhere would mean pushing out some other tribe. Certainly Spotted Tail wouldn't want them coming south of the Platte River, and up north, Sitting Bull of the Hunkpapa Sioux wasn't going to welcome them. Red Cloud must make the other chiefs see that they had to resist the whites everywhere. The least toehold these invaders got gave them a springboard to jump to the next hunting ground.

Man Afraid broke in on his companion's thoughts. "Maybe something could be arranged."

"What? How arranged?" asked Red Cloud, forgetting for a moment what they had been discussing.

"If No Water brought you many horses, would you accept him for a son-in-law? Would you talk to Black Buffalo Woman and tell her she should marry him?"

"I could tell her, but I don't know that she'll do it."

"You're her guardian, her father's brother," said the younger man impatiently. "If you tell her it's important, that it's what you want and that you won't give permission for her to marry anyone else, maybe she'll listen."

Red Cloud sighed. "It could solve a lot of problems," he admitted.

"Yes." Young Man Afraid nodded. "You're beginning to see."

"Let me think about it. . . ."

The next day word reached the village that Spotted Tail, Standing Elk and Swift Bear had signed a peace treaty with Taylor after Red Cloud and his followers walked out of the conference at Laramie.

The Oglala chiefs felt betrayed. They had held back an attack on Carrington for the Sun Dance and now these chiefs, who had agreed to the dance, had given way to the whites before they had asked Wakan-Takan which path to take.

It would now be a tug of war between himself and Spotted Tail, Red Cloud realized. He might get some angry young men who disagreed with Spotted Tail, but the Brulé chief would get the elders. More than ever Red Cloud saw that he needed entrée into the powerful chiefs' councils.

He hunted up Young Man Afraid and found him lounging in his tepee. "I'll tell Black Buffalo Woman

I want her to marry No Water. Now, what can you do?"

Young Man Afraid nodded and grinned. "I heard the news too. Listen, I have a plan. . . ."

Chapter 6

Crazy Horse sat in front of Red Cloud's tepee playing his flute and chanting, the way Old Hump had told him to:

> This song is a web;
> Listen to it, wild heart.
> Become entangled in these notes
> That are the strands of my heart's
> Long snares of love.

To Crazy Horse this courting was all so much nonsense. Black Buffalo Woman knew everything a woman could know about him, short of actually living with him. Hadn't the two seen each other practically every day since she was born? Hadn't they walked along the creek and talked? Hadn't they played together as children and glanced hotly at each other as they grew older? Hadn't Aunt Pretty Owl as much as told him that when the time came, Black Buffalo Woman would marry him?

A month or so before the Laramie conference,

when the women's minds were on gathering berries and fruit and the men's on hunting, Crazy Horse had actually asked Buffalo Woman to marry him.

"But you haven't courted me!" she had protested. "Not a day! Not one hour! You think you can just walk up and ask me? Look there, in front of my uncle's tepee, two suitors! Where are you?"

Crazy Horse grinned without answering. Actually, he didn't know what to say. Her words had shocked him. He had seen the lovesick puppies in front of the lodge, but he had never considered that he might have to join them.

"But you don't want one of them!" he finally managed to say.

"Well, how do you know?" she asked, tossing her head. Crazy Horse didn't know what to do. One of the suitors was Light Deer, who everybody knew couldn't hit a tepee with an arrow if it was farther away than ten yards. The other was Short Foot, ugly and from an unlucky family. Black Buffalo Woman wasn't going to marry either of them.

"Hai! I want to marry you; you want to marry me. I'm ready to give your uncle eight horses if he'll bless our marriage. Why're you acting this way?"

"Because you're not treating me right," she sniffed. "You haven't once played the flute for me or brought me a gift. Those two have helped out around our lodge, and have we seen you?"

"A man has to hunt," he argued. "And we raided the Pawnee and took twelve horses."

She looked away. The disdainful gesture told him more than if she had denounced him again.

Why did she have to behave like this? The way she talked to him, he could tell she knew everything that was in his heart. She was so beautiful. He longed to capture her the way he would run down a doe in the woods. He longed to see her swell with his child in her belly. He wanted to hunt for her and bring back so much meat and so many hides she would be delighted at the good fortune. He wanted to come back to their tepee and find three or four sets of little hands grabbing for him. He wanted to play with their children while she got him something to eat. But none of this could Crazy Horse put into words.

And none of it, he discovered, was going to come easy. Black Buffalo Woman wanted something else before she agreed to share his tepee.

Crazy Horse had taken his problem to Old Hump. Two blankets pulled around him to keep off the May chill, the medicine man had listened and cackled, "She's not a bear, Curly! Or a Pawnee either."

What did that mean, Crazy Horse wondered. "I would rather go against ten Pawnee than go through this with her."

"You don't have any love wakan," the old man grinned, the creases on his wrinkled face deepening.

"No." Crazy Horse groaned. He saw what was coming. "What do I need? How much will it cost?"

"A love flute. Some charms. A love chant. Gifts. A horse ought to do it, but not over five years old."

"Mooning around her tepee is not for me," Crazy Horse protested. "I'm a warrior. I don't blow a flute at a Pawnee, I shoot him with an arrow. I jump him and stick him with my knife."

"Are you going to stick a knife in her?" Old Hump jeered. "Or an arrow?"

Crazy Horse laughed. "No, I was thinking of something else!"

The old man laughed along with him, then sobered. "Before you do that you must get her to agree. And you must win her heart or she will never be your wife."

Crazy Horse didn't like it, but finally he gave in. When he returned from Fort Laramie, he joined the other suitors in front of Red Cloud's tepee. By then there were seven including No Water. Crazy Horse wondered why Black Buffalo Woman encouraged them. Was she only trying to make him jealous, or was she really looking for another husband? He blew harder on his flute and endured the snickers of passers-by. He would rather face a bear or Pawnee any day.

Crazy Horse had borne three weeks of this when No Water remarked one day that he had been sitting there a long time now and was growing stiff. Why didn't they get a few other braves together and see if they couldn't grab some horses from those Crow the scouts had spotted last week only fifty miles south?

No sooner had he said it than every brave there was all for it—everyone but Crazy Horse.

"I don't feel like going on a Crow raid." He figured to convince Black Buffalo Woman to marry him in their absence.

"I heard you were a good fighter. I didn't think a few Crow would scare you," jeered No Water.

"No Crow frightens a Kit Fox. Neither does a Brulé Lakota."

For a moment nobody said a word. They all knew that Crazy Horse was one of the leaders of the Kit Foxes war society. Even a stupid Brulé like No Water could see that Crazy Horse longed to settle this thing over Buffalo Woman with a fight, which was his element. They also knew that he would obey the rules against fighting a visitor to the camp. But if No Water wanted to push things, any way would be better than sitting in front of a tepee blowing on a flute.

The Oglala had many war societies, but none was braver than the Kit Foxes. Foxes were the two stake-holders for the camp. Their duty, if the camp was attacked, was to care for the helpless, to guard the rear while the others retreated and to rescue any women and children taken prisoner. The stake-holder got his name from his pledge to stake one end of his deerskin sash to the ground and not leave that tight circle until he was relieved, the battle was won or he died. Only the bravest society provided stake-holders for a camp. They had to be ready to do anything for their people. A Kit Fox song went:

> I am a Fox.
> I am supposed to die.
> If there is anything difficult to do,
> If there is anything dangerous,
> That is mine to do.

The Foxes were such a fierce group that when a young man prepared himself for the initiation ceremonies, he prepared himself as if for death, wearing his burial clothes, giving away his horses and singing his death song.

So No Water wisely deflected Crazy Horse's challenge. "I always heard you were a good fighter," he repeated, but lightly this time. "I'd like to ride on a raid with such a famous captain, but only if he fights better than he blows the flute!"

Everybody burst out laughing, even Crazy Horse.

"*Hai!*" he shouted to all the young men gathered around them. "Do you want to go?" From their excited shouts, they certainly did.

The next day was a fever of work. For a Sioux youth, war and its heroics came close to being the only purpose in life. In this venture, in addition to the glory of adding coups, there was the powerful lure of the horses, Sioux wealth. Even if one of the suitors managed to win Black Buffalo Woman's hand, still he had to give Red Cloud enough horses to get his blessing. A raid was the only way to get them.

With more joy than he had felt in weeks, Crazy Horse packed his best leggings, his bone breastplates, his otterskin braid wraps and his bladder food bags filled with pemmican. In addition to his bow and arrows, he took his shield and the lance he was entitled to carry as a member of the Kit Foxes.

The raiding party had kept its plans a secret, sneaking out of the village at midnight. Actually, Red Cloud, Old Man Afraid and the other elders knew what they were up to but closed their eyes to it.

Away from camp Crazy Horse set a slow pace, for he didn't want to tire the ponies on the way over.

The next night when they found a convenient flat spot at a bend in the river, it was Crazy Horse who gave the band of twenty-five instructions for making camp. Some of them had expected No Water to assert his leadership and were surprised when he didn't. After watering the horses, they picketed the pack horses and hobbled the mounts to graze.

Dog Leg, one of the two boys who had tagged along with them, asked Crazy Horse if he should stay up all night and keep guard. Dog Leg would have flown off a cliff if it could gain him Crazy Horse's approval.

"Thank you," Crazy Horse said solemnly. "I'll share part of the watch with you."

How much better he felt out here! This was where a man belonged, not in a camp full of gaggling women.

He told Dog Leg and the other boy so at midnight. "This is where a man is at his best." Around them the others slept rolled up in blankets. "Counting coups and taking prisoners are what make a Sioux a Lakota. You must take risks in battle, throw yourself into danger, push yourself when your heart quivers with fear." The pair solemnly stared at him. "You can escape death only by becoming its lover."

"Its lover?" repeated Dog Leg, puzzled.

"Slide right up next to it, tickle it, give it a chance to roll over and crush you the way a dog sometimes crushes its puppies."

"But—" Dog Leg began and stopped.

"I know," Crazy Horse smiled. "It doesn't make sense. It isn't reasonable. An old man would tell you the chances aren't good. But it's often then that you can snatch the most honor."

Their eyes glowing, the two boys listened and absorbed the wisdom of the leader of the Kit Foxes.

By dawn the camp was awake. When all the horses were gathered and the saddle horses readied, Crazy Horse had everyone eat some pemmican. They mounted and rode slowly till noon, when they stopped for water.

No Water and Blue Chest, an Oglala brave and not a suitor for Black Buffalo Woman, asked Crazy Horse for permission to model their battle dress. Crazy

Horse gave it, knowing they were looking forward to counting coups. They went off and came back shortly dressed in full battle regalia and singing "Sotka Yuka."

No Water walked up to Dog Leg, who stared admiringly at the warrior's leggings and breastplate. The Brulé punched him so hard with the butt of his lance that the boy fell over backwards.

Everyone except Crazy Horse laughed, knowing that No Water was only joking, showing them all what he would do to the Crow in battle.

Blue Chest strutted around the camp chanting:

> I'm going into battle;
> I'll use my horse there.
> I'll show them my horse
> Is better than their horses.
> I'll run their horses down.

Having made the desired impression, No Water and Blue Chest withdrew to change back into their travel clothes.

The noon meal finished, the raiding party moved on. The route now led to the lowlands and through wooded draws. They approached the barren flats slowly, Crazy Horse carefully surveying the countryside before allowing them to proceed.

Dog Leg, to his credit, sighted a small herd of buffalo. At once everyone wanted to go after it, tired of eating pemmican, but Crazy Horse wouldn't allow them to hunt until the area had been scouted for enemies. When they were sure there were none, Crazy Horse, to impress No Water with the prowess of the Oglala, told Blue Chest to go get them a buffalo, but to take only one arrow. By this, No Water knew that

Crazy Horse had chosen one of the best men. If Blue Chest failed to kill with that one arrow, he would be shamed before all of them and someone else, perhaps even No Water, would be picked the next time.

Blue Chest took his arrow and slowly rode his war horse toward the herd. After a quarter of an hour studying the huge animals, the Oglala chose his victim. Holding his horse's reins in his mouth, he charged.

Crazy Horse and the others watched. This was the sort of challenge that made a Sioux a Lakota. Blue Chest's horse, trained to run close to the galloping buffalo, made his work easier. Aiming at the heart of a fat cow, he killed her with the single shot.

The rest of the party rode out, hooting and howling, Crazy Horse leading the way, to help Blue Chest butcher the cow. No Water suggested that they make soup, which was enthusiastically seconded. They carefully removed the cow's paunch, and when the meat was cut and the tongue, liver and kidneys removed, they headed for a nearby creek.

Dog Leg, his friend and a couple of the younger braves heated stones while No Water stretched the cow's paunch over a frame of four sticks and filled it with water. When the stones were hot, they were carried to the paunch one by one on a forked stick. After a dozen stones had been thrown into it the water began to boil and No Water dropped strips of meat in to cook.

Drinking the soup from his horn cup in the shade of the scrub pines by the creek, Crazy Horse was filled with a deep feeling of contentment. The men he was with, except for No Water, of course, could all be counted on, and what in life was more enjoyable than being on the trail with other Lakota?

It was several more days before the raiders reached Crow country. Now it was important to keep moving, not to sleep for more than a few hours a night. That way if the enemy did spot them, by the time an attacking force returned they would no longer be there.

Crazy Horse sent out scouts in several directions. By noon they had all returned, two with the exact location of the Crow village. Crazy Horse filled his pipe, offering it first to the Four Winds, the Earth and the Sky, then presenting it to the scouts. Smoking it was their vow to tell the truth. The two scouts who had gone south reported a medium-sized Crow camp at the fork of a creek. For their efforts each was now entitled to a scout feather.

It was time to dress for battle. Some put on fine buckskin shirts and leggings; others, quilted armbands and bone breastplates. But while some dressed in their finest, the best way to die in battle, others wore only moccasins and breechcloths, preferring the freedom of movement.

Each warrior prepared his amulet and painted his horse and himself according to his wakan formula. Dog Leg and his friend watched all these preparations closely, seeking to learn, but asked no questions. They knew that at this time the men must concentrate on their chants and prayers. Those who owned war bonnets put them on; the power of eagle feathers would somewhat protect a man. Those who carried lances attached otter skins and feathered trailers to them. Some fastened feathers in their horses' manes and tails to protect them. Others tied up the tails with strips of red flannel.

As always, Crazy Horse dressed simply, putting

on only a breechcloth, painting first his and then his horse's chest with the mark of thunder and making sure his wakan blue stone was securely tied behind his left ear. He looked in the sky for a hawk, his power animal, but saw none. This made him anxious. Had he somehow offended his wakan bird? Would he lose men today? He would make sure to ride at the head of any action today.

The plan was to ride all night, enter the village at daybreak and run off the horses and retreat. When chased, they would turn and put up a fight. This would give them the chance to count coups.

After Crazy Horse explained the plan, each warrior rode off a little distance and blew through an eagle feather, asking Wakan-Takan and his own power animal for help, making promises: "If I am successful today, I will give up a robe in an offering to you." Each then sang a song to the four sacred directions before rejoining the others.

Night was falling and it was almost time to leave when Crazy Horse noticed that No Water was behaving strangely. He held his head at a funny angle. When anyone looked at him, he forced it up as if he had been doing something he didn't want anyone else to know about.

"What's wrong with your neck?" Crazy Horse finally asked him.

"Nothing," No Water answered, but his manner made Crazy Horse suspicious. Something felt wrong.

The others gathered around them. "*Hai,* let's go on," No Water said impatiently. "I expect to get myself half a dozen ponies."

"Your jaw doesn't hurt, does it?" asked Blue

Chest. He leaned forward over his horse's neck to stare at No Water's face.

"What if it does?" Crazy Horse demanded.

"He told me his power dream. If his jaw hurts, it brings bad wakan in a battle."

"Does your jaw hurt?" asked Crazy Horse.

"Only sometimes." No Water looked away from him.

"It does!" shouted one of the braves near him. "Look how swollen the left side is!"

Crazy Horse looked and saw that the whole lower left ridge of the jaw protruded. When he reached out to touch it, No Water pulled back.

This stopped them, for this was truly bad wakan. Several wanted to call off the raid. Others were for going through a sweat bath to cleanse themselves. But the most favored suggestion, put forward by Blue Chest, was to send No Water back. After all, their goal was so near, and it wouldn't be much fun to return with nothing to show for their trip.

No Water argued that he had had these attacks before, that the pain often went away in a few hours and that he certainly had more sense than actually to ride into battle with bad wakan. But the more he protested, the more certain Crazy Horse became that for No Water to ride with them would be bad wakan and that he must leave the war party.

As darkness fell, No Water finally gave in. He silently turned his horse and rode back the way they had come.

Chapter 7

Leaving Dog Leg and the other boy behind to look after the extra horses, Crazy Horse led the attack party toward a tall butte about a mile from the Crow village.

Silently they led their horses up the mountain trail and waited. Crazy Horse was conscious of the old familiar excitement. Fear, tension and eagerness fought in his stomach. He took deep calming breaths, as Old Hump had taught him to do when he was still a boy.

All night the warriors sat their horses, hardly moving and making no noise. Just before dawn each man took a pinch of medicine from his wakan pouch. He offered this to the Four Winds, the Sky and the Earth, then put some on his horse's mouth and nose to make him long-winded. This done, the warriors walked their horses to get them to make water. This would keep them from getting colic and help them hold out longer.

At daybreak the unsuspecting Crow turned their horses out to pasture, leaving only a few prized mounts picketed within the camp. The horses headed down to the river to drink, then moved north to graze.

Crazy Horse looked up at the sky. In the east wheeled two hawks, making his heart leap and promising him good luck. He had been right to send No Water back.

As the last of the horses left the river Crazy Horse gave the order. Leading the warriors down among the willows, he drove the stragglers towards the flats, where the raiding party surrounded the herd and headed it northeast toward Dog Leg, his friend and the supply horses.

Crazy Horse was pleased. So far no one at the Crow camp had noticed them, though any moment someone would. He assigned Blue Chest and Kicking Bird to hang back and keep a lookout.

The main party reached the base camp unmolested. Warning them to keep to low ground, Crazy Horse sent the boys and two warriors riding ahead toward home with the pack animals and the stolen horses. Now the trick would be to keep what they had taken.

Loping their war horses easily over the high ground where they would be seen, the rest of the raiding party waited. Soon they saw Blue Chest and Kicking Bear galloping toward them, and then some twenty Crow came into view. Spotting the rest of the Sioux, they began to ride faster.

This was what Crazy Horse had been waiting for. The Sioux picked up speed. As expected, before long some of the Crow began to fall by the wayside, victims of winded horses.

Crazy Horse kept glancing back at the pursuers. When their ranks had thinned by half a dozen men, he suddenly wheeled his horse around and signaled the others to follow. Each rider made a short, quick circle back toward the advancing Crow. Leaning off to the side, using his horse as a shield, each man shot one arrow, then another. The riders wheeled again and rode back in their original direction, then repeated the maneuver to strike again at the advancing Crow. On the third execution the pursuers became the pursued.

Crazy Horse nocked an arrow and hit the nearest Crow in the stomach. He rode up to the warrior, who was still clinging to his horse, struggling to remove the arrow. With his Kit Fox lance Crazy Horse knocked him to the ground, counting coup. He hit the horse with his lance for another coup, then jumped down to scalp the dead Crow. Around him rode the rest of his party, intent on their coups, and more of the enemy fell. It wasn't long before some of the survivors headed for a hill while the rest scattered.

Satisfied, Crazy Horse turned his men toward home. They had killed three Crow warriors and captured many horses. Before leaving, they rode back over the battlefield and touched the fallen enemy, sharing coups among them.

They rode home slowly, unafraid. It was good to ride with Crazy Horse, many were thinking, for again under his leadership no one had been lost.

The next day they caught up with the rest of the party and divided the stolen horses before moving on again. As they rode they worked red paint and grease into the scalps they had taken and tied them to long poles. Nearing home, they camped for the night. At dawn, stripped of their clothes, faces blackened and bodies painted red, they charged into the village waving the scalp poles and shouting. As they circled the center of the village, they cried out their names and their boasts: "I'm Blue Chest. I made a kill and took horses."

As usual, Crazy Horse rode in last and did not prance, but stayed modestly to one side.

A feast of jerked tongue, pemmican and young dog was prepared in honor of the victors. The horses they had captured were given to their sisters and other female relatives, who in turn gifted the warriors with embroidered moccasins and leggings and other personal items.

By midmorning Crazy Horse was weary of all the celebrating. Too much food put you to sleep, and as for telling and retelling your exploits, what did that give a man? All that mattered was being in harmony with the wakan around you.

He hadn't seen Black Buffalo Woman yet. It occurred to him that his hero's welcome and the good feelings aroused by the celebration might have lowered her guard. He just might persuade her to marry him.

Buoyed by this thought, Crazy Horse stopped three women in turn to ask where Black Buffalo Woman might be found. Each said she didn't know, and by the time he asked the third, he knew something peculiar was going on. The women always knew the business and whereabouts of every other woman in the village. He asked one more, Yellow Leaf, a close friend of Black Buffalo Woman. She didn't know either.

Crazy Horse rushed to Red Cloud's tepee. It was empty; probably the entire family was off celebrating, he thought, Black Buffalo Woman chaperoned by Pretty Owl.

He had no trouble locating Red Cloud, who sat

in Young Man Afraid's tepee feasting on dog meat and listening to Blue Chest repeat the story of his kill and his fifteen coups for what Crazy Horse figured must have been the fifth time that morning.

"Yes, I know where she is," Red Cloud nodded. "She's with No Water at Spotted Tail's camp. They were married yesterday and left right after the wedding."

"Married!"

"Married," confirmed Red Cloud.

"To No Water!" Crazy Horse was dimly aware of laughter around him.

"Sit down and have some dog," offered Young Man Afraid. "You'll just have to find another lodge to blow your flute in front of."

There was more laughter then.

"Married! But she was going to marry me!" Crazy Horse protested.

"A bullfrog was going to fly, but he bumped his ass and couldn't get off the ground," said Young Man Afraid.

"She was just trying to make me jealous."

Red Cloud shrugged; things happened the way they happened.

"Get another woman," advised Young Man Afraid. "A year after you're married, you'll find they're all the same."

The other men hooted and began to tease Young Man Afraid about what his wives would do to him when they heard what he had just said. Crazy Horse glared at them. He wanted his lance. He wanted to beat them all, knock those silly grins off their faces. He wanted to kill No Water!

Then suddenly he wanted to sit down and cry,

wanted to hear Buffalo Woman's voice telling him it wasn't true. Hadn't she said dozens of times when they were growing up that she would be his wife?

He turned and stumbled out of the tepee. Black Buffalo Woman was gone, gone from him forever, as if dead, and he knew he would never stop mourning.

The morning of the day the raiding party left the Bad Face camp, Black Buffalo Woman received a summons from her uncle. She entered the tepee to find no one there but Red Cloud, and this made her uneasy. She could not remember ever being alone with him there. Always Pretty Owl or one of his other wives or his daughters were about.

"What is it, uncle? Pretty Owl said you wanted to see me."

"Sit here. On my right." She sat on the buffalo robe and waited nervously for him to continue.

"No Water, the brother of Black Twin, has offered me a large number of horses as a gift. Will you have him?"

"No Water? No, I do not care for him," she answered.

Her uncle sat thinking about her answer for such a long time that she grew even more nervous. She knew how fond of her Red Cloud was. She had long suspected that if she had not been his niece, he would have asked her to be his fourth wife. Of course, she had never told anyone this. So knowing how he cared for her, how kind he had always been to her since he had taken her to raise as his own, she was shocked at his answer.

"No matter," he said. "I want you to marry No Water."

"But—" She was stunned. She couldn't believe it. He must be teasing. "No, it's Curly I'll marry, when he's shown me that I'm not just some Crow woman he can snatch up and put to work."

"This village needs to be connected to Black Twin's," Red Cloud insisted. "I've made up my mind. You'll marry No Water."

"No, Uncle!"

"Yes. I'm sorry, but it has to be."

For a while then neither spoke. Black Buffalo Woman wasn't used to rebelling against him, and Red Cloud hardly knew what to say. His own daughters wouldn't have dared argue with him. In fact, they would have been delighted to please him. He sighed. Why couldn't No Water have chased one of them?

Neither looked at the other, but sat staring at the walls of the tepee.

"Tomorrow," said Red Cloud. "I've already told Pretty Owl. You'll marry him tomorrow afternoon, and he'll take you away to his camp."

"Tomorrow!" she exclaimed. "Leave all my friends? Give up Curly? No!"

She wanted to scream, to weep, to tell him that he was talking about the rest of her life, her happiness, the father of her children and the man she would make a lodge for. She opened her mouth to say this and more, but he spoke first.

"I have provided for you since your parents died. You have eaten the game I've provided and have slept inside the lodge Pretty Owl made. Very little has been asked of you in return. Now something is being asked. You have no right to say no."

This argument stopped her. Still, she couldn't

give in. She stared stonily at the tepee wall. After a while, Red Cloud dismissed her, telling her to prepare for the wedding. She clenched her hands, wanting to beat them against his face and chest. His stern face frightened her. She knew her uncle. Once he took a stand he did not change it. She silently left the lodge.

She left the village and wandered in a daze most of the afternoon. When she returned she searched out her best friend, Yellow Leaf, who offered little help.

"What can you do?" Yellow Leaf asked. "If you don't marry No Water, your uncle may marry you off to some back-end man." Black Buffalo Woman shuddered. These were Sioux who lived in small tepees on the outskirts of camp and rode at the end of the tribe when it traveled.

"I won't marry No Water. I'll wait for Crazy Horse. We'll get married and then what can they do?"

"Without Red Cloud's blessing?" Yellow Leaf was shocked. "How could you? How could you live here?"

"After a while people forget."

"No. Crazy Horse wouldn't be allowed to lead raiding or hunting parties if he disobeyed Red Cloud. He couldn't stay in the Kit Fox society. And he's an officer too."

Black Buffalo Woman's heart fell. Yellow Leaf was right. The men's war societies depended on a man's doing the right thing. A man who went against Sioux custom was stripped of his office and membership.

"Would he be willing to go off with you and leave all that?" asked Yellow Leaf.

Black Buffalo Woman shook her head. "I don't

95

know." But even if Crazy Horse could be induced to go against her uncle, to give up the male fellowship he loved, eventually he would probably hate her.

"Oh, what am I to do!"

Yellow Leaf took her hand and pressed it gently. "No Water isn't so bad. He's good-looking and I hear he's a good hunter. He comes from a much better family than Crazy Horse. You'll be his first wife and I know I wouldn't mind living in a Brulé camp!"

"But you don't understand!" Buffalo Woman wailed. "I want Crazy Horse! I should have married him when he asked me instead of trying to make him court me."

"Well, there's no help for it now," her friend said.

Black Buffalo Woman stood up. "There is."

Yellow Leaf rose and looked at her closely. "What do you mean?"

But Buffalo Woman ignored the question. "Good-bye, Yellow Leaf. We've been good friends, but we won't be seeing each other again."

"Oh, I'm going to be in the wedding party. Pretty Owl has asked me."

"There's not going to be a wedding. Good-bye." She hugged Yellow Leaf tightly and walked out of the village, not looking back.

She hoped Yellow Leaf had understood her. Her uncle meant what he had said that morning, but she had too. She would not go through with this marriage.

As she walked away from the village, Black Buffalo Woman thought about what other girls in her situation had done. In particular she remembered the story of a Minneconjou girl who had been courted by a man her family objected to. They wouldn't take his gifts, even moved to another village where they chose her a husband they thought more suitable. She rejected him, threatening to kill herself, but even that hadn't stopped her parents. In the end she was forced to marry.

On her wedding night she crept out of her husband's lodge. He was awake and watching, and when she left the tepee he followed her. The girl went to the top of a high cliff and sat down on a flat rock. As Buffalo Woman climbed the rocks north of the village, she pictured the maiden in her mind's eye, undoing her braids, covering herself with her long heavy hair. She pictured the girl's husband, hiding behind a tree, spying on her. . . .

The husband makes a sound. The girl turns, sees him and says, "I don't want you, yet you follow me." She picks up her shawl, wraps it around her face and begins to sing a death song. Then she leaps off the cliff before her husband can reach her. He leans over the edge, sees that she has landed in a spruce halfway down. Cradled there, she finishes her death song, then flings herself into space to smash against the rocks in the water below. . . .

Buffalo Woman sighed. It was said that for years if anyone passing the spot mentioned the girl's name, the waves below rose so high no canoe could pass.

It took Black Buffalo Woman some time to find just the right place, one with so much wakan that those who passed would feel it and be reminded of how her uncle had crushed her and how strong her love for Crazy Horse had been. The wakan of the site she finally chose, a ravine with sharp, jutting rocks at the bottom, might even be so strong that when Crazy Horse came to see where she had died, he would be so overwhelmed with grief that he would throw himself off the cliff and join her. That would show Red Cloud!

She looked around her. The ravine was a good choice for another reason. It wasn't so lonely that she would never be found. If they never found her, then Red Cloud and No Water and all the others would never know how wrong they had been. But to be sure, she would leave her belt and her moccasins behind.

She had walked slowly up into the hills, and if she had figured correctly, No Water or Red Cloud ought to be not too far behind her by now. She wanted them to see what she did, just like the girl in the story. She had no death shawl to pull over her head. She would simply close her eyes. Until she had peered over the edge of the ravine she hadn't understood the point of the shawl in the story, but the dizzying drop and the ugly fanglike rocks at the bottom made it plain. She wondered how much it would hurt when she hit the rocks.

Carefully she undid her hair and began to sing a death song, loudly, for it was beginning to get dark and she wanted to make sure that Red Cloud or No Water found her before nightfall. Supposing the old stories were true and if she fell off this cliff at night she would stumble around paradise in the dark for the rest of time. Besides, it was scary out here. Who knew what spirit or wakan demon might carry her off?

Then she saw him! No Water! Yellow Leaf had done just what Buffalo Woman had hoped. She closed her eyes and made sure she didn't betray herself with a smile as she sang the death song more loudly still.

She heard him cry, "No, don't move! You might fall off! I'm coming."

How stupid he was! He had no idea what she was about to do. They would talk about her for years to come, telling her story over and over. She peeked through the veil of her hair and saw No Water charging across the clearing toward her.

He would be sorry for what he had done! She waited until he was within a few yards, then took a step backward toward the ravine edge, then another. Closing her eyes, she pictured the dizzy drop behind her. . . .

Her right foot wouldn't move. She stopped singing and concentrated on picking it up, but it was rooted in the ground. She struggled to pick up the left foot, but it too refused to budge. No Water was almost on top of her. She desperately leaned back.

No Water grabbed her around the waist and flung her to one side. She hit the ground and the skin on her elbow and knee tore. He dragged her away from the cliff edge toward the woods. As he pulled her along, the pain and frustration inside her exploded in harsh sobbing. She knew what had happened and she hated it. She had told herself she wanted to die, had even gotten as far as the cliff, but her body, knowing better, had refused to obey. Some wakan had kept her alive.

No Water carried her weeping back to the village and into Red Cloud's tepee. She had fallen, he said. Red Cloud didn't ask questions.

Full of shame for her lack of courage, Black Buffalo Woman could hardly speak. Pretty Owl was making buffalo stew and gossiping with the other wives

99

about the wedding. They looked curiously at her. Did they know what had happened? Did they guess? If so they said nothing.

That night she couldn't sleep and one of the women stayed up with her. Buffalo Woman said nothing, but she knew she would not try to escape again. If she couldn't kill herself, what escape was there? To convince Crazy Horse to marry her and ruin himself? That would be no victory.

Maybe Red Cloud did know what was good for her and for the tribe. How much choice did she have?

The next day she did what the women asked. She dressed and learned what to say during the ceremony. When the time came she went as docilely to No Water as a puppy to the feast pot.

Chapter 8

It was time. Red Cloud dressed carefully, threw a thick-haired buffalo skin over his shoulders and mounted his best horse. Accompanied by Young Man Afraid, he rode stern-faced and silent, holding his pipe filled and sealed before him, toward the lodge of Old Hump.

The two held their horses to a slow walk. Had Hump lived in another village, they wouldn't have gone faster, nor would they have eaten if it took all day to get there. To do so would have invited bad wakan on themselves and on all those who danced the Sun Dance.

News of his coming had already been sent to the shaman, who sat waiting in his tepee with his herald. After Red Cloud entered and laid his pipe in front of the old priest, the herald called out, "All come home," a summons to the entire council waiting nearby. When they had assembled, Hump purified Red Cloud's pipe in the wakan incense of sweet grass and prayed, holding the stem to the west:

O great mystery, grandfather, you will be the
       first to smoke this pipe.
Wing Flappers, you in turn will smoke.
This day may the Sioux nation live,
A blue day will you hold before my face.

He gave the pipe to each of the others to smoke.
As it passed around, Red Cloud grew increasingly
solemn and attentive. How much wakan he could feel
here. How good to be Lakota!

Hump smoked the pipe in the proper manner and
made sure its contents were emptied into the fire so
that no one could step on them and offend Wakan-
Takan. When the pipe was smoked this way, the spirit
in the smoke went into the mouth and body and then
came out and went upward. While this spirit was in
the body it soothed the smoker. As the smoke went
upward, it soothed Waken-Takan. Now the smoker
and Wakan-Takan were as friends.

Hump asked Red Cloud to stay till morning.
Throughout the night the old man sang song after song
over the chief of the Bad Faces. As morning dawned,
Hump refilled the pipe and placed red paint before
him. Red Cloud felt both sleepy and restless. He wanted to lie down by this old man and sleep. At the same
time he wanted to get up and go hunting or run. He
had thought all night long about the Sun Dance, as
Hump had told him to, and he was certain he still
wanted to do it. But he wasn't so certain he could
stand up under its rigors.

Red Cloud rubbed the red paint on his palms and
smeared it over his face and body.

"Man Afraid, wait outside," Old Hump ordered.

As Young Man Afraid scrambled up and reverently walked backward out of the wakan man's tepee, Red Cloud watched the shaman. This wasn't part of the usual ceremony, sending out a candidate's companion, but then a priest could do whatever was necessary to make sure the Sun Dance worked. There had never been a Sun Dance in which something new had not been added to the old to handle some new problem that had come up.

"You're taking on a role for younger men." Hump referred to Red Cloud's decision not only to call the dance but to act as chief dancer.

"I know."

"Why are you undertaking this dance?"

"These intruders have run off our buffalo. They'll starve our women and children. We must drive them back. I want wakan power. I want the other chiefs to see what I see." He lowered his head. "And I want to know if I am doing the right thing or if bad wakan has entered my heart."

For some moments the old man seemed to turn the answer over in his mind. He was old, Red Cloud thought. He looked like a stalk of sagebrush about to be blown away until you looked into those eyes, deep, sad eyes that never looked away, but searched you for the truth. Red Cloud wanted to wriggle away from the old man's scrutiny as he had wanted to wriggle away from his father's as a child.

"Chief dancer, though," said Hump. "You should get one of the younger men to do that for you."

"If I'm to lead them, if I'm to know, I must be the chief dancer."

"When you come back from presenting the invitations, I want you to put yourself under my instruction until the dance starts."

"Fine."

Red Cloud knew leading the dance would be difficult. But many Sioux would come just to see how well such an aged dancer performed, how much wakan he carried. He wanted to show them that he had plenty, more than enough to beat the whites.

"I never knew a man as old as you to be the lead dancer," said Hump. "I can't make it easier for you."

"I don't expect that."

That day, again carrying the pipe, Red Cloud and Young Man Afraid rode on in the same slow, measured way to the next Sioux village. When they entered the tepee of its chief, he promptly summoned the old men of the village.

The chief first offered Red Cloud's pipe to the Mysteries of the Four Winds, the Sky and the Earth. Then he passed it to the old men.

"What did the priest say to you?" asked the chief.

Red Cloud gave the ritual answer. "That they would move to the ground in four days."

"Then we'll all move at that time," came the old response.

The chief's wife brought in food and water. Afterward, Red Cloud and Man Afraid rode on to invite the other villages to the Sun Dance.

When at last they rode back to their own camp, Red Cloud felt both elated and anxious. All the tribes of nearby Sioux, Brulé, Oglala and Minneconjou as well as some Cheyenne had agreed to come to the dance. But for him to lead it? At his age? Did he still have the strength? He had taken part in the Sun Dance when he was twenty, then again at twenty-four. Now he was almost twice that. Many warriors never participated, and most did only once. But three times! And at his age to lead!

"Will you attend me, Man Afraid?"

"This is such a hard thing you're doing, brother," said Man Afraid. "But yes, I'll be with you the whole time. You can count on me."

Under Red Cloud's direction, the young men at the village planted green cedar branches two to three yards apart to form a circle about a mile in diameter and open to the east. In the following days the tribes arrived. Each pitched its tepees in a circle on the edge of the huge cedar one. Inside their smaller circles each village erected a sweat lodge for the use of the men who would take part in the ordeal. Around the bottom of this tepee they piled thick branches to prevent the entrance of any cool air. That evening they started a fire. The dancers entered and must not leave until the actual dancing began. Nor could they scratch their heads or any part of the body with their fingers, each man having been provided with a forked stick for this purpose.

Under Old Hump's direction, medicine men from the other villages coached the participants. The next few days were spent in the Imitation Dance, the rehearsal of the Sun Dance songs.

While the dancers prepared for their roles, the assembled camps mixed freely. The first four days of the Sun Dance were a festival, and this was a time to see old friends, look up relatives and give gifts.

In the second four, Old Hump and the other leaders made sure the dancers were well instructed. Hump had already selected his lay assistants, a Hunter, a Digger, an Escort and a Singer, all great honors.

The last four were the holy days, the height of

the Sioux religious year. On the first of these, criers
rode through the camps asking the men to assemble.
From the hundreds who came, Hump and his assistants selected four to act as scouts. These picked four
more. As previously arranged, one was Black Twin,
who became the scouts' leader.

The eight scouts, dressed and painted as if for
war, prepared to begin the search for the tall, straight
cottonwood that Young Man Afraid, as assistant to
Red Cloud, had selected and marked by leaning two
poles against it.

Drums beating, drummers singing, the scouts
formed up in single file and rode four times around
the mile-long cedar circle, then away towards the timber, accompanied for a distance by horsemen dashing
around in circles.

From the camp came the song of the drummers:

He has gone again,
He has gone again.

This symbolized that Black Twin, the leader, was
in enemy territory.

A couple hundred yards from the camp, a group
of young warriors set up a bundle of branches to rep-
resent the enemy. The scouts appeared and Black Twin
gave a thin, piercing coyote cry. The eight scouts zigzagged single file toward the camp, signifying that they
had sighted the enemy.

As with one impulse, hundreds of youths on
ponies rushed Black Twin and the other scouts. Four
times they circled them in a great seething mass, then
suddenly veered away toward the bundle of branches.
The goal of each youth was to reach the enemy bun-

dle first. No risk of riding was too great, and it was hard for those watching to understand why none of them fell under the hooves. In a burst of speed, Otter Lance of Spotted Tail's band struck the bundle with his bow and in triumph shouted, "*Anke!*" He was assured now of achieving the first coup in the next battle he fought.

That afternoon the assembled tribes joined together to perform the Buffalo Dance, a great processional saluting the Buffalo and the Whirlwind, patrons of the lodge and of lovemaking. A Buffalo Dreamer supervised the pageantry and blessed the dancers.

For four days now Red Cloud had not left the sweat lodge. Young-Man-Afraid-of-His-Horses attended him, bringing in the hot stones, dropping them into the water to make steam, making sure that the flaps of the sweat lodge were firmly tied down and keeping stray dogs and children away from the chanting chief dancer. Hump and the best shamans from other tribes came and went, checking on Red Cloud's progress.

By now he had put aside his worldly concerns. Quarrels with Pretty Owl over how often he slept with his other wives, arguments with Spotted Tail over what was the right Sioux course, questions about whether he had been right to force Black Buffalo Woman to marry No Water, all such things were forgotten. They no longer distracted him from what he should have seen but had failed to keep his eyes on: that the Sioux had been placed on this earth by Wakan-Takan, the Great Father, to guide and preserve the life he had set here. You could walk north for hundreds of miles and see his face in the trees, in the animals and in the pattern the rocks made as they fell from the cliffs. Wakan-Takan had laid out the lakes and planted the forests. He had sent the buffalo in a great dance of migration from north to south and back again. No man could penetrate the mystery of his purpose, for if a man knew it, it would burst his brain and heart, its wakan was so strong.

If Red Cloud could prove himself strong enough in the Sun Dance, perhaps Wakan-Takan would give him the strength to hold back the destruction the whites made.

Hump came in to give him a new chant. "And now no food for the next three days," he told Young Man Afraid. "You'll think you're doing him a favor to sneak him some pemmican, but he's likely to suffer more if he eats."

"I won't eat," Red Cloud snorted.

"You keep on chanting," Hump said sternly. "This is between me and Young Man Afraid."

The second of the four holy days was devoted to the capture of the cottonwood tree that Man Afraid had marked out. Hump and the other medicine men first cleansed the camp of evil spirits, then formed a procession of some five hundred villagers to go into the woods. Included were the women who wanted to have their children's ears pierced at this wakan time, which would give the children power to ward off evil.

At the fourth resting place before the procession reached the cottonwood enemy, Hump chose four warriors. Each recounted the hunting and battlefield exploits that entitled him to strike the tree. When the procession finally reached the cottonwood, the four warriors struck it with axes to subdue its enemy *nagila*. Then Hump ordered the tree to be killed and each

woman in the procession took a turn at chopping it.
When the tree was ready to fall, the woman chosen
for the greatest honor struck the final blow, and everyone sang and cheered with joy.

The woman who had felled the tree gathered her
assistant. They peeled the limbs and bark off the foot-
thick trunk to a point just before it forked, leaving
the top branches entwined. Other women gathered the
discarded twigs as a protection against Anog-Ite, the
devil who tempted women. Now only shamans and
men who had previously danced the Sun Dance could
touch the tree. A delegation of them stuck poles under it and picked it up.

Carried to the cedar circle, the cottonwood was
painted so that when standing the west side would be
red, the north blue, the east green and the south yellow. To the fork were attached black rawhide figures
of the demons Iya and Gnaske, their breasts, vulva,
hips and penis exaggerated to indicate their sexual
licentiousness. To the top of the tree were tied sixteen
cherry sticks enclosing tobacco offerings, a leather buffalo effigy, an arrow for buffalo and a picket pin for
securing a captured horse. The stripped and painted
tree was raised in four stages. On the last heave it was
dropped into the wakan hole.

As soon as the pole was raised, the throngs around
it hooted at the two libidinous demons.

"Hey, Iya, come down here and spread your legs!"
came a shout.

"Let's see what you can do with that thing, Gnaske, you foolish woodpecker!"

Normally the Sioux were as prim in public as
Puritans, but now, while Iya and Gnaske ruled the
camp, all verbal bounds were down.

"Say, woman, would you like to go lie down with me?" asked Otter Lance. "Turn over and open up your hole to the biggest prick you've ever seen."

The mother of four giggled boldly. "I bet that little thing you got wouldn't fill up my infant daughter."

One Minneconjou warrior went from maiden to maiden, asking them to come off into the woods with him. He stopped after three told him what they would do to him in such graphic detail that he was afraid if he took them up on it their enthusiasm might wring his penis off.

The village shamans, Old Hump at their head, watched the men, women, youths and maidens cavorting around the cottonwood pole.

"It turns my stomach to see all this," complained a Cheyenne medicine man. "I don't let this part go on for so long."

Hump sighed and smiled. "I want it to go on until they get sick of it. The longer they keep it up now the less they'll sneak around the tepees during the year."

After two hours of it, Hump gave a hand signal. A group of warriors came together to dance the War Dance. They shot their arrows at the two obscene leather figures of Iya and Gnaske at the top of the pole until they fell to the ground, where they were kicked about and trampled into the dust by the dancers.

The end of the third holy day was spent in final preparation of the Dance Lodge. Hump directed forty young men to build a leafy roof supported on two concentric circles of forked sticks. The walls of the Dance Lodge were of loose, leafy boughs and vines so spectators would have no trouble seeing the dancers within. Finally Hump sent a younger medicine man for a dried buffalo skull. This he placed on a bed of sage just west of the wakan pole. He painted it with stripes of red to assure a successful dance and an abundance of buffalo in the fall.

In the meantime, fifty young men had painted their faces white. Those who had earned them donned war bonnets and honor shirts. At a shout from Hump's crier, these now came trooping single file into the Dance Lodge to perform the Dance That Smooths the Ground. As the drummers pounded and sang, the warriors danced toward the wakan pole, shooting at the rawhide effigy of the buffalo, retreating and again advancing. With a storm of war cries, the buffalo was soon brought to the ground.

The sun was almost down now and the dancers filed out of the dance lodge. Hump wanted to be alone there, saying his own prayers, listening to his heart and the wakan of the place to make sure that it had been properly consecrated. The next day so much wakan would be called for that if the power wasn't well balanced it could slip, fly around and destroy half the people there.

Satisfied after an hour's chanting, Hump went to check on Young Man Afraid and Red Cloud. He found Red Cloud sitting motionless in the dark sweat lodge.

"He hasn't moved or said a word all afternoon," Young Man Afraid whispered.

"What was he doing?" asked the medicine man.

"He did that series of chants you gave him, then started singing to the eagles."

111

"Did he do all the eagle chants?" The eagle was Red Cloud's power animal.

"Almost all. He got to the part where he thanks the eagle."

Hump peered through the gloom at Red Cloud's face. The chief sat cross-legged, staring straight ahead. Hump waved a hand in front of Red Cloud's face, but the eyes didn't blink or waver. "Then what happened?"

Man Afraid looked down. "I'm afraid I fell asleep."

Hump smiled. "Of course. Look." He pointed at the smoke hole at the top of the tepee. It was torn and was more than half again the size that Man Afraid had made it.

"What! Something came in through there while I slept!"

"The eagle," Hump nodded. "Red Cloud's power animal heard the call and came in to take him."

"Take him?" Young Man Afraid stared at the old medicine man. "But he couldn't get through that hole! Besides, no eagle is strong enough to pick him up."

Hump smiled. "He's away now."

"But—"

Hump motioned him to be quiet. Man Afraid, shivering from the sudden knowledge that more wakan than he knew how to deal with was present, moved away and sat against the sweat-lodge wall. Hump began to chant softly.

Chapter 9

Before dawn the shaman rose and nudged Man Afraid awake. "Give him some water, nothing else, and prepare him."

Red Cloud was smiling, his face as relaxed as a child's. No one spoke, although Young Man Afraid was bursting with questions. He did as he'd been told while Hump purified the sweat lodge with sweet-grass smoke.

Hump now painted Red Cloud with a black semicircle from the forehead down each cheek, others at his shoulder joints and full circles at the elbows and wrists.

"I saw so much yesterday," Red Cloud murmured.

"You should have a good dance," Hump said.

"I saw the whole world. I flew around it on the back of an eagle."

"I know. I saw you."

"If we don't stop the whites they will destroy us. They will destroy the very face of Wakan-Takan."

"Easy," Hump soothed him. "You have a hard day coming up."

A vision of the ceremony sent a shiver through Red Cloud. His glance fell on Young Man Afraid, watching frightened and bewildered.

"Brother, what's the matter?" Red Cloud asked.

Man Afraid tried to smile and failed. Hump answered for him. "The wakan is very strong here. He's never been around so much."

"It is?" Red Cloud looked surprised. "I don't feel it."

"No? You're the source of it."

Red Cloud shivered again. The old man's words silenced him and he simply watched while Hump painted the rest of his body in red. Rolls of buffalo hair were tied to each elbow and wrist. The rolls at his wrists carried small pieces of Indian scalps with long flowing hair. At Hump's order, Man Afraid fastened a single eagle feather in Red Cloud's hair.

At daybreak, when all the other participants filed into the dance lodge, Red Cloud, Man Afraid, Hump and the other medicine men were waiting for them. The dancers wore double aprons of deerskin from waist to knee and buffalo skins, hair out, over their shoulders and belted at the waist. Around each man's neck hung a whistle made from an eagle's wing bone, the mouthpiece wound with sage and the other end adorned with an eagle feather.

After the dancers had been painted by the medicine men, they rose and dropped their buffalo skins. Old Hump, standing beside Red Cloud, pointed his eagle-bone whistle toward the east and blew a shrill note beside the chief dancer's right ear, then another by his left and as Red Cloud stooped, a third over his head. These were the three calls to the wakan of the sun.

The other dancers held their right hands outstretched toward the rising sun.

Hump now led everyone to the south, the west and finally north of the wakan tree, following the sun's course and sounding his whistle at each stop. The dancers stationed themselves around the cedar circle, grouped by village and facing east. Their leaders took posts between the wakan pole and their people, who stood watching on the outside of the great circle.

Hump shouted from just west of the buffalo-skull altar and the drummers began to play and sing. The dancers went up on their toes in time to the beat and began to chant.

This part of the dance demanded that they not leave the spot where they stood. They moved only to rise to the balls of their feet, legs and body rigid, right palms extended toward the rising sun. Each man concentrated on the one thing he wanted most. In Red Cloud's case it was the strength and clarity of mind to lead his people on the right path. Others there wanted powerful wakan, or many coups in battle, or children in a barren marriage, or a particular woman for wife.

Each song was chanted four times. As the sun rose the dancers craned their heads to keep their eyes on its lower rim, chanting and moving up and down on their toes, concentrating on their purpose.

This dancing continued from sunup until noon. The intense light and concentration after the days of preparation, the chanting, the rocking dance step, the rising wakan of the ceremony lifted Red Cloud to an inner place from which he could clearly see the past and future movements of his people. His heart was full of grief at the many dead Sioux he saw; his rage and anger at the white ghosts were so palpable he could have fired them like arrows from his bow. But how to get the others to see?

When the sun reached its zenith, Hump signaled and the drummers ceased drumming. The chanting stopped and the dancers dropped back on their heels. Hump waited, letting the silence take hold, permitting wakan to enter. His old eyes could not see clearly, but he knew that some of the dancers had tears streaming down their faces.

When he felt it was time, he filled a pipe and handed it to Red Cloud, who turned and offered it to Young Man Afraid. He refused it. Red Cloud attempted to force it on him, striving to open his friend's hand and put the pipe in it, but Man Afraid kept his fist clenched.

Red Cloud turned to Hump, who sternly ordered, "Go again!" Twice more Young Man Afraid refused the offer of the pipe, but on the fourth attempt he accepted. "Ho! It's hard, but if you want it I'll do it, my brother."

He lit the pipe and the two of them shared it, signaling agreement. Red Cloud returned to his dance place. Man Afraid took a wooden picket stake and split it into quarters, two of which he whittled down into smooth six-inch triangular skewers.

Around the circle, inside and out, dancers and spectators held their breath. The only sound was the wind moving across the grass.

Man Afraid put the skewers on the ground next to Red Cloud and stood erect. He began to pray: "Wakan-Takan, this is Man-Afraid-of-His-Horses who prays. I'll do this thing, although it's hard. He requests it and I'll do it for him."

Man Afraid spread sage on the ground south of the wakan tree. He led Red Cloud there, lifted him bodily in his arms and hurled his friend to the ground. Man Afraid next selected an assistant, Moon Rim, one of the younger medicine men, who stationed himself on Red Cloud's left and began to whet a knife with a stone.

Red Cloud knew what happened next as well as anyone there, and he fought the urge to jump up and run away. Surely Wakan-Takan had shown him enough! Suppose he screamed and disgraced himself? He was old and soft. Suppose he asked to be cut down from the wakan tree? Could he ever hold his head up again? It was one thing to be an ordinary dancer and suffer pain. You could even ask to be cut down. But it was quite another to be chief dancer. He was expected to show the others how to endure.

Above him, Red Cloud saw Moon Rim sharpening the flint knife. He felt the hot July wind blow over him. The heat of the sun warmed his chest. After the morning's concentration, how pleasant to lie there and listen to the wind. Why did anyone have to fight anyone else? In that peaceful interlude, the idea that anyone could settle anything by fighting seemed stupid.

Man Afraid and Moon Rim had now finished their preparations. A part of Red Cloud still wanted to jump up, to push back the knife and say, "I've seen what I needed to see. Thank you for what you've done for me, but I'm not going to need the rest." But what a fool he would appear! What a coward! He would lose his value to his people and his people would lose themselves because of it. Such thoughts were one of the very enemies he had come here today to vanquish. He pushed them away.

Man Afraid knelt, grabbed the skin of one of Red Cloud's breasts with his thumb and forefinger and pulled it out. Old Hump wailed in mock sorrow, feigning tears with a bit of sage before his eyes. Moon Rim, who had been chewing on sage, spit on his knife before he thrust it in two quick motions through the fold of skin that Man-Afraid held. Pain shot through Red Cloud, shaking him to his toes. Moon Rim picked up one of the wood skewers and with considerable force shoved it through the cut. The same process was repeated with the other breast.

Red Cloud felt as if a lizard of fire writhed under the skin of his chest. There was no way to escape the agony, and it took everything he had not to move. Sweat ran down his face. After what seemed like a long struggle, Red Cloud finally gave up and allowed the pain to dominate him; oddly, that seemed to lessen it.

Man Afraid and Moon Rim lifted him to his feet. Man Afraid whispered, "Your eagle chant! Sing!"

Red Cloud dimly remembered he was supposed to chant, but he was so busy hiding his agony that he couldn't be bothered to ask his power animal for assistance. Nothing was going to help.

"Sing!" ordered Hump. He stood before Red Cloud, piercing him with eyes that now looked exactly like the yellow and grey eyes of an eagle. Frightened by the old wakan man, Red Cloud opened his mouth and sang:

Hai! Feed me your heart when mine turns weak.
Hai! Give me your eyes when mine tire.

Hai! Give me your power when I falter.
Hai! Help me soar above as you do,
Help me plummet to earth with courage. Hai!

From the fork of the wakan tree dangled two
plaited rawhide ropes terminating in stout thongs. The
loops of these Moon Rim slipped over the ends of
the skewers in Red Cloud's breasts. His arms around
his friend's body, Man Afraid pulled him back four
times, drawing the loops tight. Each time Red Cloud
fainted for a moment before the pain roused him again.
Take this from me, he longed to shout to Man Afraid.
But he couldn't shame him so.

Hump, chewing on a piece of flag root, spit toward Red Cloud's face. A wave of coolness swept over
him. Hump blew four long notes on his bone whistle.

Leaning back against the ropes like a captured
animal, Red Cloud was dimly aware of shouts of approval from the watchers. His legs wobbled and it was
all he could to do to remain standing. With great effort he raised his own bone whistle and blew it at
the sun. Then he threw himself back against the ropes.

Several times he leaped clear of the ground and
fell back against the ropes with his whole body, but
the skewers held. That morning the sun had mounted
steadily across the sky, but this afternoon Red Cloud
thought the sun had stopped, so slowly did it crawl
down its path. Sometimes the pain seemed as big as
a mesa inside him, as if it would choke him if it stayed
there a moment longer. Other times it receded to a
pinprick.

In midafternoon Hump gave Red Cloud five small
sticks. He couldn't remember what to do with them
until the old medicine man whispered instructions.

Then he•threw them among the spectators. Everyone who caught one would get a horse from Hump. Hump then went around behind Red Cloud and pulled back to see if he could tear him free of the skewers. After four futile tries to release him, Hump gave up.

He took his place at Red Cloud's left. Filling a pipe, he placed it on the ground. Pretty Owl and Red Cloud's daughters came forward leading horses packed with buffalo robes, tanned skins and leather bags stuffed with pemmican.

"We want you to cut the flesh of our father," they told Hump, for it was clear that not even with the old medicine man's help could Red Cloud tear loose.

Red Cloud knew what would happen next. Hump would accept the horses, take a knife and cut the skin so that only a small flap was left, easily broken through.

"No," Red Cloud told him. "Don't cut me loose. Start the other dancers."

"It's time to let go," old Hump protested. "You've done very well."

The pain screamed to be ended, but some other voice told him that he must gather all the wakan he could. "This is the will of Wakan-Takan. Start the other dancers."

Hump looked at him appraisingly. "You're not some young brave trying to prove how strong he is. Let it go."

"Wakan-Takan will free me when it is time. Do not interfere."

"You're too stubborn for your own good." For a moment it looked as if he would cut him down anyway, but then the old man moved away.

There was a roar of approval from the onlookers

when they realized that Hump wasn't going to cut Red Cloud down. What a Lakota!

Hump called on the women to bring their babies forward. To assure them good fortune, infants would have their ears pierced.

They were placed on the beds of sage in the dance lodge. The men chosen to do the piercing first recounted the coups and exploits that confirmed their right to carry out this operation, then advised the parents of their obligation to rear the child as a Sioux. Finally, each man knelt beside an infant and pierced its ear lobes.

Warriors who had already performed the Sun Dance were called on by this year's dancers to act as their captors. In a mock battle, they attacked the youths and captured them by throwing them roughly to the ground as Man Afraid had done with Red Cloud. Singing victory songs, the warriors then ritually tortured the captives. The young men who were to perform the "Gaze at the Sun Buffalo" dance had the skin below the shoulder blade raised, slit and a skewer inserted. Candidates for the "Gaze at the Sun Staked" were also pierced below the shoulder blade and through the skin of each breast. For the "Gaze at the Sun Suspended," wounds were made only through the breast. While the captives underwent this torture, they sang songs of defiance. Female assistants wailed and encouraged them and wiped the blood from their wounds with bits of sweet grass. Incense made with these swabs of sweet grass would make sure a lover didn't stray.

Some of the seventy dancers were tied by thongs to the wakan tree. Others had buffalo skulls attached to their skewers and dragged these about the dance lodge. All afternoon the youths tried to pull out the skewers, but not very hard, for it wouldn't look good to end the dance too soon.

Most of the candidates had suffered nowhere near the depth or width of cut that Red Cloud as chief dancer had endured. By late afternoon, after a third rest period, several had managed to pull away from the wakan tree. Hump's assistants trimmed the ragged flesh with a sharp knife and wrapped the wounds.

Red Cloud continued to pull against his thongs and chant his eagle songs, his voice rising and falling. By late afternoon the skewers had torn half through. No one there could remember anyone lasting so long. Red Cloud was so filled with wakan that afternoon that many later swore they had seen him as a giant eagle.

Red Cloud soared with the eagles that afternoon, seeing clearly why Wakan-Takan had sent him and his people to earth. He flew on Wakan-Takan's back all around the world, then away from the world, where he saw all the winds poised to do their master's bidding. He heard the roar the stars made, smelled the thunder as it played around them.

Red Cloud laughed at Grandfather's toys, for that was what the elements and the sky were to Wakan-Takan. He screeched when he saw the way men and animals were tossed around by Grandfather, but finally he understood the reason for all the suffering, although he could not afterward explain it to Hump.

The sun was setting when Hump told him he must cut him down. Red Cloud again said no; he would break through himself.

"You're too weak."

"When they're all done," Red Cloud said, nodding toward the other dancers, "then I'll break loose."

"You can overdo this. The eagle may carry you off. Don't destroy yourself."

But Red Cloud was firm. "I have more to see."

Finally just one young brave and Red Cloud were left and the torches had been brought out. With not much grace, Hump insisted that the protesting youth have his flesh cut. Afterward he easily pulled out the skewers. Then the old priest turned to Red Cloud.

"Now they're all loose, you fool," he growled. "I'll cut you free."

"No, now I'll break loose."

"You can't. You're too weak."

"Get away. Man Afraid, keep him away."

The watching crowd was quiet. Red Cloud began his eagle chant and the watchers picked it up to help him:

> Hai! Feed me your heart . . .
> Hai! Give me your eyes . . .
> Hai! Give me your strength . . .
> Hai! Help me to soar . . .

There was a loud rustling in the top of the dance lodge. Red Cloud looked up to see Wakan-Eagle coming through. He laughed to see him, for the power animal was huge, at least the size of a buffalo, its wings as long as a grown man was tall and its claws like arrows. The huge bird settled down over him, its giant wings beating in a flurry that drove back the crowd. Hovering there, the eagle took a skewer in each claw and pulled them through the flesh as Red Cloud screamed. His whole body felt crushed as the eagle began to eat him the way he would have eaten a mouse—bones, hair, skin, flesh and all. Red Cloud laughed down a long dark tunnel of black relief, letting himself go. All around him rang his laughter, which echoed his own sudden knowledge of himself, of all men. Nothing could happen to him that he couldn't bear. When it did he could die. While he was alive, he could do whatever he chose, which was why he had been sent to earth. He had forgotten that.

Darkness closed over him and he knew he was in the belly of the eagle, where he could dream until he passed back into the light of ordinary day. Red Cloud abandoned himself to dreams of soaring.

Chapter 10

Colonel Henry Carrington realized that his assignment was going to be more difficult than General Cooke had led him to believe. He hadn't enough men or supplies to carry out his mission. Before he left Fort Laramie he wrote to his headquarters in Omaha:

> I find at this post a supply of hard bread for only four days for my command, and . . . only a thousand rounds of ammunition, caliber .58. I shall find thirty-six thousand rounds at Fort Reno, giving me a total of sixty thousand rounds, obviously very inadequate. . . .
>
> The entire supply of .58 caliber ammunition at Laramie being only one thousand rounds, the troops will be almost powerless in case of delay of supplies. . . . All the commissioners who are negotiating the peace treaty with the Indians agree that I go to occupy a region that they will surrender only for some great equivalent; even my arrival has started among them many absurd rumors, but I apprehend no serious difficulty. Pa-

tience, forbearance and common sense in dealing
with the Sioux and Cheyenne will do much with
all who really desire peace, but it is indispensable
that ample supplies of ammunition come promptly.

The march seemed to bear out Carrington's conclusion of no serious difficulty, for while the ferryman
at Down's Ferry complained that the Indians had run
off two of his horses, the overland circus saw no Indians on its four-day march there. At Fort Reno itself,
it soothed Carrington to find life so quiet that the sutler did not even guard his herd of mules when he
turned them loose to graze outside the fort.

For three days Carrington's command camped
next to Fort Reno, made repairs and rested. Carrington discussed district policy and regulations with Major John Sanders, the camp commander. Since Carrington had been appointed regional commander of
this entire mountain district, Sanders would be report-
ing to him.

The feature of the country that most thrilled Carrington also troubled him: its emptiness. Fort Reno
was not much more than a wall three hundred by four
hundred feet. As Sanders put it, it provided "months
of boredom with twenty minutes a year of terror"
from Indian attack.

"We're going to build the strongest fort west of
the Mississippi," Carrington promised him.

Sanders smiled strangely. "I'd think in terms of
getting through the winter, sir. Big plans have a funny
way of collapsing on you out here."

The next part of the trip would be the hardest;
Carrington and Sanders agreed on that. From Fort

Reno, the last army outpost on the Bozeman Trail, the wilderness stretched four hundred miles to Bozeman City, Montana. Carrington was expected to keep order in an area some twenty-five hundred miles square with fifteen hundred troops. Of course he would not be expected to keep order among the Indians. Let the Sioux, Crow and Pawnee kill each other off if they liked. His principal mission was to guard the road between Fort Laramie and Bozeman City, making it safe for the tens of thousands of emigrants who headed west each year.

On the third day at Fort Reno, a Sunday, the sutler came running into the fort shouting about an Indian attack, sending a shudder of apprehension through Carrington. This was the first violent episode under his command. The sutler described the trappings of the Indians and their ponies to John Richards and Jim Bridger and the two men declared the Indians to be Sioux.

Carrington was reluctant to disturb the newly made peace. Just yesterday word had reached them that Spotted Tail had signed the treaty. Sanders, however, prevailed over him.

"Get thirty men, saddle up and get those mules back," Carrington ordered Captain Fred Brown.

"Yes, sir!" Brown was obviously pleased. He saluted smartly.

Before the troop rode off, Carrington warned Brown not to kill any Indians "for the heck of it. Just bring back the mules, you understand?"

The captain looked sulky, like a schoolboy admonished before he had done anything wrong, but he nodded. "Yes sir."

127

Carrington paced and fretted all day while they were gone, wondering if he should have sent more troopers or none at all.

When they returned at dusk they led no mules, just one Indian pony laden with trade goods that had been given out at the Fort Laramie treaty signing.

"Couldn't catch up with them, sir," reported Brown, "and you didn't want us to stay out too long."

"No, we have to get upcountry." Carrington fingered the buffalo-skin saddle pack on the Indian pony. "Where'd you find this specimen?"

"We caught sight of them, sir. This one got away and they didn't have time to chase it before we got it. They slipped across a river."

"I don't like it," said Jim Bridger.

"What don't you like?" asked Carrington.

"Well, if this pony's carrying trade goods, it means they came right from signing that treaty and stole the sutler's mules."

Carrington nodded, his face creased with worry. "It certainly looks that way, but let's hope for the best. I shall report this as an isolated incident."

A wave of optimism had swept the country over the prospect of reopening the Bozeman Trail, and several emigrant trains were already at Fort Reno, waiting impatiently for the escort to Bozeman City they had been led to believe the army would provide. To these trains Carrington issued a set of regulations instead of troops for their passage through Indian country. He declared that since the road would be made perfectly secure, no escort would be necessary. He told the wagon masters that he expected them to organize and stick together and that they must take care not to annoy the Indians.

"Annoy them!" one leader shouted back. "What do you mean, don't annoy them? You got troops. You come up here to keep the peace. Give us some till we're at least past the Sioux and Cheyenne."

"I mean what I say, sir." Carrington was determined to bring a measure of common sense to the mountain district. "The big trouble with the Indian out here is that we've given him too little respect. My orders are for you not to venture farther than five hundred yards from the trail, not to shoot at Indians unless you are fired on first and to shoot no game."

"But we have to eat!"

"Buy what you need from the sutler before you pull out. We now have a treaty with these people that allows you to make your trip in peace under those conditions. If my patrols find fresh meat in your camp, you'll be turned around and escorted back to Laramie."

The wagon masters stared at him.

"No use to get riled up, gentlemen," Carrington adjured them. "We've made a deal with the savages, and if we don't keep up our end of it, how can we expect them to learn what's civilized?"

"Didn't they carry off them mules Sunday?" pointed out one wagon master, a big man with a long scar down the side of his cheek. "Was that in the treaty too?"

"An isolated incident, sir. We're going to show Christian forbearance over that."

"Well, it's a good thing they didn't steal my mules," the man went on. "I don't know if I got enough Christian forbearance to last me more'n a minute or two." From the mutterings of the other wagon masters, Carrington saw that they might not have much either. "I'd just have to kill me some Indians to show how forbearing I can be."

On July 10, 1866, Colonel Carrington marched from Fort Reno. Nine days later he reached Piney Fork, two hundred thirty-five miles from Fort Laramie and about the same distance from Bozeman City. Here he would build Fort Phil Kearny.

Carrington decided on the spot after long debate with Jim Bridger and his officers, who favored higher ground. He chose it not so much for safety as because the pass controlled the movement of the Sioux between their northern and southern hunting grounds. It would make the assignment easier.

"But you're going to have to get wood to build the fort," Bridger argued, "which is going to expose you and your men. And you're going to need hay." He pointed to the surrounding ridges. "They're going to be able to watch you and attack at just the right time."

"I'm sure we'll do fine," Carrington answered. "The Indians aren't attacking the wagon trains as they pass through, so they aren't likely to attack armed soldiers."

Bridger sighed. It didn't feel right to him, but Carrington was in charge. "Yes, sir. How can I help?"

Fred Brown hated to build. It reminded him of the sort of work he had escaped when he left his father's farm for the army. He longed to be out riding his stallion Rooster on patrol. On the long march out he had assumed that that was what he would be

130

doing. This job, supervising the log-cutting operation, chafed him.

"But we have to have a fort before winter," George Grummond reminded him. "You wouldn't want to spend a winter without a fort, would you?"

"I'm a soldier, damnit, not a wood-chopper," snapped Brown. "If you like it so much, you volunteer for it."

Grummond smiled sweetly. "I've got my job."

"You're just lucky you had some carpentry experience."

"Maybe you'll get lucky and the Sioux will attack you."

Brown snorted at that. "They're not stupid enough to attack soldiers. They're going to wait and hit one of those wagon trains. It's going to be a long, boring two years till my enlistment's up."

Using the few officers who had any kind of building or organizing skills, Carrington marked off the six-hundred- by eight-hundred-foot site for the fort. Using plans he had brought from Omaha, the officers and soldiers pounded stakes in the hot sun and laid out the buildings: Carrington's quarters, the kitchens, the storage rooms, the powder magazine, the barracks, the bachelor officers' quarters, the parade ground, the stables and the mess hall.

The first project was the walls, some ten feet high, but as these would take three thousand logs, every one of which had to be hauled in from two to eight miles away, it would be months before the stockade was completely enclosed. Grummond had gone through the woods tying a piece of white string on each tree that was to be felled and brought in.

Sioux Arrows

* * *

Captain Tenodor Ten Eyke had taken civil engineering at Virginia Polytech, so in the construction he was Carrington's right hand. He worked with a dogged methodical energy, all the time brooding on and struggling to bury what was growing inside him: his obsessive attraction to Cynthia Simmons.

He had been careful all the way out from Omaha, stopping by her wagon only twice a day and allowing himself only as much time there as he gave the other wagons, so no one, especially the other unmarried officers, would guess his feelings for the minister's wife.

Once they camped at Piney Fork, he had to be still more careful. Already that ass Brown was ribbing him about having eyes for Cynthia. The last thing he needed was rumors about it throughout the new camp.

He had never felt anything like this before. Another man's wife! Why couldn't God have given him this feeling for some unmarried girl? What was wrong with him? He found he wanted to wring the plump neck of the Reverend Simmons. Half a dozen times he caught himself figuring ways of luring the minister out on patrol and getting rid of him.

Ten Eyke forced himself to pay attention to the construction of the fort. Carrington was intent on making this as solid and secure as any fort in the country.

Like the other officers, Ten Eyke often thought Carrington behaved more like a fussy schoolmaster than a military commander. Still, there was nothing wrong in building well. So every day the captain rose early and pushed the gangs digging holes, stripping logs and tamping sand till the last light of day. Then he pored over the plans with Carrington till late at night.

It was hard, exhausting work, yet he never got enough done in a day to suit himself. Winter would arrive in a few short months. Once the snow fell there would be precious little they could do till spring, and from what he'd heard, no winter back East could prepare you for the howlers on the plains.

Cynthia took a keen interest in the building. She had found that there were villages of friendly Cheyenne nearby and she talked excitedly about starting a school for the children. Ten Eyke didn't think much of the idea; he reasoned that trying to teach a savage child to read and write made about as much sense as giving lessons to a mule. But all he could do when she came over and spoke to him about it was smile and nod enthusiastically.

There were so many eyes on them! He had to be so careful, when what he really wanted to do was take her down to the creek and talk, and then perhaps go swimming together the way he and Nelly had, not so many years ago. Nelly . . . it still hurt to think about her. What bliss it had been, drifting in the water, stroking each other, afterward bouncing around in the grass like a couple of young goats. They had joyfully gotten married as soon as they found out she was pregnant and had four children, three of whom lived, before war came to the South.

Nelly . . . the wire was still in Ten Eyke's wallet. Fleeing Virginia before the advancing Union army, Nelly and the children had died in the collapse of a weakened bridge.

He missed the feel of her and the children, how it felt to touch them, more than anything. Not that he didn't miss their voices, their smiles and their laughter, but the main thing seemed to be that he would no longer caress the chubby small ones who had clambered giggling all over him nor the long sloping curves of Nelly's lean body. He hadn't cried when he got the telegram; he had never been able to cry. But in his mind he wept continually for what he had lost.

The impossible thing he ached for now was to make Cynthia Simmons swell with his child, for the two of them to play with the baby, and then for her to have another. Maybe then the terrible ache in him would ease, though it might never disappear. He suspected that even if he had a hundred more children, he would carry this ache till he dropped into his grave.

"We're going to need some idea from the reverend about the chapel layout," Carrington mentioned one day. "I think the Simmonses want it to double for a school. Go see them, will you, Tenodor? Find out if we need to modify these plans."

That afternoon Ten Eyke couldn't keep his eyes off Cynthia as he sat with her and the reverend discussing the chapel. She wore a long white dress embroidered with blue cornflowers, smooth around her waist and flowing across her rounded hips and breasts. She sat poised and ladylike, now and then giving him such a sweet smile that Ten Eyke had all he could do to keep from gathering her into his arms. She didn't look a bit like Nelly, but she was as big a woman as Nelly had been. Tenodor wasn't quite sure what he meant, but it had something to do with a capacity to enjoy life.

"When the time comes, I'll work with the men on the chapel," Reverend Simmons said.

"You, sir?" Ten Eyke eyed him doubtfully. The portly minister looked as if he had never pounded a nail in his life.

"Wasn't our Lord Jesus a carpenter?" Simmons asked. "I shall be happy to wield a hammer in His service."

Cynthia smiled her sweet smile. "Do you think I could get an escort to visit the Cheyenne camps, Captain?"

"Visit? Why?" Ten Eyke's heart quickened at the idea of offering service to such a lovely creature.

"She wants to round up her pupils," smiled Reverend Simmons. He laid his hand fondly on his wife's arm. Ten Eyke wanted to smash the man. What right did a pudgy sheep have with such an eagle of a woman?

He choked back the impulse. "We can ask the Cheyenne to come and see you," he muttered.

Cynthia shook her head. "No, I must go to them. You see, that's part of the problem. We assume the Indian will come at our beck and call. It's important that we go to them."

"Well, I don't know if the colonel can spare anybody for escort duty. We need every man, six days a week, to cut logs and work on the stockade."

"Will you ask him for me?" she pleaded. "Perhaps you'll know how to persuade him." She touched his sleeve lightly and a thrill shot through the captain.

"Of course," he answered, dizzy with delight. "I'd be glad to help you."

But two days later he still hadn't said anything to Carrington because he couldn't understand the strange excitement her request had produced in him. It had something to do with the idea of her riding a horse down a long avenue of lush oaks. . . .

* * *

The Cheyenne sent a messenger to ask if Carrington wanted peace or war. The colonel sent back an invitation to come in for food and gifts.

Toward the end of July a party of Cheyenne arrived, twelve chiefs and fifty braves, many of them decked out in new buffalo leggings, honor shirts and war bonnets. Guided by their officers, the soldiers kept their distance, but even at long range they made reckonings of how much damage those lances, knives, arrows, tomahawks and guns could inflict.

In a gesture of good will, Carrington sat down with the chiefs and his own officers to a Sunday dinner at a long outdoor table. Reverend Simmons' grace and wishes for peace between the two peoples, translated by Jim Bridger, went down well. So did platters of turkey, deer and pressed vegetables they had brought from Laramie.

Several of the chiefs asked for whiskey, but Carrington said they had brought none, a lie of course, but one he had been advised to tell by everybody from General Cooke in Omaha to John Sanders at Fort Reno.

"The chief here wants to know what you're putting on your meat," Grummond relayed to Brown, who was spreading yellow mustard on his venison.

Brown glanced at the head of the long table, where Colonel Carrington sat nodding at Owl Tongue, the principal chief of the Cheyenne.

The captain rubbed his stomach and said, "Ummm, ummm," with an exaggerated expression of delight. He held out the mustard pot to the inquisitive Bull Horn, a Cheyenne chief with a face that Brown thought looked like the rear end of a buffalo. The captain punched Grummond in the ribs with his elbow as if to say, "Watch the fun!"

Bull Horn took the mustard pot and sniffed it. Brown put on another dumb show of a man eating something delicious. The attention of the Cheyenne chiefs around Bull Horn was caught by their neighbor's activity. The one next to him asked something, and Bull Horn went through the same dumb show, adding something in his own language.

The two officers jabbed those next to them with their elbows, hardly able to keep a straight face. Shortly all seven officers at the lower end of the table watched goggle-eyed as Bull Horn's neighbor stuck a grimy finger into the pot and took it out covered with mustard. He glanced at it and popped it into his mouth.

At first, the chief opened his eyes wide and smiled, as if his finger had been coated with honey, but that lasted only a second or two. With a howl the chief jumped straight off his bench into the air. Holding his jaws in his hands, he began to run around in circles.

Immediately every Cheyenne at the table jumped up and grabbed his bow. The seven white officers were laughing so hard that two of them fell over backward off the bench. Twice, when he tried to explain to the puzzled and alarmed Carrington what had happened, Brown collapsed in laughter.

Gradually the chiefs were made to realize that their friend hadn't been poisoned. Colonel Carrington himself ate a little mustard to show the chiefs how it was meant to be used, but while this demonstration mollified the Indians, none tried any more of the yellow fire.

Before Owl Tongue left he informed Carrington through Portugee Phillips that he had seventeen lodges and that his people were hunting on Goose Creek and the Tongue River. He said that the day Carrington had arrived at Piney Fork a party of Sioux from Red Cloud's camp had come to him and told him about the march, describing Carrington's movements in detail and demanding that the Cheyenne help them fight the troops. The Sioux had said that if Carrington would go back to Fort Reno and not open a road through their hunting grounds, they would leave the troops alone. The chiefs stated that Red Cloud had five hundred warriors, which indicated a camp of two hundred fifty lodges, and that Old-Man-Afraid-of-His-Horses was camped on the Tongue River one day's travel below Red Cloud with another two hundred fifty lodges. Owl Tongue also reported that the Sioux were all busy just now holding a Sun Dance.

The account of the peace council at Fort Laramie worried Carrington. So did the news that Red Cloud and Old Man Afraid had so many warriors with them. Back at Laramie, Maynadier had led him to believe that Red Cloud was a sort of renegade chief with no more than his family supporting him. But it would be hard to call a man with so many followers a mere outlaw.

Owl Tongue said that Red Cloud and Old Man Afraid claimed the peace commission had tried to deceive them. They cited as proof the arrival of Carrington and his soldiers to build new forts and open a new road through their hunting grounds.

"Ask the chief if he understands what I am doing here," Carrington told Bridger.

The Cheyenne answered that they didn't want

war, that if the Little White Chief didn't attack, his people wouldn't either. They would even help him, for they had no wish to antagonize anybody, white or Sioux.

"Because there are so few of them," Brown muttered to Grummond. "You can bet we'd be ducking arrows and clutching our scalps if those ugly bastards had the manpower to make it worth their while."

Chapter 11

Before the Cheyenne chiefs left the Sunday dinner table, Reverend Simmons asked that he and his wife be allowed to visit their camps and talk to the parents about taking reading and writing lessons, which they understood to be magic or power or spirit-talk.

After some discussion with his chiefs, a few of whom were obviously against the idea, Owl Tongue said in his gracious way that his people would be honored to have such a visit. He even offered to send an escort. When would they like to come?

Carrington said he couldn't spare any men for an escort until the fort was finished. Neither could he allow the reverend and his wife to go with no military escort.

"Perhaps I could go with the Reverend and Mrs. Simmons," volunteered Ten Eyke.

"You, Captain? You of all people have too much to do for me to spare you."

"Not Sunday, sir, if they don't mind traveling on the Lord's day. We don't work on Sunday."

Carrington looked dubious. "But I can't order

any of the men to go with you. They must have a day to rest."

"Of course, sir. I'm sure we'll manage."

So it was arranged. The following Sunday Reverend and Mrs. Simmons, a well-armed Captain Ten Eyke and twenty Cheyenne braves would travel the two hours to Owl Tongue's village, where the reverend and his wife would strive to impart some enthusiasm for Jesus Christ as well as literacy.

That Sunday Clarence Simmons woke at four in the morning with severe stomach cramps. When Ten Eyke and the twenty braves from Owl Tongue's village arrived at the tent, they found him sitting on a bench wrapped in a blanket; only Cynthia was dressed for the two-hour ride.

"Why, Mr. Simmons, you look terrible," Ten Eyke exclaimed.

The minister's face was pale and drawn, his voice weak. "I'm afraid the Lord has spoken to me."

"Sir?"

"Going off on the Sabbath. Not preaching today. Leaving my flock just to accompany Mrs. Simmons."

Cynthia was wearing a sensible dress of dark blue cotton. She stood by her husband and demurely looked down.

"Mrs. Simmons," Ten Eyke asked, "do you still want to go?"

She looked over his shoulder at the tribesmen who stood waiting by their ponies. "They've come a long way for me. I don't want to disappoint them."

"But alone? Without a chaperone?"

Clarence Simmons smiled weakly. "She has you, doesn't she?"

Ten Eyke's head spun. He wanted little else in

the world than to spend the day with this wonderful creature, but he didn't want to compromise her reputation. Contrary impulses battled within him and kept him rooted there speechless.

"Go, Captain." Simmons made as if to shoo them. "I'll recover from these cramps in time to hold services this morning, and I can't think of anyone I'd trust more with Mrs. Simmons."

"It's all right, Captain," his wife added. "Hank, would you bring my horse?"

The black servant brought the horse. With Ten Eyke's help Cynthia got up sidesaddle, which set the Cheyenne agog. Ten Eyke mounted his mare Belle and the party set out.

The ride through the forest was without incident and they were at Owl Tongue's camp by eight. Jim Bridger had taught Cynthia a few words of Cheyenne and the universal sign language. With these she was able to convey her good feeling toward the bashful mothers and children.

She had brought bead necklaces to give the girls and pocketknives for the boys. To Cynthia's horror, a boy of about eight managed to cut halfway through his right forefinger with his new knife. Instead of sympathy he got anger and insults for his stupidity. This appalled both Cynthia and Ten Eyke, but not two hours later they saw the boy playing contentedly, his injury forgotten.

Early in the afternoon, with Owl Tongue's amused permission, Cynthia gathered forty Cheyenne children under a tree for an English lesson. It proved to be even more of a challenge than she'd expected. No child sat still for more than ten minutes, and Cynthia knew she didn't have a dozen of the original forty by the end of the day. Still, soon the camp rang with "Hello!" and "Good-bye!" and "I am an American!"

The lesson was interrupted by one of the hard thunderstorms that lash across the plains. It drove everyone inside to listen to it walk up and down the walls. Cynthia and Ten Eyke shifted from puddle to puddle, thinking how ill suited to such a downpour a tepee was.

Owl Tongue made them understand that because of the storm they must spend the night; crossing the swollen river must wait until tomorrow.

Ten Eyke was taken to the chief's own tepee, where he sat by a smoky fire and ate whatever the boiled stuff in the stewpot was. He didn't try to identify it. Cynthia, if he understood Owl Tongue correctly, was eating with the women of the tribe. It was several hours before they were reunited. Ten Eyke was taken to another tepee and found Cynthia there alone, seated by a small fire.

"Are you all right?" he asked when his escort had left them.

"I'm fine," she said gaily. "How about you?"

"I can't say I care much for Indian accommodations," he grinned, "but I suppose one night can't hurt me."

She laughed. "They're very sweet, the ladies, but awfully curious. I gave them my brooch and let several try on my blouse. My word, they smell!"

Ten Eyke smiled, beguiled by the flush in her cheeks. "I think we had dog for dinner, but I kept hoping it was buffalo."

She pretended shock. "Tenodor! You're just trying to upset me."

"No." He looked around the tepee. It was bare

143

except for some buffalo rugs, firewood and clay pots. "Whose lodge is this?"

"I have no idea."

"I'll go to the chief and ask him if I can stay in his tepee tonight. I can't stay here all night alone with you."

"What? You're going to leave me?" she exclaimed. "Suppose some brave comes in? You can't leave me here."

He squatted down. She had a point. "But what will people say?" he asked. "What will your husband say?"

"I don't know," she shrugged. "Well, yes, I certainly do know. But they don't have to know. I slept with the women tonight and you with the men."

He thought about it. "Are you sure?"

He thought he saw her tremble.

"I'm sure I can't spend the night here alone," she answered, her voice calm, "and I'm willing to tell a white lie about it."

"Suppose your husband asks?"

"That's my problem, isn't it, Captain?"

He couldn't see her face too clearly, but from the tone of her voice and the way she lifted her head he understood that he was to inquire no further. He built up the fire, hoping to create a draft and clear the air of smoke.

From his saddlebag Ten Eyke took a silver flask. "Here, this will warm you," he said, offering her the whiskey.

"Captain Tenodor Ten Eyke! My husband is a founder of the Boston Temperance League!" But she said it with such good-natured mockery that they both

144

began to laugh. He poured a tot into the tiny silver cup that lidded his flask and tossed it off.

"I will take one of those," Cynthia decided, "to ward off the chill of this damp ground." The fire was burning hot and bright and the air began to clear. "It's not so bad in here now. It's rather cozy. I wonder what the Cheyenne are doing to amuse themselves?"

In the distance they heard the sounds of laughter and shouting.

"Telling stories and playing games, I imagine," Ten Eyke said.

"Let's tell each other stories to pass the time."

The suggestion made him feel awkward. "I'm afraid I don't know any stories."

"Of course you do! You know the story of your life. That's one of the greatest things we have to give each other, the story of our pilgrimage on earth."

"I don't have much to tell."

"You do, but I'll start first." She went right to it. Born in Boston to a prosperous merchant, she had been schooled at a private grammar school, then at a finishing school for young ladies, the same one her father had sent her sisters to. She had showed an aptitude for classical languages, and when the bishop had needed someone to help him prepare sermons, she had been delighted to offer her assistance. It was in the bishop's office that she had met her husband. Her one great sadness was that she had not been able to give him the children he so desperately wanted.

Her touching candor moved Ten Eyke. To his surprise, he found himself telling her about Nelly and the children, about his firstborn, Danny, who had died when he was still a baby, about the tragedy that had taken his entire family from him.

"You must marry again."

"I suppose," he answered. "But I don't know if I can. I couldn't take a loss like that again, and I couldn't marry a woman who didn't mean as much to me as Nelly meant."

"Of course not."

The compassion in her voice, the whiskey and fatigue, the eighteen months of grief over Nelly and the children rose within him. Tears surged up and out of him with all the intensity of the afternoon's storm.

Cynthia was immediately by his side, holding him against her, urging him to let go, to cry. Though he felt ashamed, a boy and not a man, he was helpless to stop himself. Holding her, rocking against her, he allowed his grief to spill onto her shoulders.

When at last he stopped, he pulled back, reached for a handkerchief, blew his nose and dried his face.

"I'm sorry," he whispered.

"Don't be."

Something in her voice made him look up. Her face was wet with tears.

"Why are you crying?" he asked.

"Because you loved her and the children so much."

"No more than any man would have. But certainly no less."

"But you can weep for them. Clarence, now, he couldn't."

"Your husband? What's he got to do with it?"

"It grieves him that we have no family, but he won't let me comfort him." She turned her head away. "I wish he would leave me—I know it's that important to him—but he won't. He'd never be elected bishop if he left his wife." She sobbed and he handed her his handkerchief. She blew her nose. "He cares more about being a bishop than having children of his own. Sometimes I could kill him for it."

This time he was the one to offer comfort. Before they knew it they kissed, and then they kissed again.

Ten Eyke drew back. "This isn't right."

But she reached over and began to unbutton his shirt. "Come to me. Comfort me."

"You're sure?" He wanted nothing else but this woman, but he feared to harm her.

"I'm sure."

"I wouldn't want—"

"Are you as big a fool as Clarence?" she asked bitterly.

Then he took her in his arms and kissed her long and hard. Within him something sighed. He felt her unfold against him and caressed her through the thin cotton of her dress. Their mouths couldn't get enough of each other and soon she had the shirt off him. The touch of her fingers on his bare back inflamed him.

He began to undress her. When she was down to her chemise, he picked her up, put her down on a buffalo robe and threw another over the two of them. Guided by her, he drove himself gently into her. She welcomed him with an eagerness that momentarily embarrassed him and then filled him with delight. She kissed him and he kissed her back. The world, he thought, was all right after all. It had more than one woman in it.

They didn't sleep. They lay in each other's arms and talked about the first time they had met and what they had felt then and now.

"Now that I've found you, I can't let you go," she purred.

"I can say the same thing."

"Then do say it. For God's sake don't make those halfway noises Clarence makes."

He groaned. "Don't compare me to that nincompoop."

Cynthia laughed. "Then don't play the nincompoop with me. Be the soldier you are. March like you mean business, sir."

She pulled him to her. "Come on. Take me. It may be weeks before we have another chance."

Chuckling with delight, he complied.

Chapter 12

When Colonel Carrington released the emigrant wagon trains from Fort Reno, the word rolled back eastward the length of the trail. Within weeks it became a river of wagons. No sooner did one white line of prairie schooners disappear over the hill than another hove into view.

By the end of July you could not stand anywhere on the five-hundred-mile trail and fail to see a wagon train. Captain James Powell, in charge of records at Fort Kearny, estimated that at this rate fifty thousand emigrants would pass during 1866.

The trains stopped for a day or so at Fort Reno for rest and repairs, then pressed on. Several nights later they would camp near Fort Kearny, still under construction. When travelers asked about the Indian situation, they got Carrington's lecture and rules on how to behave toward their red brothers.

Later Captain Fred Brown gave them his scornful interpretation as he escorted them five miles west. "Don't shoot any game, the colonel said! Doesn't that strike you as plain dumb? How does the man expect you to eat?"

He got no argument from the wagon masters, who were hard-pressed to stop the rough men and youths who traveled with the train from foraging for deer, buffalo, rabbit and elk. As for Indians, hardly anyone on the Bozeman had seen one for almost two months. The Laramie treaty had bought them all off and was proof that the peace party, which now dominated Congress, was right. The way to deal with the Indian was to pay him, not fight him. Fifty thousand dollars in goods had accomplished what several millions in men and arms could not. Who could find a better argument for peace?

"But suppose one of them snoops of the colonel's finds us with fresh meat?" a wagon master would inevitably ask.

Brown would wink. "You tell him to report to me when he comes in. You think our men don't know the schoolmarm's got a glass butt?"

"Is that what you call him? The schoolmarm?"

"You seen them pretty blond lashes of his, didn't you?"

"And the glass butt?"

"If he fell on it, he'd break it, wouldn't he?" This always set the wagon masters to laughing and slapping their thighs.

The buffalo, alarmed by the wagon trains' noisy passage, the rattle, the crack of whips, the rifle shots, the smell of so many people, the endless cloud of dust, started to avoid the line that the Bozeman Trail cut across Sioux hunting country. A creature of habit, the American bison in herds of millions ate its way from north in the summer to south in the winter, then turned with spring to march back north. It had to keep moving, for herds of several hundred thousand rapidly ate all the grass wherever they stopped.

For years the Sioux had made their winter and summer camps along these migratory paths. Before they dared to hunt, the Sioux went through elaborate purification and propitiation rituals. The buffalo was the most powerful expression of wakan that Wakan-Takan had set on earth. Man was a fool to approach it with anything less than awe.

Certainly the look of the buffalo confirmed such ideas. Often standing seven to eight feet high at the shoulders, tapering to a rather dainty rump, the American bison gazed on his attackers with an expression of benign disdain. Only after you begged him not to take offense could you safely kill such a creature and bring its flesh, bones, horns, hide and innards back to camp, where your wife and children would handle the remains with reverence.

The wagon trains cut across the paths of the buffalo as they drove through Red Cloud's Oglala country. Frightened, the creatures turned back south and milled around looking for forage or headed out toward the drylands, where tens of thousands perished from thirst.

Red Cloud and his people were aware of this, but not in detail. They knew only that before the white man had come they had been able to get what buffalo they needed. Now there were wagons and white troopers strung out along the road leading west, and the buffalo herds weren't where they were supposed to be.

Captain Brown would have told them to eat deer, but deer didn't satisfy buffalo-hunger any more than

Brown would have wanted cake instead of bread. The Sioux not only lived off the buffalo, they were also its keeper. They had been placed on earth by Wakan-Takan to worship, tend and live off Brother Buffalo. If the Sioux failed to rescue their beleaguered brother, they would be as guilty as Captain Fred Brown would have been not to object to the Sioux's burning down his church.

Red Cloud had no trouble calling to war the members of his and Old Man Afraid's band after the Sun Dance. He had shown such strength of wakan that mothers brought him infants to name. For two weeks he lay recovering in his tepee. In the second week he sent runners and criers to villages of the Cheyenne, the Minneconjou and the other Sioux tribes asking them to join him in driving back the white man. Some elders still would not, but hundreds of young braves picked up their best lances, bows and shields, left their villages and assembled with the Oglala.

From an obscure captain in a secondary Sioux tribe nine months before, Red Cloud had risen to leader of the largest Indian army on the American continent. He and the other chiefs argued endlessly in council over what to do. Attack Fort Kearny? Attack the new one farther west that the Little White Chief was building, the one called C.S. Smith? Attack the new railroad to the south? The singing wire? The wagon trains? The settlers? What Red Cloud wanted now was a strategy that would drive the troopers back, but each chief had his own idea of what that strategy should be.

Red Cloud got word that the Cheyenne chiefs had talked to the Little White Chief and made peace with him. Soon after came an invitation from the Little White Chief asking Red Cloud to come and talk. Gifts and a feast waited for him.

He sent the messenger, a Laramie loafer, back with no reply. A meal and a few knives to buy hundreds of miles of hunting grounds? Did the white ghosts think they were dealing with a Crow or Pawnee or Cheyenne? The Little White Chief would learn.

As the two stagecoaches carrying nine passengers rolled westward out of Fort Reno late in July the drivers and their reliefs stayed alert, their guns ready. The sergeant major at the fort had repeated rumors of Sioux restlessness, although there had been no attack in months.

All at once, the man riding shotgun on the box of the front coach shouted, "Injuns is coming!"

A war party of six Sioux, bold white and red slashes painted across their faces and chests, galloped up the road directly at them. The four men on top of the two boxes cocked their two shotguns and two rifles, not knowing whether this was an attack or a begging expedition looking for a few pounds of coffee and sugar, which often worked wonders on the savage temperament. Better to keep your gun cocked and be ready for anything.

Shots suddenly rang out from along the sides of the road. In an instant the coaches were surrounded by howling painted savages. An arrow struck a driver in the chest. One of the mules was hit in the mouth and wheeled crazily. The drivers frantically urged their panic-stricken teams to a slight knoll above the road. They released the mules while the passengers threw out mail sacks, buffalo robes and cargo crates and barricaded themselves under and between the coaches. Concealed in the brush, the Sioux rained bullets and arrows on the defenders. One man was shot in the face, another in the leg. Three times the Sioux rose from cover and charged. Each time they were turned back.

The next rush would be the last. By now the little group of defenders was down to a dozen shells and had suffered three more casualties. Late in the afternoon the Indians, robbed of an easy victory, withdrew. After they had gone the able-bodied survivors helped the wounded to their feet and they set out back to Fort Reno. When they had disappeared over the hill, the Sioux returned and set fire to the coaches.

The next day an army wagon train from Fort Kearny that carried thirty-five troopers and three officers was attacked near Crazy Woman Creek. Caught by surprise and pinned down, the train would have been wiped out but for a detachment of troopers on their way to Fort Reno from Kearny. At the sight of the reinforcements, the Sioux broke off the fighting.

Lieutenant George Grummond described the action in a letter to his brother. He concluded, "Don't believe those lies the so-called peace party puts out about how the poor Indian wants nothing but peace. He may lie low for a while, but what he wants is your hair for his belt. He is going to have to go some to get mine!"

Chapter 13

Not long after the Sunday dinner with Carrington, Owl Tongue and his council visited trader Pierre Gratteau, a swarthy Frenchman who had lived there with his Sioux wife and children for fifteen years. The Cheyenne hoped to get shot and powder from him.

As the Cheyenne sat on Trader Pete's front porch talking to him and his men, Crazy Horse and a party of Sioux rode up.

"Hey, Owl Tongue!" Crazy Horse shouted in Cheyenne. "Is it true you met with the Little White Chief?"

Owl Tongue glanced around at the nine chiefs and warriors with him. They all sat gazing impassively at the Sioux warriors.

"Crazy Horse," said Trader Pete, "come back tomorrow. I have some new goods I want to show you."

Ignoring him, Crazy Horse concentrated on Owl Tongue. "Well? Did you meet him? What did you promise him?"

"I met him," Owl Tongue said cautiously. Word had come to the Cheyenne that Crazy Horse had gone wild over the loss of some woman and was behaving with no care for his life. A wise man would tread carefully around him. "We talked. He gave us presents. The Little White Chief said there are presents waiting for you at Fort Laramie, Crazy Horse, if you will touch the pen."

"Presents!" Before anyone on the porch could move, Crazy Horse and his warriors had leaped off their mounts and were standing among them, strung bows in their hands.

"Presents!" Crazy Horse began hitting Owl Tongue with his bow, shouting, "Coup! Coup! Coup!" as if he were in battle and these seated Cheyenne were beaten enemies. His men joined him, striking the other Cheyenne with their bows and shouting, "Coup! Coup!"

The Cheyenne sat as if frozen, bearing the insult in silence. After several minutes Crazy Horse broke off the attack and stepped back.

"Hai, Lakota! Come on, let's leave these women to sit here and stitch their moccasins."

He jumped on his horse. The others followed and in a flurry of hoofbeats the Sioux rode off.

Trader Pete spoke first. "I never seen that before and I been around Sioux a long time."

"We should have killed them," said Bull Horn.

"What? They would have killed *you*," Trader Pete exclaimed.

Owl Tongue shook his head. "It would have been better to die. In my life, in my father's life, no Cheyenne has ever been so insulted."

"But that Crazy Horse ain't one to mess with," Trader Pete pointed out.

Owl Tongue was silent. He was filled with shame. He knew the lodge of respect he had been building for all of his years had been pulled down. It would be best to step down as head of the council and let a younger man take over. Sadly, he rose to leave.

"You get your people over to the soldiers' camp," Bull Horn told Trader Pete.

"I'm married to one of Old Man Afraid's cousins," the Frenchman protested. "Don't worry about me."

Owl Tongue also warned him to leave, but old Pierre felt secure. At dawn the next morning Crazy Horse and his warriors came back and killed him and all his men. His wife and children escaped into the woods and were later rescued by Carrington's men.

In his reports to headquarters in Omaha, Colonel Carrington called these attacks isolated incidents. He concentrated on building his fort. He seemed to be everywhere at once, making sure the postholes for the stockade were a full four feet deep, that the roof of the powder magazine got three sets of shingles, that no man or mule shirked his job and that every regulation he posted was obeyed to the letter. He didn't want soldiers walking on the grass in the square and he wanted every man out of the mess hall by eight in the evening. He found the practice of sitting there drinking coffee "ragged and unsoldierly."

He had sent two companies, about one hundred and fifty men, to the Bighorn River to build a post, Fort C.F. Smith, which would give the emigrant wagon trains more protection. These troops for the Bighorn and the first group of trains got safely by the Sioux. But soon afterward the Indians began raiding every wagon train on the Bozeman Trail. This was the cornerstone of Red Cloud's strategy. If he made the whites see that they would surely be attacked, and attacked hard, it must discourage them and stop travel on the road. His warriors boldly pushed in close to the forts, running off cattle, mules and horses and attacking smaller detachments of troops wherever they met them.

Still Carrington's reports to Omaha were optimistic. He considered the situation good. He told General Sherman in an August 29 report that the wagon trains would be safe if they were well organized and used proper precautions. But in that same despatch he stated that thirty-three white men had been killed along the road in the past five weeks and that the Sioux made daily attacks.

During the raiding in late July and August, Fred Brown led the officers in pleading with Carrington to take the offensive, but Carrington did not seriously consider their advice. He had been sent there to keep the Bozeman Trail safe for travelers. This did not mean attacking Indian villages. Like many others, he figured the whole problem with the Indians over the past two hundred years was the white man's too-ready use of the gun.

Captain Brown held court nightly in the bachelor officers' quarters about his commanding officer's wrong-headed notions of their situation. Hardly any order Carrington gave suited him.

"He's got the soul of a goddamn quartermaster," Brown raged one hot summer night. "Mitty tells me he's written Omaha to close Fort Smith."

Grummond's jaw dropped. "Close it? Why? That's crazy. That's where the redskins are, on the Tongue and the Bighorn."

"Sure," Brown sneered. "That's part of his clever plan, see? The result is that the trains will ride unprotected right into the biggest pack of hornets the country's ever seen. Red Cloud and his red-rumps will get so tired of stinging they'll give it up."

Most of the officers groaned or laughed at this. Powell and Ten Eyke didn't laugh much at Brown, but the rest of the officers more than half agreed with him. Life at the fort was mostly hard work and boredom except when they were called out to fight attacking Indians.

In late summer Carrington recruited Jim Bridger to get in touch with Red Cloud and see if peace could be arranged. The scout attempted to open communications through the Crow. Apparently, however, over the summer Red Cloud had attempted to induce the Crow to abandon their traditional hostility toward the Sioux and join them in turning back the white men. The Bad Face chief even offered to return part of the Crow hunting grounds they had taken from them between 1856 and 1863. Bridger told Carrington he thought the Crow were stalling, waiting to see which way the struggle went. It seemed that most of their young men were in favor of joining the Sioux against the whites and a few already had.

Both the Crow and the Cheyenne told Jim Bridger that the Sioux were planning two big fights, at Pine Woods near Fort Kearny and Bighorn near Fort C.F. Smith.

It didn't take long for disturbing rumors about Indian attacks on the Bozeman Trail to filter back to Washington. Opposition to Peace Party policies began to build. The Indians were as hostile as they had been before the Laramie treaty. Travel on the Powder River road was as hazardous as it had ever been.

When Nathaniel Taylor, in Omaha, heard the rumors he wired President Johnson:

SATISFACTORY TREATIES OF PEACE HAVE BEEN CONCLUDED WITH THE UPPER PLATTE SIOUX AND CHEYENNE AT FORT LARAMIE. CONTRADICTORY REPORTS ARE WITHOUT FOUNDATION.

Still the rumors of trouble did not die.

In late August, the Department of the Interior asked Taylor for a special report. He had no trouble lacing one together. Yes, Indians had performed certain depredations, but these had been the "work of . . . desperate characters of various tribes of Sioux who refuse to recognize the authority of the tribal leaders. . . . They are known as Bad Faces and are composed of the most refractory . . . characters of the tribe. . . ."

Interior thought it could bring these "refractory characters" to terms. On October 18 the new Indian agent for the Upper Platte, M.T. Patrick, telegraphed Taylor that Red Leaf's band was on the way to Fort Laramie to touch the pen and that Red Cloud himself would come in to sign the treaty. On November 19, Patrick wrote to Major James Van Voast, the new commander of Fort Laramie, that he was about to move Red Cloud, Red Leaf and Man-Afraid-of-His-Horses with their bands from north of the Powder River to Bordeaux Ranche and negotiate a peace treaty with them.

On that same day, Nathaniel Taylor wired his superior in Washington that all previously hostile Sioux now wanted to sign the treaty.

These bursts of optimism from the men in the field made a strong impression on the men who ran the country. On December 5, 1866, President Johnson in his State of the Union message assured Congress and the country that the Indians had "unconditionally submitted to our authority and manifested an earnest desire for a renewal of friendly relations."

Red Cloud's strategy of guerrilla attacks on the white troopers and settlers had baffled the army commanders. Because he didn't launch a full-scale attack, as they would have, they didn't think he was serious.

By the end of the summer it was obvious that Carrington couldn't guarantee the safety of the road. Every campsite between Forts Reno and C.F. Smith, some two hundred miles apart, had served as a burial ground.

In September the attacks became even more frequent and were carried out by ever-larger war parties. On the eighth the Sioux attacked a wagon train just four miles west of Fort Kearny, killing two men and a woman and driving off forty mules. Three days later they attacked the fort's own herders, driving off thirty-three horses and seventy-eight mules.

On the thirteenth, Carrington received word that a civilian hay party was under attack. Riding out to the rescue, Brown found that one man had been killed and a mowing machine and much hay burned. The Sioux had also run off more than two hundred head of cattle.

That same day the Indians stampeded an army herd near the fort and wounded two of the herders. Grummond pursued them, but only for the ten miles permitted by Carrington's regulations; he failed to retrieve any of the herd. The next morning a soldier's bloody uniform was found; the body was never recovered.

Red Cloud continued to gain new allies. Entrenched in the last buffalo country north of the Platte River, he was giving the rest of the Sioux a hard choice: join him or starve. Even the Brulé Sioux and the northern Cheyenne, who had gone south to the Republican valley, had found poor hunting. The last of their young men broke away and joined Red Cloud.

By now Red Cloud's camp was reported to number a thousand lodges, two thousand warriors. The friendly Crow rumored that Red Cloud had counseled with the Sioux of the Black Hills and the tributaries of the upper Missouri, whose great war chief was Sitting Bull. It was said that some of these Minneconjou and Hunkpapa had smoked the war pipe with Red Cloud.

The fort itself seemed safe, particularly because of its mountain howitzers, which the Sioux rightly feared. But late in September, Captain Brown got the battle he thirsted for when he and his men caught up with Crazy Horse's band. The Indians turned, shouting, whooping, dodging back, and soon surrounded the patrol. In half an hour of close fighting Brown and his men killed six Sioux. Only one trooper was wounded, and Brown returned triumphantly to the fort. Carrington later reported to Sherman that the incident had "inspired my men with new courage."

From Reno to C.F. Smith, the Bozeman was so much under siege that the troops were little more than prisoners in their own stockades. In less than five months, the Sioux had killed sixteen soldiers and fifty-six civilians and made fifty hostile moves against the men of Fort Kearny alone. As one report stated, they "attacked nearly every train and person who attempted to pass over the Montana road."

Van Voast had difficulty getting anybody to run messages from Laramie to Carrington. "I don't suppose I could hire a citizen to go to Phil Kearny for any price. Even my Indians could not be induced to make the trip," he wrote his superiors. "The more money we offer the more frightened they are."

"Did you see the new men?" George Grummond asked Brown over dinner.

"You call them men?" Brown sneered. "Those recruits are boys."

"They've got no training," Captain Powell put in. "Half of them don't know where the trigger is on a rifle."

"And the schoolmarm is going to keep them so busy building they won't learn anything about fighting." Brown was disgusted. "What we need is to take a force right into the Sioux villages and take them apart. Then they'd leave us alone. It's the only way to stop any Indian war, including this one."

"Not according to Colonel Carrington," Grummond sighed. "He says that's not the way this one will be fought."

"Maybe we need a new commander," Brown hinted.

Back at Fort Laramie, Major Van Voast volunteered to undertake a winter offensive against Red Cloud. One thing the army had learned in seventy-five years of Indian fighting was that the Indians didn't like or expect to fight in winter. Winter was time for huddling in tepees and telling stories, for playing games and making weapons. Summer was time for hunting and war.

On November 12, General Sherman wrote Colonel Carrington, "You are hereby instructed . . . to turn your earnest attention to the possibility of striking the hostile bands of Indians by surprise in their winter camps. . . . Major James Van Voast has volunteered . . . to make such an expedition from Fort Laramie. Perhaps a pincer movement by the two forces would expedite success."

Clarence Simmons read the orders and frowned. "What will you do, Henry? You can't attack innocent villages."

"I may have no choice," Carrington sighed.

"It's wrong. A Christian always has a choice. Women and innocent children will be killed. Besides, you don't know which villages the men who made these raids came from."

"Or even what particular tribe was involved."

"No, not even that." Simmons shook his head over the injustice of it. Dozens of times over the last fifty years army troops had attacked Indian villages in revenge and wiped them out, only to have it proved later that none of the victims had ever lifted a bow in war.

"I can't go," Carrington decided. "I'm not a combat officer. I'll have to send someone."

"But, Henry, you must resist such an order!"

"Resist? In the army you don't resist orders like this. See this line about Van Voast? It's a dig at me. He wants to know why I haven't volunteered."

"I think I'll send a few telegrams." Simmons was proud of his influence. "I'm not without friends in

Washington and Boston. This is the time to use them."

"If ever there was, this is it," agreed Carrington. "The peace policy can't work if we don't give it a chance to."

Clarence Simmons sighed. "If only we had another twenty officers like you out here, Henry, this country wouldn't be in the mess it's in now."

Carrington smiled wryly. "I don't know about that, but thanks anyway."

Chapter 14

When Cynthia Simmons missed her monthlies for the third time she knew for certain that she was pregnant and Clarence wasn't the father.

She was both elated and fearful. The prospect of a child at last delighted her, but she was afraid she must stop the affair with Tenodor. God knew what he would do, because the truth was that she had started it in the first place to find out if it was she or her husband who couldn't conceive. Now that she knew the truth and had the new life firmly started within her, she was ready to abandon her lover and return to Clarence's side.

But the thought of having to deal with Tenodor filled her with terror. As the weeks passed, the captain had become more and more ardent. He had even asked her to leave Clarence and marry him. How that had tempted her! But the idea also chilled her. No woman on this or any other army post would speak to her again. The whole country wasn't big enough to hide from such shame. No, she had married Clarence Simmons. She would bear him the child he wanted and they would grow old and she hoped happy together, particularly if he got the bishopric. The child, at least, she could give him. But she didn't feel at all right about it.

As she waited for Tenodor, she puttered around the combination schoolroom and chapel. She could still taste the bile from that morning's sickness. What did the father matter? It was the baby who mattered. It must have a good life. All very well, but then why was she cold with terror? Why did her limbs feel like lead? Was it only morning sickness that made eating so difficult?

She hung the children's drawings on the wall and cleaned the mud off the floor. She started at the least noise, expecting Tenodor to walk in the back door at any moment. Sometimes he had to wait for the little alley behind the building to clear. She thought it a miracle that their affair had not been discovered, especially when she considered that they met twice a week. But after today all that would be over.

Cynthia sighed. She had grown to love the very feel of Tenodor, his hard muscles compared to Clarence's soft flesh; his proud blond mustache instead of her husband's pink upper lip. And Tenodor smelled like a man, of rum, horse and pipe tobacco. Clarence used talcum and seemed more like a boy groping his way. She was sure that Tenodor sometimes saw and felt more than she.

That their affair hadn't been discovered had a lot to do with Tenodor's forethought. He had turned himself into something of a recluse, refusing all invitations from the ladies of the post to Saturday night socials and Sunday afternoon teas. To Clarence's disgust, Ten Eyke wouldn't even set an example for his

167

men by attending Sunday services. In this way Cynthia had been spared the danger and awkwardness of meeting him in company.

She heard the door open and close as Tenodor came in from the alley. He wore his riding uniform, and his brisk walk and confident smile did nothing to ease her fear. He looked as if nothing and no one could get in his way. Glancing about to make sure the shutters were closed, she embraced him but held herself a bit away and made her kiss cool.

"Sorry," he said. "There was a private out back tending the smokehouse."

"Did he see you?" All the fears of the last months made her voice shake.

"No, of course not." He pulled her toward their nest in the closet.

"No, wait." She put her hands against his chest, her heart beating wildly. "Tenodor, we have to talk."

"Talk?"

"Yes. Sit down."

Not understanding, frowning, he sprawled in the front pew.

"What's wrong?" he asked. "I saw it when I came in."

She struggled to calm herself. She wanted to put this in such a way that the break would be clean and permanent. She didn't want him to think that he had any claims on her. She had foolishly failed to consider the possibility that she might fall in love. She had chosen Tenodor because he was the most attractive bachelor officer on the post. She had imagined going back to Clarence afterward with no real feelings about the man or the affair.

168

But Captain Tenodor Ten Eyke was more of a presence than she had bargained for. He was obviously so in love that more than once she had considered scuttling her plan, but a few of Clarence's long-suffering glances in her direction changed her mind. Besides, she wanted a child if it was at all possible. She must know, once and forever.

"We have to stop seeing each other," Cynthia blurted. "I have to stop." She turned away, unable to bear the look in his eyes, that blaze of hurt.

"Stop?"

"Yes. Clarence suspects." It was a lie.

Surprisingly, Tenodor laughed. "Good. He has to know sometime."

"No, Tenodor. I don't want to hurt him."

"No! What's this?"

"I don't want to go on. I can't. It's tearing me apart."

"Then tell the fat little reverend how it is and I'll marry you the day you're free."

"It's not that simple. You—you want a child too." She hung her head. "I can't give you one any more than I could give Clarence one."

That stopped him, as she had known it would. She saw him frown as he turned her speech over in his mind. He nodded slowly, as if reluctantly coming to a decision. A rush of dark grief rose in her, but she forced herself not to give way to it. She longed to throw herself on that uniformed chest and tell him she was carrying his child, to beg him to take her off to some place without marriage or divorce where the two of them might raise this and other children. But they both knew that such a place didn't exist on this earth. They had talked about it. Besides, Tenodor planned to stay in the army, which demanded proper conduct. He worried about what he would do if he had to make any kind of living in the shattered South. His family had lost everything in the war.

He squirmed on the pew. She knew what bothered him: he loved her, but she couldn't replace his lost family. She saw acceptance on his face and thought with a pang that she had succeeded. She was wrong.

"It's all right, Cynthia. I mean, that you can't have children." He sighed. "I'll marry you anyway."

She felt cold all over, as if her whole being were shriveling away from him.

"No. I won't do that to you. You'll get over me and find someone else. I won't leave Clarence. And now that he suspects, I must stop this."

"No! You can't!"

"Tenodor, we knew from the beginning it couldn't last!"

"I won't lose you, Cynthia. I'll go to Clarence myself if you won't listen."

"No, Tenodor, you can't do that to me."

"You can't just walk away from me!"

But in the end, she could walk away and he couldn't go to Clarence. It took her an hour, but she finally made him understand that it was better for them both if they didn't meet privately. Cynthia had learned her lesson. How possessive Tenodor was! Still, she could understand, for how she longed to possess him!

She was to learn something else too. Over the next few weeks, before she saw the post doctor early in December, she found herself mooning over memories of Tenodor, the one night and the many afternoons they had had together and how she, Tenodor and the baby might have lived together.

The pleasure her husband took in her pregnancy didn't ease her feelings. Clarence Simmons wasn't going to take any chances on her losing the baby. He insisted that she give up her duties at the school, stay around their quarters and get plenty of rest.

Certainly Cynthia liked the attention and solicitude that a mother-to-be got from everyone on the post. But as the days passed her uneasiness increased. It was a lie that grew within her. She was deceiving Clarence and betraying Tenodor. She hadn't calculated on so much guilt. But given Clarence's inability to father a child and his urgent wish to have one, what else could she have done?

On November 16 six young replacement officers arrived at Fort Kearny from Omaha. One of them was William J. Fetterman, a thirty-three-year-old West Point graduate who had attained the brevet rank of lieutenant colonel during the Civil War. Although he was now carried on the army's books as a captain, like many other brevet officers including General George Armstrong Custer, Fetterman still wore the eagle and uniform of his temporary higher rank. General Cooke had led Fetterman to believe that he might replace Carrington if the colonel should be transferred elsewhere.

Carrington received Captain Fetterman and the other new officers the day after their arrival at Fort Kearny. He gave them a briefing on what they might expect at the fort. "The red man is all around us, as I'm sure you gentlemen are aware, but we have a treaty with him. Shortly he will want to live up to it in order to return to his more peaceful pursuits and receive his annuities from the government. Our job is to hold steady here till he comes to his senses."

There was a surreptitious exchange of glances among the six slim young men.

"Are you saying, Colonel, that we aren't to give pursuit if the Indian fires on us?"

The question came from Fetterman with more than a touch of arrogance.

"I suspect you are already aware of my rules in that regard."

"Begging your pardon, sir, if the savages know they can attack with impunity, it hardly makes sense for us even to man the fort."

"I hardly think it wise for you to question how we do things until you have been here a while, Captain," Carrington snapped. He could see that the rot of insubordination that infected the BOQ had already set in with these six. He asked Fetterman to stay behind and dismissed the others.

"I don't approve of your uniform, *Captain*. On my post, a man wears the insignia and uniform of his rank."

He was gratified to see the officer redden.

"Sir, this is my rank. The army has ruled that an officer may wear the uniform of the highest grade he has obtained, provided he has not lost it dishonorably."

"Just where do regulations say that? I haven't seen it."

"Begging your pardon, sir," Fetterman sneered, "but possibly you haven't received the latest regulations yet."

"Haven't received—?" Carrington was struggling

172

to figure out how to put this swaggerer in his place.

"I intend to continue to wear the uniform of the rank I obtained in the late war, sir."

"Even if I order you to wear the uniform of a captain, Fetterman?"

"I would respectfully refuse, sir, and I understand the army would support me."

Carrington struggled to remain calm in the face of the contemptuous gleam in Fetterman's eye. He realized suddenly that the captain was enjoying himself. If it hadn't been for the uniform, he would have found something else to antagonize his superior.

"Well, since you feel so strongly about it, I'll allow it, pending the arrival of those regulations. Which I shall write for today."

"Yes, sir." Fetterman's voice dripped scorn. Carrington ignored it.

"I know that your rank would ordinarily make you second in command here, but you have little experience in Indian fighting, so Captain Ten Eyke will continue as my executive officer."

That got him. He stiffened and flushed a little, Carrington saw. "Whatever you say, sir. What will be my duties?"

"What do you think you're best fit for, Captain?" Carrington's voice was mild. He dropped into the chair behind his desk and regarded the junior officer. *Pity the fellow has to act like such an ass,* he thought. *I could certainly use a first-class fighting man.* "In what do you excel?"

"I'm sure you have my record, sir. Don't I see it there on your desk?"

"You try my patience, Fetterman. Damnit, we

have to live together. Now, I'm asking you what duty you'd like to have."

Carrington thought he saw the young man thaw a bit. "I'm a soldier, sir, and what I'm best at is leading troops into battle."

"We have plenty of that for you. Think you can get some of these recruits that came with you trained to shoot and ride before the snows?"

"Make cavalry out of them, sir?" Fetterman frowned. "Not before four months, and six would be more like it."

"Out here we measure these things in weeks, Captain. Are you up to it?"

"I'll do my best, sir."

"Good. Take that latest batch and find out from Ten Eyke if he can give you another twenty-five or so of his less experienced men. See if you can make something of a special unit out of them. Spend a lot of time drilling them and teaching them how to fight. I'll even lend you my scout, Jim Bridger. He'll give you some idea how these Indians scrap."

"Begging your pardon, sir, I don't need some old drunk's idea of how to fight savages. I learned my methods at the Point."

Carrington gave him a twisted smile. "I can see why Cooke sent you. You take Bridger anyway, Captain, and you listen to him too. Maybe then you'll live long enough to learn something. Now, get out of here and get busy."

"Yes, sir." Fetterman executed a fancy salute, clicked his heels and left.

Carrington sighed. He had never met a West Pointer he liked, and he probably never would.

* * *

As the cold winds of November began to blow harder, the soldiers at Fort Kearny prepared for winter. The men hurried to finish the south wall, filling the last chinks with mud as the skies grew daily more threatening.

Ten Eyke and Carrington pushed the work crews harder than ever. Ten Eyke had a look of pain these days, as if a pair of giant pliers were squeezing his face. The colonel got even more schoolmarmish as the pressure from the Indians increased. They were in evidence whenever the men went out of the fort, as they had to do for wood, hay and water.

Fetterman, whom almost everybody called "Colonel" to annoy Carrington, turned out to be a pistol. He might have started with a hundred of the rawest recruits, but he got Fetterman's Raiders, as his troop came to be called, the newest rifles, the finest horses and the best of the younger officers, including Brown. He and Fred became fast friends, seeing eye to eye on what ought to be done to keep the red man at peace: namely, exterminate him, and the sooner the better.

Accompanied by Brown, Fetterman went to Carrington's office with an offer to take a hundred men and wipe out all the hostile tribes on the Tongue River. The colonel refused, and quite a bit of yelling ensued. In the end Fetterman insisted that his request be put into the official log and the weekly report that went to General Cooke.

In the officer's mess, Fetterman boasted, "A company of regulars could whip a thousand savages, and a regiment could clean out the whole array of fighting tribes."

Jim Bridger chuckled. "And I suppose a hound

dog can whip a grizzly, too! You men who fought down South are crazy. You don't know a damn thing about fighting Indians."

But the captain paid him no attention. Both Brown and Fetterman openly sneered that Carrington had "no more liver than a yellow-haired virgin choirboy." As Fetterman put it night after night, "There's not an officer on this post who has any confidence in him. He's afraid. He doesn't know how to maintain morale and he's too jumpy to command."

In truth, Carrington's reports to Cooke hardly inspired confidence. He wrote like a man who had been pulled in different directions for too long. He was bombastic in one paragraph and cautious in the next. He warned of the dangers along the Bozeman Trail, only to declare how safe he had made it. He complained of his weak forces, then boasted of their strength.

Near the end of November, Carrington addressed his second in command. "Tenodor, I hardly know what to do. Omaha wants us to attack Red Cloud and Man Afraid. We both know we're too weak for that."

"Yes, sir. Being caught between Red Cloud and General Cooke isn't what I'd call enviable."

"With those morons in the BOQ pushing me for some military adventure."

"Why not let them have one?"

"Let them ride into Red Cloud's camp?" Carrington shuddered. "I hate to think what would be left of them."

Ten Eyke smiled. "Fetterman says he could do the job with eighty troopers."

"Eighty troopers? Fetterman's an ass."

"Yes, but the men need an outlet. They're stir

crazy from sitting here in the fort for weeks and months without ever meeting the enemy on their own ground. All they do is go out to rescue some poor muleskinner who's been ambushed, and they usually get there too late."

"What do you have in mind?"

"Fetterman has an idea for a midnight ambush of the Sioux. Set mules out for bait. The moon will be full tomorrow night. It would give those red horse thieves a bit of their own medicine."

"Hmm. Caught in the act, so to speak."

"Yes sir, in the act."

"I like it. Tomorrow night?"

"Yes sir."

"Set it up, Tenodor."

The next night, led by their brevet colonel, Fetterman's Raiders sneaked out of the fort before the moon rose and hid themselves in front of the fort in the cottonwood thicket along Big Piney Creek to watch the mules the herders had hobbled there as live bait.

"Pass the word, Fred," Fetterman whispered, "to keep it down. Tell 'em they could get scalped."

The chill moon rose. Nine o'clock melted into ten, which slid into midnight. Up and down the line the men grew restless. The mules could be plainly seen; occasionally one strayed into the shadows of the cottonwoods. Even in the darkness they could be followed by the jingle of their harness bells.

In the small hours of the morning ten men were sent back to the fort crippled with cold. The remaining men surreptitiously stamped their feet and rubbed their hands.

Dawn came at last and ninety raiders came back to the fort stiff, cold and hungry. Despite their lack of success, Fetterman was full of enthusiasm. He strode around the enlisted men's mess asking the troops and noncoms how they felt and slapping them on the back, but they seemed more interested in hot coffee.

Within three hours of the men's return to the fort, Crazy Horse's band appeared not a mile off and ran off a herd of horses. The six herders considered themselves lucky to get away with just one man wounded, an arrow in his thigh.

"I'll bet those savages knew we were there. They were watching us and laughing," Fetterman raged at Brown and Grummond. "They're out there somewhere now, whooping and dancing around their fire, gloating over how they got the better of us."

"Well, they did," said Grummond.

"But never again," swore Fetterman. "You can count on that."

In December one of the oldest, most respected chiefs of the Missouri Sioux died. The Minneconjou, Hunkpapa and Sans Arcs, who were camped with Red Cloud on the Tongue River, so far had not participated as tribes in his attacks on the whites, although some of their young men had joined him.

But as White Swan lay dying, he gathered the war chiefs about him and spoke. "I have tried to keep you from fighting the whites, but now I am going to die. If you want to fight them, pull yourselves together and go out and satisfy yourselves—fight once more!"

The deathbed lecture made such an impression on his followers that many did indeed decide to join Red Cloud. The greatest number were Minneconjou, headed by Chief High Backbone. With them came some Hunkpapa and Sans Arcs warriors.

They were in the force that marched south toward Fort Kearny. The Bad Faces and the Oglala of Old Man Afraid's tribe had also collected Red Leaf's Brulé Wazhazka and scores of other Brulé as well as a number of Arapaho and some northern Cheyenne. These last had turned hostile after Brown and several other officers from the fort got drunk one night and shot up their camp.

Red Cloud did not plan to huddle in his tepee that December. He was about to launch a winter campaign.

Chapter 15

As Jim Bridger had tried to convince Carrington back in the summer, Fort Kearny's location on low ground gave it a strategic disadvantage.

On the other side of North Piney Creek lay Lodge Pole Ridge, which separated the drainage basins of the Powder and Tongue rivers. This was higher than any of the land near the fort, so it blocked the view of all the terrain past its spine. Red Cloud could hide as many warriors as he wanted there and no one inside the fort would know it.

Perpendicular to this ridge lay another, called Turkey Ridge because the rock at its top looked like a turkey's head. The Sioux could hide on its east and west slopes even from troopers who had crossed Lodge Pole Ridge.

On December 6, as usual, the woodcutters were attacked some four miles from the fort. They sent up their alarm flag, and the man on Signal Hill rapidly semaphored. Inside the fort, Carrington ordered Fetterman to take a company of infantry and another of cavalry out. They were to rescue the woodcutters and drive the Indians back across the creek.

At the same time, feeling that he must do something to keep up with the bold Fetterman, Carrington himself decided to take thirty men across the creek to cut off the attackers' retreat.

"Remember what I told you!" Fetterman shouted to his officers. "Grummond, you come at them from the left, Brown from the right. Don't give your men time to think or they'll bolt. Just press the hell out of the red-rumps. Ride right through them and let the infantry come in behind to kill."

When Fetterman's Raiders met the Sioux, the beleaguered woodcutters cheered raggedly. At first they just squatted behind their wagons but had to move as Fetterman led the cavalry through them toward the Sioux, who had pulled their ponies to the edge of a field near the creek. It looked to Fetterman like a rout in the making.

He shouted and waved his saber, but when he turned he saw that more than half his troopers, mostly the youngest recruits, had bolted from the hail of arrows and were urging their horses back toward the fort. These animals, as green as their smooth-cheeked riders, reared and whinnied and circled.

"Shoot those cowards if they don't get up here and fight!" shouted Fetterman.

Brown immediately turned his long-barreled revolver on the recruits, who were so busy struggling to control their horses that they hadn't retreated far. Following Brown's example, Grummond threatened his men; Fetterman fired over their heads.

Arrows rained down on them all. The small force

of Indians melted into the forest. Seemingly from no-where some two hundred Sioux rode across the blue-coats' rear, shooting arrows from horseback. By the time the troopers turned the Indians had ridden into the draw and disappeared.

Carrington had taken his thirty men over Lodge Pole Ridge and dropped down into Peno Creek, hop-ing to surprise the Indians and keep them from escap-ing Fetterman's attack. No sooner had Carrington's men forced their horses into the icy creek than a hun-dred Indians surrounded them, whooping, hollering and panicking the horses.

"Ride up on the bank!" shouted Carrington. He soon saw that a third of his men were frozen while another third stuck closely to him. The rest were eager to fight and looked as if they might hold firm. As for himself, the colonel didn't like the noise, the confusion or the lack of control. The savages were trying to sur-round them and he had no idea what to do.

"Fight the Indians!" he roared. The sergeants and lieutenants with him repeated it to their men.

Fetterman, meanwhile, had managed to clear his field of enemies and he began to pull the woodcutters out. He sent Brown over the hill with twenty troopers to see how the colonel was doing.

Brown rode up just as Carrington's men, finally organized for defense since they couldn't get up the hill without being slaughtered, managed to push back their attackers. Brown and his men soon put the Sioux on the run.

"Let's go get them, shall we, men?" shouted Brown.

A cheer went up. The troopers who had dismounted so as to fire without panicking their mounts shouted agreement and got back on their horses.

"Do you think it's wise to chase them?" asked Carrington. "They might have reinforcements."

"Sir," Brown cried, "they need to be taught a lesson and we are the men to do it."

"All right, Captain," Carrington conceded. He had never in his life ridden in combat. "You lead and we'll follow."

The troops plunged into the woods, came out into a little clearing and without hesitation rushed up the hill that lay before them. From both sides and the front came whoops and war cries.

"We're surrounded!" someone shouted. The Indians had whirled and flanked the troopers. The Indians rode through the party trying to lance the men. One of the new replacement officers took an arrow in his throat and fell from his horse. In the time it took the men to reload their muskets, one warrior rode four times through the troops, finally killing a sergeant with his lance.

"That's Crazy Horse!" shouted Brown. "See if you can get him!"

But the charging Sioux warrior, a jagged streak of lightning painted on his chest, passed through them again without getting hit.

Brown himself was surrounded by six Indians. His pistol was empty, he had to fight his way out with his saber. The captain escaped with a gashed arm and rode back to where Carrington was making his stand.

Suddenly the hillside was deserted. "Where'd they go?" shouted a sergeant.

Nobody answered him.

"Let's get back to Fetterman," Carrington ordered. The colonel led the party back, their two dead slung over the back of a horse.

As they came over the top of the hill they saw Fetterman's men surrounded by more Indians. Before Carrington could say a word, Brown shouted, "Attack!"

Excited by their taste of action, the men followed him. Charging from the rear, they broke the back of the attack and the Indians scattered. Carrington and Fetterman's forces joined.

"Let's go get them!" Fetterman roared. "We've got them on the run now!"

"Hold it, Captain!" ordered Carrington. "You're not to chase them."

"I'm not to what?"

"You're not to chase them," the colonel repeated.

"Damnit, man, what are you saying?" Fetterman glowered at him. "You afraid? You take the dead and wounded back to the fort, Colonel *sir,* and we'll just finish up the lesson we've started to give these savages."

"No, sir!" Carrington glared back. "You just call your men together and get ready to head back. We've done all the fighting and taken all the losses we're going to take today."

The other men and officers listened with mixed feelings. Yes, a real battle after so many frustrating skirmishes with the savages felt good. But what didn't feel good, what in fact was damn scary, was to start out fighting sixty or seventy Indians and turn a corner and find hundreds. No sir, that didn't feel good at all. Better by far to talk about what you would do the next time, to curse their spineless commander and ride back to the fort than to ride into the bush to face God knew how many red men.

"This is going in our reports, Colonel," Fetterman warned.

"As a victory," Carrington smirked.

"Victory! We haven't begun to fight."

"I count ten Indians killed, Captain, and we have only three dead."

"We have eight wounded and we're afraid to give chase."

"Captain Fetterman, we are not *afraid* to give chase," Carrington explained patiently. "It's just not wise. In a few days we'll haul in the last of the wood and then the fort will be finished and we'll be snug for the winter. This is not the time to go gallivanting after Indians."

"They won't respect us if they think we're afraid to chase them."

"It's my decision, Captain."

Fetterman muttered into Brown's ear, "Only for a little longer. Only for a little while longer."

The wind blew cold across the plains, but to a man intent on hot revenge it merely stirred the blood.

It had taken Red Cloud weeks to regain his strength after the Sun Dance, but by the end of the summer he was himself again. The ordeal had been worth it. He got new respect from the other chiefs, who could see the powerful wakan that had settled on him.

Even now, five months later, the memory of what the Wakan Eagle had shown him stirred him. He had seen Indian babies starving, mothers weeping, fathers discouraged and destitute. He had seen a mountain of buffalo carcasses, whole forests leveled and proud

185

mountains whittled into hills by the evil white ghosts who had come to steal the Powder River hunting grounds.

The marriage of Black Buffalo Woman to No Water had helped Red Cloud too. Now when he sent messages or spoke in council he was listened to. True, Crazy Horse would not speak to him, but he followed the council's battle orders. Well, that was all right. All that mattered was to keep the pressure on Little White Chief.

And he had. The white men scurried from the shelter of one fort to another, from Laramie to Reno to Kearny to C.F. Smith, like a rabbit struggling to escape the hunter.

Red Cloud now commanded all the warriors from Red Leaf's band as well as those of White Bull of the Minneconjou. It thrilled him to lead such a brave assembly of chiefs and warriors. This army was the most powerful Indian army he or anyone else alive had ever heard of. Besides Red Leaf and White Bull, there were He-dog and his brother Short Bull's Oglala band. High Backbone of the Minneconjou had led several raids. So had Crazy Horse. No Water and his brother Black Twin had pushed many settlers from their homes. Old Two Moon of the Northern Cheyenne had brought his people, and no one could ride and think in battle like that wily old man.

Red Cloud had asked Young-Man-Afraid-of-His-Horses to take charge of the attacks on Fort C.F. Smith and the countryside around it. The two hadn't wanted to part. They had become even more like brothers since the Sun Dance. But Young Man Afraid knew that Red Cloud needed someone he could trust or the distant attacks might falter. It was hard enough to keep the bands together and concentrated on a single purpose and every week some chief pulled out to go hunting. But fortunately, so far every week some other chief joined them. If only the whites didn't have those log-sized rifles that shot twice, once inside the forts and again in the air over the victim's head. Without that defense Red Cloud could have led his warriors to victory right over the stockade walls.

Those warriors had not done well today. Ten dead! They would talk of bad wakan. They would think of going hunting, anything to get away from a war party with bad wakan. Red Cloud would have to explain in council why so many had died and answer questions about whether he was fit to continue to lead.

"This war is not fated to be successful," High Backbone complained that night. The Minneconjou chief resented Red Cloud and wanted to take over.

All the great chiefs of the expedition were present. White Bull, He-dog, Short Bull, Crazy Horse, High Backbone, No Water, Black Twin and Two Moon of the Cheyenne—all made sure Crazy Horse stayed a safe distance from young No Water.

"The warriors didn't stay in line," Old Two Moon said in his reedy voice. "We had them outnumbered."

No Water's men had broken and run when the white reinforcements showed up. "It was the guns," he complained. "It's useless to fight the whites when they have so many guns."

Silence followed; Red Cloud knew why. Nobody believed him, but they didn't want to come right out and call No Water a coward.

"My people are upset. My warriors want to go hunting," He-dog put in. "So many dead! When we fight the Crow, it's a big day when three die. These people are devils."

"Are you leaving, He-dog?" asked Red Cloud.

He-dog sidestepped. "My council is discussing what to do."

Red Cloud saw that if something wasn't done soon, he would lose his army to attrition. A band here, another there, and shortly he would have only the Bad Faces, arguing among themselves. Red Cloud nodded at Two Moon. He thought now was a good time to present the strategy he and the old chief had decided on earlier.

"Hai, Crazy Horse," said Old Two Moon. "Can the Kit Foxes lead the next battle?"

"The Foxes will do what the Sioux need done," their curly-haired young captain said. He chanted:

"The Foxes are ready to die if dying is what is needed.
The Foxes love death, for death shows what kind of Sioux is a Fox.
If there's any dying to be done, Foxes are ready to do it."

"All very well," said Chief High Backbone. He looked out through the eyes of the wolf, his power animal. "Crazy Horse is brave and the Kit Foxes the bravest of Sioux societies. We can do no better than to have them police the warriors. But unless we have wakan with us, it is useless to go into battle. I lost three men today, and I will not go back and face those guns unless Wakan-Takan himself has filled the air with enough breath to blow away their bullets."

"Hai, don't you have a *berdache* in your camp?" Chief Two Moon asked High Backbone.

"My wife's cousin's husband's brother," High Backbone admitted. "Why, do you want to lie with him? And you such an old man!" The council roared, for berdaches were half man and half woman, hermaphrodites who wanted to be the wives of other men, like women.

The Sioux had great respect as well as scorn for them and often consulted them, especially in matters of war. For all the tribes except one, the Sans Arcs, they proved powerful in predicting battle success.

The Sans Arcs Sioux, however, had once been induced by a crazy berdache to place all their bows on a hill while he performed a ceremony that would bring them much wakan. A force of Crow appeared, caught the Sioux without their weapons and drove them away in wild flight. This event so amused the other Sioux bands that it gave the tribe its name: Sans Arcs, no bows.

"I'm not a Sans Arc," Chief Two Moon smiled. "Besides, I have more wives than I can feed now." The council laughed again. "But maybe we could get the berdache to find out how we'll fare in the next battle."

"What do you think, Red Cloud?" asked Hedog.

"I'd like to know what Wakan-Takan has in store for us," Red Cloud answered.

"If we see their iron hornets killing us, I'm for returning to the hunt," High Backbone maintained.

"Of course," Red Cloud agreed. "It would be foolish to fight without wakan."

189

* * *

Sashay the berdache didn't like anything about the idea. He looked down at the eyeless black hood old Two Moon held in his hands. "Why can't I just spin around in a circle and see what happens?"

He glanced around at the chiefs surrounding him; they stared impassively back. Actually, Sashay made them uneasy. Only a few berdaches had both male and female organs. Most were just crazy men who thought they were women, like the one who had led the Sans Arcs astray. What an idea! Better to think you were a wolf or a buffalo.

Some berdaches took men for lovers, but rarely openly. Berdaches usually lived on the outskirts of the village with each other.

"No, you have to be on a pony," Red Cloud told Sashay. "We talked to the shamans from two camps and both agreed. Men fight battles on ponies."

Sashay looked from one to the other with fearful, pleading eyes. "But I'll fall off and hurt myself!"

"If you don't get on that pony and ride up the hill, you're likely to fall off a cliff," High Backbone threatened.

Red Cloud thought this a little strong. He tried another tack. "Hai, Sashay. Only you can keep the Sioux men from dying."

"Dying?" Sashay had been a nurse for the wounded warriors who had been brought back last week. He shuddered at the memory of those terrible wounds. He looked at Red Cloud. "So many were hurt."

"Many more will be hurt if we don't know how much wakan we'll have with us."

The berdache's slender form trembled. "Put the blindfold on. I'll see what I can see, but I don't promise anything. It's so cold I can't feel much of anything."

Red Cloud took the black hood and pulled it over Sashay's head. The others backed away. With the hood on Sashay looked like some dreadful being from the world below.

Red Cloud took the berdache's hand and pulled him toward the pony, which the shaman had chanted and prayed over all last night. He helped Sashay up and settled him there.

Sashay reached blindly. "Where are the reins?"

"There aren't any."

"But how can I control the pony?"

"With your wakan power!"

"But I'll get hurt!"

The warriors smiled and shook their heads at this fear of pain. A Kit Fox would have welcomed the chance to prove how brave he was.

As the medicine men had told them to, the chiefs pointed the pony up toward the top of Raven Hill, took off its leather bridle and hit it hard on the rump. The animal shot forward and the chiefs laughed at Sashay's efforts to hold onto the horse with his knees. The pony ran to the top of the hill and disappeared.

"Get your ponies!" shouted Red Cloud. "Let's go!"

They galloped after the berdache.

On the third hill they found Sashay stretched out on the ground, the pony grazing a little further on.

"He's asleep," He-dog said.

"No, he hit his head when he fell," Red Cloud replied. "Let's see how bad he's hurt."

It took them several minutes to revive Sashay,

who tried to huddle against Red Cloud when he realized where he was. The chief pulled away as if the touch was distasteful. Sashay smiled up, sweetly confused.

"What did you see?" asked High Backbone.

"I have ten soldiers in each hand," replied Sashay.

"Ten! Wonderful!" He-dog exclaimed.

"Do it again," High Backbone and Red Cloud urged.

Although Sashay protested, resistance was useless. Again he was blindfolded, again he was set on the pony and again it was hit. This time the chiefs followed at a more leisurely pace.

When Sashay fell off this time, he did not hit his head, only knocked his breath out. They asked him again how many soldiers he had seen.

"I had twenty in each hand," he gasped.

"Not enough," agreed the chiefs. Once more Sashay was blindfolded and set on his horse.

"You'll kill me!" he squealed.

"Grab more soldiers when they come by you," shouted He-dog. "Be a Sioux!"

That set the others to laughing. Red Cloud gave the pony a hard whack with the halter.

It shot away and again they followed. This time they thought Sashay might have hurt himself badly, for as they came up to him they saw he was bleeding from a gash in his forehead. They put a cloth over the wound and again Red Cloud worked to bring the she-man around. Gradually Sashay regained consciousness.

"Fifty soldiers!" he shouted.

"Fifty!" they echoed. "Is that all?"

"I mean, fifty in each hand," Sashay corrected himself.

A murmur of approval rose from the chiefs. One hundred white warriors in his two hands! There was a battle worth fighting! What power! What glory! What wakan rode with them if they killed a hundred white soldiers!

News of the divination ran through all the camps before noon. All afternoon runners came to Red Cloud with messages from various chiefs who wanted to take part. It was obvious that the Bad Face chief had strong wakan.

A war council was held. Red Cloud disagreed with High Backbone and He-dog, who wanted to attack the fort directly.

"They have the double-tongued guns as big as logs. We wouldn't get anywhere. Besides, the Crow and Cheyenne told us they have a whole house full of powder and shot inside the fort."

"Then how do we kill a hundred soldiers?" Short Bull demanded.

"It's ridiculous to take a thousand warriors out to attack only those few who cut trees," White Bull pointed out. "And most of them aren't soldiers."

"We saw how recklessly they came on to fight last week," Red Cloud observed. "That's what we will use against them, their own foolishness."

"But how?" asked He-dog.

"Here's my plan."

Red Cloud went on to outline a strategy to lure the whites into an ambush.

"But what will we use for bait?" Short Bull asked.

193

"Isn't it the Foxes who sing that if a job with death needs doing to call them?" said High Backbone.

"Crazy Horse!" cackled He-dog.

"Yes, Crazy Horse," Red Cloud grinned.

"Ask him if he would come into council," said Two Moon. "We certainly do have a job for the brave Foxes."

Chapter 16

John Richards arrived at Fort Kearny in December and was put up in the bachelor officers' quarters for the night. He'd had no luck persuading any of the fort commanders from Laramie to C.F. Smith to let him trade with the Indians. This was the third time he'd come to speak to Carrington about it. He planned to try and bribe the colonel, though he had little hope of success.

Richards enjoyed visiting the forts, talking with the soldiers and hearing the latest gossip. He would have enjoyed it still more if he'd been able to trade. He liked sitting around the BOQ after supper, pulling on a jug and sucking on a pipe, which was where he was the evening he got to Kearny.

"Heard you boys had yourselves something of a shoot-out with Red Cloud last week," he said to the six officers sitting around in their suspenders before a fire.

"You heard right," said William Fetterman. "We sent them packing, too, didn't we, Fred?"

"I think that's fair to say," Brown drawled. "The

Indian doesn't understand anything about modern warfare. A really good volley from riflemen who'll stand their ground will stop any Indian attack."

"That so?" Richards' tone said he didn't believe a word of it.

"What we've needed all along is someone like Fetterman here," Brown added. "Right, George?"

Lieutenant George Grummond, over for a pipe and a glass before he went back to his young wife, grinned and guessed so.

"Damn right," Brown went on. "Why, if Bill here had been our commander, we wouldn't have been in any of the trouble we've had this year."

"Shit," Richards snorted. "You don't know what you're talking about."

Fetterman pricked up his ears. "What makes you say that?"

"You ain't going to listen to this fellow, are you, Bill?" Brown interrupted. "All he's interested in is getting a trading permit."

"Isn't he the man who lives with the Sioux? Let's hear what he's got to say." Fetterman nodded to Richards.

"I say you ought to leave Red Cloud alone," Richards asserted. "I say you ought to pull back to Fort Reno and let him have this part of the country."

"Do you?" Fetterman turned to the other officers and winked. "You don't think a hundred troopers with the right training could wipe out any Sioux village within two hundred miles of here? I could take eighty troopers and break up any Sioux fighting force if I had my pick of men."

"Eighty troopers!" Richards shook his head.

Fetterman smiled cockily. "With modern rifles and proper military discipline, we'd go through a redskin village like a dose of salts."

"Not with no eighty troopers. Not unless they're dressed in them iron suits I've seen pictures of. You got no idea how many warriors there are within a few miles of here."

"How many?" asked Fetterman.

"Upward of six or seven hundred."

All the officers laughed. "Mr. Richards," Fetterman smiled patronizingly, "we have had our little skirmishes with the savages, and I think I can safely say there aren't many more than a couple hundred red braves within a hundred miles."

"Look." Richards leaned toward them. "The Indians could take over this fort any time they wanted to."

For a moment the officers looked at him in astonished silence; then they broke into hoots of laughter.

"Take us over!" cried Fetterman. "If they could have they would have!"

"Yes, why haven't they?" Brown could hardly talk for laughing.

"It just ain't come to them yet. I don't think a Sioux has ever attacked a fort. He don't know it can be done."

Grummond eyed Captain Powell, who was suddenly looking thoughtful. "You think that's possible?"

"Aw, come on, George!" Fetterman hooted. "We're going to teach these redskins another lesson or two, and the quicker we do, the fewer casualties there'll be all around."

197

* * *

On the morning of December 19, 1866, Colonel Carrington visited the woodcutting party. The half-hour ride with his escort of ten troopers took them through acres of cut stumps that had been laid bare that summer.

The weather looked threatening and Carrington congratulated himself on his foresight in pushing the construction schedule. Without the hard effort of the summer and autumn, the fort never would have been finished by the time the first heavy snows fell.

Very likely this would be the last time the wood-cutters would be out until spring. To finish up the south wall of the fort, they had been sent out seven miles to bring in the larger trees that had already been cut down.

Glancing up at the sky, Carrington remarked to Ten Eyke that it certainly looked like snow.

"Yes sir. I think it's wise you're stopping the woodcutting for the year," the captain answered. "It's so cold the men can hardly hold an axe anymore."

When they reached the woodcutters, Carrington gave his orders and rode back to Fort Kearny. He felt good. Without too many casualties he had accomplished what he had been sent out to do, build a secure fortress that would help make the wilderness safe for travelers. The effort had tried him, but the year's hard work was over now. Winter was almost on top of them and they had survived in pretty good style. When the bad weather hit the Indian raids would stop.

All morning long, in little fits and starts, the snow whipped at the woodcutting party. They had been glad to see the colonel ride off, for Captain Powell didn't push them quite so hard when the school-marm wasn't around. The blowing snow stung their faces as they grappled with the huge logs. Despite three pairs of socks, their feet were wet, cold lumps of pain. They had built a fire, but Captain Powell wouldn't allow anybody more than five minutes to warm up.

About eleven o'clock, eight men hoisting a log into one of the wagons let it slip out of their frozen hands. The waist-thick fifteen-foot log crashed down on the foot of an enlisted man.

He screamed and the others raised the log. Blood oozed from the cracked wet leather of his boot.

"Jesus, that's nasty," one of the men shuddered.

"Cut off his boot," ordered Powell.

The others had crowded around to watch when suddenly they heard a shout: *"Injuns!"*

They looked up. Standing in the woods not fifty feet away was a line of some thirty Sioux on horse-back, silently watching them. The sight so frightened most of the men that they couldn't move. The Sioux had painted their thighs, chests, arms and faces with savage patterns of red, white, grey and yellow. They looked as menacing as demons out of hell.

"Hey, do something about my leg!" shouted the man on the ground, but nobody paid him the least attention.

Captain Powell quietly ordered, "Get your guns."

The men moved slowly toward the wagons some ten feet away.

With no word of command the Sioux began to gallop toward them. They were almost on top of the woodcutters before they swerved off, narrowly avoid-ing the wagons and the men scrambling into them to bring up their muskets. Several arrows thunked into the wagon beds and clattered against the frozen ground.

Powell shouted, "Pull those wagons around! Ernst, get that signal flag up!"

When the spotter on Signal Hill caught sight of the flag, he semaphored the message to the fort and pandemonium broke out. Colonel Carrington rushed out onto the parade ground and shouted at some of the sergeants to saddle up their units. Catching sight of Ten Eyke, Carrington put him in charge of the rescue party.

Ten Eyke was standing at the edge of the parade ground stolidly calling out orders when Captain Fetterman arrived, buckling on his pistol and saber.

"Colonel Carrington," Fetterman declaimed, "I ask for command of the rescue party."

"Captain Ten Eyke is in command."

"I outrank him," Fetterman pointed out, "and if I request it, since you yourself are not going to take charge, I believe I should have the privilege."

For a long moment the two men stared at each other. Carrington knew very well what Fetterman's game was. Proving that he was the best battle officer in the fort, he would not only earn the advancement in grade he sought, but eventually get Carrington's job. Still, it wasn't the sort of request a commanding officer could refuse. "Go, then, but no adventures, you understand me?"

Fetterman drawled, "Of course, sir, no adventures."

Carrington's voice was cold with anger. "You'll relieve the woodcutting party and bring them right back. Is that clear?"

"Yes, sir." Fetterman sounded somewhat chastened. Brown and Grummond exchanged amused glances.

By the time Fetterman had his horse brought around, more men had joined him. In fact, when he was finally ready to ride out, he had just the eighty men that he had boasted would be all he needed to wipe out any hostile Sioux.

But he was to have more help. At the last minute Larry Tierney and Bry Benjamin, two civilians on their way to California, asked if they could come.

They held up two rifles as they made the request. "We want to try these out on some real game," Tierney shouted.

"What the hell is it?" Fetterman asked, taking Tierney's weapon.

"A Henry, sir," Benjamin beamed. "Holds sixteen shots. A repeater. Load it on Sunday and it shoots all week."

Fetterman handed the weapon back. "Well, come on. With any luck we can find you a month's worth of game today."

But before they left the fort, Carrington grabbed Fetterman's reins, making the gelding rear. "You did understand my orders, didn't you, Captain?"

"Release my horse, Colonel! Men may be dying out there!"

"You're not to go over Lodge Pole Ridge, do you hear me, Captain?"

"Yes sir. Now let me go!"

"Not over Lodge Pole Ridge, no matter what." Carrington still clutched the reins. "Repeat that order, mister."

Fetterman used a look and a tone that said he would do anything to satisfy such a fool. "Yes, sir, not beyond Lodge Pole Ridge."

Carrington released him. Forty men on horses, cavalry of sorts if recruits not three months in the army could be called cavalry; another forty infantry; two civilians in three mule-drawn wagons moved out. The infantry was armed with Springfield muskets and the mounted men with seven-shot Spencers. The entire command had perhaps twenty-eight hundred rounds of ammunition.

Crazy Horse sat in the forest watching Chief High Backbone and thirty Sioux attack the woodcutters. He and the ten Kit Foxes with him had run their horses up and down the short hill to get them limber and now walked them back and forth to keep them warm and active as well as rested.

A Kit Fox herald came up. "They've left the fort," he announced, "one hundred of them."

A hard light flashed in his captain's eyes. "Just as the berdache promised."

Since he had lost Black Buffalo Woman to No Water last summer, Crazy Horse had become even bolder. Many called him reckless, yet the missions he led were always successful. Rarely was anyone injured and certainly not Crazy Horse. Strange that such a great Lakota should look so little like a Sioux. He lacked the high cheekbones; that, combined with his sandy curling hair and light complexion, made many whites think he was a captive or a half-breed.

Crazy Horse and the other Kit Foxes had spent the last two nights in the sweat lodge chanting and concentrating on their power visions till they were filled to bursting with wakan. Beside Crazy Horse now sat his best friend Young Hump on his war pony. The yellow paint on Hump's body, face and arms showed that he was a Kit Fox; The red on his hands, that he was entitled to handle wakan things and lead a war party. The red paint on his thighs, legs and feet meant he had danced the Sun Dance. Stripes around his forearm indicated that he had once been captured by Pawnee but had made his escape; the black around his mouth, that he had returned from a war party bearing an enemy killed in battle.

Across his right shoulder and chest Young Hump wore a sash of antelope hooves, a charm prepared by his father to protect him against wounds. Crazy Horse thought his friend looked magnificent. He loved and respected him. Young Hump could be counted on; riding into battle, there was no man on earth Crazy Horse felt safer with.

This morning as he steadied himself in the gusts of icy snow, the air around Crazy Horse felt warm with wakan. "Today bullets will melt in the air."

Young Hump answered with the old Sioux battle cry, "It's a good day to die!"

Crazy Horse nodded gravely. "Yes, it's a good day to die."

As they rode away from the fort, Grummond, Brown and the troopers with them welcomed the chance for action, particularly action led by Fetterman. They'd had a taste of it a few days before, though three men had been killed. Usually the Sioux disappeared before troops arrived at a raid site. They wouldn't stand and fight; it was always hit and run.

"Some glass-ass, the colonel, isn't he?" Fred

203

Brown called to Fetterman as they cantered along.

"Grummond's wife would take a tougher stance than the schoolmarm," Fetterman answered. "The trouble with these redskins is they haven't had their butts bloodied."

"Any luck and we'll bloody some today."

"Just push your men forward," shouted Fetterman. "That's what will turn the tide, hot lead."

When they rode into the woodcutters' camp some minutes later, they saw about thirty Sioux riding around the circled wagons. Fetterman swung to the right, Brown to the left. Behind them, perhaps half a mile off, came the infantry wagons.

The Sioux were riding in two circles around the woodcutters' wagons, in opposite directions to confuse the riflemen's aim. Fetterman urged his men forward and was pleased to see the revolving circles of Indians begin to break up.

"We've got 'em on the run, boys!" he shouted. "Push on!"

Forgotten were the stinging snow and icy wind, the jolts of the gallop. The two lines of troopers cut through the Sioux, shooting at close range. Once beyond the milling clumps of Sioux, they paused and pumped new shells into the breeches of the seven-shot Spencers. Tierney and Benjamin went on firing their Henrys.

The Indians suddenly broke and wheeled toward light cover on the other side of the clearing.

Now that the men had reloaded, Fetterman shouted to both commands, "They're on the run! Let's get them, boys!"

* * *

So far the battle had gone according to plan, Crazy Horse observed. He could feel the wakan surging in him. It always did before battle, but never before had he felt it so strongly, as if it might burst from within.

The thirty warriors on the battlefield had faked panic, not a difficult feat with horse soldiers bearing down on you shouting and firing their guns. As these warriors swept by, Crazy Horse signaled the nine Kit Foxes with him. Together they rode to the edge of the wood and fired their bows at the approaching horsemen. Each of the Kit Foxes held three arrows in his left hand along with his bow, an arrangement that would allow them to fire rapidly.

"There they are!" shouted a trooper. The blue-coats veered in their direction.

"White man!" Crazy Horse shouted in English. "We're going kill you!" He released two arrows in quick succession.

He shouted at the other Foxes to turn; appearing to ride hard, the ten warriors zigzagged their ponies between the trees so they actually made little speed.

As they crisscrossed up Lodge Pole Ridge, they heard the cavalry crashing through the woods behind them. Up the slope in back of the horse soldiers came the infantry, ready to rush up to give supporting firepower.

At the top of the ridge Crazy Horse pulled up his pony and dismounted, exposing himself to the approaching soldiers' fire as he picked up the pony's front hoof and pretended to pick out a pebble with his knife. His hands trembled as bullets clicked around him and spun away. Struggling to hold his trembling hands still, he chanted against the bullets:

Hawk, beat them away with your wings!
Beak, catch them with your hardness!
Claws, deflect the hornets of death!

The whine of bullets around him grew angrier as they looked for him in vain. Today his wakan was so strong it blinded the deadly hornets.

"Stop!" shouted Fetterman. "It's that son of a bitch Crazy Horse up there! Get off your horses and make sure you hit him."

Fetterman's sergeant major ordered three of his best shots to dismount. To keep from getting hit by their own marksmen, the captain and the rest of his men circled to the right and charged on up the hill. But by the time they reached the top, Crazy Horse was a third of the way down the back side of Lodge Pole Ridge. Fetterman could see that the riflemen had scored, for the Sioux's pony was limping and Crazy Horse himself slumped over the animal's red-painted mane.

"We got him!" Fetterman exulted. "Sergeant, signal the infantry to advance. Tell them to make all possible speed. I want Crazy Horse!"

Fetterman was in his glory. Next to Red Cloud, Crazy Horse was the name the newspapers most liked to cite as a warrior who could outfight the cavalry. If he, Fetterman, brought Crazy Horse in dead, Carrington's job wouldn't be safe for a month!

His plan, carefully worked out with the other officers on whiskey evenings in the BOQ, was to bring the infantry up to the top of the hill, rush them over, then swing the two units of cavalry to the sides and trap the Indians with a pincer movement at the bottom of the ridge.

It delighted Fetterman to see his plan working so well. Two of the retreating warriors near him had disabled horses and two others appeared to be wounded. As the somewhat winded infantry reached the bottom of the hill they saw the five able Sioux turn back to aid their stricken comrades. The sight raised the soldiers' spirits. They were within minutes of wiping out this band of savage marauders.

Of course, going over Lodge Pole Ridge, Fetterman briefly reflected, was disobeying Carrington's orders. But any reproach would be light if he could capture Crazy Horse.

"Charge!" He waved his freshly loaded revolver as he led his men down the other side of the ridge.

To Fetterman's surprise the lame Indian ponies instantly regained their strength, and their "wounded" riders, including Crazy Horse, sprang to able-bodied life and sprinted out of firing range. They were criss-crossing in front of Fetterman in some wild pattern when shouting made him turn his head to the left.

Over the edge of Turkey Ridge suddenly appeared hundreds of mounted Indian warriors wearing bright paint. Fetterman at once realized what had happened: Crazy Horse had lured him into a trap.

Furious at first, he felt a stab of despair as he thought of sending a messenger back to the fort for help and realized that no one could ride back over the ridge and live. Well, the battle wasn't over yet. They had firepower, and those two civilians with the Henrys might be enough to do the trick if they could shoot straight and didn't lose their nerve.

If they were all prepared to sell themselves dearly, they might not have to sell a damn thing. The only thing to do was make a stand, for rushing back up Lodge Pole Ridge would be suicide. The Sioux would chase them up the slope, picking them off with arrows and running them down with their ponies.

Fetterman shouted at the sergeant major to bring the horses around and prepare to make a stand in a little hollow surrounded by granite boulders. Below them, some four hundred yards down at the edge of the creek, the infantry was overrun by more Sioux than any soldier had seen in one place since the peace conference at Fort Laramie. Fetterman felt sick for a moment when he realized that every time a blue uniform went down it meant one of his men had died. Like a swarm of angry ants over a stricken bee, in five minutes the Sioux had the infantry pulled apart. The panicky recruits disobeyed young Grummond's orders to hold the line. But everywhere they ran they found a savagely painted devil with a raised lance or tomahawk. Armed with the single-shot muzzleloading Springfields, they got off only a few shots before they all fell.

Caught on the slope above the main body of infantry, pressed by hundreds of Indians coming at them from three sides, the cavalry wheeled in panic. Fred Brown and half a dozen veterans who knew that retreat meant certain death threw themselves off their horses. The seven-shot Spencers and the sixteen-shot Henrys surprised the Indians with firepower and drove back the first onslaught.

Two Sioux horsemen who weren't stopped by this volley rode straight over the cavalry, lances outthrust, yelling fearfully, only to drop dead ten yards beyond.

Given the circumstances, Fetterman had managed to choose a strong position, the giant granite rocks shielding the natural hollow. He felt a surge of hope as he realized that well-armed men just might hold off an army from there. Outside that circle, all was rearing horses, falling arrows and shrieks.

"Shoot the horses," Fetterman ordered. With Brown and the sergeant major's help, he plugged up the few holes between the rocks by pulling the frantic beasts over and shooting them dead where they would be most needed.

It was so cold that bleeding wounds froze in minutes. With stiff, slippery hands and numb fingers the men hung themselves over rocks glazed with snow, ice and oily blood and shot at the Indians. The weather worked for the troopers as well. The attacking Sioux slipped when they charged up the icy slope.

"They're getting ready to charge again," shouted Brown. Fetterman and the men at the upper side of the fifteen-yard ring rushed to the lower side.

"Springfields, fire the first volley!" commanded Fetterman. This was the order he had drilled the most.

Ten men from Brown's squad stood up to get a clear shot at the charging Indians, while ten riflemen from Fetterman's group dropped to one knee, ready to rise and fire after the first group.

As Fetterman shouted "Fire!" a wave of arrows hit the firing line. Two of the ten riflemen screamed, staggered back and fell. Four others clutched their chests and arms. "Springfields, fire the second volley!"

But having seen his men hit, Brown shouted, "Down, you fools!"

For the next quarter-hour Fetterman found it hard to follow what was happening. But when he had a moment's reprieve to assess his position, he found himself in command of a fifteen-yard circle of man-sized boulders and horses' carcasses containing thirteen dead men, eight so severely wounded they were useless, four loading and firing with one hand and four able-bodied soldiers. Four! How had it happened? He couldn't hold this position with four soldiers. Miraculously, Fetterman had not been hit. Brown was still alive despite three arrows in him, one entirely through his throat and two in his chest. Fetterman hesitated before giving his next command. Had it all come down to the end? "The next charge will be the last," he said quietly during a lull.

Six men turned to look at him as if to ask what that meant. Looking at their pale, frightened faces, Fetterman thought, these are just boys. He had to prepare them for the inevitable. He gave the order. "Kill the wounded."

The four young men, pinched white as whey by fear and cold, only stared at him.

"Shoot the wounded!" he shouted, but they stared on.

Fetterman aimed his service revolver at the wounded sergeant major, who was breathing with difficulty, an arrow through his chest. The sergeant nodded at the sight of the pistol's black open circle.

"Yes, sir," he wheezed. "Thank you, sir."

Fetterman fired. A hole appeared in the sergeant's forehead; his body shuddered and he sank into death.

"Hurry up! We don't have much time. I'll take care of the captain," Fetterman promised. Brown had watched all this with a slack, sick face.

But still the recruits just stood there frozen.

"Damn it, shoot the wounded or I'll shoot you!"

"You do it," gasped Brown. "Children."

"Then shoot the goddamn Indians!" Fetterman aimed his revolver at another wounded soldier and shot him. When he looked up he saw two of the recruits still watching him. He turned his pistol on them.

"Shoot the Indians, damnit, or I'll shoot you, so help me God!" Finally they turned and started firing at the painted bodies creeping from rock to rock up the icy hill.

Fetterman kept on shooting the wounded, killing seven. When he got to his friend Brown, he knelt beside him. "I waited till the last for you, old scout."

Brown nodded weakly and licked a piece of ice off his lip. "It's all over? No use?"

"No use. Almost all dead."

"Don't let them take you, Bill."

"No, of course not." He and Brown had seen too many burned bodies and hacked-up corpses to allow any such fate to befall them. Fetterman was fulfilling a promise they had made to each other many times back in the BOQ on cozy evenings with a glass in their hands. Of course they hadn't ever really thought it would come to it.

"Good-bye," Fetterman whispered. "I'll be with you soon."

"Good-bye." Brown closed his eyes. Fetterman shot him cleanly through the temple.

When he looked up, only one of the recruits was still standing. Even as he watched that one took an arrow in the eye. Now more wounded lay writhing on the ground, one moaning horribly.

Pulling Brown's pistol from his hand, he checked it and shot the last three wounded.

Except for the angry whine of the wind and the

sharp clack of arrowheads hitting the granite rock, Fetterman heard nothing. He seemed to have an unhurried hour, so surely and easily did his hands do their work as he checked his pistol. He considered waiting for some Indian to appear, shooting him and then himself. But he knew if he failed he would pay the price in hours, perhaps days of agony.

He put the muzzle of the gun against his temple and pulled the trigger. The barrel slid off his head and the pistol fired against a rock. His hand had refused to obey him. He suddenly felt weak and faint. A little surge of panic rose in him. He had to die, and quickly, or he would die a thousand times at the hands of these fiends.

With a little inward sob at the coward in him, he stuck the icy barrel into his mouth. His tongue froze fast to the cold metal. In a panic he wanted to pull it away before it froze so tightly it would rip the tender flesh, but then the pointlessness of that asserted itself. He gave a shrug of indifference and concentrated on getting his index finger to pull the trigger.

He seemed to be pushed backward down a long, narrowing well. With a shudder of profound relief, he found he was able to release every responsibility of a long and heavy life. His last thought was more of a feeling: Well, at least that's over.

Whooping triumphantly, Crazy Horse, High Backbone, Red Cloud, Two Moon and their warriors overran the troopers' position. They searched for survivors. Finding only two with any life, and that feeble, they quickly dispatched them with tomahawks.

Those who arrived first counted coup on the bodies, striking them with their bows and coup sticks and shouting, "Coup! Coup!" Down the hill, other warriors

212

savagely dismembered the bodies of the foot soldiers to make sure that in the next world these enemies would have no fingers, feet, eyes, tongues, hands, arms or genitals.

"Hey, look at the dog!" He-dog shouted, spotting a yellow mascot of the soldiers sniffing the corpses.

"Hit him!" shouted High Backbone. "Let him go back and tell them how strong are the Lakota."

"Kill him!" shouted Crazy Horse, nocking an arrow and drawing back his bow. He shot. "Don't let even a dog escape."

The arrow caught the dog in the hind quarters, knocking him to the ground. The animal spun around to see what had happened. Ten other arrows caught him in the side. With a soft, muffled yelp he dropped as dead as his masters. The Sioux laughed and set about finishing the preparation of their enemies for paradise.

Chapter 17

"So many shots," Ten Eyke mused. He and Carrington stood on the parapet of the fort gazing after Fetterman.

"That damn fool," Carrington remarked. "What's he got himself into?"

A chill wind blew across the two officers. Ten Eyke saw Henry Carrington touch his forehead and blink, as he always did when he wasn't quite sure what to do.

"Shall I ride out, Henry?" Ten Eyke volunteered, trying to make it easier for him. He didn't so much like Carrington as sympathize with him. Henry hadn't much to carry out his mission, either men and guns from the army or the right character from the Creator. A man commanding a fort under siege needed both.

"He's probably shooting turkeys," Carrington snorted. "Yes, go out, but be careful. Get everybody back safely."

Galloping out with sixty men, Ten Eyke led his troops across Big Piney Creek. Up the Bozeman Trail they rushed, only to hear the sound of the heavy firing die.

"Listen! What's that?" a young trooper asked Ten Eyke.

"What does it sound like?"

"Groans, moans and screams," the soldier quavered.

From the top of Lodge Pole Ridge Ten Eyke and his men saw nothing of Fetterman's command. The wind blew even stronger here, a north wind with the cut of a sharp knife. Across the roiling sky ran low, heavy clouds.

"Do you see anything?" Ten Eyke asked the sergeant.

"I see a bunch of Indians milling about down there." The sergeant was a regular who had spent the last ten years on the frontier and whose face looked like the fatty side of a leg of mutton. "Hear them shots? That's Captain Fetterman, probably cleaning up a pocket of them redskins somewheres, got them cornered somehow."

"Let's go around the turn," Ten Eyke said. "We'll be able to see the whole valley then."

The sight astonished them. They could see the valley of Peno Creek clear across to the opposite buttes and the back of Lodge Pole Ridge. Below them the slope was covered with Indians dashing about on horseback.

"What are they doing? Where's the captain?"

"I'm afraid Captain Fetterman is in the middle of that swarm of Indians you see there, Sergeant," said Ten Eyke.

"Dear God!"

"Yes. Dear God." Ten Eyke shuddered. He knew

at once that Fetterman and all the men who had ridden out with him must have been killed, and the cold wind seemed to shriek into his stomach with the realization.

Shouts drifted up from the bottom of the valley and they saw the Indians looking up at them.

"Come down!" some of them shouted in English. "Come down and fight us!"

"They've killed Captain Fetterman!" The sergeant was horrified.

They heard hoofbeats behind and turned to see a messenger from the fort.

"Bulletin from the colonel," he shouted. He handed a note to Ten Eyke.

> Proceed with caution. You must unite with Fetterman. Fire slowly so as not to use up ammunition and keep your men in hand. Send this man back with a report.
>
> Henry

On the back of the note Ten Eyke scribbled that the situation looked unclear but grave. Fetterman was in trouble, he wrote. He would see if he could relieve him.

They fired as they moved down the ravine toward a circle of rocks where the blood-spattered blue uniforms looked thickest. The Indians near the rocks moved away and a scout came rushing back up the slope to report, "The men down there are all dead."

Behind Ten Eyke and his troopers the wagons rumbled up with another forty soldiers. Seeing them, the Indians scattered.

The sight of so many dead around him appalled

Ten Eyke. There lay Smitty, the musician from Philadelphia, his harmonica slipping out of his pocket. Not ten feet away sprawled Tony Lynch, the meanest man in "A" Company. Around him Ten Eyke heard his men gasp and retch as they recognized one after another of their bunkmates.

The sergeant had been studying the ridges above for signs of hidden Sioux. "I don't like it, Captain." He shaded his eyes and squinted. "They've got blood up their noses. That's what they were doing riding up and down the hills as we came up, playing out their victory over and over again."

"I want the dead picked up, Sergeant," ordered Ten Eyke.

"Begging your pardon, sir, but we ain't got time. Soon as they figure out there ain't no howitzers in these wagons—that's what made them run off so fast —they're going to be right back here."

Ten Eyke thought about it. The sergeant likely was right. "All right, but pick up these men right here anyway. We'll come back for the rest later."

It was dusk when Ten Eyke and his men got back to Fort Phil Kearny, their wagons loaded with dead soldiers. Every man, woman and child came out to watch them unload. Their gasps and groans faded to grim silence as the forty-nine blood-soaked corpses were laid out in the stable.

Frances Grummond had to be pulled away from the body of her husband and carried to bed. In such a small community, every survivor had lost someone, husband, lover, friend or enemy, and every slain trooper was at least familiar to all eyes.

As bad as the corpses were, even worse was their

217

mutilation. Jim Bridger said it was nothing; wait for the bodies that had been left behind, he cautioned.

That night there was a good deal of speculation about the still-missing thirty-three men. Could they be alive? Had Captain Ten Eyke been at fault in not scouting farther for them? They also wondered at length what the Indians would do next. Surely they would attack the fort, and from what Captain Ten Eyke said, not hundreds but thousands of savages were running up and down the valleys, exulting at getting their knives and arrows into so many whites.

That night Carrington, Ten Eyke and Powell met in the colonel's office to make plans. An hour later they still didn't see how to prevent thousands of Indians from storming over the fort's walls. Ammunition was down to thirty rounds per man and twenty rounds for each of the three mountain howitzers.

"Damnit," said Carrington, "if Van Voast at Laramie can boast about a winter offensive, he can send over some troops!"

"But only General Cooke in Omaha can order that," objected Powell. "And the only way to reach him is through the telegraph at Laramie."

"Laramie?" Ten Eyke scoffed. "We can't get anyone to Laramie through those Indians. Besides, the weather's kicking up."

That afternoon snow had begun to fly more thickly, and judging by the way the clouds kept getting lower and blacker, they were in for a severe storm.

"Powell, go double the patrols around the walls," Carrington ordered. "And have the men build another barricade around the powder magazine and stock it with food and water."

"Tonight? In this weather?" Powell exclaimed.

"What for, sir?" asked Ten Eyke.

A shudder passed over Carrington. "So we can put the women, the children and the sick in the magazine, Captain, and when we are overrun, blow it up."

For several moments no one could say anything. Ten Eyke looked at Powell and saw the same sick fear he felt in his own stomach. Had it come to this? Was he so near the end of his life? Had he gone north to fight for the South, then come all the way out here to die in this frozen nowhere, bereft of real friends and mourners? Well, there was Cynthia, damn her!

"Oh, my God," Powell choked. "You don't expect them to take over the fort!"

"Isn't that what they've wanted all along?" Carrington demanded. "What's to stop them? We're down to a few rounds apiece and we can't put more than three hundred men on twenty-eight hundred feet of wall. If they charge, what can three hundred do to stop thousands?"

Neither Powell nor Ten Eyke answered. Both knew there was damn little to be done. Ten Eyke marveled at how well Henry was doing. It was uncharacteristic for him to outthink them in war.

"Let's prepare for the inevitable, gentlemen," Carrington concluded in his softest voice. "But quietly. I don't want any hysteria."

During the night the temperature fell just below zero from the mid-twenties and the wind increased to thirty miles an hour. Carrington struggled to sleep but kept popping awake, thinking he heard Indians breaking down the main gate of the fort.

Sioux Arrows

* * *

Cynthia Simmons, four months pregnant, sat up with her husband. He kept babbling that the savages wouldn't kill their baby; no man would commit such a barbarity. He didn't mind dying, he said over and over, and he would watch out for Cynthia and the baby from heaven. From time to time he broke down and cried, shamefully out of control, and Cynthia silently comforted him.

Captain Ten Eyke gave his orders for the night and retreated to his room to get some sleep. Was this it? he asked himself again, sitting before the fire with his last bottle of whiskey. Was this strange up and down life of his to end tomorrow? Would it come to an abrupt halt at a tomahawk's blow? What would come after, a mess of singing angels, or a fire in hell, or cold, black nothingness? What could he believe? If he trusted Clarence Simmons, he was in trouble. He smiled wryly. In the war, hadn't he seen many smile as they died? Could it be so bad?

Ten Eyke sighed. Death would be a relief. Cynthia's betrayal had torn him in two. He had wanted to confront her and demand that wed or unwed, in the army or out of it, they live together, for he knew that the child in her swelling belly was his, and he wanted it.

What had happened? Nelly had been cruelly snatched from him with all his children. He hadn't even been able to bury them. He sighed as the old grief rose anew.

He had thought when Cynthia first pushed him away that it wouldn't last, that she would call him back. Then, two weeks later, he had heard that the reverend's wife was pregnant. The news had hit him like a brick. He'd known at once it was his child, but his every effort to see Cynthia alone and speak to her had failed. On the public occasions when they met she refused even to look at him. But now, before the walls of the fort crashed in on them, before everyone was slaughtered, he must speak to her. She couldn't do this to him, to their child. She owed him something and he was going to make damn sure she knew what before he left this world for the next.

Having arrived at this decision, Ten Eyke poured himself a double shot, drank it in one gulp and dived into bed still fully clothed against the cold.

Several doors down from Ten Eyke's room, Jim Bridger also had a bottle of whiskey. He whistled as he filled the brass shells for his two revolvers, cleaning them and wiping all the oil off. He didn't want them to freeze in tomorrow's battle. He had lived on the frontier for sixty years, had faced death a dozen times, but the end of his life had never looked more nearly certain than it did now.

That damn fool Carrington hadn't listened when he told him where to put the fort. Then he had thrown all his efforts into building it instead of escorting the wagon trains and making it unprofitable for Red Cloud to attack them, which would have been the fastest way to discourage the Sioux. They would have grown tired of Red Cloud and gone after buffalo. The war would have petered out.

But no, to Carrington's mind it wasn't a war, just a hundred outlaw braves. Bridger knew these weren't outlaws, not the thousands Ten Eyke had seen out there today. No, sir, that was the whole Sioux nation, and if the whole Sioux nation wanted this little piddly-ass fort, these peashooters he was cleaning weren't going to do shit to stop them.

But it made him feel better to get ready. It gave him something to do while he got drunk enough to get some sleep on the last night of his life.

The next morning after breakfast Colonel Carrington summoned Ten Eyke, Bridger and Powell to his office.

Ten Eyke first checked the officer of the day to see what had happened during the night. He was puzzled to learn that no one had sighted an Indian all night.

"You won't, neither," Bridger commented when he heard. "Sioux don't do hardly nothing at night. Figure some night ghost will take them off. Night's the time for sitting around the tepee letting the fire keep away the evil spirits."

"I thought maybe it meant they've pulled out," Ten Eyke hopefully suggested.

"Maybe; maybe not. What we got to do today is go get the rest of our dead."

"Go get our dead!" exclaimed Carrington. "Let Fetterman bury his own dead."

"Yes sir," Bridger nodded. "As a general rule that suits me fine, but if we don't go, the Sioux are going to know how weak we are."

Ten Eyke saw it. "That's what they're waiting for!"

"Yes sir, could be." The old woodsman's face looked hard and red this morning, as if the cold had done a bad job of polishing its broken surface.

Carrington seemed to be struggling with an idea. "If we don't get our dead as we always have,"

Ten Eyke explained, "they'll know we're short of men and powder."

Carrington looked pained. He had understood perfectly. "Yes, but if we do go out, no matter how many men we take we can't pick up our dead and face all those savages you saw yesterday."

"That's it exactly. We lose either way."

Powell's eyes had been getting bigger and rounder. "My God, what do we do?" he quavered.

"I'll go." Carrington squared his shoulders. "You and I, Tenodor."

"You, sir?" Ten Eyke tried not to sound incredulous.

"I feel responsible."

"It's not your fault," Bridger put in. "That damn fool Fetterman brought this down on us. You told him not to go over the ridge." He wanted Ten Eyke in charge of the party.

"I should have had Captain Ten Eyke lead the rescue."

Ten Eyke kept quiet. He was glad Fetterman had replaced him. He didn't know precisely what had happened to the dead captain, but he wasn't at all sure he could have escaped the same fate.

"Captain Powell, you'll be in charge here." Carrington gave him a long, steady look. "Put the women and children into the powder magazine. Run a fuse out and make sure it's not left unattended."

"Good God, sir!"

"And I want you to swear by God you'll blow it up if the savages come over those walls."

The two junior officers sat in stunned silence, for the colonel's wife and two boys would be in the magazine. Still, they recognized the terrible necessity of the order. A fast death was far preferable to falling alive to the Sioux.

"Captain Ten Eyke, pick seventy men and get six wagons ready," Carrington commanded. "We're going to bring back our dead."

Two hours later Carrington and Ten Eyke arrived at the spot by the creek where Fetterman's infantry had died.

To the horrified Ten Eyke this more than anything else showed the difference between red man and white. In just three bodies he counted one hundred sixty-eight arrows. Teeth were chopped out of every skull. The joints of most fingers had been hacked off and brains spilled on nearby rocks.

"Why did they put so many arrows into these men's buttocks?" Ten Eyke asked Jim Bridger.

The scout gave him a grim smile. "Now where they're going they won't have the pleasure of taking a good dump."

The sight of so many mutilated bodies made Ten Eyke sick. He had been at Gettysburg and much of the later fighting in Virginia. Terrible as that carnage had been, it was nothing like this. Only the fear of unseen Indians surrounding them kept the soldiers grimly at work loading the wagons.

"So where are they?" Carrington asked Bridger as at last they started back to the fort. "How come they haven't attacked us?"

Bridger shrugged. "They're in camp bragging about their victory," he guessed. "When the ones who didn't get any coups get mad enough, they'll all be back."

He looked up at the black, threatening clouds.

"And when they do come, they're going to walk in on us."

"Walk in? What do you mean?"

"I've seen clouds that looked this full just once before." The scout squinted up. "Made drifts twenty feet high."

Carrington stared at him. "My God, of course! The stockade walls will catch the snow."

"Yes sir. Be a natural place for snowdrifts."

"Is that what they're waiting for?"

"I don't know, but I don't see how a few hundred soldiers are going to stop several thousand savages from running up the drifts on, say, two sides of the fort." Neither could Carrington.

Back at the fort, the colonel had a long shallow grave hacked out of the frozen earth next to the parade ground. Into this the contents of the wagons were hastily unloaded. This time only a few came out to watch.

That night Carrington had Ten Eyke redouble the patrols to combat the menace of the snow, for Bridger had correctly forecast the extent of the storm. The temperature dropped steadily to forty below and the north wind rose. So fierce was the gale that the guards could remain outside no more than twenty minutes at a time, and Ten Eyke doubted whether they could see enough in the storm to act effectively as sentries. Every fourth tour the men took turns shoveling the drifts outside the stockade walls, but through the night the snow rose steadily and they appeared to be losing the struggle.

Chapter 18

The morning after the mass burial, Ten Eyke came to the front door of Reverend Simmons' quarters. He hesitated before he knocked. He knew what he wanted to say, but he was torn between desire not to hurt Cynthia and anger at her. Twice he turned away and twice he turned back. An enlisted man at the corner seemed to stare at him curiously and finally made him knock.

Cynthia answered the door. From her frightened look Ten Eyke knew she realized why he had come.

"What do you want?"

"To talk."

"He's here."

"Come away then," Ten Eyke demanded.

She looked so scared he might have been Crazy Horse or Red Cloud come to drag her from the fort. "No, I can't. I told you, it's over."

"Either you come or I march right in and talk to the reverend."

"No!"

"Oh, yes. I'll tell him the whole thing."

"You'll break him!"

"What do you think you've done to me?"

From the sitting room Simmons called, "What is it, dear?"

"Tell him you have to help at the hospital," Ten Eyke whispered. When she hesitated, he gripped her arm. "Tell him!"

"They want me to help out at the hospital," she called back.

Simmons appeared at the sitting-room door. "My dear, you should stay here and rest. I'll go."

Ten Eyke longed to shake the little man. How he hated him! If only he would drop dead!

"Oh, Clarence!" Cynthia pouted prettily. "He treats me like an invalid," she told Ten Eyke.

"But we don't want you to overexert yourself in your condition." Her husband smiled smugly. Ten Eyke clenched his fist.

"Clarence, I'm going to the hospital," Cynthia insisted. "Tomorrow we may all be butchered. Any relief I can give a soldier today I consider it my Christian duty to provide. If you'll be kind enough to escort me there, Captain Ten Eyke, I'll just get my coat."

They went to their old haunt the schoolroom. Outside a winter wind now howled. Inside their breath steamed.

"I can't be a party to this any longer," Ten Eyke rasped. "That's my baby, isn't it." He watched her closely. "Isn't it!"

Under his stare something in her seemed to crumble. Finally she admitted it. "Yes, it's yours."

"What are you going to do about it?"

"What can I do? I'm married!"

"You lied to me. Is that what you really are? A liar?"

He knew her. He knew she wouldn't cry, but he saw the lines of pain in her face.

"Tenodor, I didn't know what to do. Believe me! I'm worn out with thinking and praying about it. Please believe me."

Despite his anger he was moved—but not enough. "I am not going to let you steal my child."

"What does that mean?"

"Come away with me."

"Come away! You don't want me. I lied to you. What kind of woman would lie to a man about such a thing? I can hardly stand myself."

"I do want you—and I don't," he admitted. "I don't know what I want. You lied to me and you've avoided me. Why? *Why?*"

She turned away from him. "It was wrong for me to come here. We've nothing to say to each other. I have to go."

"No! Talk to me!"

"I've nothing to say."

She turned and walked toward the door. Behind her he shouted, "Damnit, you walk out of here without talking to me and I go straight to Clarence."

"Tenodor! You wouldn't!"

He hated this, but the weeks of frustrated rage were too much for him. "Why didn't you tell me why you didn't want to go on seeing me—the real reason?"

She seemed to shrink from him. "All right, I will tell you. But you have to promise me just to listen."

He didn't want to give her anything, but he nodded.

228

She told him again about her supposed inability to have a child, but this time all of it, how Clarence made her feel she'd failed him, how desperate she'd been to know the truth: Was it she or Clarence who couldn't conceive?

"It seemed just a lark at first, you and I. My marriage was a millstone and—well, I was bored out here." She saw the stricken look on his face. "Tenodor, I didn't want to hurt you. You don't know what a shock it was when I realized I was pregnant. I hadn't really considered that it could happen to me, nor how important it would suddenly be to see that the child had a good home to grow up in. I knew I couldn't tell Clarence the truth for the baby's sake. I hoped by breaking off with you the way I did I wouldn't hurt you too much."

"You should have told me. I felt betrayed when I heard—heard! I heard a rumor about my own baby, Cynthia!"

Cynthia sighed. She looked pale and grey. He wanted to take her in his arms and comfort her, but she wasn't his. She belonged to that fat white worm. Damn him! Damn her! And inside her was his child.

But Cynthia had more to say. "I saw you more than I planned," she confessed. "I cared more for you than I planned. I grew to dislike Clarence more and more. Tenodor, I love you. I'm miserable now, but I'm a pregnant woman with a large, respectable family back East. What would my father say if I left my husband to have another man's child? And Clarence! This child means so much to him; what happens to him if I tell him the truth? If I leave him?"

"Do you want to live with me?"

"What are you asking?"

He seized her by the shoulders. "Let's make right what's ours and damn what others think."

"No! We can't make it right. It's impossible." She shook her head.

"Not having you and my baby is impossible."

"Oh, Tenodor, it's all I've thought about. If you only knew how much I've suffered! But Clarence—"

"Clarence will just have to manage." Ten Eyke pulled her toward him. "What counts is that we want to be together. That's true, isn't it?"

"Yes!" she breathed. "Yes, oh yes! But we have to think carefully about what to do and how to go about it. Let's talk again in a week."

"We may all be dead by then."

She shuddered. "Then none of this will matter. But if we survive, then we must make plans. We must do the right thing as far as possible. I need time."

"All right, but only a week."

"A week," she echoed, "to make things right. Right for you, for me and for the baby."

Ten Eyke, Bridger and Powell met with Carrington in his office that night. "We don't have enough men and we're low on ammunition. If only we could get a message to General Cooke in Omaha, maybe we could get some reinforcements from Laramie," the colonel said.

Outside, the storm raged unabated. Not only was ammunition low, but so was food. The last of the carefully conserved pressed vegetables were being used up now. Christmas, if it occurred at all at Fort Kearny, promised to be about as bright as a funeral.

"I've asked a couple of the civilian scouts." Bridger puffed on his pipe. "Portugee Phillips says he'll make the ride."

"In this weather? Through the redskins?" Ten Eyke protested. "No one can make it."

Bridger smiled grimly. "Better'n staying here to die with the rest of us."

"If he wants to go, let him go," voted Powell.

"Which one is he?" asked Carrington. "The tall dark-bearded fellow?"

"That's him. Calls himself John Phillips, but he was born in the Azores. Sailed to California for the gold rush. He's worked for us driving mules and scouting."

"Why's he going?" asked Ten Eyke.

"Wants a hundred dollars in gold."

"A hundred!" exclaimed Carrington. "I don't have it."

"Tell him yes, but only if he gets through." Ten Eyke looked at Carrington.

"I don't think this is the time to worry about spending, sir. If we have to we'll take up a collection."

"Where is he?" Carrington asked Bridger.

"Right outside, sir," the old man grinned.

Carrington burst out laughing. "All right, I know when I've been outflanked. Bring him in."

Portugee Phillips, who except for his curly black hair seemed made of the same dark leather he was wearing, had one other request.

"I want your horse, Coronel." He meant White Hawk, Carrington's pride and joy.

"He'll be ruined," Carrington protested. "It's over two hundred miles through snow, wind, sleet and Indians." Then his eyes glazed over. "All right. What's the difference?"

Portugee smiled. "Thank you, sor."

"When will you leave?"

"Near dark. Pass the Indian at night."

"I'll have the telegrams ready."

"Yes, sor."

With the telegram to Cooke Carrington enclosed another to General Ulysses S. Grant in Washington. It read in part:

> I WANT ALL THE OFFICERS I'M SUPPOSED TO HAVE. I WANT MEN.

By nightfall Phillips was ready. He wore a massive coat that he had sewn himself, heavy gauntlets and a huge shaggy helmet, all of buffalo skin. He put a dozen hard biscuits in one pocket and stuffed his saddlebags with oats for the stallion.

Standing at the window watching Phillips saddle up, Powell remarked to Ten Eyke, "That's one poor bastard we'll never see again. Even if he only gets a mile away, I don't see how he could find his way back in this weather."

Ten Eyke silently agreed.

At the gate, Carrington patted his white stallion on the rump and took out his service revolver. "Here. You may need this."

"I have a gun, sor."

"Take it, man. You never know," Carrington said gruffly. "And may God be with you."

He stood watching until Phillips disappeared into the storm and then came back into the warmth. "He took the softer ground at the side of the trail. Maybe he knows enough to get through at that." He sighed heavily.

* * *

Phillips rode south in this fashion, off the road, keeping away from the dangerous areas and crossings where the Indians might lie in wait. Remembering the Bozeman Trail with some exactness, thanks to his mule-driving days of the past fall and summer, he often moved as much as ten miles off the road. Though he encountered drifts up to four feet high, he urged the colonel's horse forward.

The first night he kept moving, guided by the wind and hoping that it wouldn't shift. If it did, he and the horse would wander off to die.

He felt good. His coat, helmet and gloves did a fine job of protecting him. He didn't believe he would die out here, but if he did, it was better than waiting for the savages to come over the walls. The urgency to keep his heading straight kept his head clear. He concentrated on remembering every turn in the road.

The next day he rested and got some sleep in a natural cave, daring to lay a fire with the tinder he had packed and light it with his flint and steel. He kept the fire small, feeding it dried dung he found inside the cave.

When night fell he moved on regretfully. He might not find another place half as good next morning. He fed the colonel's horse before he set out, chewing on a biscuit.

That night it was so cold it stopped being just cold and became painful. It hurt to move, hurt even to breathe, the air cut his mouth and nostrils so. Every step of his horse jarred right through him.

In the middle of that night he pounded on the gates of Fort Reno, where he was greeted with astonishment, warmed and fed before being brought before the new commander, Brevet Lieutenant General George Connor.

Phillips saw a bear of a man with a mane of long greasy hair. His left arm was missing.

"What the hell are you doing wandering around in this weather, man?" One Arm Connor roared at Phillips.

"I come from Phil Kearny. Much trouble, sor. Here. You read what the coronel say." He fumbled inside his several shirts, to find Carrington's telegrams.

"Never mind that. What's happened? Talk to me."

So Phillips told him about Fetterman; about how many troops had been lost and about the sorry state of the fort's defenses.

"What does Henry Carrington want?" Connor asked. "I can't send him troops or ammunition, not without orders from Cooke."

"You send somebody with me to Laramie?" asked Phillips.

"Through this storm? No sir." Connor grinned angrily. "And don't tell me you're going!"

Afraid the man might stop him, Phillips protested, "Sor, I must send the telegram to Omaha for Colonel Carrington."

"Let me see it."

From under his bundle of clothing, Phillips finally managed to dig out the dispatches, sealed in oilskin, and gave the packet to Connor. As the general opened it, it suddenly struck Phillips that it might not be quite right for him to read the dispatches, but Connor didn't seem like someone to argue with.

"That damn Carrington!" Connor snarled. "He

doesn't even say here what happened to Fetterman and his men. So you're going to ride on to Laramie?"

"Yes, sor."

"You're not going to make it."

Phillips' teeth shone. "I get here, sor."

"To Reno? That's only fifty miles. Laramie's another hundred and eighty-five."

"Yes, sor."

"If the storm don't get you, the Indians will. If they don't the wolves will."

"I'm going, sor. Coronel Carrington and the ladies and all the men and children depend on me."

"You're a bigger fool than I am; I'm only going to write a couple of letters. One is for Major Van Voast and another for the post telegraph office. You aren't to let anybody read them. They'll be sealed. If I find out you did I'll horsewhip you with this one good arm I got left. You savvy me, muleskinner?"

"You know me, sor? That I drove the mules through here?"

"I know you, all right. I know a muleskinner when I see one," replied Connor. "Who but an idiot who never looks at anything but mules' asses would be stubborn enough to tackle this weather!"

That night, after sleep, a big hot meal and oats for White Hawk, Phillips rode south. Now he was far enough away from the forts to risk the road, but still he often floundered in drifts four and five feet deep.

North of the Platte, when he figured he was out of danger from the Indians, he took to riding by day as well as by night. Near noon, two days out of Reno, he spotted five braves coming down the road. They saw him about the same time. One of them whooped and reached for his bow. All five picked up speed as they headed toward him.

He was tempted to ride through them, pistol blazing like a cavalryman's, but he couldn't get either gun out from under his coat fast enough. Besides, on the slippery snow the startled horse was liable to somersault if he fired, and the braves would be on top of him in a flash.

He jerked the horse to the right and rushed up the hill. Dismounting, he pulled White Hawk as he dodged along the ridge top, using the two revolvers and his Springfield to keep the five braves at a distance.

At dusk, exhausted, he crept back along the ridge the way he had come, hoping the braves would assume he was still going in the direction he'd been heading. After he'd covered a mile or so, which took him a couple of hours, he remounted and got back to the road. The ruse must have worked; he didn't see the Indians again as he drove himself and his mount into the teeth of the blizzard.

The bachelor officers' quarters at Fort Laramie were ablaze with light. It was Christmas night and New Bedlam didn't look much like its name. A holiday ball was in progress. The men wore their regimental best and the ladies their finest gowns. The band was sweating under the strain of playing for two hours now without a break, for the crowd cried "No, no!" whenever it looked as if the music would stop.

Portugee Phillips rode onto the parade ground toward the only light he could see. Beneath him White Hawk barely responded to his prodding. He moved inch by inch across the parade ground, an ice-covered apparition on a ghost horse. As in a dream the shapes of the buildings around him seemed to fall into each other in jumbles. He swayed and could barely hang on to the reins. The sight of the lights, the thoughts of being warm again and of something hot for his stomach made him want to slide off the colonel's horse and lie in the snow, but he forced himself to go on. He could lie here, a hundred yards away, and be a corpse by morning.

"Halt! Who goes there?" A figure materialized out of the swirling snow. The guard stared up at Portugee, teetering on the stallion's back. "Gawd! What is it?"

Phillips slid unconscious to the ground. The guard called for help and they carried the traveler into New Bedlam's hallway. The blast of warm air revived Phillips, who asked to see the biggest man there.

"Biggest man?" asked a soldier.

"That'd be General Palmer. He's visiting from Omaha," offered another. "But he ain't for the likes of you to jaw with."

"That's him. That's who I want to see," Phillips insisted.

While the soldiers stood looking doubtfully at the bearlike figure, Phillips lunged to his feet and moved under his own steam through the door into the ballroom. There the officers were about to choose new partners. The sight of the bearded, snow-covered specter staggering into the room set several ladies squealing.

"General Palmer!" cried Phillips, blinking snow-blinded eyes. "Show me General Palmer."

Up marched a ruddy-faced man with a chest full

of medals and ribbons. He looked like a puppeteer's idea of a general.

"Sir! What can I do for you?"

"Dead, sir!" gasped Phillips, his eyes wild and his frozen face cracked in a demented smile. "Fetterman's troopers, sir, all dead."

"Haskins! Kirby-Smith!" shouted the general. A captain and a colonel stepped forward smartly.

"Here, sor," said Phillips, handing over Carrington and Connor's dispatches to the general.

It wasn't long before news of the disaster on the Bozeman Trail spread through the holiday crowd. The band never struck up another tune.

The telegraph lines between Fort Laramie and Omaha were busy all the next day as Van Voast and Palmer at Laramie and Cooke back at headquarters considered what to do.

That Carrington needed reinforcements went without saying. It also went without saying that it was time to get rid of Henry Carrington, or at least pack him off to a post where he couldn't do any more damage.

They also needed the right way to present news of this defeat to the newspapers, for the generals wanted to discredit the policies of the peace party. A defeat like this, if not properly exploited, might discredit the army's methods of dealing with him.

The next day news of the disaster was wired to Washington with recommendations from officers on the scene for certain changes in troops and command. General Sherman made a few minor adjustments in those orders and wired back approval.

The newspapers had the Fetterman story the next

day. The western press used it to show that the Indians had been given far too much leeway. The *Omaha Herald* called it "the worse massacre of soldiers to date" and warned that "a nation that would allow savage rebels within its borders to treat it like this in modern times betokens a lack of self-respect on the part of its leaders that fills us with foreboding . . . for the future of this country."

The eastern papers declared that Fetterman and Carrington had provoked the attack. The *Boston Globe* added, "Some will see this as an excuse to exercise still more savagery on the innocent people whom we discovered on arriving on these shores. . . ."

General Palmer remained at Laramie to direct efforts. When the weather cleared he would send one hundred troopers to Fort Reno, where they would pick up Connor and ride on to Fort Kearny to give Henry Carrington his new orders.

One thing Sherman, Palmer and Cooke were all sure of. No Indian would fool with Carrington's designated replacement, old One Arm Connor, who'd lost his arm charging Rebel artillery. Yes, sir, you'd have a hard time finding a better fighting man than old One Arm.

Chapter 19

Sated with victory and stopped by the blizzard, the forces under Red Cloud scattered.

High Backbone took his people back south, where they hoped to escape the worst ravages of winter. Two Moon took his to the west, to a high canyon that was sheltered from the storms. Red Cloud prepared to lead his people fifty miles toward the Big Horn River.

The tribes were well satisfied with their victory. In his mind Red Cloud played over and over again the picture of the troopers coming down the hill after Crazy Horse and his limping pony. When surrounded, the soldiers had fired and run at them with their long knives, as if that would save them. But you couldn't stop the Lakota when the power of wakan was in them.

But now the problems of winter were no less urgent than the problems of war. The whites got their food from the wagons that came from the big waters they talked about, but since the Bad Faces hadn't touched the pen, Red Cloud's people couldn't take the meat and parched corn that Big Mouth, Big Ribs and the other Laramie loafers drew from the whites.

With the guns and ammunition they had taken from the dead soldiers at Lodge Pole Ridge, the Bad Face braves were able to bring down two dozen deer at distances they could never have reached with bow and arrow. The women folded the buffalo-hide tepees and loaded the travois and the tribe set out on its cold march to Big Horn Canyon.

Following the routes made by their scouts, Red Cloud's people moved slowly through stinging swirling snow, all they saw for the first days of the march. With them rode John Richards Jr. and his Sioux mother, who was the niece of a cousin of Red Cloud. The young man gave the tribe the feeling that he was fleeing from some demon, but all they knew for sure was that he had just come from Fort Laramie.

The third night out, with the storm raging and no possibility of pursuit, they made camp for what they hoped would be several days, provided they found food. At the chief's request John Richards came to eat with Red Cloud.

Young Richards was a sullen youth who hated anyone in authority, be he red or white, chief or father. As usual, he made Red Cloud uneasy, but the chief resolved to put the feeling aside. He needed answers; what should be done once the warm weather returned. This half-breed might be able to teach him something, for he had spent as much time at Fort Laramie among his father's people as he had with the Oglala Sioux who were his mother's. Hiding his revulsion wasn't easy, for Richards' face told the story of the worm that gnawed within him, a many-toothed worm of hatred for anything weaker than himself, a worm that fawned on those more powerful.

"What's happening in Laramie?" Red Cloud asked. They spoke in Sioux, for Red Cloud knew only a few words of English.

Richards laughed. "What do you think? They're figuring how to get back at you."

Red Cloud swallowed his anger. "They see now that the Lakota aren't men to trifle with." He was thinking that young Richards was like a camp dog who hadn't learned not to piss on a brave's leg.

The pup laughed again. "Naw, not them soldiers. You ain't done nothing but stir them up some. Just shooing flies off buffalo dung."

The barking laughter deepened Red Cloud's dislike, but he persisted.

"Now they'll leave the road," he suggested. "We fought them through the summer and fall and now winter. We took their cattle, horses, mules; we killed their men."

"You don't know nothing about soldiers, do you, Chief? Where you been?"

"Not sitting on my rump around Laramie." Red Cloud longed to kick him.

"Yeah, I know. You're better'n Big Mouth and Big Ribs. But you don't see them running away from the soldiers, do you?"

"Running? I'm not running."

"Naw, because of this weather. But just as soon as it breaks, just as soon as spring rolls around, you're going to be chased all to hell and gone by more troopers than you've ever seen."

"Then we'll just bring the tribes together again.

The white chiefs can't be that stupid. I've shown them that they cannot use the road unless I allow it."

"Red Cloud, you don't understand the least thing about white people. They play *for keeps*." Richards used the English phrase.

"What does that mean?"

Richards shook his head in that insolent way that so infuriated Red Cloud. If he hadn't been the son of the trader and if the Bad Faces hadn't traded so much over the years with his father, this pup wouldn't last through a meal in Red Cloud's camp.

"Like when you play bones for money and you don't give back what you win. That's how they play war, not the Indian way."

"What do you mean, not the Indian way?"

"When you fight the Crow, do you kill their women and children? Do you kill the grandparents? The babies?"

Red Cloud was outraged. "No, it's a good day's fighting if three, four Crow braves are killed. Killing children isn't the Lakota way."

"That's what I'm talking about."

"But we killed a hundred soldiers not a week ago. That should teach the white chief our strength."

"Didn't my father ever tell you how many were killed in their war?"

Red Cloud waved his hand. "He told us many things we could not believe."

"You were stupid not to believe him."

Red Cloud struggled with his temper, wondering how this insolent cub had managed to live so long.

Richards sat up on the buffalo robe. His eyes gleamed as if he had some particularly good news

243

to impart. "You know the leaves on a tree? Think of how many leaves on a tree and how many there would be if every leaf had a tree full of leaves."

Red Cloud tried but his head began to spin and he shook it to clear it.

"That's how many the bluecoats killed when they fought the people in the South. And about as many of their own people were killed."

The same kind of wild story Trader Richards had told. Red Cloud regretted thinking he could get any answers out of this lying youth.

"Why are you telling me this?"

Young Richards leaned towards him, eyes dancing. "Because if they'd kill so many of their own people, what will they do to the Sioux? You've killed more soldiers at one time than any Indians ever killed before. Do you think they can leave that alone? What did they do to Black Kettle and the Cheyenne?" He paused. "Wiped them out, and they're going to do the same to you."

Pictures of evil jumped around on the boy's face, pictures of night demons, flapping bats and the impish love of things going wrong.

"Ah, but the Sioux aren't Cheyenne."

"You'll see, Chief." Richards was full of delight; Red Cloud couldn't understand why. "Come the spring, when the troops can ride, you'll see. They've finished their own war and the North and South of the whites have united. They're going to fall on you like a dog on a mouse."

"I'll be ready, but I still can't believe they'd be so stupid."

They dropped the subject as Pretty Owl and the other women came back from visiting at the other end of the village. Red Cloud wondered if Richards was lying. Was he trying to stir up hatred because he was that kind of boy? The chief sighed. White people were as bad as the Crow, the Pawnee and the Arapaho. They did not use words like the Sioux, placing them as straight as possible along the edges of the world, but twisted them to make other men give them things Wakan-Takan had not meant them to have. What a better place the world would have been if Wakan-Takan had simply filled it with Sioux!

What Crazy Horse had felt for Black Buffalo Woman he could feel for no other woman. Though he rode into battle with Red Cloud, he had lost none of his rage nor any of the desire to have her for his wife.

When occasionally a hunting party took him through Black Twin's village, he saw her. Their eyes would meet and lock and he knew she felt as he did. Though no word passed between them, he knew she cared for him and hated her husband. He wanted to go to her, touch her cheek, press her to him. He wanted to pull her down on his bed and plant his seed in her. That fall when he rode through Black Twin's village and saw Buffalo Woman's belly swollen with No Water's child, he almost fainted. Only a supreme effort kept him from falling off his pony.

After that the war chiefs noticed that Crazy Horse took more chances in battle than ever. He had always been bold, but now he charged into the horse soldiers with a recklessness that made everyone believe Wakan-Takan had placed him under special protection, for only once had he been wounded in three months of almost daily battle.

When he wasn't preparing for a raid, Crazy Horse

spent his time with the young boys of the tribe, who revered him. Most of the warriors would occasionally help a boy who wanted to learn more about the Lakota way. But Crazy Horse spent all his free time with his apprentice Dog Leg and his friends.

He showed them how to make a buffalo shield by hardening the leather so it would deflect bullets and arrows. He taught them how to ride on the side of the horse away from the enemy and how to hit a moving target with their arrows. He helped them discover their power animals. Dog Leg's was the badger, which disappointed him until Crazy Horse pointed out its marvelous qualities of persistence and endurance. Once he took all of the youths who hung around him out on a raid against the hay gatherers working out of Fort C.F. Smith.

As the tribe set out on its fifty-mile march to the Big Horn, Old Hump and Old Crazy Horse cornered Young Crazy Horse in his father's tepee one night.

Something in their look alerted him and he rose to leave as his father and Old Hump positioned themselves by the fire.

"Sit down," commanded Old Crazy Horse. His voice had a hard edge.

Crazy Horse hesitated, definitely wary now.

"Sit down and talk to us," Old Hump said mildly.

Crazy Horse looked at the wrinkled face, every crease of which he knew and loved. As a boy he had looked to that face for approval hundreds of times. Slowly he sank back down on the buffalo robe.

The two old men seemed to be in no hurry. Old Crazy Horse fed the fire some buffalo chips and Hump pulled his robe close with elaborate care. For some minutes the three sat in silence. Crazy Horse stilled his impatience. He knew these two. They would wait until the air around them settled before they acted. Old Hump, with some amusement, had struggled and failed to teach Crazy Horse to do the same.

"That time when you were a boy and your father and I found you in the hills," the medicine man began, "I saw around you as much wakan as I'd ever seen around a warrior, and I knew you were destined to bring many great victories to the Oglala. That has come true."

Old Hump sounded slow and rasping. He gazed into the fire as he spoke, as if he could read the words there. If anyone else, including his father, had spoken so slowly, Crazy Horse would have lost patience. But now the old man's pace soothed him and he began to relax.

"You have brought great honor to your father, as he knew you would when he gave you his name," Old Hump went on. "You have made the Kit Foxes the greatest warrior society anyone has ever heard of. With some envy I and the other shamans watch your wakan practices and listen to your chants to learn from you. You have grown bolder and bolder and have led your men over and over again into the bear jaws of death."

Crazy Horse saw it coming. He didn't know what it was, but he knew he wouldn't like it. He tried to deflect it by saying, "Successfully, too. When I lead a raid we kill the enemy and those who ride with me can't be killed."

"Yes, all this is true," agreed Hump, but now he

gave Crazy Horse a smile full of sadness. "Over the last few weeks I have watched you closely, and I see that your wakan has worn thin."

"Thin!" exclaimed Crazy Horse, determined to challenge this. "Which warrior drew the horse soldiers over Lodge Pole Ridge? Which one allowed them to get within an arrow's flight and still the bullets melted before they hit him? Who rode up the slope into the face of their fire without getting more than a scratch on the left forearm? Which warrior counted fifteen first coups in that battle? And who counted more coups on that slope than I?"

"No one," conceded Old Hump, "but a tree can't bend too far in one direction without breaking."

These words meant nothing. They only clattered around inside him. Old men lost their courage, he thought. Young men like himself often had sounder judgment without all this talking and sitting around waiting for the right thing to land on a man's shoulder.

As yet, Old Crazy Horse hadn't spoken. Now he said, "A man needs to temper his nature with a woman."

Curly wanted to laugh with relief, but he was too polite. So that was what these two old buffalo wanted. He smiled at his father and said nothing.

The old man took the smile for encouragement and went on. "Every animal and plant accepts the nature of its other sex. Even a berdache needs its opposite nature."

Old Hump spoke again. "Only Crazy Horse has tried to break the way of the world, living with his brothers entirely, never coming near a woman."

Crazy Horse was exasperated with the pair. "Both of you, I found a woman, remember? For weeks I sat in front of her lodge, blew silly tunes on my flute and had my blanket ready for her to sit under. But I was tricked and she was given to another, remember?"

"Who she was given to was for her uncle to decide," Old Crazy Horse maintained.

"And it's for me to decide not to take any other," answered Crazy Horse. "She wanted me. She still wants me, to judge by the way she looks at me."

The two thin old men glanced sharply at each other. When they looked back at Crazy Horse their expressions had hardened.

"Only a thief takes what belongs to another," Old Hump said sternly, "not a Sioux warrior."

"I've found you a woman," his father announced. "Don't encourage a married woman to lust after you. Only disaster follows."

"I don't want a woman."

"Of course you do," his father answered. "You're older now, a leader and a man of means. It doesn't look right for you to live in your father's lodge. A woman would make you a tepee, cook for you and make gifts for you to give others. A warrior as brave as you will be a chief one day, a far greater leader of our people than I have been. Such a chief should have a wife, perhaps several. This would bring even more honor on our family."

Crazy Horse nodded slowly to show that he had heard and understood their words. Yet for all the politeness he tried to maintain, he still answered with anger in his voice. "I don't want several wives and all that bickering. I want one woman, the one I always wanted, and she wants me." His voice rose. "She's carrying a child now, Father. My insides burn when I think that it's not mine. When I think of it I don't care for anything— not my life, not my honor, not the Kit Foxes, not coups, nothing." His voice sank to a whisper. "What I wanted most has been taken from me. Red Cloud has traded away our lives for nothing. My spirit has withered. It's as dry as an ear of corn in winter."

Old Crazy Horse shook his head sadly. "My son, you are a great warrior. You know more about fighting at your age than I've learned in all my long years. But about women you know nothing. The truth is—and I know this is hard for a young brave to understand— after years of marriage a man finds that all women are more or less alike, in the same way that all horses are alike. If you want to ride somewhere, it's much better to have a horse, even though it's not the one you want. Even a lame horse is better than none at all."

"You found me a lame wife?" Crazy Horse smiled, hoping to ease some of the tension.

His father smiled back. "No, not lame. A strong young woman of a good family who is also handsome. One who'll do for you as your mother did for me. One who'll bring you children and me, grandchildren. A woman who has, your mother tells me, crafted many moccasins and parfleches for her father's lodge."

"No, Father. If I can't have Black Buffalo Woman, I don't want anyone."

"You'll eventually kill yourself in battle," Hump warned him.

Crazy Horse responded with the old Sioux adage: "Better to die on the battlefield than an old man in bed."

"My son, forget this woman," Old Crazy Horse pleaded.

"I'm not being willful, Father. I can't stop the feeling I have. The spirit has gone out of me."

"Following the wrong spirit will kill you," warned Old Hump.

"No. I'm not marrying just to have a servant for my tepee. Losing Buffalo Woman I lost laughter. Only she could make me glad again."

There things stood for a couple of months, but Old Hump and Old Crazy Horse did not stop trying to change his mind. Even his mother began to scold him. It got so bad he stayed in the Kit Fox lodge half the nights of the week.

He knew he could not remain there forever. Eventually he would be forced to marry, but he would never, never stop wanting Black Buffalo Woman.

During these winter months the whites sent messengers asking Red Cloud to come in to touch the pen, promising him many gifts and rations if he would come to Fort Laramie. At the same time he received dozens of other chiefs and their emissaries as he struggled to keep together the coalition he had forged the past summer and fall.

It was not going to be easy. When Red Cloud argued in council that the Sioux should keep a permanent force to patrol the Bozeman Trail and see to it that the whites didn't use it without permission, the other chiefs wanted to raid the Pawnee, hunt winter deer and go to Laramie to ask for rations.

When Red Cloud suggested that they send a combined expedition to Mexico to barter for rifles and shot with the buffalo hides they hadn't been able to trade because of the army's ban, each chief wanted to do what he had done every year since he had been a boy: hunt and raid other tribes for women and horses. And when Red Cloud wanted representatives of the Oglala, Minneconjou and Brulé to travel north to parley with Sitting Bull of the Hunkpapa for a possible raid together against the whites in the spring, he could get only four chiefs to agree, and these disagreed over what the message should say.

Although the younger warriors announced themselves ready to follow him into battle at any time, the other chiefs seemed jealous and resentful of Red Cloud's leadership. They argued that he didn't come from a good family and asked what made his ideas better than the suggestions of those who had set in council for years.

So as winter softened into spring and the bare trees put forth delicate buds and then strong young leaves, as was the way with the Sioux, the chiefs argued and came to no decision.

Spotted Tail twice made the trip to attend the council. He recounted all he had been given by the whites since he had touched the pen last summer, but Red Cloud's opinion of Spotted Tail was that the whites were buying him off till they decided what to do with him.

"It doesn't do any good to take these gifts from the white devils," he argued. "What happens when our young men forget how to hunt or can't be bothered to try anymore? Do we become like the Laramie loafers?"

No Water and Black Twin came to the council too. No Water was tactless enough to bring Black Buffalo Woman, six months pregnant. Young Hump persuaded Crazy Horse to leave the village while she was there and join the other Kit Foxes in a hunting party.

* * *

That spring, under the guidance of Old Hump, Red Cloud and Man-Afraid-of-His-Horses led two hundred braves on a buffalo hunt that was so successful Crazy Horse even killed a white buffalo, further proof of how much wakan he carried. The Bad Face tribe spent a week in ceremonies designed to assure Wakan-Takan that they were grateful for the gift. The hide was particularly wakan because Crazy Horse had managed to kill the beast with a knife in the belly and leave the skin whole. He wrapped it in a special deerskin pouch and gave it to Hump to keep with Crazy Horse's other wakan objects: his buffalo-skull altar, the herbs and paints he used in ceremonies and his feathered head-dresses.

When the snows were almost all melted, Trader Richards turned up at the Bad Face camp one morning, riding a horse and leading six mules laden with goods.

Red Cloud thought Richards looked old and haggard. Although it was conducted in English, Red Cloud gathered from the tone of the conversation between father and son that the two were discussing a matter urgent to them both. Something about the trader's visit made Red Cloud uneasy. What surprised him and the other chiefs, however, was the man's generosity. In a day or two Richards had uncharacteristically given away half the goods he had in his packs, including cloth, knives, metal pots, salt, coffee and sugar, in an apparent effort to insure their continued welcome with the tribe. As Richards put it at several times in his broken Sioux, "Me and Johnny here don't want to be mistaken for no horse soldiers."

Without Red Cloud's knowledge, Richards traded a three-gallon keg of rum to Eagle Beak for twenty buffalo robes, the profit of three years' hunting by him and his two sons. A sly, crafty man, Eagle Beak waited until his sons went on a horse raid with his brother-in-law and would be away for some days. Then he made the trade. He asked his oldest crony, Three Legs, to join him in drinking the rum.

Giggling over their good fortune, the two sat in Eagle Beak's tepee, the rest of the family on the other side of the fire, dipping deerskin cups through the smashed-in top of the keg and drinking. Eagle Beak's fat wife screeched at him as often as she dared, demanding that he share the rum with her. Hadn't she scraped and pounded the hides? By her side sat her three youngest children, a boy of nine and two girls, seven and thirteen, who demanded a taste of the liquor from her whenever Eagle Beak grudgingly passed her the cup.

Within a half an hour, the two men were falling down drunk. An hour after that they were quarreling over which one of them had shot the arrow that killed the deer they had brought in from Hawk Point the year before.

Eagle Beak told Three Legs that from now on they were no longer friends: he didn't ever want to see him again; life in the camp would be better if an eagle were to pick Three Legs up and eat him the way she ate a mouse, hair, skin, flesh, bones and all.

"And since you aren't my friend anymore, get out of my lodge."

"No, I'm staying here." Three Legs was a solidly built man of about thirty with a wide square face and belligerent eyes. "You invited me and I'm staying."

"My tepee," Eagle Beak belched. "Can't stay 'less I say so. Now get out."

254

The quarrel continued, with Eagle Beak hovering over the keg with a hatchet, refusing to allow Three Legs another drink. Finally, with the help of the three children and his wife, Eagle Beak managed to push Three Legs out of the lodge. In return he filled a small metal pot half full of rum and gave it to his wife and children, who promptly made such a squall over it that he regretted his generosity.

Suddenly his children shouted, "Daddy! Daddy! Three Legs!" But before Eagle Beak could react, Three Legs lifted the dew cloth and drove a war lance through his back. Beak's wife and children, cut off from the entrance of the tepee by the wild-eyed Three Legs, cowered against the wall and watched Eagle Beak thrash. Finally, with huge gasping sobs, Eagle Beak heaved blood and died. A wail went up from his wife, for she had no brothers who would hunt for her and she had had some feelings for Eagle Beak, who from time to time had treated her with more kindness than a wife might expect.

"Who did he think he was, pushing me around?" mumbled Three Legs. Wielding a hatchet, he staggered over to the rum keg.

A face appeared at the entrance to the tepee. Three Legs lunged toward it, roaring like a bear disturbed in hibernation, waving the hatchet. The face pulled back.

Richards was in Red Cloud's lodge, invited to a meal with the chief, Man-Afraid-of-His-Horses, Old Hump, Black Twin and High Backbone, when the young brave who had poked his head into Eagle Beak's tepee rushed in.

"Something has happened in Eagle Beak's lodge. There is blood everywhere!"

The others rushed outside and across the camp to find a crowd standing around the lodge. From inside they heard the cries of the wife and children.

"Who's in there besides his family?" Red Cloud asked the young brave who had alerted him.

"Three Legs."

"Three Legs!" Red Cloud called. "Come out here!"

Silence. Around them in the gloom the crowd grew.

Red Cloud called again. There was no response from Three Legs, but there were shrieks for help from Eagle Beak's wife and children.

"What's he doing to them?" Red Cloud wondered aloud. He asked Richards if he could borrow his pistol.

The trader pulled it out and made sure it was loaded and cocked. "Be careful," he cautioned Red Cloud. "He could be waiting to jump you in there."

Red Cloud knelt and reached for the flap covering the opening to the tepee. He jerked it open and slid inside and to the left.

What he saw sickened him. On the other side of the tepee, Three Legs had herded the wife and two youngest children into a corner. The thirteen-year-old girl was half under him. From the way her skirt was bunched up around her waist, it was clear that Three Legs was raping the child. He had his hatchet raised, waving it at the shrieking woman and children.

"Three Legs!" shouted Red Cloud.

The heavy face turned to look at him. "She's mine. Go away."

"Let her go," ordered Red Cloud. "What happened to Eagle Beak?"

"Now *you* want my whiskey," Three Legs muttered.

Red Cloud saw the keg then and knew at once what had happened. Damn Richards! Damn all white men! Red Cloud knew rum well enough; it had destroyed his father.

"Put down the hatchet, Three Legs."

"You want my drink, Red Cloud."

"No. You've killed Eagle Beak."

Pulled by the two pleasures, the girl beneath him and the keg two armlengths away, Three Legs was clearly torn between which to guard in a fight.

"Get out, Red Cloud."

"Put down the hatchet and let's talk, Three Legs."

"No. Out." He waved the hatchet and Red Cloud pulled back. Three Legs laughed and lunged towards him.

"I've got a gun, fool!" shouted Red Cloud.

"Kill him!" shrieked Eagle Beak's wife. "He murdered my husband!"

Seeing that Three Legs was distracted by Red Cloud, she pounded him on his back. He whirled and smashed her arm with the hatchet. She shrieked and shrank away.

In an effort at control, Red Cloud pointed the gun at the smoke hole and pulled the trigger. The bullet sliced into the thongs that held the circle of lodge poles together, cutting them, collapsing the lodge around their ears. In the resulting melee Red Cloud reached toward the keg to tip it over, figuring it had caused enough trouble. Three Legs, seeing him reach for it, roared and lunged for him.

Tangled by the falling poles and tepee walls,

Red Cloud was helpless. Three Leg's hatchet crashed twice next to the chief's foot. The maddened Three Legs leaned back to strike at Red Cloud's head, but before he could bring the hatchet down, the chief raised the pistol and pulled the trigger. The bullet hit Three Legs in the throat and tore off half the right side of his neck. He fell like a tree.

That night Red Cloud had Richards bring him the other three kegs of rum and smashed them to pieces. Richards looked distressed but he didn't protest. He saw clearly that the situation called for him to keep his mouth shut.

"How did Eagle Beak get that liquor?" asked Red Cloud.

"He must have stolen it," Richards lied.

"Didn't he trade hides for it?"

"No. It's true I took some of his hides, but I gave him several knives and two axes for them."

Red Cloud didn't believe him. He wanted both Richardses out of the village. "Take your son and leave. You're no friend of the Sioux."

"But I've been trading with your people for years." Richards was alarmed now.

"Go!"

Richards wanted to argue, but he saw that Red Cloud wouldn't listen. "At least let me trade the rest of my goods and leave with a full load of robes."

After some discussion Red Cloud gave in, but he wouldn't give in on the boy. The chief learned from his father that he had made the soldiers so angry he couldn't return to Fort Laramie.

"Better your son isn't with us. He causes trouble."

"But you are his people too, Red Cloud."

"He'll go with you," the chief answered coldly. "I don't want any whites with the Bad Faces."

Spring eased into early summer. A small herd of buffalo crossed the tribe's path and Red Cloud led fifty warriors on a successful hunt. Crazy Horse raided a Pawnee and a Crow village and lost a man in the latter raid, an event so rare that it plunged him into gloom.

When June came, Red Cloud was again ready for battle. He had heard from the Crow and from Richards that the Little White Chief had fled after the beating he had taken last year and that there was another chief at Fort Kearny now.

That too was all right. Even fools could see that the soldiers could not beat the Sioux. Shortly the whites would come to their senses and abandon the road. Only a few more attacks would be needed to drive the soldiers back to Fort Reno, which was where Red Cloud had told them from the beginning they must remain.

The braves he needed for the last battle were already assembling.

Chapter 20

Part of the two cavalry companies General Palmer picked to relieve Fort Kearny plodded out of Laramie on January 2, 1867, into a world of white. Two days later four companies of infantry, four hundred well-armed troops commanded by Major Van Voast, followed.

The younger, newer troopers set out in good spirits. The more experienced noncoms and officers didn't at all like the idea and the conditions they met on the way bore them out. Snow was piled up on the road to a height of five feet. In order for the infantry to make any time, the cavalry had to push through the snow a quarter of a mile at a time, then turn and ride back over the same section to tramp down the snow for the foot soldiers. At least once every half mile snow had to be shoveled to make a way for the wagons.

They staggered into Fort Reno nine days later needing a rest. But General Connor, after reading his orders from Cooke, roared that they needn't bother to unpack. If it had been anybody but old One Arm the officers might have protested.

One of them asked about provisions.

"Didn't you bring any?" Connor asked. "Not enough here to last the winter."

"Gettin' real low, sir."

"Come on, boy, we'll make do! If they killed off all them horses at Kearny they'll have more than enough for all of us!"

On the second day out of Reno the hay gave out, and many of the mules and horses went wild with hunger. Some broke free and pawed the snow for grass. Some chewed on the wagon tongues and feed troughs or bit the manes and tails of the other animals.

The creeks were frozen clear through to the bottom and except in the deepest streams, water was almost impossible to find. It was no easy task to hack through a foot and a half of ice twice a day to get water for a hundred fifty men, seventy mules and seventy-five horses, particularly with a one-armed maniac roaring the injunction to "Move your asses, damnit! They may be burning down the fort!"

Ten men were so badly frostbitten they had to ride in the wagons. The cold was so intense, the men so weary, many wondered if it wouldn't be worth it to swap a couple of toes in order not to have to take another step.

January 16, fourteen days after they had set out, the troopers reached the gates of Fort Kearny looking as much in need of rescue as those they had come to save.

The command at Kearny busied itself setting up quarters for the relief troops, a difficult feat, for the fort hadn't been built to accommodate double its normal population.

If Connor's troops were in bad shape, conditions at the garrison were even worse. The only wood the post had for heat was green oak and cottonwood, and the hospital was crowded with scurvy victims.

Connor went straight to Carrington's office. When the two were alone he handed Carrington his new orders.

"Relieved!" Carrington looked shocked.

"What did you expect?" Connor chuckled mirthlessly. "A medal? You had the worst defeat in the history of our scraps with the Indians."

"I? I had nothing to do with what happened. It was that damned Fetterman who led the men into that trap."

Connor produced a belly laugh but he still sounded cold. "Who was in command here, Colonel, you or Captain Fetterman?"

"He disobeyed me!"

Connor eyed him with disgust. Such mishaps didn't happen under his command. He'd roast any son of a bitch who didn't obey his orders. "Dismissed, Colonel."

"Dismissed?" Carrington looked around his office in bewilderment.

"Surely you know the meaning of the word? Take a half hour and get all this junk out of here. I need a place to work, and I assume that this is the best office."

Carrington looked at him. "But I didn't do anything!" he protested.

"I presume a court-martial will decide that."

"A court-martial!"

"Colonel, I expect you to leave in a few days, just as those orders say," the general told him. "In my experience it won't do you or the men any good for you to linger."

"My—my wife," stammered Carrington.

Exasperated, Connor asked, "What about her?"

"She's here with me," said the prim Ohioan. "And my two boys. This is awful weather. They can't travel."

"And why not?"

"I saw your men when they came in. It's too much of a hardship."

Connor lost patience altogether now. "Colonel, you're leaving! I don't give a damn if your missus goes or stays. She should have thought twice before she came out here. A post in the middle of wild savages ain't no place for a woman. The army doesn't give me jurisdiction over how she comes and goes, but I do know this: you're leaving."

Captain Ten Eyke had heard enough about Connor in the general's first two days at the fort to dread his first meeting with the man.

When he arrived at the commander's quarters he saw at once that changes were being made. On one wall of the reception room two lieutenants who had come with Connor were drawing a map of the entire Platte country with the help of Jim Bridger and John Richards. The new orderly at the desk sat up straighter than Sergeant Meadows ever had and stood to ask Ten Eyke what he could do for him.

"I'd like to see the general." In a few moments he was shown into Carrington's old office, but what a difference! Where Carrington had covered the walls

263

with an engineer's renderings of fortifications, floors, beamed ceilings and stockade walls, Connor had put up three regimental flags, four rifles, three shotguns, a brace of pistols, two sabers and all the tack and paraphernalia a proud cavalry officer can collect over twenty years.

Carrington had worked at a large desk supported by two sawhorses on which he could spread out plans and study them. Now the room was bare of any work surface and had been furnished with a long leather sofa and a couple of comfortable armchairs.

"Delighted to see you, Captain." Connor waved him into a chair.

Knowing the general wouldn't be so delighted to see him when he heard him out, Ten Eyke sat.

"I've looked over your record, Captain. You seem to be a sound combat officer, although you were stupid enough to choose the wrong side in the last war."

Ten Eyke forced himself to smile politely and remain calm. He saw why Connor had a reputation as a hard man to deal with. The general gave the impression of boiling, as if some internal ferment was continually rising in him. Connor didn't sit; he strode restlessly about the office.

"I know you people have had a rough time here. I don't expect to change things overnight, but we're not going to have any more foolishness from the Indians."

"Foolishness?" asked Ten Eyke.

"Letting them play with you like puppets. Letting them run over you."

"Our orders were to defend the road, not pursue the Indians. I don't think anyone could say we had enough men or arms to do that."

"You lost eighty-two men in one engagement, Captain. How many Indians did they kill first?"

"I don't know. Nobody knows."

"Guess, damnit!"

"Ten, perhaps. They took their dead, but that's a good guess."

"Only ten?" The bearded general shook his head in disgust as he paced. Ten Eyke saw a barrel of a man, in his forties he guessed, his wiry black hair shot with grey. He looked like a well-fed grizzly.

"Only ten?" Connor repeated.

"It sounds bad, I admit, General, but don't forget, Captain Fetterman rode into a trap."

"I can't imagine Union troops not accounting better for themselves."

Ten Eyke decided it was time to steer the conversation to the purpose of his visit. "Sir, I've come to ask permission to leave with Colonel Carrington."

"Leave? Why, sir?"

"It's a bit awkward, but I'd like to resign from the army."

"Permission denied. I want you for my second. We're going to make those red rascals pay for this blood bath."

"I don't know that I can be useful here, sir."

"Why not?" Connor glowered at him. "Spit it out, man. Don't talk in riddles."

"Yes sir." Ten Eyke took a deep breath. "It's my relationship with Mrs. Simmons."

"Simmons? Who's that?"

"The minister here. His wife—"

"Yes?"

"She's leaving her husband for me."

Connor stared, then burst out laughing as if he

had never heard anything so funny. After some moments, he wiped a couple of tears from his eyes and calmed down. "So, what's wrong? You won."

"Mrs. Simmons is expecting a child."

"Yours, I suppose." Connor laughed again. "Well? So what?"

"I would like to take Mrs. Simmons with me, leave with the colonel and resign from the army."

"I already told you." Connor was no longer laughing. "Permission denied."

Ten Eyke felt cornered. "I must, sir. Don't you see her position? I can't subject her to the men's snickers and the scorn of the ladies here."

"Hang 'em all, Captain. You're staying. Tell you what I will do, though. I'll send the minister away. Never did like those pious bastards."

"Send Reverend Simmons away?" Ten Eyke's head was beginning to swim.

"That's right," Connor nodded. "Out of sight, out of mind. You and his wife stay here. Be over in no time."

"Hardly a solution."

"It's the only one you'll get from me," Connor snapped. "I need you, and you won't get a better deal from the army wives no matter what post you go to."

"That's why I want to resign."

"I don't think the army's going to let you, Captain. Now, you won, and you got the man's wife, so enjoy the spoils of war!" Connor flung his arm out in an extravagant gesture. "Get out of here and go to work. I want a report of what we have in the way of guns, ammunition, fighting infantry and cavalry, and I want it by tomorrow morning, along with your recommendations for additional men and arms. We'll send out our requisitions with the departing colonel—and the preacher."

Four days later at daybreak, Hank knocked softly on the door to the two rooms Tenodor and Cynthia had managed to get from Frances Grummond.

Cynthia woke feeling her gorge rise and dashed out of bed to the washbasin, where she vomited, as she did every morning. The water in the basin was frozen and she shivered in the frigid air. All she wanted was to get back into bed, snuggle up to Tenodor and sleep.

But she knew she must go and say good-bye to Clarence and she dreaded it. She didn't want to see him again after the horrific scene when she told him it wasn't his baby and she was leaving him for Tenodor, but she felt she owed him at least a good-bye. Perhaps he would relent and change his refusal to give her a divorce.

"You want to be an imp of Satan, you'll live in sin like one, Cynthia," he had declared. After two hours of confrontation he was speaking as if from the pulpit. "If I don't give you a divorce you can't marry him, and the world will condemn all of you no matter where you go."

He remained firm no matter how much she pleaded with him. She had rarely seen such stubbornness in him.

She dressed quietly in the morning gloom. Tenodor stirred. "You're really going to see him off?"

"I must."

"I'll come with you. You shouldn't face him alone."

"No, it's my battle. Stay here."

Tenodor groaned and pulled himself up to sit on the edge of the bed. Yes, she wanted him to come with her, but she wouldn't let him. She pushed him back into the warm bed.

"You're only going to say good-bye, aren't you?" he asked.

"What do you mean?"

"There's no chance you're going with him?"

"Is that what you're worried about?"

"Yes."

"No, silly, there's no chance I'll go with him. You and I are married by more than words, Tenodor." She patted her belly. "This little fellow marries us in a special way."

Her voice must have carried conviction, for Tenodor lay back without another word and watched her pull on her warmest coat. She blew him a kiss and left the room.

Out on the parade ground the snow lay piled in high drifts. The wind made Cynthia shudder as she walked toward the fort gates, where three wagons and a dozen mounted horsemen were preparing to leave in the damp morning darkness.

As Cynthia approached the group she saw Colonel Carrington and his wife Margaret come out of the headquarters building and climb into a wagon. They saw her but looked away without speaking. The dozen mounted soldiers eyed her slyly. It was something she still hadn't gotten used to and it would be her lot for months or years to come. She would be whispered about as if she had a scarlet "A" branded on her forehead.

At that moment Clarence, walking between two

soldiers, came out of the quarters they had shared. Cynthia saw that his head was bowed in shame. At once her heart went out to him. What had she done? She realized what Tenodor had sensed, that she still cared for this half-man she had lived with so long.

Apprehensive, Cynthia edged closer to the wagons. Clarence looked up, saw her and hesitated. The soldiers pushed him forward by his arms, much as they might have forced a man forward to his execution. Suddenly angry with the way they were treating her husband, Cynthia strode forward.

Clarence swung onto his horse, gave it a little kick and rode away from the soldiers to meet her halfway. Her purpose for being there shifted. Now she wanted to make sure he understood that she hadn't meant to hurt him.

For a long moment they stared at each other. From the look of his face, she knew he had spent the entire night awake and crying, probably struggling to pray and failing. She knew what he needed, which was for her to soothe him, but giving wasn't enough for her now. She needed something for herself. She was only dimly aware that the cavalry escort, the Carringtons and the drivers of the wagons, just out of earshot, were watching them curiously.

"I didn't expect this." She meant she hadn't expected General Connor to throw Clarence off the post.

"I can still forgive you. Get in the wagon. Come with me."

"No, I can't."

"Get in the wagon, Cynthia. I'll raise the child. It might be mine. You can't really know."

"No, Clarence."

"You're my wife, Cynthia!" He looked like a stout young pig who saw that he was about to be penned up and was wild with alarm. "How can you throw everything away?"

"I *was* your wife, Clarence. Please. We went over all this."

"Don't do this to me," he pleaded.

"I didn't want to hurt you, Clarence, believe me."

"I loved you," he whined. "I loved our child."

"Oh, Clarence, can't you understand? It never was ours. If we lived that way, we'd be living a lie."

For a long moment they looked at each other. Seeing him, his unhappiness, his childlike bewilderment, she wavered. After all, the service that married them had said in sickness and in health, for better or worse, till death do you part. What she was doing was wrong, wrong, wrong, wasn't it? She pictured her father and mother commiserating with Clarence when he got back to Boston. In the wind she heard the gales of gossip that would blow about them for years.

"Let's go, preacher!" shouted the sergeant.

"You're still my wife," Clarence insisted.

"Good-bye, Clarence. Let me go. Give me a divorce."

He shook his head. "You'll come to your senses, Cynthia. When you do, I'll be waiting in Boston."

"Clarence, it's over. Let me go!"

"No."

The sergeant shouted again and Clarence gathered his reins. "I'm not going to make it easy for you, Cynthia."

"Please, Clarence. Please, please, please."

"Come back to Boston and we'll talk about it."

"No, I can't."

"Then good-bye. In my eyes you're still my wife and always will be. I'll be waiting for you to come to your senses." Having had the last word, he wheeled his horse and joined the others. The wagon drivers cracked their whips over the mules. As the first wagon lurched forward Cynthia wanted to shout for it to stop, but she knew it was too late. She had glimpsed something in her final encounter with Clarence that she had rarely seen, a fighting spirit. She wished more of it had emerged during their years together. If it had she might have made a life with him after all.

The wagons disappeared through the huge gates of the fort. Glancing around, Cynthia saw the soldiers and officers starng openly at her. Tears and a sense of a cherished something lost forever rose in her. She wanted to shout at them not to stare. One soldier leaned over and whispered something to another; they both snickered. At that, she drew herself up, gave an angry flounce of her coat, spun and marched back to the cabin she shared with Tenodor.

That walk back across the parade ground in the dawn's raw gloom was the bleakest moment of her life. Was the rest to be the same?

As Ten Eyke knew only too well, the post didn't have enough ammunition to fight off an Indian attack, much less any to spare for target practice. His report to that effect put off Connor's plans to whip the garrison's forces into shape and take them out after the enemy. As a compromise he called a meeting of officers and instructed them to train their men in the use of the bayonet.

271

"I'll not have soldiers who can't attack!" he roared at them. "And you, Powell, I want you to train a man for every horse on post. Fire half-charges next to the horses while they're being trained. We can't have them bolting in a fight. Ten Eyke, you organize this ragged-looking crew of officers for me. Make sure that each one heads a combat group. Gentlemen, we're going to have roast red man this spring, and I expect every one of you to help me push his butt to the fire!"

But continued snowstorms and freezing winds in February allowed little of the training the general had in mind. In March the weather cleared and the snow began to melt. The mushy ground provided little better training conditions, but that didn't stop Connor from pushing his officers and men.

"We got a massacre to avenge, damnit!" he would shout when anybody questioned the orders of the day, which six days a week read that every company would be on the parade ground, out on patrol or practicing against sack dummies painted to look like Indian braves.

In April the ground firmed up. Patrols were increased, but they had little to protect; what wagon master would be fool enough to bring a train over the Bozeman Trail after the slaughter of last year?

Connor himself often rode with these patrols obviously spoiling for a fight. He rode with two pistols strapped to his right side, Black Bear's reins looped around his chest to leave his hand free for shooting. Next to him rode an officer and two enlisted men whose strict duty was to make sure the general's pistols were always loaded and his rear and flanks covered. This duty frightened every man just to think of it. As one veteran said, the only thing worse than riding at old One Arm's side into the jaws of Hell was his wrath if you left him undefended in battle.

The Sioux battle tactics infuriated Connor. "The damn cowards won't stand and fight!" he roared every time they melted away from one of his mounted attacks. Because so few wagon trains came through, giving the Indians few targets to attack and Connor few raiding parties to chase, such encounters were rare.

In a way, both sides' strategies were working. Settlers, miners and other white travelers were afraid to use the road, which was a victory for the Sioux. On the other hand, the army still held three well-fortified garrisons in the heart of their hunting grounds.

From Boston to San Francisco the Sioux Red Cloud, who had defied the army, was the subject of countless editorials. Much of the Eastern press hailed him as the most brilliant Indian commander of all time, while papers in the West vilified him as an outlaw who should be shot on sight. Spotted Tail was painted as a model of the same Indian. Crazy Horse and Man-Afraid-of-His-Horses were puppets of the devil Red Cloud.

The only travelers who braved the trail these days were freight haulers, who were paid four times their usual wages to make the run. No more than three quarters of the trains reached Bozeman City.

One brilliant day in late April, out on a patrol with ninety troopers, Connor arrived too late. Before them lay the smoking wreckage of eleven wagons and the bodies of twenty men.

"Jesus Christ, what happened to them, Ten Eyke?" Connor asked.

The two gazed down at the victims' bodies, strewn about like so many large broken dolls. Several of the dead men looked to have had their feet burned off in nearby fires that still smoldered. They had been shot, cut and clubbed before and after death. Feeling sick himself, Ten Eyke couldn't blame the men for hesitating to begin the burial.

On the way back, not five miles from the scene of the attack, the patrol came upon a small group of Indians. Three women, an old man, two children and a brave were crossing a creek as the cavalry rode up.

The Indians hadn't heard them over the sound of the rapids. The troopers captured them as they tried to flee. "Finally caught some of the beggars!" the jubilant Connor shouted.

The seven Indians struggled against the soldiers, who pummeled them with every move they made.

"Take them back to the fort, sir?" asked Radcliff, the sergeant major, a beefy man with the red face of a boozer. He was struggling to hold on to a kicking child or four or so.

"Hell, no! String them up!"

Silence fell. Most of the men in the patrol looked at each other. What did he mean? It was one thing to hang this brave, who had probably been in on the raid, but this old man and these women and children, weren't they a different matter?

"Sir!" said Ten Eyke. "These aren't Sioux, they're Pawnee."

"I don't care if they're snakes or buffaloes, ain't they redskins?" Connor's guffaw shook his horse.

274

"We're not at war with the Pawnee," Ten Eyke pointed out. "They've been our friends ever since we came out here."

But Connor didn't even seem to hear.

"No prisoners, sir?" The red-faced sergeant major held out his squirming captive.

"Sergeant," Connor barked, "surely you've heard that big lice grow from little nits."

At this the sergeant threw the child up in the air, caught him—or her; the horrified Ten Eyke couldn't tell—by the heels and swung the screaming child in a circle around his head twice before leaning forward to dash its brains out against a granite boulder.

The wails of the women and the screams of the other child mingled with the gurgle of the rapids. The soldiers stared silently at the sergeant and the small form on the ground at his feet. They heard General Connor laugh, heard him say, "What are you waiting for? We ain't taking no prisoners, goddamnit!"

"No!" shouted Ten Eyke, by now thoroughly sickened. "These Indians haven't done anything."

Connor's face pinched into a hairy sour ball. "And how would you know that?"

But Ten Eyke couldn't answer, so stunned was he by the sight of the yelling, jeering soldiers. They had seized the other child, who couldn't have been more than six, and were holding it underwater by standing on the struggling body. They bound the hands and feet of the protesting old man, the sullen brave and the three women. In another joyous minute they had them all dangling and jerking from the tree that shaded the creek.

"Leave them there!" shouted Connor. "It'll teach them not to mess with us. Goddamn thieving stinking son of a bitching no count redskins, they're what's wrong with this country!"

From that day on Connor's standing order to the men was to kill any Indians they came across. Whenever he was with them he made sure the order was carried out to the letter.

Ten Eyke objected, knowing the killing of so many innocents couldn't possibly lead to any good. Actually, few Indians were killed in Connor's campaign, for word soon spread how dangerous the Bozeman Trail was for Indian traffic, which was what the general wanted. Of course this policy flew in the face of the peace policy as outlined by Congress, the Department of the Interior and the Bureau of Indian Affairs, but Connor knew that if he stayed on top in the conflict with the Indians, the War Department would support him. Despite all the pious squalling of the schoolmarms and preachers, what the country wanted was to subdue the savage. Besides, who back East knew what the hell went on out here in the woods?

"It reminds me of what the Union did to the South," Ten Eyke wearily told Cynthia one night late in May.

She cradled his head, which lay on what was left of her lap, for she was expecting their child any week now. They spent most of their time in the two-room apartment they had inherited from Frances and George Grummond. They had no social life, for the ladies wouldn't speak to Cynthia and his fellow officers ignored Ten Eyke when he visited the bachelor officers' quarters.

Connor, knowing how strongly Ten Eyke felt about his Indian policy, kept a close eye on his second in command. In an effort to counter the general's orders, Cynthia wrote long eloquent letters back East to churchmen, politicians and newspaper writers who supported peaceful treatment of the Indians.

By June 1867, Red Cloud still had not beaten the whites. They remained in the hated three forts that broke up his hunting ground; heavily armed wagon trains still traveled the trail and troops of soldiers patrolled. The Sioux still attacked work parties from the forts, small troop detachments, travelers and what few settlers remained. All the fighting of the past two years, its pain, grief, agony and six hundred dead had achieved no more than a stand-off.

Chapter 21

In June, Nathaniel Taylor arrived at Fort Kearny from Fort Laramie with Big Mouth and Big Ribs, the Laramie loafers. He'd enlisted them to go about the countryside with gifts of tobacco to persuade the leaders of hostile bands to come in and sign the new treaty.

At dinner the night Taylor arrived, Connor declared, "You ain't doing nothing more than bribing them."

Taylor found the general objectionable and nightly prayed for him. Why did soldiers have to think the only answer to the Indian problem was extermination? Couldn't they see that the Indian was as much a man as they were?

"They come in here and you give them powder and shot. All you've done is paid them off, not brought them to their knees," Connor growled. He leaned forward confidentially. They were dining alone in the general's quarters. "And that's what's going to happen to these people in the long run, sir. They will be brought to their knees before the might of a great nation marching west! We're going to make this a single country from sea to sea! Might as well get them ready for that now as later."

Connor rattled him, but Taylor was used to standing up to the devil's bullies. "Sir, I take offense. We have a moral duty to nurture these natural children of God, particularly to shield them from our rapacious society, against which they stand helpless."

"Helpless! You should hear what they did to Fetterman's little party last year not seven miles from here."

"Provoked by Captain Fetterman, I believe."

"Indians are just out to make all the mischief they can, a bunch of wild boys who live in the woods with nothing to do but hunt and fool around. I'd love to live that way myself, if I didn't have some Christian conscience and a call to serve my country." The general looked wistful enough to have Taylor believing him for an instant, but then the peace commissioner remembered that he was talking to the scourge of the Powder River, who was not to be trusted, and he went back to his venison steak.

A week later Taylor had his hands full. A number of the chiefs who had signed the treaty the year before had heard about his offers and they turned up at the gates of the fort wanting to sign again and receive presents. These chiefs got angry when they heard that they wouldn't get presents for signing again. After all, hadn't they been cooperative for the last two years? Why should they be punished now? It would have been better not to sign last year, for they would have received powder, shot, cloth, salt, sugar, coffee, kettles, axes and the other supplies that the Bureau of Indian Affairs empowered Taylor to give out.

Taylor relented, sensing that either decision was wrong. He endured endless ribbing from the officers at Kearny for giving out treaty gifts to "tame" Indians.

Of course Taylor wanted Red Cloud's Bad Faces and the other Oglala to sign the treaty, but he could find only a village of twenty-eight lodges whose chief would sign and accept presents. Still, it allowed him to tell the Interior Department and the Bureau of Indian Affairs that he had gotten Oglala signatures.

"The trouble with you peace-policy fellows," complained Connor to Taylor one night, "is that you're like a ball and chain around a man's ankles. I could clear this whole country of Sioux by winter if you'd just turn your backs."

"Which we have no intention of doing. Depend on it."

Connor sighed. "Oh, I will. I've had my orders. I know Cooke and Sherman's hearts aren't in them, but I've had my orders." He leaned across the little space between the two men on the veranda. "But depend on this, sir: you are making a fool of your country and your own people."

In the third week of June, Big Mouth returned to Kearny without the tobacco and said there was an excellent chance that Red Cloud and Old-Man-Afraid-of-His-Horses would come to Kearny to talk to the commissioner. They could meet in a mutually agreeable place, perhaps just outside the fort, with equal numbers of armed warriors from each side looking on.

Of course this excited Taylor. Getting Red Cloud and Man Afraid's signatures on the treaty was what he had come thousands of miles and waited all these weeks for. He gave Big Mouth more tobacco to take back and made plans for when and how to meet the Oglala chiefs.

Before the Laramie loafers left the fort again, General Connor ordered him to come and see him.

Big Mouth, who had acquired his name through his relentless bragging, came into the general's office quaking with fear. Knowing Connon's hatred of the Indian, none of them liked to be in his presence. Big Mouth strove to keep his fear off his face and out of his stomach, half-convinced he would never leave this demon's presence alive.

"You're going out to find Big Chief Red Cloud?" asked One Arm.

"Yes sir." Big Mouth aped the accents of the answer that he had heard the soldiers give so many times.

"How long will you be gone?"

"Week, maybe more."

"Could you find me a girl?"

"A girl?"

"Sure, a girl."

Big Mouth's heart leaped and he thought swiftly. "Yes, sir. You want a girl to marry?"

He looked round the general's room wondering what she would do, for the general had many men who kept his rooms clean and cooked for him. Then it hit him. He knew that soldiers sometimes liked to take Sioux women under their blankets.

"Not marry," the general grinned. "Or anyway, only for a little while. Can you bring one back?"

Many Indian fathers would be delighted to sell a daughter to an important chief like the general, and many girls would be delighted to have such a chief for their protector. Big Mouth knew he could profit from such a transaction. He would insist that the father give him a pony.

"Only for a little while?" asked Big Mouth. "Father no like that."

"Don't tell him."

"Yes." Big Mouth grunted. "How much you pay?"

"Two ponies."

"No, no good."

"Four and no more."

"Four no good."

"Listen, you rascal, don't tell me some dumb little squaw's worth more than four ponies, goddamn you!"

The general's roar frightened Big Mouth, who grinned and nodded in agreement. "Four ponies."

Connor calmed down. "Now, a couple of things. One, I don't want anybody to know about this."

"Sir?"

"And two, I want a fresh girl, savvy?"

"Fresh?"

"Clean and fresh," roared the general in his usual impatient fashion. "And if one word of this gets back to me from somebody else, I'm going to wring your head off your fat little neck. Get me?"

Connor reached over with his one huge hand and pinched Big Mouth's fat neck so hard that tears spurted from his eyes. Big Mouth nodded vigorously.

"That's just two things." The general let him go. "Think you can remember them?"

"You pay some rum?"

"How about we make it two small kegs of rum and three ponies?"

As he had seen the soldiers do, Big Mouth stuck out his hand to seal the bargain. "You got a deal, sir."

Hesitating a moment, Connor finally grasped the hand. "Done and done."

Several days later John Richards and his son turned up at Fort Kearny. Nathaniel Taylor asked the father if he would come and see him. The two met the next morning in the office that General Connor had had to give the man from the Department of the Interior.

"I need your help," Taylor appealed to the big-bellied backwoodsman.

Richards hadn't shaved or trimmed his beard in weeks and looked sour and weary, very different from the confident man who had served as translator last summer at Fort Laramie. "What for?" Richards warily regarded the Easterner.

"Sit down," Taylor invited him. "You don't look at all well. Trouble?"

Richards sat, exuding a long weary sigh. "Ah, preacher, you don't know the half of it."

Taylor nodded. He thought he did know the half of it. At Fort Laramie he'd heard that John Richards Jr. was wanted for killing one of the sutler's men in a barroom brawl and that the youth had fled to his mother's people to escape trial at Laramie. Why had father and son come to Fort Kearny?

"Business not good?" asked Taylor.

"What business?" Richards snorted. "Things were fine till you government folks came messing around."

Taylor frowned. "What do you mean?"

"I ain't traded more'n a wagonload of hides in two years," Richards complained. "I'm so close to broke you might as well call it that. I can't get a permit to trade from the jackasses that run these forts, and without a permit I can't bring in goods. Old One Arm there would confiscate them if I did."

Taylor thought the situation was even better than he had figured. "You know, you could help resolve things and then go back to trading."

"That's what you said last year when I agreed to translate."

"We almost had a treaty."

"Would have, too, if you had dickered honestly and hadn't run that fool Carrington in on them," Richards groused.

"I'm afraid a lot of people back East don't know much about Indians," Taylor smiled weakly.

"That's certain," Richards agreed dryly.

"But we're out here learning, and we're trying to do the right thing."

"The right thing would be to keep the whites away from these people. Nothing from the whites does them much good. Sometimes I don't think I ought to trade with them myself."

"They wouldn't even have horses if it weren't for us."

Richards nodded glumly. "What do you want from me?"

"I want you to help me get the rebel bands to sign a treaty and settle down."

"I told you over and over again, they want the land they're on and the whites not to ride through it like they do."

"That's not possible, Mr. Richards. Have you ever heard of eminent domain?"

"Yeah, you can take a man's property for a road. Oh, Jesus, is that what you call this? You expect them to understand that?"

"We want to offer them something much better. We want to give out the richest presents they've ever received, including guns and powder plus annuities if they will move to agencies on the upper Missouri."

"Upper Missouri?"

"Where they'll be well fed and cared for."

"Cared for? They don't want to be cared for. They're men. They'll care for themselves."

"If they don't move," Taylor went on as if Richards hadn't spoken, "although I don't approve, a force of several thousand cavalry will be sent against them."

"They beat federal troops here two years running," Richards pointed out.

"Ah, do you really think they can keep on doing that?" Taylor gave Richards a knowing look.

The trader was silent.

"Do you?" Taylor pressed him.

Richards looked uneasy. "Just whose side are you on?"

"I know it sounds as if I'm on the side of the army, but I'm not. I'm pleading with you, Mr. Richards." Taylor had Richards' attention now and there was nothing to lose. He dropped all pretense and spoke the whole truth. "If we don't get these rebels to work with us, I'm afraid of what may happen. How many blood baths like Harney and Chivington's will it take before we all wake up? These people will be slaughtered if we don't head off the confrontation. Putting them on their own reservations is the only answer. Congress has agreed and we're proposing land on the upper Missouri."

Richards shook his head. "Yes, but it's not their land. The Powder River country is. They won't understand going somewhere else. All they want is what they've got. And they've heard so many stories about Indians being driven off their land, they're determined to stick with their own."

"But we'll promise to deed them this new land forever."

"Who's we?"

"The Congress, the President, the whole country."

Richards laughed and stood up. "How come? How come all of a sudden Powder River country is so important when for the last hundred years nobody wanted it?"

"The country has pushed west. The government doesn't want the Union Pacific Railroad molested anymore."

"What the hell's the railroad got to do with anything? That's seventy-five miles south of here."

"The Cheyenne got encouraged by the Sioux. They've been disrupting the track-laying."

"So? Let the railroad hire guards."

"Mr. Richards, the government guaranteed the railway's bonds. It can't allow the road to lose money or not finish on time. While they can't ship freight, every day it costs hundreds of thousands of dollars just to maintain the company."

Richards sighed. "But that don't mean the Sioux need to leave the Big Horn. In fact, once the railroad is done I don't see that the government's even going to need the Bozeman Trail. Why not give them the damn road and avoid a war?"

"Because of the Northern Pacific."

"The what?"

"The Northern Pacific will be built along the northern edge of the Powder River country."

"They'll never let you do that!"

"Of course not."

Richards looked staggered. "Do you have any idea what that'll do to the buffalo migrations?"

"Disrupt them still more, I should imagine."

"Jesus Christ! The herds are already only half what they once were."

"Some people say it's a good thing, too."

"Good thing?"

"No buffalo, no Indians."

Richards stared at him and shook his head. "Whose side *are* you on?" he wondered.

"I'm trying to tell you what your adopted people are up against." Taylor shrugged. "I'm not for any of these things. Another thing. A lot of people have gotten the notion that there's gold up in the Black Hills and the Big Horn mountains."

"Aw, Jesus, not gold!"

"Yes. You know what that'll do to the region." In the gold rush of '49, the flood of immigrants had trampled everything in California. Taylor continued, "The government doesn't want to find itself in a few years' time having to be the arbiter between the Indians and the gold prospectors."

Taylor thought Richards could see it, but just to make sure he added, "In the end the government would have to use troops to drive back either the Indians or its own citizens."

Richards responded sullenly, "They ain't likely to shoot their own people."

"You see my point." Taylor smiled sourly. "Now, I can't do anything without getting in touch with Red Cloud."

"He ain't that big a chief."

"Perhaps not, but to judge by the newspapers and the talk in Washington, I need his name on the treaty or it just won't have happened."

"I'll try to find him."

"Try? I'm trying to avert a war, Mr. Richards. I saw enough mangled bodies in the Civil War. Our side was right and we won, but if you had seen the carnage you would have to ask yourself if the price was worth the victory."

"All right, all right, I said I'd help, but I think you're wasting your time. The Oglala and Arapaho are fighting for all they've got left, their last hunting grounds, and they're not going to be bought off easily."

Taylor played his trump card. "Maybe I can help your boy when he comes up for trial."

Richards looked startled. *"When?"*

"If and when."

"You'll help him?"

"I said I would, sir."

"Thank you, Mr. Taylor," Richards said warmly. He stuck out his hand. "Thank you very much. I'll help you too."

Taylor shook the offered hand and watched Richards shuffle out. He sighed. Why did men fight instead of sitting down and working out their differences? Sometimes very little of what men did made sense to him, especially the way they fought and schemed for what they wanted.

* * *

"Sure I can do it." Sergeant Smithers, the head carpenter at Fort Kearny, looked at the general's rude drawing and scratched his head. "But I can't see the sense of it." The sergeant was regular army and one of the few people on the post who dared talk back to Connor. "Why do you need a room there? Why connect the back of the hospital with your quarters?"

But as he asked the question he glanced slyly at a red-headed woman standing by Connor's desk. Nurse Selena Crawford had come out from Fort Reno at Connor's request to help reorganize the hospital. Gossip among the troops had it that she was there primarily to minister to certain needs of the general's.

Connor saw the sergeant's look and thought, old fool, let him think what he wants to. He leaned across his desk and stuck out his bearded chin.

"That's a military secret," he whispered, grinning.

"Military secret?" Smithers blinked watery eyes and glanced again at the nurse, wondering what old One Arm saw in her. Too old and skinny. "In the middle of the wilderness?"

"Never mind," Connor snapped, losing patience. "Can you build the room?"

"I already told you."

"Then do it and keep your mouth shut about it. Put a door there." He pointed to the wall behind him.

"Everybody coming in here will see it," Smithers pointed out.

"I'll put a screen in front of it. Now get going before I change my mind about that keg of rum I promised you and drink it myself."

* * *

Crazy Horse arrived at Black Twin's camp two days after No Water left it to go hunting. He knew No Water would be gone because he had given a young Brulé brave named Sleepy Tree three buffalo hides to come over to Red Cloud's camp and tell him.

He rode through the village, aware that heads were turning to watch. But no one greeted him and no one tried to stop him. He almost wished they would. Now that he had made his decision he would have liked to reinforce it through opposition.

Black Buffalo Woman's tepee was near the center of the village, close to her brother-in-law Black Twin's, the largest one there. She was outside working on a pair of moccasins, her baby son playing in the grass beside her, when Crazy Horse rode up.

The joy in her face when she saw him pierced his heart. "Curly," she said. Her voice licked at his spine. He slid off his pony.

For what seemed like endless time they stood silently looking at each other.

"Do you still find me a joy?" her eyes asked.

"My life has been empty," his replied. "There is no woman like you."

The silent dialogue went on.

"I'm married now. I have this child you see here."

"I don't care. I've come for you if you'll have me."

"Our tribes will cast us out."

"Is life worth living without each other?"

"Mine isn't."

Then Black Buffalo Woman spoke aloud.

"You took a wife!"

Crazy Horse shrugged. "My father and Old Hump found her. They said my wakan was leaving me."

She stood looking at him. "I wanted to be your first wife," she said sadly.

"You are, in my heart. It has always been that way and always will."

She laughed that wonderful rich sound he loved. The June sun danced on her face and her eyes shone. Crazy Horse knew then that what he was doing was right. He didn't know where it would lead and he didn't care. It had taken him months of agony to arrive at this decision. What had troubled him most was giving up his Kit Fox brothers. No matter what tribe he went to now, what war society he joined, it would not be the same. But his love for this merry creature had tugged and tugged at him and now here he was. Well, every man had to bear some sadness in his life. He would bear the sadness of never again riding into battle with his friend Young Hump and the other Kit Foxes.

"I'll leave the child with his grandmother." Buffalo Woman glanced over at Black Twin's lodge, where a toothless crone looked up and nodded pleasantly.

"You can bring him."

"No, I don't think of him as mine." He saw she was crying. "He is No Water's child."

Crazy Horse didn't know what to say. He had never before heard of a mother leaving her child. "Hurry," he urged. "Pack quickly and take a horse."

They took two horses, one for Black Buffalo Woman to ride and another for her household goods. She had wanted to pack the tepee itself, which of course belonged to her, but Crazy Horse pointed out that it would slow them down.

For the rest of that day they rode hard. Near sunset they reached a spot in the hills by a waterfall. Crazy Horse often visited here when he needed a power vision.

He helped Black Buffalo Woman down off the horse and stood holding her, his hands on her waist. She reached up and brushed his lips with her fingertips.

"My husband," she murmured.

Crazy Horse caressed her back; his hands moved to her hair and undid her braids. The black silk cascaded over her shoulders. Gently he undressed her, then scooped her up in his arms and carried her to the shade of the trees.

"My husband," she said again when he placed her down on the soft grass.

He nuzzled her cheek. "My wife."

When he took her and she moaned softly, her arms clutching him, her eyes glowing, it was as if there had never been another for either of them.

For two days they stayed there making love and talking about how lonely the last year had been. Buffalo Woman confessed that she had been a prideful fool to toy with him when she was being courted.

Crazy Horse admitted that he had been too aloof, refusing to acknowledge how important she was to him. Well, he had learned his lesson and if it meant fighting No Water to the death for her, he would do it.

For a moment her merry look darkened. "He'll come," she predicted. "Though I've divorced him now and left his child, he'll come."

They were lying in the pool at the bottom of the waterfall, drifting lazily in each other's arms.

"He was always questioning me about my feelings for him, always asking me about you. He thought the child would hold me. The other men teased him. Twice he whipped me. The second time Black Twin caught him and was very angry, because of my uncle I suppose."

"Whipped you?"

She turned so he could see her back. The hard little welts were almost invisible.

"I'll whip him!" Crazy Horse turned her back toward him, gripped her tightly.

"He almost killed a brave last fall because he spoke to me at the well. He's tricky. He crept up on the brave and hit him from behind with a rock. When the man's family found out they made No Water give them three ponies."

"I hope he tries sneaking up on me," Crazy Horse raged.

"No," she protested, "I don't want you hurt. I want to go where he can't hurt you."

"Hai! I'm Crazy Horse, woman. I can't be hurt. Arrows and bullets melt in the air around me. No Water would be a fool to attack me."

She put her arms around his hard muscular body and squeezed him tight. "I don't doubt it. Still, let's go somewhere safe."

They rode north toward the hunting grounds of the Hunkpapa. Crazy Horse had heard that these Sioux were rich, that they killed many buffalo and owned many horses. Perhaps he and Buffalo Woman could live with them.

A week later they reached a small Hunkpapa camp on the outskirts of a larger village and explained their situation to the tribe's Big Bellies. The elders questioned them closely. At last they were satisfied that Black Buffalo Woman had properly divorced No Water, doing the right thing by leaving the child with the man's relatives. They invited them to stay. They had heard about Crazy Horse. Having a warrior of such bravery with them would bring honor to their band.

With apologies for its location on the edge of the camp rather than in the center, the Hunkpapa gave them a tepee. This would serve as their lodge until Black Buffalo Woman could make them one.

"It isn't so bad." Black Buffalo Woman looked about the tepee when the elders had finally left them alone. "Of course it's not up to Pretty Owl's standards, but I'll soon have it looking like home."

Crazy Horse laughed and pulled her down beside him. "The most important thing in a home is love." He pushed her back against the buffalo robe.

When Black Buffalo Woman woke, dawn sunlight was already filtering through the walls. She lay drowsily listening to Crazy Horse's breathing and the sounds of the waking camp. Women laughed and talked as they prepared the morning meal. A child cried, which brought a tear to her eye as she thought of her own left behind. A dog barked excitedly.

She heard someone approaching the tent and stirred guiltily, knowing she should have lit the cookfire by now. Before she could rise the tent flap jerked open and a figure loomed over her.

"No Water!" She screamed and rolled away from the pistol she saw leveled at her. It went off and she saw Crazy Horse stagger to his feet, blood gushing from his face.

No Water stood there grinning inanely. Buffalo Woman threw herself on him, pounding his chest with her fists. Let him use the pistol on her! Crazy Horse was hurt. She didn't want to live without him. Maybe No Water would kill her too.

He did turn the pistol on her, but it only clicked like a cricket when he pulled the trigger. No Water dropped it.

The sound of the shot had brought men from the lodges nearby. They seized No Water but he wriggled out of their grasp and ran out of the camp before anyone could block his way.

Black Buffalo Woman knelt beside Crazy Horse. His head was covered with blood. She tried to staunch it with a buffalo robe. It seemed his strong heart was pushing his life through her fingers.

She felt herself roughly pulled away and struggled to get back to Crazy Horse, who moaned and thrashed. Over him knelt the village shaman, stuffing into the terrible wound what looked like dried sage and sweet grass.

"No, no," Buffalo Woman cried, "let me help him!" But they wouldn't let go of her.

"Let Karat see what he can do," someone said kindly. Finally exhausted, she stopped struggling.

That night they told her. With such a wound no power was likely to save him, although three shamans were trying. He might linger for days, for they had stopped the bleeding, but the bullet had entered the right side of his head and torn away much of his upper jaw. No man could live with such a wound.

She began to grieve then, and of course none of them could help her. She sat by Crazy Horse's side and cried until everyone in the camp thought there could be no more water in her body. Still she cried, as if the only proper end to such grief was her own dissolution in tears.

A runner was sent to her uncle and a few days later Red Cloud and a dozen of his band arrived.

"It's all your fault!" Black Buffalo Woman screamed at him. Her voice was like the screech of an eagle furious over an attack on her nest. "You gave me away. It wasn't right. It never was right."

Red Cloud was ashamed. He tried to quiet her but she was beyond quieting. After another outburst she fell into a crying spell that lasted the rest of the day. The men who had come with Red Cloud tried to carry her away, for Red Cloud wanted to take her back to the Bad Face camp, but she resisted.

"No, no," she shouted. "If you take me away I'll kill you! I'll kill myself! He's my husband!"

"I may have made a mistake," Red Cloud told the warriors who had come with him. "We'll wait."

He visited with the Hunkpapa for another week. He even went north for two days to talk to Sitting Bull, who made him welcome and gave a feast in his honor. They spoke about the buffalo herds, how the last two years' hunts had gone and whether the white devils should be allowed to take more land. Red Cloud learned that the Hunkpapa had seen relatively few white intrusions, which Sitting Bull attributed to his reputation.

"I have many powerful warriors," he said, exuding the power and authority of strong wakan. Red Cloud could see how Sitting Bull, whose name meant "buffalo bull who has come to live with us," had gotten his reputation.

Red Cloud told him about his biggest concern,

keeping the Minneconjou, the Brulé and the Oglala together to resist the whites. Sitting Bull at once saw the problem. "They'll say Wakan-Takan has fled you because Crazy Horse, who headed many of your attacks, has been wounded."

"Yes. Worse still, his father, his uncles and his Kit Fox brothers will want revenge. They'll go after No Water, and if they can't find him they'll go after Black Twin and all their relatives."

"You'll have your hands full with a blood feud. Maybe the No Water's family will make restitution if not No Water himself. But you don't know if Crazy Horse's people will accept any presents."

"Would you?"

Sitting Bull shook his head. "I would find No Water and kill him if I were Kit Fox. It was done so cowardly."

"Crazy Horse isn't dead yet."

Sitting Bull gave Red Cloud a scornful look. "Don't think like a child or a woman, Red Cloud. No man can live with such a wound. A pity. We heard wonderful things about him. It is a tragedy for all the Sioux."

Chapter 22

For days Crazy Horse lay in a feverish coma. Black Buffalo Woman stayed by his side and nursed him. Six times a day she bathed his wound in water soaked with seven herbs and once a day she applied a clean bandage. The sight of the terrible gaping wound in his jaw frightened and sickened her.

All night for four nights two shamans and a wakan woman sat in the tepee chanting and crooning their songs while Crazy Horse babbled. None of the healers liked this task, for it did a shaman's reputation no good to take hopeless cases, but Black Buffalo Woman had promised them so many ponies from her uncle's herd that they could not refuse.

Something worked. By the time Red Cloud returned from his visit to Sitting Bull, Crazy Horse had regained a measure of consciousness, although he still could not talk and could barely take soup through a hollow reed.

Red Cloud backed up his niece's promise of four ponies for each of the healers and gave orders to have them delivered from his herds. He and Buffalo Woman stayed in the village for another week. Each day Crazy Horse gained strength, but it still wasn't clear if he would regain his spirit. Perhaps he would be like a child for the rest of his life, or perhaps he would suffer a relapse and die.

In the third week, Red Cloud had a travois made and they prepared for the long, slow trek back to the Bad Face camp. On the way Red Cloud had his niece tell him the whole story and it saddened him. Clearly No Water was in the wrong. A man had every right to take vengeance because of a woman if that woman was his wife, but Black Buffalo Woman had done enough to show No Water that she no longer considered herself his wife. That should have ended the matter. If compensation could not be arranged, Red Cloud would have to raid the Brulé camp of Black Twin and No Water. It was just this sort of feud over a woman, when Red Cloud had helped Old Smoke kill Bull Bear for stealing a wife, that had separated the Bad Faces from the Brulé twenty-five years ago. This time the consequences cut deeper. Not only would it delay the struggle against the whites, but a feud among the Sioux might wreck their chances of winning it.

But Red Cloud had hardly reached home when a messenger from Black Twin arrived with a conciliatory message. No Water realized that he had done wrong. Black Twin regretted his brother's mistake. Would the gift of a number of horses make up for No Water's rash behavior?

With relief Red Cloud sent back word that some horses would go a long way to heal the hearts that could not be healed—provided there were enough of them. How many did Black Twin have in mind? Even in the midst of his own grief—for Red Cloud felt that

299

all this trouble was the result of his own ambitions for a unified Sioux nation—he didn't forget how much better it was to get the other side to name a figure first.

A week later a messenger returned from the Brulé camp with the answer that Black Twin would send over eighteen war ponies. By now he had heard that Crazy Horse was still alive and inquired if he would regain his former strength.

Red Cloud replied that twenty-two ponies would be acceptable and that it wasn't clear whether Crazy Horse would recover completely, although recently he had made much progress.

When it rained it sometimes seemed as if a river was falling out of the sky. The guards at Fort Kearny had taken shelter from just such a downpour when they heard someone pounding at the gates.

Cursing, sliding through the ankle-deep mud, they opened the little door in the gate to admit Big Mouth. He told them he wanted to see General Connor.

"See old One Arm?" incredulously asked a guard named Grimes. "He don't want to see no mangy Injun like you."

"He wants to see me," Big Mouth assured them.

"Aw, shit, Big Mouth," Grimes said, "you drag me out in all this rain to get my ass kicked? Go on back to your wigwam."

"No, no, you tell him," Big Mouth insisted.

The guard turned to his buddy. "What do you think, Sam?"

"What does he want to see you about?" Sam asked.

"Must tell only him."

"You don't tell us, you don't see him," Grimes drawled.

But Big Mouth would neither tell them nor leave, so finally they passed the word up to the officer of the day and to their surprise were ordered to get Big Mouth over to the general's office at once.

The three set out through the rain and mud across the parade ground.

"He's going to have you shot and he's in a hurry to get it done," Sam shouted at Big Mouth, who didn't think the joke was funny. He didn't like being here at the general's mercy. One Arm reminded him of a crazy chief he had once known who had little fighting ability but who was so unpredictable that you never knew whom or how hard he would strike. That instilled so much fear in those around him that it always got him what he wanted.

The two dripping guards followed Big Mouth into Connor's office. The general glared at them. "What the hell are you two doing in here?"

"Escorting the prisoner, sir."

"Get out of here!" Connor snarled. "No, get this redskin a blanket before he shivers to death. And bring him a glass of rum. Not one of those little thimbles either. A water glass."

"Yes sir!" chorused the guards, which pleased Big Mouth.

Finally he was alone before the fire with the general, two blankets wrapped around him, seated in a chair. The general strode around the room behind him.

"You get her?" Connor asked.

Big Mouth was proud of himself. "Yes sir."

301

"Where is she?"

"Outside, sir."

"Outside? Outside where?"

"Outside the fort, at the bottom of the ravine to the north."

"Jesus, she's liable to drown."

"No sir. Her father's there with her."

"Her father?"

"Yes sir. He wants to get paid."

"What did we say?"

"Three horses and two kegs of rum."

"We didn't!"

"Yes sir, we did."

"What's she like?"

Big Mouth looked enthusiastic. "Very young. Very pretty. Not fat, not skinny. Her mother say she works hard."

"She ever been with braves?"

"Oh, no sir. Her father says his wife has watched and two aunts live with them who watch too."

"If they're lying I'll take my horses back."

"Yes, sir."

"And I'll wring my rum out of their balls."

"Yes sir."

"You tell him that."

"Yes sir."

The general paced while Big Mouth gulped his rum. He wanted to get the drink down while he still had the chance, for any minute the general might tire of his presence and order him out.

"Two horses and a keg of rum." Connor glared at Big Mouth.

"I tell them three, sir, just like you say."

"But these are army horses, big animals, not them

302

little ponies you people are used to," Connor argued. "He'll see the difference."

"I don't know, sir. I can ask him."

"Two horses and two kegs of rum," cried the general. He rubbed his hands. "That's it. Go talk to him."

"Yes sir." Big Mouth raised the glass to his lips to finish off his own rum.

"Now! Get out of here."

Big Mouth stood, dropping the blankets. He was halfway to the door when the general stopped him.

"Wait. Here's what you do. I'll have an ambulance with four horses issued to you. Inside will be the two kegs of rum and a big empty barrel. You'll leave the kegs and two of the horses with the father and put the girl into the barrel and close the lid. You'll bring the barrel here to me. The girl is to keep quiet."

"Quiet?"

"Yes, *quiet,* Big Mouth."

"It is a strange way to bring in a new wife, sir."

Connor took a menacing step toward him. Big Mouth said quickly, "She be quiet, sir."

"Quiet in that closed barrel. Not one word. Quiet in here and quiet in the new room we built for her. Not a word, not a sound, you hear me?"

"Yes sir."

An hour later Big Mouth and the two guards at the gate returned to the general's office struggling with a heavy flour barrel.

"Sir, he says we ain't to look in this here barrel, but I wouldn't trust him." Grimes was eaten by curiosity. Something was going on if he didn't know what it was.

"Get out of here," Connor growled, and the two guards were gone almost before he stopped speaking. Big Mouth, afraid to turn his back on the general, started backing out too, but Connor stopped him.

"Hawkins!" he shouted to the officer on duty outside.

"Sir!"

"Go tell Mrs. Crawford to get her fanny in here."

Big Mouth tried to make himself as small as possible. The general put another two logs on the fire and Big Mouth crept closer to the blaze to warm himself. Soon steam rose from his clothes. He wanted to tell the general that it might be a good idea to open the barrel, that maybe the girl couldn't breathe in there, but he was afraid it might make him angry.

A tight-faced woman with orange-red hair came into the office. Big Mouth looked at her curiously. He recognized the nurse from the hospital and he had heard the white soldiers talking about her and the general. He could see why the general wanted a young Indian wife. This woman looked like a doe antelope that had seen many winters.

"Where is she?" the nurse asked.

The general pointed to the barrel.

"Get her out." The woman looked impatient.

"Get her out," the general ordered Big Mouth. "Selena, lock the door."

When the lid of the barrel was pried up with the poker, they found inside a cowering slip of a girl. Selena Crawford reached down and eased her to her feet. Big Mouth told them her Sioux name.

General One Arm looked annoyed. "What is it in English?" he growled.

"Little Owl."

The girl stood in the barrel and looked around, wonder and fear in her huge black eyes. Her black hair was plastered to her head and her deerskin dress was soaked through. She shivered as she gazed about. Big Mouth knew what she saw, for she had never been inside a white man's house before and he could remember his first time. The roaring fire should but didn't burn the place down. The room didn't feel so safe and cosy as a tepee. It was too large. The tables and chairs were strange. There were cloths on the floor instead of soft buffalo robes. Mysterious white skins with black marks hung on the walls.

When Selena reached for her the girl drew back in terror.

"Tell her I'm not going to hurt her," Selena told Big Mouth. He spoke to the girl in Sioux and she relaxed slightly. The nurse went on, "Tell her that I want to help her out of this barrel, warm her and dry her off and get her some dry clothes."

Again Big Mouth translated, adding that the girl was very lucky to be marrying such an important man and to stop acting like a three-year-old.

Out of the barrel and by the hot fire, the girl relaxed a little more, although obviously she was still frightened. Selena gave her a small glass of rum and had to coax her to drink it.

"Tell her to take off those wet clothes," the general leered.

"Not now," Selena objected.

"Now. I bought her; I want to see what I'm getting."

"With him here?" Selena glanced at Big Mouth.

"Who else is going to tell her what to do?"

Under Big Mouth's repeated instructions, Little

Owl reluctantly untied her dress but didn't remove it. She spoke softly to Big Mouth.

"She says she would offend you if she took it off," he translated.

"Goddamnit, take it off!" shouted One Arm. He stepped forward and jerked the garment free.

He revealed a thin child's body, breasts barely begun and hips no bigger than a boy's. The girl spread her hands over her and tried to block their vision with her elbows.

"Tell her to turn around." The general licked his lips. Slowly the naked girl turned. "I think she'll do fine. What do you think, Selena?"

"You're a better judge than I am, sir. It's you she has to please. Now if you're finished surveying the merchandise I think I should get her dressed, fed and into bed with maybe a couple more tots of rum before she comes down with pneumonia."

"Bah!" the general sneered. "She lives in the wilderness. A little rain is what she thrives on."

Selena looked at Big Mouth, who was following all this intently. "He does understand he's to keep quiet about this?"

"Don't worry, he's going to keep his mouth shut, ain't you, Big Mouth?" asked the general.

But the nurse was still looking at him. "I hope so. I can't help wondering where Chief Big Mouth got his name."

"With me his name's No Mouth, ain't it, No Mouth?"

"Yes sir."

At that point the girl began to speak rapidly in Sioux.

"What does she want?" asked One Arm.

"She says she hopes to make you a good wife," translated Big Mouth, "that she will do a better job if you allow her to dress."

The girl said something more. "She want to know if this is the fire she will use for cooking and where the meat is kept, and can she get some buffalo robes for the floor, for a person will get cold and dirty sitting there without them."

Connor grinned. "She ain't gonna be exactly that kind of wife. Tell her that she won't have to cook or wash kettles or haul wood."

Big Mouth told the girl this and she answered him. "She wants to know what she's to do then. A wife must take care of her husband's lodge."

"This isn't that kind of house," Selena put in. "The general here has many soldiers to cook and clean for him."

The girl answered that such a great chief needed many gifts to pass out, and that she would begin tomorrow to make parfleches, leggings, moccasins, shirts and headdresses.

"Stop all this," interrupted the general. "Selena, you tell her what I expect of her. Big Mouth, you translate good, hear me?"

"Yes sir."

"And remember, some of the things that white people do with their wives might not be what the Injun would do," One Arm went on.

"Yes sir."

"I hope not," Selena sniffed.

The general turned and glared at her. "You forgetting that one word from me could get your thievin' husband court-martialed and kicked out of the army?"

She flinched. For a moment hate flared in her green eyes, then died.

"Why don't I go get this girl some dry clothes? When I get back, Big Mouth and I can explain to her what her duties will be."

With that she turned and walked out of the room. The general watched her go, his face sour.

Chapter 23

When Old Hump examined Crazy Horse on his return
to Red Cloud's camp, he shook his head in sorrow
over his friend's son. "This boy will never do battle
again. He is lost to the Sioux."

"Hump, will you sing over him?" asked Old
Crazy Horse.

"Look, my friend," said Old Hump, "just look
at that wound. It would be a waste of your ponies to
give them to me."

Old Crazy Horse hired Hump anyway, deciding
that it was worth two ponies to make sure his son had
the best attention, as he didn't trust the wakan of the
Hunkpapa tribe. While Old Hump sang and danced
over Crazy Horse, Black Buffalo Woman continued
to nurse him.

From the beginning, she and Senla, Crazy Horse's
first wife, were in conflict. Black Buffalo Woman
had been through too much to allow this girl from a
not-so-powerful family to get in her way. After three
days of arguing, Buffalo Woman established that she
was Crazy Horse's first wife and that if Senla wanted

to stay around as his second wife, with Buffalo Woman giving the orders, that was her business. Obviously Crazy Horse hadn't ridden off and risked death over Senla, so that it ought to be clear even to her whom Crazy Horse preferred.

"But listen, Senla," Buffalo Woman proposed. "That's his child you're carrying. I can love it as much as mine. We can get along, or we can fight, or you can leave. It's up to you."

The girl thought that over for a full day. Then she returned her answer. "You're right. I knew when I married him that he had you in his heart. I thought I could make him care for me. I accept you. Let us be sisters."

Black Buffalo Woman pulled her into her arms and gave her a hug. "Hai, we must get him well. At best we're not likely to have much of a man to provide for us."

So the two set about nursing him. They changed the hot compresses covering the gaping wound many times a day. They went to the most powerful shamans for their best herbs and medicines to combat infection, heal head wounds and drive away bullet sickness. By the time they finished paying for all this Red Cloud's herd was down another dozen ponies, but he said nothing. As Pretty Owl had repeatedly told him, he had brought this all on himself by being too concerned with his own affairs and not listening to how strongly Black Buffalo Woman had wanted to marry Crazy Horse in the first place.

"He's getting better," Old Hump told Buffalo Woman one morning as he examined Crazy Horse. "You're giving him excellent care."

310

"He knows I'm here. He wants to live with me. He's fighting."

"Yes, something wakan is at work," the old man agreed. "He is a great warrior. Maybe Wakan-Takan still has something special for him to do."

As would happen half a dozen times over the summer, Red Cloud's Bad Face camp packed up and moved, putting the infants, the wounded and the elderly on travois and pulling them to the next site. They followed the buffalo herds and camped where they could find grass for their ponies, wood for their fires and shelter against attacks.

A dozen camps gathered to hold a Sun Dance in July. Again during the dance Wakan-Takan confirmed the rightness of keeping the whites off the road and away from the buffalo grounds. As the tribes moved across the plains they attacked any white travelers they came across and any soldiers who strayed outside the fort in small enough numbers.

This eventually forced the white soldiers to come out in larger and larger groups until General Connor was sending as many as forty men at a time out on patrol, fifty or more to rescue a wagon train the Sioux had pinned down.

Traffic on the Bozeman that summer dropped to only one wagon train every three or four days. Only two years before, fifty thousand travelers a year had used the road.

The Sun Dance had brought together many bands of the Black Hills, but they couldn't stay together too long, for their four thousand ponies rapidly ate all the grass for miles around and their campfires consumed every stick of firewood. The tribes moved out, keeping on the move to find grass, wood and buffalo. Where they found many fruits and berries they stopped to pick them; whenever a buffalo herd was sighted they organized a hunt. If weeks went by without sighting buffalo and a lodge's food supply ran low, a family hunting party would leave the main body of travelers to forage the surrounding countryside for game.

The Moon of Ripe Juneberries moved into Cherry Ripening Moon and into midsummer, the Moon of Ripe Plums. The women had gathered strawberries, plums, cherries, squash and cabbage. As the men came back from the hunt with bison and deer, the women ground up the vegetables and meat and pounded them into pemmican. This they stored in parfleches in layers protected by animal fat.

Red Cloud attended many council meetings at which he urged the other chiefs to continue to attack the road and the soldiers, though all the tribes were being bombarded with messages from the peace commission to come to Laramie, touch the pen to the treaty and receive many gifts. Red Cloud found his task increasingly difficult. Old Man Afraid, who last year had been Red Cloud's staunchest ally, this year considered that the whites had been taught their lesson. He argued that they should go in, make the best possible bargain and sign the treaty.

Spotted Tail, who had already signed, urged the same thing. He warned that it was only because the policy of the whites at this time was to treat the Indian with some restraint that the army chiefs did not pour troops into the villages and wipe them out.

"I will come in and touch the pen," Red Cloud announced in council a few weeks after the Sun Dance.

A surprised murmur rose from the assembled chiefs.

"This is such a change," Spotted Tail marveled. "You'll sign a treaty saying that you won't fight the whites?"

"Yes, but only when the forts come down."

"The forts!" exclaimed Spotted Tail. "What forts?"

"The three in Powder River country."

"But the whites won't pull down those forts."

Red Cloud shrugged. "That is when I'll come in and touch the pen."

The council of twenty chiefs didn't stare at Red Cloud; that would have been impolite. His announcement gave them much to think about, though. The whites abandon the forts! What an idea! Who had ever heard of such a thing? Was it possible?

"But they won't leave," Spotted Tail predicted. "I've never heard of their doing that, not in all the time I lived with them at Fort Leavenworth."

"Nevertheless, if they want me to touch the pen that's my price."

"It's only going to anger them, telling them that sort of thing," said Spotted Tail. "You're going to make it harder for every Sioux to deal with these people."

"Haven't I made it much more dangerous for the whites to use the road since they built the forts?" asked Red Cloud. A number of the men looked up.

"Yes, but—"

"Well, if they want the road to be safer, they must remove the forts. We'll go back to the old way."

It seemed logical. To Spotted Tail's obvious annoyance, some of the chiefs began to chuckle quietly. After another week's argument, Red Cloud's suggestion was established as the position of half the council over the protests of Spotted Tail, Black Twin and Old-Man-Afraid-of-His-Horses, who declared for the treaty.

It was three weeks later that a messenger brought Red Cloud's latest demand to Fort Kearny.

Connor roared when he heard it. "Think I'm going to have some half-assed savage make a monkey out of me?"

But the peace commissioner, Nathaniel Taylor, was overjoyed. "Don't you see?" he told the new Indian agent. "Red Cloud's talking to us at last."

"Yes, but look what he's saying."

"Oh, nonsense!" exclaimed Taylor. "Never mind what he's saying. He's saying he wants fifty dollars, and we're saying we will pay two. Now all we have to do is sit down and work out an agreement."

The Indian agent looked doubtful. "Suppose he doesn't see it that way? Suppose he means what he says?"

"He's just beginning the bargaining process," insisted Taylor. "I know these people. I've dealt with them for two years now. They take their time. This is the beginning of the end, I tell you. It may take a month, two months, maybe even six, but Red Cloud's sick of this whole mess just as we are, and he wants to settle it."

Taylor composed a reply to the latest message from the Bad Face war chief that told in detail what ground-clearing equipment, seeds and so on would be supplied to the Sioux at the signing of the treaty. He managed to catch John Richards on one of his supply trips and asked him to translate it.

"Yeah, I'll do it," Richards said when Taylor

showed him the message. "But it's the biggest damn fool thing I ever saw."

Taylor pulled back, shocked. "Why, sir?"

"The Sioux aren't interested in farming."

"But this will solve their problems! They'll be able to feed themselves without hunting."

Richards sighed. "You know, Reverend, you don't know the first thing about the red man."

"Don't start that again, Mr. Richards," snapped Taylor. "I've been out here eighteen months now, and I'm sick and tired of being told I know nothing about the Indian. I'm offering them plows and planters and all the seeds they want. Cattle and horses even, virtually everything they need to get started farming."

"It's an insult to them."

"Insult!"

"You married, Reverend?"

"Yes. What's that got to do with this?"

"Where's your wife?"

"Back in New York."

"When you're home, do you do the dishes?"

"We're fortunate enough to have help."

"All right, who does them?"

"The help, the domestic."

"And you have children."

"Why?"

"Answer, please."

"Yes, two girls and a boy."

"You change the diapers?"

"Not very often."

"Your wife does?"

"Yes, she and the help."

"You put up jams, Reverend?"

315

"That's my wife's job."

Richards pressed on, "Maybe you make the fire in the kitchen stove, draw water and sweep the floors?"

"No, no, none of those things is my job," said Taylor impatiently. "I'm the pastor of a large congregation, or I was till I took on this duty."

"And you don't want to do any of those things, am I right?"

"No, they're women's work."

Richards smiled, exhibiting a mouthful of stained and rotting teeth. "Yes, and that's what farming is to the Sioux. Women pick berries and vegetables. Women plant seeds whenever the tribes are in one spot long enough to plant. And women chop firewood and draw water, not men. Men hunt. Men protect the camp. Men raid for horses."

"Well, they'll just have to learn how to farm."

"And what about you, Reverend? Suppose somebody came along and told you you had to learn how to make jam, sweep floors, do laundry, wash dishes and change all the diapers, how'd that make you feel?"

"I'm not in that position."

"But answer me. Suppose somebody told you you had to stop being a preacher and go be a housemaid, how would you feel?"

"But I've years of education! That is a silly analogy."

Richards leaned forward and roared, "What do you think a brave has, if not years of education? His father and the village spend his whole boyhood training him to hunt and fight well. They pound it into him that he'll only be a real man, a Lakota, if he hunts and fights all his life. Now you come along and tell him you want to make a woman out of him, and you don't understand why he doesn't jump at the chance. That's dumb, Reverend, if you don't mind my telling you the truth."

"He'll have to learn that it's just as manly to plant crops as it is to chase animals," Taylor said stubbornly.

"I don't know how anybody's going to make an ignorant savage see anything," replied Richards, "when even an educated preacher is blind as a bat."

As the report of Red Cloud's demand rose through the hierarchy of the United States Army, it produced howls of outrage and the itch to send more troops and weapons to protect the three forts.

But the Bureau of Indian Affairs used the demand to show that it had been the army that had provoked the Indians into attack. It was clear that if the military were curbed the trouble on the Powder River would soon be over.

Neither the Interior Department, the parent of the Bureau of Indian Affairs, nor certainly the War Department ever considered meeting Red Cloud's demand. In fact, no one in authority in either chain of command even suggested taking such action.

Taylor got a few more signatures that summer for the treaty he was promoting. The most important signatory of all was a real coup, Old Man Afraid. By now, however, nobody would believe in any Sioux treaty that didn't contain Red Cloud's signature. While he was damned in the western press, he was lauded in Boston and New York as a far-sighted Indian leader who didn't intend to get kicked around.

John Richards tried again to explain the Sioux position to Nathaniel Taylor. "See, what Red Cloud wants is to go on like he's going. He wants to hunt buffalo, move his camp when the spirits tell him to, have his Sun Dance every July, raid the dumb Crow for horses and trade with me or somebody like me. That's what he wants and that's all he wants, but with whites filling up this country, there ain't much chance he's going to get it. He wants more years of his way of life. His people have had it for God only knows how many hundreds of years."

"The arrival of whites in this country is a fact of history, Mr. Richards," Taylor stated. "I can sympathize with him, but he's got to recognize that he's just run smack into historical necessity."

"That's fine for you to say, for you ain't the one run into it. Red Cloud now, he don't see it as necessary at all, and I can't say as I blame him. After all, how many wagons has the army been able to get through that road this year? What purpose are those three forts serving out there?"

"I'm not a general, Mr. Richards."

"And I'm not a peace commissioner, but it looks to me as if Red Cloud has done himself pretty well."

Taylor's face tightened. "Good for him. But if I were a friend of his, Mr. Richards, I'd tell him he'd be wise to negotiate while he has the strength he has now, because nothing lasts."

The fourth batch of new soldiers that General Connor asked for arrived at Fort Kearny at the end of August. With them came more repeating rifles and breechloading howitzers on wheels. The general kept Captain Ten Eyke and the other officers continually busy on the parade ground and in the woods near the fort training the troops for Indian fighting.

Such training consisted of having the recruits ride their horses directly at other recruits who were waving blankets, shouting and shooting their guns in the air to simulate a Sioux attack. Many of the army horses couldn't be conditioned to attack under these conditions. Those that passed the test had powder charges shot off next to their heads to accustom them to gunfire. The horses were taught to kneel in the thick of battle so the troopers could get behind them or shoot them where they might need battlements. This never proved practical. It was one thing to get a horse to kneel but quite another to keep him there with bullets flying around his head and a soldier leaning over his back and shooting a Henry rifle. Any horse with sense got up and ran. Besides all this, the troopers practiced how to ride hanging off their saddles on the side of the horse away from the enemy, a trick they had often seen the Sioux perform but that no more than half of them could master.

Ten Eyke put in for a transfer again after Cynthia gave birth to a healthy boy, though she had to go through the entire pregnancy and the difficulties of birth without any of the support or help women usually give each other.

Connor, however, seemed to take a perverse delight in finding Ten Eyke indispensable. He made sure the captain understood that Ten Eyke's personal problems were no concern of the general.

"Even a flea can see the dog he's jumping on," was the general's favorite way of putting it. Afterward he would produce a belly laugh that made Ten Eyke want to shoot him.

Opposition to the general's Indian policies didn't

increase Ten Eyke's chance of a transfer either. Connor was firm. "I don't care whether you like 'em or not. You're my best officer and you signed up for a tour of duty. Till it's over you belong to me. Drill those recruits. Patrol. Keep this fort safe and make sure C.F. Smith and Reno aren't taken over by redskins either."

The Indians' hit-run attacks on the few civilian wagon trains and the army supply trains continued. Connor lived all that summer in a fury because the Sioux wouldn't give his boys a stand-up fight, as he put it. It was something his often-frustrated troops wanted too. Until they squared off in a knock-down drag-out fight, who could say who was the stronger, the Sioux nation or the United States Army?

Wasn't it important to settle that, damnit?

Chapter 24

Red Cloud told himself that summer that he was winning the war against the whites, but in his heart he wasn't so sure. Actually he was having trouble keeping his forces together. After a successful raid the warriors were in no hurry to fight again. They had shown the whites how brave they were. Now they would go to the mountains and hunt with the guns they had captured.

Even Crazy Horse—whose miraculous recovery over the summer had Old Hump shaking his head and brought shamans from miles around to Red Cloud's camp to look and marvel at the power of so much wakan—even Crazy Horse often chose the hunt over battle these days.

Things went no better for Red Cloud in the tribal councils. The arguments continued. Most of the opposition to his actions still came from Spotted Tail; of all the chiefs he was the most difficult to deal with. Late in August their frequent clashes came to a head.

To rekindle interest among his backsliding warriors and increase the pressure on the white soldiers,

Red Cloud announced that he was preparing to launch two large attacks, one against Fort Kearny and the other against Fort C.F. Smith. Young-Man-Afraid-of-His-Horses would take on C.F. Smith; Red Cloud himself, with Crazy Horse, would lead the raid on Kearny. They would look for a great victory like the one that had driven the Little White Chief from Fort Kearny.

At once Spotted Tail objected. Attacks on the forts would not force the whites out, he insisted; it would only make them angry and bring more troops. "You are dealing with as many whites as a hill has leaves of grass," Spotted Tail warned. "Best that we make our peace with these people. Your warriors have done well. They've showed the whites how we can fight. But if we do not stop they'll kill us all. I've lived among them. I know that they are people like us."

"That's not true," said High Backbone. "They are not like us."

Red Cloud saw that some of the others in council had been disturbed by Spotted Tail's statement. "The whites are not Lakota." It wasn't polite to use the Sioux term in front of the two Cheyenne chiefs, but Red Cloud's anger set him beyond caring. "They are a species of white grub, the kind you find when you dig into an anthill."

A murmur of laughter encouraged Red Cloud. "If we listened to you," he told Spotted Tail, "we'd ask them to take care of us like children and forget that we are Lakota."

Spotted Tail sighed, his whole attitude that of a father dealing with a stubborn child. This infuriated Red Cloud.

322

"My friends, I was sent to Fort Leavenworth to die. Instead of hanging me, the whites found it interesting to talk to me. I found them interesting as well. . . ."

Red Cloud listened impatiently to the old familiar story. Spotted Tail was like an old man no longer able to hunt or do battle, forever reliving the past.

". . . I do not believe we can win against the whites."

A stony silence greeted this assertion. Red Cloud held his breath. How could Spotted Tail take such a stupid position? Hadn't they all but closed the road?

"I think that while we are still strong, before we are weakened by attacks the way our friends the Cheyenne and the Arapaho were, we should make our peace with these people," Spotted Tail went on. "Many of us see this as a challenge to our way of life, perhaps our greatest challenge, but it is not the end. The problem is that there are too many whites for their leaders to control. They will come here from the East as they fill the land there, like water pouring out of an overflowing cup. They will force us off our hunting grounds unless we now make peace with the strongest tribe, which they call the government. I have spoken."

Red Cloud didn't come right out and call Spotted Tail a woman, but the suggestion was there. "Spotted Tail wishes to die safe in his tepee."

Spotted Tail responded with a hot speech in which he pointed out that he had hunted with every man present and that except for Red Cloud, he had more coups than any other chief there. Did a woman count coups? He led the Brulé and he must do what was right for his people, which was to take the whites' latest offer and move to the upper Missouri. This, the whites promised, would be theirs as long as the grass grew on the hillsides.

Spotted Tail's position provoked a week's discussion in the Sioux council. Most of the chiefs opposed such a move, but Spotted Tail remained firm.

That week Red Cloud listened to Spotted Tail's words more than ever before. At times he found himself almost believing the impossible claims Spotted Tail made for the whites: houses that moved on logs as fast as birds, canoes as tall as trees, branches that could bring the image of a man from a mile away to within a hundred yards, guns that shot three miles. Certainly the whites had much wakan. Any creature who could make a gun must have that. But was it good wakan or bad?

While these discussions among the chiefs continued Red Cloud sought to create as much interest as possible among his followers in the two raids he had proposed. He paid more ponies to have not the usual two or three shamans but six at each attack site. He had them arrange not one but three days of ceremonies to make sure of the best auguries. No sooner did a noted warrior or band declare its intention of joining him than Red Cloud sent heralds to the surrounding camps to announce it. This brought in more celebrated warriors.

Finally, with warriors from all over the Powder River country arriving daily, Red Cloud addressed the assembled chiefs again and presented the details of his plan.

"I have listened to Spotted Tail talk of the whites. He knows much of their ways, but I have learned much too. I have learned that if they don't gather hay, bring in wood and haul water from the river, they can't survive the winter. What we're going to do is destroy those who gather the hay and cut the wood. This will force the others to abandon the forts and leave the Powder River."

Red Cloud knew no more than a tenth of all the warriors on the expedition really understood his reasoning, but every one of them was excited about being in on a glorious attack.

A week later the two forces set out, one to Fort Kearny, the other to Fort C.F. Smith.

Crazy Horse was elated. Black Buffalo Woman was expecting a baby, and this would be his first big raid since No Water had wounded him. Taking Young Hump and Dog Leg with him, he had spent the last ten days studying Fort Kearny, trying to understand more of the enemy's ways. Red Cloud's idea was a good one. The whites built their lodges out of logs and used logs for fuel. If they couldn't get out of the fort and didn't have trees to cut inside, what would they use to keep from freezing to death?

During this scouting trip Crazy Horse with difficulty kept scattered bands of braves from attacking the woodcutters outside the fort. He saw that after many weeks of no attacks the whites began to spend the night at their base camp rather than travel the eight miles to and from Fort Kearny. Crazy Horse discovered that the cutters actually had two camps: one on Piney Island in the north fork of Piney Creek and another on a small plateau on the mainland overlooking the river. From this camp they had a good view of the surrounding countryside and it served them as

325

a jumping-off place for parties going deeper into the forest to cut wood. Around this main camp the whites had placed the wagon boxes in a circle to contain the mules in a makeshift corral. When the time came, Crazy Horse thought, it would be easy to overrun this little camp despite its elevated position.

Red Cloud had gathered six hundred warriors in a draw some ten miles to the rear of the wagon-box camp. Messengers were sent to Crazy Horse for information and Red Cloud himself slipped up to the scouts' position to study the camp.

"How many are there?" he asked Crazy Horse.

The side of Crazy Horse's face was still swollen and red, but the young Lakota seemed to have recovered his full strength and cunning. There was still some animosity between the two men because of Black Buffalo Woman's marriage to No Water, but they needed each other to drive out the whites so they put their personal feelings aside.

"Maybe thirty," said Crazy Horse, "no more than forty."

"It should be easy."

"We'll overrun them with the first pass."

"Let's attack in two days."

"I'd prefer to wait," Crazy Horse demurred. "The longer we wait, the more careless they'll be about watching for us."

"I can't hold these warriors together long without something to attack. They're restless now, beginning to scrap among themselves."

"We may lose more men by attacking too early."

Red Cloud sighed and nodded. "But if we wait too long we won't have any warriors left to attack with. Half of them will go off deer hunting or over to Black Twin's to race horses or some other fool things. Besides, Young Man Afraid will attack at C.F. Smith any day. Once word of that reaches here they'll be on their guard."

"Two days, then. Not one of them will escape." Crazy Horse turned and stared down at the hated camp.

At dawn on the chosen day, Crazy Horse watched two men on horseback come from the direction of the fort past the woodcutters' camp. They carried rifles across their saddles as if they were going hunting. Behind Crazy Horse, spread out on the other side of the hill, lay just over four hundred fifty warriors in attack groups.

Beside Crazy Horse were Young Hump and their Kit Fox brothers. Nearby was Dog Leg, who served as Crazy Horse's personal messenger.

"Let's take them," whispered Young Hump, watching the two men. "We can sneak up on them when they go around that second hill."

"No." Much of Crazy Horse's leadership lay in resisting such temptations. "It'll make too much noise. Let them move more men away from the protection of the camp."

They watched the two men pass by. Shortly thereafter the camp awoke and a party of ten woodcutters in two wagons drove off to the east.

"How many?" asked Hump.

"More today. Ten just left and it looks like there are about thirty-five in the camp."

"We shouldn't have much trouble."

"It depends on how good they are with those rifles, and how brave."

From behind them they heard a long whoop and holler. At once Crazy Horse knew what it meant. One or more of the braves, seeing the two whites on horseback and unable to restrain themselves, had disobeyed orders and attacked before the signal.

From around the hill galloped the two whites, followed by seven warriors on foot. The men lit out for the fort. An arrow hit one of the horses in the rump and a man took an arrow in his back. They cut across the meadow to the right of the camp, but they were no more than halfway across it when a handful of warriors rose from behind the hills to cut them off from the fort. They veered toward the left and rode into the wagon-box camp, yelling as they came in.

Crazy Horse gave the signal for the general attack and Red Cloud confirmed it. Some of the warriors went for the two wagons that had left earlier and others attacked the camp. As agreed, Red Cloud stayed back with half the warriors so the ponies and men would be fresh, although it wasn't easy restraining them.

As planned, the group led by Young Hump went directly for the mules in the corral while Crazy Horse led a large party toward where the men in the camp lived.

Young Hump's forty or so foot warriors were driven back by a strong volley of shots. Alarmed by their retreat, Red Cloud, who sat his horse on a hill overlooking the scene, sent word to Blue Chest to drive off the mules so the whites could not use them to escape.

As Blue Chest rode into battle every warrior watching saw how powerful his wakan was. The very air around him was so dark with it that it shimmered like the heat rising off a pond in summer and spread back over the Lakota who galloped behind him.

Into the circle of wagon boxes rode Blue Chest's thirty warriors. The guns of the whites were powerless against such wakan, which melted the bullets before they hit. Blue Chest and his men drove off all seventy mules. The whites were trapped, Red Cloud noted with satisfaction. Now they would be taught a lesson.

The ten whites on the two wagons had turned them and struggled to get back to the corral, but Crazy Horse and the Kit Foxes managed to wound a mule in one rig and two in the other, and the wagons were stopped. The men jumped out and ran back toward the base camp, half a mile away. On their first pass Crazy Horse and the Kit Foxes killed two of them, but on their second they were met by a new strategy. Two men knelt while the rest kept running toward the camp. The two left behind fired steadily at the pursuers, who had to swerve not to be killed. As it was, three Kit Fox horses fell, spilling their riders. One of them, Lone Beaver, was shot in the head.

When the other woodcutters reached a spot a hundred yards off, the two left behind sprang to their feet and ran to join them. Now two other men formed a new rear guard. This maneuver proved so successful that the whites lost just one more man. The other seven reached the camp safely.

Angered by the loss of Lone Beaver, the Kit Foxes counted coups on the three dead whites amid a hail of bullets from the base camp even though a coup on a white didn't count for much.

The surviving whites gathered in the corral made

of wagon boxes. The Sioux, led by Crazy Horse and Red Cloud, made pass after pass at the flimsy fortification. A well-driven arrow shot from twenty feet away went almost through a box.

Over the next two hours Crazy Horse led charge after charge. His personal wakan proved strong enough to protect him but not those beside him. Each charge met withering fire. Worse still, assuming that the whites would have to pause to reload, Crazy Horse led in a wave of warriors only to have them cut down; the firing continued as if the whites had an unlimited supply of muskets at hand.

For the first time they left dead and wounded behind them as they withdrew out of range, which distressed them all. They went back to rescue them, galloping up in pairs and grabbing a fallen man by the arms, carrying him off between them to safety. When the whites saw what they were doing, they killed every fallen Sioux.

By midmorning Red Cloud knew he had lost at least two dozen men. Neither he nor any of the other chiefs could understand why the enemy's wakan was so strong this morning. It made the whites brave, and that made it easier for them to shoot down the Lakota as they attacked.

An extra difficulty was that the white camp was surrounded by level ground that offered no cover for the attackers. But on the north side of the corral where the plateau dropped off into the river was an overhang. Red Cloud had Young Hump and the few warriors with guns take up a position there and fire at the whites. They were no more than seventy-five yards from the corral, and to Red Cloud's satisfaction, their steady fire dropped four of the whites.

He sent word to Crazy Horse that the maneuver was working and suggested that he hold off his frontal attacks to give Young Hump's group more time. Blue Chest didn't receive this suggestion, or if he did he ignored it. He regrouped his warriors and they rode down on the corral, each brave with five arrows in his left hand. In a fast pass they fired every one of those arrows into the corral.

From where he sat on his war pony, Red Cloud saw that the arrows did little harm, for the whites shielded themselves in the hollow of the wagon boxes, but Blue Horse lost five men. Every fallen warrior was the object of intense fire from the whites, so rescue of the dead and wounded was foolhardy, though half a dozen youths were ready to try.

Red Cloud ordered fire arrows shot into the corral, but all these did was set piles of mule manure next to the corral burning. Still, this produced a thick black smoke that Red Cloud hoped would make defense still harder for the whites.

Suddenly three whites broke from the corral and headed toward the camp where the men slept and ate. Shouting orders, Crazy Horse advanced on the three. A fourth man joined them, and the whites still inside the corral fired at any Lakota who dared move to stop the four.

Young Hump and his people began to fire from the overhang. Now Red Cloud saw what the men had gone after. Water! They were struggling with two large kettles. Thanks to young Hump's marksmen, one of the kettles had sprung a leak.

Red Cloud would wait. Time was on his side. The men in the corral couldn't leave. Sooner or later their food and this last kettle of water would give out. If the horse soldiers at the fort didn't suspect these men were in trouble, by nightfall he and Crazy Horse would have wiped the earth with them. But why had Wakan-Takan allowed so many brave warriors to be killed? Red Cloud pushed the worry away. To justify such a loss they must crush the whites in this corral, but how?

He sent messengers to Crazy Horse, Blue Chest, Young Hump, Chief High Backbone and Red Leaf. As the sun climbed toward its zenith the six debated the problem. They had battled now for half a day against a handful of white men and hadn't dented their defenses. No matter how the day turned out it would not be a victory.

"We need something new," suggested Crazy Horse. "Something to surprise them."

The others turned to look at the corral far below. Its circle of grey wagon boxes was surrounded by the brown- and wheat-colored plateau. At some distance from the corral, out of reach of its defenders, warriors stood shouting and occasionally loosing an arrow that fell yards short. Across the face of the plateau the rains had cut a defile that ran into the valley to the side. With rising excitement, Crazy Horse saw that this defile ran close to the corral. He might be able to use it as cover to reach the corral.

He described his plan to the others. Red Cloud asked, "How many warriors do you need?"

"It's dangerous," warned High Backbone. "If they don't capture the corral, many will be shot."

That brought silence. Crazy Horse knew the chief was right. He could not lead just anybody up that defile.

"I'll take the Kit Foxes." He repeated part of the war society's chant: "A Kit Fox is ready to die."

No one said a word, but they all looked down at the plain again. From that vantage point the risk was plain to see. The attackers' only advantage would be surprise. Once the whites spotted them they would rush to that side of the corral and lace them with rifle fire. Searching like a hornet, each bullet would come buzzing in to sting to death its target.

Crazy Horse looked at the men around him and saw many eyes clouded with fear.

"You're Kit Fox Lakota!" he barked. "What is death?" He laughed wildly. "It's all that can happen to you, and it's going to happen to you anyway someday! Hai!"

With that he turned and shouted to Dog Leg to assemble the Kit Foxes.

"On the other side of the wagon boxes," Red Cloud asked Blue Chest, "can you come in with horses as Crazy Horse comes up out of the defile? It'll divide the whites' fire."

Blue Chest saw the cleverness of this plan and left to brief his warriors.

Crazy Horse gathered forty Kit Foxes and several other braves. Blue Horse assembled his horse soldiers and began the ride around the edge of the battle area to get into position.

Red Cloud and the other three chiefs stayed on the hill. From there they saw Crazy Horse and his men creep down by the river and up into the defile. When they reached the spot closest to the corral the forty Foxes stripped to loincloths for greater freedom.

Crazy Horse softly chanted a Fox song, then put three cartridges for his single-shot rifle into his mouth, where he could get at them quickly. Around him he heard his Fox brothers chanting their death songs.

Dog Leg had persuaded Crazy Horse to allow him to be in on an attack. The youth moved with the calm precision of a warrior twice his years.

"Hai, little brother," said Crazy Horse. "Is the badger with you?"

"I'm full of wakan." Dog Leg's eyes shone and Crazy Horse knew that even if this little Fox brother should die today, he would have known what it was like to be a real man, a true Lakota.

"It's a good day to die." Crazy Horse chanted the old refrain and held out his hands palms up.

Dog Leg put his hands in them and responded, "Yes, it's a good day to die."

His men were ready. Crazy Horse looked up to where Red Cloud watched, a speck in the distance, and raised his hands twice in the agreed signal. Red Cloud signaled that Blue Chest was also ready.

"Hai!" Crazy Horse shouted. He charged up and out of the defile.

As he came over the top, Crazy Horse felt a moment of panic. What was he doing? These people had killed more than two dozen Sioux already that morning. The image of Black Buffalo Woman's swollen belly flashed before his eyes. The thought that he might never see their child made him want to dive back into the safety of the defile. But as he turned his head he saw his Kit brothers scrambling all along the length of the gully, screeching as they rushed forward in a long line. With a pang of remorse Crazy Horse looked back at the corral. He zigzagged toward it, outdistancing the others and reestablishing himself as their leader. They were halfway across the open area before the startled whites began to fire at them. They were twenty feet away when the first of the Kit Foxes fell. Crazy Horse turned his head to the left. The ragged look of the line shocked him. He glanced back and saw at least a dozen bodies sprawled on the ground. A dozen down! Even when wounded a Kit Fox would attack. It could only mean that they were dead or had taken too many bullets to get up again. A blow like a bear's swipe spun Crazy Horse even farther around, so that suddenly he realized he was running sideways to the corral. He turned back. More of his men were falling and no one was nearer to the corral than ten feet.

"Back! Back!" someone shouted. "They'll kill us all!"

Half of the warriors nearest the corral turned and retreated. Several stopped to pick up fallen comrades and ran back with them, weaving to avoid the volleys that filled the air around them.

Back? No! No Kit Fox ran back! Who had ordered that?

"No! Attack!" Crazy Horse turned to wave his men on toward the corral when another bear swipe got him, this time in his thigh, and knocked him to the ground. He struggled to pick himself up again and fell over.

Something strange happened then, something that had never before happened to Crazy Horse. He felt a blow in his chest like a hawk striking him in full flight. Then, as if he were a rabbit, the hawk picked him up and carried him off. He soon reached the height of several trees, from which vantage point he could see the entire battlefield.

His vision had become that of a hawk. He could see everything in great detail. Below him he saw Dog Leg carrying his own lifeless body away from the corral. From his hawk's height Crazy Horse strug-

335

gled to order Dog Leg to return him to the battle so he could continue the fight. But while he had a hawk's vision, Crazy Horse seemed to have no tongue.

In mute horror he saw three of the soldiers in the corral carefully aim their long-barreled rifles at Dog Leg's back. Suddenly Crazy Horse realized that he had broad wings with long talons that could reach the ground. With these he struggled to keep the soldiers' bullets from hitting Dog Leg. He saw that his frantic efforts were moderately successful, but with these long spider-like fingers that he wasn't used to handling, he couldn't stop all three riflemen. With a sob and a shout he watched a bullet trace a long lazy path from the end of the cruelest-looking white's gun toward Dog Leg's back. Crazy Horse's long fingers got caught up with themselves as they strove to deflect the bullet; it was impossible. The bullet tore into the middle of Dog Leg's back, crushed the boy's spine and ricocheted into his lungs. Crazy Horse saw the boy fall . . . and then the hawk fell too.

Dog Leg had run almost out of range when the bullet got him. Others ran out and picked up Dog Leg and Crazy Horse and carried them to the safety of the defile.

Red Cloud had seen it all from the hill. The attack plan had been a good one, but the defenders had proved stronger. As Crazy Horse and his men had come up out of the defile, on the opposite side of the corral Blue Chest and his horsemen had shouted and charged across the plain. Watching, Red Cloud had seen Blue Chest sway and clutch his chest. Next to him his Badger Society brother Long Branch had pitched off his horse as both he and his mount went down.

Blue Chest now rode around in circles struggling to stay on his horse. Around the two leaders the twenty horse warriors circled, uncertain what to do. Finally one of the men jumped down and picked up Long Branch. Red Cloud saw that the whites had the range and that the warriors were an easy target. As they pulled Blue Chest and Long Branch onto Blue Chest's horse two more were wounded. The survivors rushed back to safety.

That left Crazy Horse and his Kit Foxes to attack the corral by themselves. The whites rushed across to defend it and thirty rifles fired shot after shot at the attacking warriors. Red Cloud waved for someone on the other side of the corral to attack and draw off some of the withering fire, but no one saw the signal. All but Red Cloud seemed to be watching fascinated as Crazy Horse and his men hurled themselves at bullet-toothed death.

By the time the outgunned Kit Foxes turned to retreat, Red Cloud felt numb. He rushed down from his observation post to where the wounded and dead had been gathered and looked about in horror. In no battle he had ever fought had so many Lakota died. He had pushed his people into this and death had chewed them up like so many beetles in a bear's mouth.

At the bottom of the hill he found Crazy Horse being nursed by a berdache. The warrior had taken three bullets, one in the arm, one in the thigh and one in the buttocks. Beside him lay Dog Leg.

"How is he?" Red Cloud asked the berdache.

"He'll live, but this one's gone."

"Gone," repeated Red Cloud. Gone! This boy who had joked and ridden with them all. He was stunned. How could it have come out like this?

337

A messenger ran up. "Blue Chest is dead. So are two of his men. Long Branch wants to talk to you. He'll be here shortly."

Red Cloud nodded. He wanted to talk to Long Branch and to the rest of the chiefs. Further attacks were senseless. The Sioux had shown the whites that they couldn't cut wood in safety, but at what a price! He would urge the other chiefs to pull back. The battle was over.

Chapter 25

When Connor heard about the wagon-box fight, as the men called it, he was jubilant.

"See, Mr. Ten Eyke?" he gloated, a fresh cigar glowing like a hot coal in his face. "The Indians can push inexperienced emigrants and recruits around, but against well-trained troops they don't have the chance of a snowball in hell."

He cackled and danced a little jig around his office. "We've got them on the run now, Mr. Ten Eyke, we've got them on the run! You can call Red Cloud Chief Red Smear, cause that's all that's going to be left of his red ass when I finish with him!"

"You persuade the contractor of that, sir," Ten Eyke suggested in the dry tone he usually adopted with his superior.

"Of what?"

"He refuses to take his men back out to cut wood. He says they don't have the protection the army promised them. They want to go back to Laramie."

"Back to Laramie! Horseshit! They signed on to cut wood and they're damn well going to cut it."

"Five of them died yesterday, sir," Ten Eyke pointed out. "Mr. Rankin asserts that five deaths don't constitute protection."

"We need wood, Ten Eyke." Connor glared at him. "It's going to get cold pretty quick. Remember how we froze our asses last winter?"

"Yes sir, but we can't make them go out against their will."

"Why not?"

Ten Eyke let it go. Surely not even One Arm Connor expected an answer to that one. He might get away with shoving around the soldiers under his command, but civilian workers and contractors were another story.

For a moment the two glowered at each other.

"Send Rankin to me," said Connor, finally. "He and I are going to have a little head-to-head talk." He pulled at his cigar until the end glowed hotly. "Maybe we can work something out."

Something did seem to get worked out, for while the woodcutters didn't go out for the next three days, Ten Eyke got the impression that Rankin was just resting his men. He wondered what had happened in Connor's office to change the contractor's mind about going back to Laramie.

On the fourth day after the wagon-box fight Ten Eyke was officer of the day. He'd just gone on duty when he looked up to see the long trim form of Colonel John Kirby-Smith, the commander at Fort C.F. Smith, filling the doorway.

"Colonel, sir!" Ten Eyke stood up and saluted.

Kirby-Smith slapped a pair of white gloves into his left hand. "Where's His Majesty, Tenodor? We've got a problem the three of us ought to discuss." Outside the door behind Kirby-Smith lurked Rossner, the sutler and contractor for Fort C.F. Smith.

Ten Eyke was alarmed. A camp commander didn't often leave his garrison. Not only was it against army policy, but it was also dangerous, for the commander was responsible for whatever mischief might occur in his absence. "He's going to blow up when he sees you here," he warned.

"I don't give a goddamn if he court-martials me." Kirby-Smith stood relaxed and confident, but he didn't look happy.

Ten Eyke had been right about Connor. He roared when he heard Kirby-Smith's opening remarks. "You deserted your post and came all the way over here just to tell me you have a problem with your sutler? You left the fort? What's he doing, pissing in the whiskey?"

Ten Eyke, whom Kirby-Smith had asked to attend the meeting, was amused to see that the colonel wasn't daunted by Connor's shouting. "George, cut out the goddamn yelling. Let me talk to you and I'll be right back on my way."

Ten Eyke couldn't remember anyone ever calling Connor anything but General Connor to his face and One Arm behind his back. The poised, tall, effete-looking Kirby-Smith was a thin blade compared to the general's broad saber, but his blunt, self-assured approach seemed to work. Connor settled into his swivel chair and snarled, "All right, Colonel, what's on your mind?"

"I'm undermanned. I've reason to think we're going to be under siege from the Sioux soon and I need reinforcements. Besides, if I don't give my sutler more protection, he says he's going to pack up and take his people back to Laramie."

Connor snorted. "I've heard that before. What happened?"

But Kirby-Smith wasn't to be hurried. First he folded his gloves and tucked them under his belt, then asked Ten Eyke to pour him a whiskey from the general's supply. Finally he began his story.

"Kinny chose the site for C.F. Smith well," he drawled, "and Carrington had it built with his usual thoroughness. The post is almost invulnerable to attack. For Red Cloud to lay siege to it he'd need hundreds of well-disciplined troops, which no Indian commander has. But we do have one weak point."

"Which is?" snapped One Arm.

"Like you, hay for our horses and mules, wood for ourselves. Rather than make the five-mile trip from the fort every day with his mowing machines, Rossner decided to set up camp on the banks of Warrior Creek. I supplied him with a guard of twelve to twenty men, and he's got twenty men cutting wood and twenty mowing hay."

One Arm looked exasperated. "Can't you speed this up?"

"I'm over here now, George. Let me tell it my way." Ten Eyke smothered a grin.

"From the beginning the haycutters have had problems with fires," the colonel went on. "In their way the savages are clever. They wait till Rossner and his men have cut and dried the hay, then ride in with firebrands and pitch arrows and torch it. Makes Rossner furious. He says we're supposed to protect the hay and wants to be paid every time they burn it. We had words about it, but he has a point. Much as I dislike paying for something we don't get, I've allowed his chits."

"Sherman's not going to like that, Johnny."

"I'm well aware of that, George."

"Soldiers are supposed to keep that sort of thing from happening."

"Should they protect the hay or should they patrol, George?" Kirby-Smith demanded. "I've got all of two hundred fifty men, and that means I can only field half at any time."

Connor glowered. "Go on. What the hell got you over here today?"

"We've managed to make friends with the Crow, who have no love for the Sioux. Six weeks ago a Crow came in and told us that the Sioux were having a big council about how to destroy all the forts on the Bozeman Trail."

"Hell, that's all they've had on their minds since the forts were built."

The colonel went on as if the general hadn't spoken. "Some apparently wanted to attack you, some me. Finally they decided to hit both of us."

"We got ours four days ago," Ten Eyke told him.

"So I heard from your men when I rode in."

"I wish they would attack the fort," Connor said, eyes glittering. "I'd give them a dose of our six howitzers. But they're too damn tricky to come within five hundred feet. They ride around just out of range. Now, come on, Johnny, what the hell happened over there? I haven't got all year!"

"Six days ago Rossner's men had finished breakfast and set out for the hayfield when they looked up to see Sioux charging them. Naturally they turned their mowing machines around and fled back to the corral beating the hell out of their mules. The men on foot ran like rabbits.

"The officer I'd sent out there, a young lieutenant just out of the Point, had studied his books well. He'd had trenches dug around the perimeter of the corral."

"Trenches!" Connor's voice rose. "What the hell for?"

Kirby-Smith smiled and nodded. "You'd think he was in Austria the way he had it all laid out. The trenches might have been a good idea at that, but the Sioux never gave the lieutenant or his men time to get into them. Troops and civilians fled into the corral, dropped to the ground and started firing. My lieutenant, though, didn't think this was the way a West Point graduate should fight. He stood at the southern entrance of the corral like a hero in a painting, firing away."

"Stood up!" Ten Eyke couldn't believe it. "For how long?"

Kirby-Smith held up a delicate white hand. "Please, Captain." He smiled and went on. "We suspect the Indians figured on an easy victory, for hundreds attacked then."

"Hundreds!" exclaimed Ten Eyke.

"Jesus Christ!" Connor whistled.

"One of them rode ahead of the pack carrying a firebrand. He was only a few feet from the corral when my romantic second lieutenant shot his horse. The warrior went down, his leg pinned under the horse. After some seconds he struggled to his feet. The lieutenant shot him dead. The men cheered. Then the lieutenant killed three more, which gave the men in-

344

side the corral time and courage to gather their wits and prepare to make a stand. About this time a savage aimed from a galloping horse and killed our hero."

No one spoke for a moment. At last Kirby-Smith went on with his report.

"Now the group was without a leader, but a civilian named Colvin took command. Apparently he was a captain in the war. Anyway, he organized the resistance and the Sioux withdrew for a while."

"Sioux? You sure?" Connor stood up and leaned his hand on his desk.

"Yes, George, definitely Sioux. We know the Crow and Pawnee. Besides, one of my men recognized Young-Man-Afraid-of-His-Horses."

"Red Cloud!" Connor rubbed his hands. "We beat that bastard last week. What happened next? Sent them running with their tails between their legs, I bet."

But the colonel continued to take his time. "The Indians used a willow grove for cover and shot fire arrows into the corral, hoping to set the hay burning. They killed almost all the horses and mules and finally managed to light some hay just outside the corral. It went up fast, and for a while it looked as if the whole corral would go."

"Jesus, did it?" Connor was pacing furiously. "Are you over here because we have another massacre on our hands?"

"No, no. We won—or at least we didn't lose."

Connor sat back down and waited impatiently for the rest.

"The wind shifted," explained the colonel. "It blew the smoke and flames back toward the Indians. But they'd seen that it had almost worked, so they spent the better part of the morning setting fires and my troops kept putting them out."

"Didn't you see any of this from the fort?" asked Connor. "How far is it from the hayfields?"

"That's what I want to make sure you understand."

"You in trouble, Johnny?"

"No, George, but this thing has to get out the right way."

There was a brief silence. "Go on," said Connor.

"From the observation tower the hayfield is hidden by a bluff, so my people couldn't see anything."

"You didn't hear any shots?"

"If anybody did, General, they're not talking."

"What does that mean?"

"Privately I think they heard, but publicly I don't say so."

"Explain."

"Fetterman."

"Fetterman?"

"My men, I imagine like all the soldiers out here, talk about Fetterman all the time. I think they heard and decided to ignore it."

"No trooper would fail to respond to a fellow soldier's cry for help!" Connor was outraged.

"That's what I'd like to think," Kirby-Smith said drily, "but it's not what my sutler's saying. One of the soldiers at the corral was so frightened he almost killed himself, he was so sure the Indians would overrun the place and torture him."

Connor looked disgusted. "You said you won. What finally happened?"

"It wasn't so much that we won as they gave up. One of their leaders got within rifle range and Colvin's men shot him. The Indians broke the charge to rescue him. They dragged him off. The next time they attacked, Colvin had the rest of his people—he was down to about eighteen able-bodied men—hold their fire until he gave the signal; then they all fired together. The leader of that attack fell and the heavy fire drove the rest of the Sioux back."

"That was the last big charge. Colvin saw hundreds of Indians ride away."

"Hundreds?" Ten Eyke asked again. "He's sure of that?"

Connor slapped the desk. "Kirby, we had hundreds over here just about the same day."

"If Colvin says hundreds, I believe hundreds."

"His hundreds and our hundreds sound like a whole lot of trouble," Connor's voice was grim.

"Yes, and my sutler wants fifty troopers for each of his work parties or he pulls out," Kirby-Smith added. "I've hardly got enough troops to patrol properly. I can't give him that kind of protection."

"We're having the same problem," Ten Eyke protested.

"But you've got twice the troops I have," the colonel pointed out.

Ten Eyke and Connor greeted this with silence. They didn't want to give up any troops.

Finally, Connor heaved a sigh. "Can't keep this up. I'm going to wire Sherman for more men. Time we rode into some of these Sioux villages and gave them a taste of what they're giving us."

"Just what I was thinking," Kirby-Smith agreed.

"Besides," Connor drawled, "a big victory over the Sioux could be quite a help to all our careers."

347

Ten Eyke stifled an impulse to tell him he didn't want any help with his career; he just wanted out of the army. When he looked up and saw Connor grinning at him, he knew he hadn't had to say it to be understood.

Chapter 26

Despite the so-called victories of the wagon-box and hayfield fights, as the newspapers termed them, much of the country seemed weary of the long, expensive warfare on the nation's frontier.

The Commissioner of Indian Affairs issued a report that expressed the view of many Americans:

> From the facts before me I conclude that we can have all we want from the Indians, and peace without war if we want it . . . at a cost of less than two days' expense of the existing war . . . simply by retracing our wrong steps and doing right. Pay the northern Cheyenne and Arapaho and the hostile Sioux for the trespass we have committed upon their recognized rights and negotiate with them by fair treaty for the privileges of way and military posts on their land so far as we may need them. . . .
>
> We have reached a point in our national history when . . . there are but two alterna-

349

tives left us as to what shall be the future of
the Indian, namely: swift extermination by
the sword and famine, or preservation by
gradual concentration on territorial reserves
. . . As now situated, the Indian tribes are in
the way of our toiling and enterprising population, and unprotected, they will soon be inevitably submerged and buried beneath its
confluent surges . . . unless the humanity and
Christian philanthropy of our enlightened
statesmen shall interfere and rescue them.
The sentiment of our people will not for a
moment tolerate the idea of extermination.

Using the commissioner's report as a rallying
point, Nathaniel Taylor was able to move Congress
to create still one more peace commission. For the
eight-man body Congress chose four, including Taylor, who favored peace. The President, seeking balance, appointed four general army officers who took a
hard line.

"In one way, gentlemen, the commissioner was
wrong in his estimate of the ease with which the Indian wars can be brought to a close," Taylor told his
fellow commissioners at their opening meeting in
October. "Some Indians may be willing to give up
their old hunting grounds and live on reservations,
but many won't."

"They're not going to have much choice," said
William Tecumseh Sherman, the senior general present.
"We've shilly-shallied with them long enough." Taylor
looked pained. "If they've got any sense, the Indians
will recognize the inevitable. If they don't—and I've

yet to hear of one who did—the Indian's just going to get run over."

"You want to divorce your wife, sir?" Big Mouth shifted nervously from foot to foot, anxious as always in Connor's presence.

"That's right." The general sat behind his desk chewing a dead cigar.

"Her father won't be happy, sir."

"A couple of kegs of rum should cheer him up. Take 'em, take the girl. And Big Mouth—"

"Yes sir?"

"I want you to get me another wife. . . ."

Red Cloud's army was in no mood for further battles after the wagon-box and hayfield fights. Most of the warriors had put off hunting to prepare for battle and now their families were low on meat. With sullen disappointment over their failure to gain a victory, the Sioux and Cheyenne set out across the plains for game.

Feeling the Lakota must have done something to offend Wakan-Takan, Red Cloud brooded. Last year he had participated in the Sun Dance as its chief dancer and out of his pain had come victory. Had he failed this year because he hadn't submitted again to the ordeal?

In the lodges of the Sioux and Cheyenne, instead of recounting their exploits the men argued about the battle plans and tactics their chiefs had chosen. The big difference in both battles seemed to be the bravery of the whites and the repeating rifles that had replaced their single-shot muskets. That only a few dozen men had been able to keep hundreds of warriors at bay shamed every man who had taken part in the attacks.

Late that fall Red Cloud and several friends climbed into the mountains to hunt eagles. Young Man Afraid came along and so did Crazy Horse, almost healed from his bullet wounds. Now that Black Buffalo Woman was expecting, Crazy Horse and the chief had patched up their differences. Red Cloud looked forward to the birth of the baby, which he thought of as his grandchild. The thought stirred him in new ways. Life moved on. His passage here on earth was a short one, and one of its main purposes was to pass on what he knew of the Lakota way to succeeding generations, so that the Lakota would never die. He too felt himself changing as Black Buffalo Woman's belly swelled.

I'm getting old, he thought. But he was only forty-six. He certainly didn't view others of his age as old, not in the way Hump and Crazy Horse were. "But this is how an old man thinks," he mused. "This is the beginning of that way of looking at things."

Red Cloud and the other dozen hunters set their camp in a secluded woody area at a safe distance from the crags where the trapping would take place. Perhaps if he could capture his power animal, it would show Red Cloud the true path again. He felt he was failing the vision the giant eagle had shown him last year in the Sun Dance.

At the base camp the men set up the tepee and built a sweat lodge. Up on a high, lonely ridge they marked out a rectangle six feet long and two feet wide. Chanting eagle power songs, they cut squares with their knives and carefully removed the sod and put it to one side. Next they dug a pit and piled the dirt on a buffalo robe. The loose earth they carried away from the pit and piled here and there to look like gopher hills.

When the pit was three feet deep, Red Cloud placed a nest of sage at its south end. A row of poles lay across the top to serve as beams, leaving an opening at the north end large enough for Red Cloud to climb through later. To make the roof firm, they stretched a rawhide rope along the beam ends and secured it with stakes. Finally the men replaced the sod and brought more grass to camouflage the trap.

That night Red Cloud prepared an altar in the camp tepee, placing behind the fire pit an offering stick and ten tiny tobacco offerings. So as not to frighten off the subtle powers or show disrespect, no one would touch these or make any noise while Red Cloud was out of the tepee hunting eagles.

Two hours before the next dawn Red Cloud went to the sweat lodge and took a purifying bath. Then he and Young Man Afraid went up to the trap, carrying with them the dismembered carcass of a jack rabbit. After Red Cloud had climbed into the pit Young Man Afraid adjusted the camouflage, set the bait securely on top of the grass roof and left.

Red Cloud, lying on his back, waited for the eagles. He felt excited and anxious. When a man went to eagles, he went to gain strength and the power to see. That same eagle power could eat him alive.

Under his breath he chanted his eagle song, hoping to create an atmosphere favorable to eagles around the trap. His heart pounded, for wrestling an eagle could be dangerous. Five years ago Raccoon Leaf had had an eye jabbed out in just such a trap, and a youth in Red Cloud's father's time had had a finger ripped off. Red Cloud forced himself to concentrate on what he was there for. He wanted eagle feathers and eagle power. Thinking about the danger wasn't going to get him either of those.

The November morning was so chilly he could see his breath. The frozen ground began to hurt his back. He concentrated on chanting. The sun's light streamed through the spaces in the leafy camouflage, but he could see little of the sky.

He seemed to have been there for hours when a shadow slid slowly over the pit. Red Cloud hardly dared breathe and had to stifle two great urges to sneeze. The eagle soared and wheeled over the trap, as if questioning whether the jack rabbit was safe to eat. Then gradually, warily, great black wings roared as it landed. Red Cloud saw a bit of beak at the edge of the pit. The eagle walked around the edge to the rabbit and began to tear off bits of the bait.

What a large eagle! Could he handle it? It was standing on solid ground and not on the roof of the trap, so Red Cloud couldn't grab its legs easily. He debated whether to make a lunge for the bird or wait and see if it moved to a better position. If he waited too long it would finish the rabbit and leave.

Suddenly Old Hump's voice seemed to speak into his ear. "Breathe with him."

Red Cloud stared at the black feathers, the powerful beak and the restless eyes. His breathing slowed. In a minute or so he caught the rhythm of the bird's own breast. Slowly . . . slowly . . . now!

Red Cloud thrust his hands through the camouflage and grabbed the eagle by its legs to pull the screaming, struggling bird down into the pit. The great wings beat at him and the beak jabbed at his arms as he held the bird away from his eyes. Gradually, keeping the legs grasped in his right hand, he worked his left toward the neck. Twice the bird slashed at the hand, but finally Red Cloud's fingers closed and he wrung the eagle's neck.

Breathing heavily, Red Cloud placed the eagle on the bed of sage at the foot of the trap. He chanted five eagle power songs and said two prayers for forgiveness. By then he was breathing easier.

By sundown Red Cloud had caught three eagles. He felt fortunate, for sometimes men waited a week in such a trap to capture one bird. Carrying the three eagles, he walked to the sweat lodge and placed them in a row to the left of the fire hole. He stayed all night in the sweat lodge. Young Man Afraid brought him hot stones and water but did not speak to him.

All night long Red Cloud chanted and prayed. The longer he stayed in the sweat lodge, the clearer everything became. He had been right to oppose the whites. Thy must remove the forts before he would talk to them. Old Man Afraid, Spotted Tail and the others could sign treaties, but he was a Lakota. He would not sell his way of life.

So be it, he thought as the sun came up. At the start of this new day let me gather these eagle feathers and eat these eagle hearts. I am ready.

Chapter 27

They had come through another winter. Looking out on a particularly fine April day, Cynthia Simmons thought she knew what hell was. Clarence was wrong about the fire and brimstone. Hell was cold, snow, ice, hail, sleet, freezing rain, cold mud a foot deep and never a big enough fire to warm the icy wind that whistled through the cracks.

Only at night, in bed with Tenodor under six quilts, had she been warm. Many times she had gotten up in the middle of the night to make sure Jamey hadn't thrown off his blankets and frozen to death. In winter the temperature inside sometimes fell to ten and twenty below. None of the cabins was properly chinked. Carrington's carpenters had had to build them in too much of a hurry. Despite Tenodor and Hank's efforts to correct the problem, the wind still howled through the walls.

But now it was spring again, and though she knew she would be subjected to the usual snickers and stares, Cynthia just had to get out.

"Hank! Watch Jamey," she called. "I'm going to take a walk."

"Yes, ma'am!" he shouted from the other room. "You go ahead. Don't worry, I'll keep an eye on him."

What a glorious morning, Cynthia said to herself, strolling along and looking at the budding trees. But as she passed a couple of soldiers digging near the powder magazine, they stopped work and one of them poked the other in the ribs. Damn them! she thought. Don't they ever get tired of giggling over us?

Well, her ordeal would soon be over; Tenodor's tour of duty would be up that summer. They had tentatively decided to push on further west, perhaps settle in San Francisco. Maybe the past wouldn't follow them out there. Cynthia sighed, doubting it, thinking that there was no lack of busybodies anywhere.

If only Clarence would relent and give her a divorce! But he hadn't answered any of her letters and had even refused to speak to her father, who after much pleading from her called at Clarence's parish office. Cynthia suspected, reading her father's letter, that his heart hadn't been in it. Though he had written saying he trusted her in whatever decision she made, she knew he was disappointed.

She and Tenodor were virtual recluses. Cynthia left their quarters only when necessary. When she shopped at the sutler's store, the whispers of the enlisted men nibbled at her like mice around her feet and the scornful glances of the women cut her deeply.

These days her only companion besides Tenodor was Hank, who had asked to remain behind with her when Clarence went back East. Her only joy was her son Jamey. When she felt that her life wasn't worth the candle, she had only to look at him, laughing in his crib, to know she would go through it all again. Had she not been drawn to Tenodor, Jamey would never have been born.

Passing the little addition the carpenters had built onto the hospital last year, lost in her own thoughts, Cynthia stopped suddenly. Wasn't that someone crying? Puzzled, she cocked her head to listen and heard it again. The sound rose and fell in long sobs, as if a child were rocking back and forth and crooning.

Cynthia walked to the split log wall, looking for a window, but she saw none. She pressed her ear against the cool logs. Yes, the crying was coming from the addition and not from the hospital next door.

For a few minutes she stood listening, expecting the post surgeon or that red-headed nurse Selena Crawford to come in and quiet the sobbing, but it went on and on.

Somehow it didn't sound like a soldier, but more like a child. Cynthia hadn't heard that there were any children in the hospital, but then, she reflected wryly, I don't hear much gossip anymore. Every child on the post could be sick and I wouldn't hear about it.

Eventually Cynthia walked around to the front of the hospital and went in. In the ward she found two long rows of empty beds. Spring sunlight streamed through the new glass the carpenters had put in just a few days ago to replace the oiled brown paper that had served for the fort's first year. The crying came from the other end of the long corridor between the beds.

"Hello?" Cynthia called.

She waited and called again, but still no one answered. For some reason, as if a cold draft had passed over her, she shivered.

Cynthia walked through the ward to the nurse's office at the rear. There was no one there. The weeping came through a door behind the office. She put her ear to it and listened. Yes, it sounded louder here and very much like Jamey when he had so exhausted himself that he could neither stop nor sleep.

She tried to open the door, but it was locked. The sound increased as she rattled the door. The poor child! Why was it locked up? Looking around, she saw a bunch of keys on the nurse's desk. She tried several and finally opened the door.

She stepped into a small room that got almost no light through the oiled paper in a tiny high window. A young Indian girl cowered on the floor in the far corner. As Cynthia came in the girl pulled an army blanket over her head and her sobbing changed to screams.

Alarmed and curious, Cynthia crept cautiously toward the girl. She drew back the blanket and saw a face twisted with grief and fear. She couldn't have been more than thirteen or fourteen or weighed as much as ninety pounds. She looked as if she hadn't had a good meal in days.

Full of pity, Cynthia held out her hand, but the girl pulled back afraid. Speaking in soothing tones, not knowing if she would be understood, Cynthia worked to calm her. Her touch made the girl quiver with fear but gradually the weeping subsided to a whimper.

After a few minutes of light stroking, Cynthia had the girl huddled against her. Using sign language

and her few words of Sioux, Cynthia found out the
girl's name was Squirrel Face—appropriate enough
—that she wasn't sick, that she lived in that small dark
room. Squirrel Face missed her sister and her mother
and she didn't like her new husband.

Cynthia knew about Sioux marriages. Many times
girls of fourteen or so were sent off to strange tribes
if the suitor gave the father enough ponies. But how
had this girl wound up here?

"What're you doing here?" a voice snapped behind her.

Cynthia jumped, startling the girl, who began to
wail again and pulled away in fear. Cynthia turned and
saw Selena Crawford standing over them, hands on
her hips.

"Oh, hello." Cynthia nodded. "I heard one of
your patients crying."

"That door was locked," Selena said accusingly. "I
locked it myself."

"I found the keys. I unlocked it. I thought someone needed help." She wondered why she felt she had
to defend herself.

"Go solve your own problems, *Mrs*. Simmons,"
the hard-faced nurse sneered.

Furious, Cynthia pulled away from the frightened
Indian girl and stood up. "How dare you talk to me
like that?"

"How dare you break into a locked room?"

"You neglected your patient. What's wrong with
her?"

"Not much." Selena's eyes left Cynthia for the
girl, who had by now pulled back into the corner and
covered herself with the blanket.

"What's a Sioux girl doing here?" Cynthia demanded.

"It's nothing serious. Now, will you leave so I can attend my patient?"

But Cynthia didn't budge. Something wasn't right: a girl who didn't appear to be sick, a locked door, the way Selena's eyes wouldn't meet hers.

"Why is she locked up?"

"Mrs. Simmons, please. You've disturbed my patient enough."

"No, she was already disturbed when I came in. What's she doing here?" Cynthia repeated.

"It's none of your business."

A sudden thought struck Cynthia. "She doesn't have smallpox, does she?" And she'd been holding the girl! She might give it to Jamey or Tenodor!

"No, no, nothing like that."

"I don't want to infect my family," insisted Cynthia. "I demand to know what's wrong with her!"

"I told you, nothing."

"Then what is she doing here?"

"Mrs. Simmons, go home. The girl's fine. Nothing's wrong with her that will hurt you. I'll take care of everything."

"If you don't tell me, I'll go to General Connor."

"I wouldn't do that," Selena warned her. "He wouldn't want that."

"Then tell me what's going on!"

"Nothing's going on!"

"There is! You don't keep someone locked up for nothing."

An awkward silence followed. Cynthia thought Selena was trying hard to come up with an explanation that would satisfy her. The longer the silence lasted the more suspicious Cynthia grew. Finally she made up her mind. She would go to Connor, but she wouldn't say so to Selena.

"Well, as long as you're taking care of her," she conceded, "I guess it's none of my business."

"No, it isn't," Selena agreed.

Choking back her anger, Cynthia strode out of the room, through the nurse's office and into the empty ward. As she stepped out into the warm spring sunlight she thought of the dark, airless room where Squirrel Face was hidden. None of her business, was it!

She walked around the hospital to the post command headquarters behind it.

She wouldn't tell the officer of the day what she wanted, but insisted on speaking to General Connor. The officer checked and said the general was busy, but in the instant before he closed the door to the general's office, Cynthia glimpsed Selena Crawford.

Selena? In there? How could she have gotten there before Cynthia?

Before the young lieutenant realized what she was up to, Cynthia swept by him and opened the door. The general was sitting behind his huge desk, a cigar in his mouth. Selena stood in front of it. The two silently stared at Cynthia as she walked up to them. Behind her the lieutenant was calling, "She just pushed around me, sir!"

"Get out of here, Lawson," growled Connor, "and shut that door."

For a few moments the three just stared at each other. Finally, Connor said, "What do you want, Mrs. Simmons?"

But Cynthia was looking at Selena. "How did she

get here so fast? I just came from the hospital. She couldn't possibly have—"

She broke off. Behind the general's desk stood a tall folding screen, and as she stood staring at it she heard the faint sound of weeping again. "That Indian girl's behind that screen. There's a door from that little room into this office! It was so dark in there I didn't notice it."

Selena and the general exchanged glances. "So what?" Connor yawned.

"Why does that room open into your office?"

"Mrs. Simmons," Connor pointed out, "this is none of your business, as you and Mrs. Crawford have already agreed."

"You know about the girl!"

"Let's say she's my ward."

"Dear Lord, and people think what I've done is shocking. That poor girl's in there crying her heart out. What have you done to her?"

"Not much that you shouldn't be intimately acquainted with, Mrs. Simmons," Selena gibed.

"What's your role in this?" asked Cynthia. "How could you have anything to do with such a thing?"

Selena drew herself up. "I don't think you're in any position to throw stones, Mrs. Simmons."

Cynthia, stunned, just looked at the two of them.

"I don't know why you're so disturbed, Mrs. Simmons." Connor shrugged. "The young lady is what the Indians call my wife, and I have every right to such an arrangement."

"Wife! That child? You're twice her size and three times her age. That's no marriage. You could be her grandfather."

"Call it a private arrangement then."

Connor stood up and stepped around his desk. "I hardly think you're in any position to pass judgment on my behavior. What say you go back to your husband and leave me with whatever arrangements I choose to make for myself."

"There's a difference!"

"I fail to see any, except, of course, that adultery is much worse in the eyes of everyone I know than a man marrying a somewhat younger woman."

Cynthia reddened. That was true enough, but nothing about this "arrangement" looked like marriage to her. Who but Bluebeard kept his wife locked in a dark, airless room? "How old is that girl?"

"Will you leave now, Mrs. Simmons? Or shall I have Lawson throw you out and perhaps off the post as well?"

"Off the post!"

"Into the wilderness."

"You wouldn't!"

"Military regulations say I can remove civilian troublemakers."

"Troublemaker! Me?"

"Mrs. Simmons, I assure you that your reputation precedes you. I doubt if there's an officer or enlisted man between here and St. Louis who doesn't know about you. Some may snicker over it, but most deplore it. Your motives for causing trouble might not be clear to my superiors, but no one on the general staff would blame me if I decided this post would be better off without you."

Cynthia was so outraged she couldn't answer him. She whirled from the room. She slammed the door behind her even though she'd always considered that a poor way to punctuate an argument, for all it really accomplished was to signal a retreat.

That night she told Tenodor the whole story. At first he was skeptical, but she finally managed to convince him that the general did indeed have a fourteen-year-old Sioux bride.

Several times the next day she walked by the little annex connecting the hospital with the general's office. Twice she thought she heard the girl crying.

That night Tenodor said he had some information. According to Smitty, the camp clerk, the general had had two girls before this one in the last year.

"Two!" she exclaimed. "What happens to them? What does he—?"

Ten Eyke held up his hand to stop her. "I also talked to one of the men in my troop who's worked as an orderly for Skinny Red."

"Skinny Red? Selena Crawford?"

"That's what the men call her. He says the general 'marries' them for a few months, and when they get pregnant, he sends them back to their fathers with a keg or two of rum."

"My God, it's barbaric. And he calls the Indians savages. But Tenodor, three girls in the past year! Why haven't we heard about it before this?"

Ten Eyke sighed. "You should know by now that the men don't tell an officer anything they don't have to, and Connor is enough to put the fear of God into the strongest heart. Besides, we're the last to hear any gossip. You know that."

"What can we do?"

"Do?"

"To stop it."

Ten Eyke sighed. "Cynthia, don't you think we have enough problems?"

And there it sat. Cynthia made it a point now to go out at least once a day and walk past the annex. Almost every time, she thought she heard the girl sobbing quietly. Was she being abused or did she simply miss her family and quite naturally hate being in jail?

Every night she spoke about it to Ten Eyke. He passed from indifference to irritation. At one point he even accused her of wanting to expose Connor as a way of making their own behavior look more acceptable by comparison.

"Yes, all right," she admitted, sighing. "But Tenodor, it still isn't right. You don't lock a woman up. If that doesn't go against your moral sense, it goes against every code of God or man I've ever heard of."

Tenodor had no answer to that. Later in the week Cynthia found herself talking to Hank about it and discovered that he knew all about the general's "wives."

"Where did you hear it?" she asked.

"The ladies who does the laundry." Three black women lived in a shack in the back corner of the fort and washed uniforms and did sewing for the officers and men.

"Hank, I saw that girl. She's just a child."

"Yes'm." Hank's face was blank.

She was no happier with Hank's response than she had been with Tenodor's. They wouldn't admit it, she suspected, but she sensed that the men secretly approved of the general's series of child brides.

That night she tried speaking to Tenodor again. "That girl's a prisoner, Tenodor, and I'm not very happy with you."

"With me? I don't have any Indian girls locked away."

"Don't make fun of me. What he's doing isn't right."

He lost patience. "Well, then, set her free."

"Set her free?" Cynthia stared at him. "Why, of course! Will you help?"

"Well . . . I don't know."

"Tenodor, please! You know it isn't right."

"Cynthia, it's not my business, and she is the general's property."

"Property!" she shrieked. "*Property*! You Southerners are all alike. A human being isn't property! That's what we fought the Civil War for."

He looked at her with a blaze of hatred, and then the blaze died and he turned away.

"What's the matter?" she asked, for suddenly he looked ill.

He heaved a sigh. "I'm sorry. You're right. I'm sick of Connor. I'm sick of seeing and hearing about slaughter. That man and a girl not much more than a child. It isn't right."

"We could set her free, Tenodor. What can he do to us for that?"

"A good deal," he replied dryly. "But we have to get her clear out of the fort."

"Out of the fort?"

"Yes. If you just let her out onto the parade ground, what is she to do? If you let a bird go, you let it out a window, not from a cage into the sitting room."

"But what can the general do to you?"

"He can make my life hell, not that he hasn't managed that already."

She considered the problem of what Connor could do to Tenodor. As commanding officer, he could—would, if she were any judge of character—give Tenodor the most difficult duty, perhaps even force him into dangerous confrontations with the Indians. Was this girl worth it? "If he makes your life hell, we can expose him."

"Easier said than done. On this post we're not the most respected examples of moral rectitude. But Cynthia, you're right. The girl shouldn't be kept locked up in there."

"Then you'll help me do it? You'll help me set her free?"

"We'll do it," he smiled. He drew her to him, rubbed his mustache against her cheek. "You'll have to endure whatever old One Arm chooses to do to me."

"Tenodor, I love you. When will we do it?"

"Tomorrow. I'll do a little scouting first and see what can be done."

"Tomorrow?"

"Tomorrow. Before I lose my nerve."

Chapter 28

At one o'clock in the afternoon, when most of the post was either eating the midday meal or figuring out some way to take a nap, Cynthia and Ten Eyke entered the hospital. This time, Cynthia saw with alarm, it wasn't empty. There were three patients in the ward. Two were sleeping and one raised his head weakly as they walked down between the two rows of beds. At the end of the room sat an orderly, his chair tipped back against the wall.

"Nurse Crawford in?" asked Ten Eyke.

"Yes, Captain. Want me to tell her you're here?"

"No thanks," replied Ten Eyke. He swept around the man into the small office, ready to confront Selena Crawford. But she wasn't there; the room was empty.

As they looked around the deserted office, Ten Eyke asked himself if the better part of valor might not be to let the Sioux fight their children's battles. But it was too late to change his mind now.

Cynthia whispered, "The girl's in there!" She pointed to the door in the opposite wall. They stood for a moment listening, and both heard the regular and unmistakable sounds of lovemaking.

"But where's the nurse?" whispered Ten Eyke.

"In there too!" she pointed to the open bolt on the door.

Of course. Where else could she be? The only other way out was past the orderly in the hospital ward. Ten Eyke felt sick. "Let's come back another time."

"No, let's wait," Cynthia objected. "Now's as good a time as any. After all, their offices are on either side of the girl's room. They'll always be watching her, one or the other of them."

With a sinking heart Ten Eyke saw that she was right. How had he imagined that they could sneak into the ward, spirit the girl off and get her through the gates before the nurse or the general was the wiser?

From behind the other room came a series of grunts and groans. Ten Eyke gently tried the door; it seemed to be bolted from within. Little barks and bumpings told of passion reaching its peak. *Were* both the Crawford woman and the general in there? What sort of alliance did those two have?

Cynthia started to say something, but Ten Eyke thought he heard footsteps and cupped her mouth with his hand, drawing her to him behind the door. No sooner had they crouched behind the desk than the door opened and Selena Crawford entered, her long thin red hair hanging down the back of her white uniform.

Without seeing them, the nurse crossed the room, buttoning her uniform as she walked, and peered into a mirror.

"Now!" whispered Ten Eyke. Pulling Cynthia

by the hand, he jumped up and hurried into the girl's room.

Behind them they heard Selena shout.

"Lock the door behind us," Ten Eyke instructed Cynthia. She pulled it shut and slammed home the bolt.

Selena Crawford pounded on the door and shouted for them to open up. Ten Eyke, peering into the gloom, heard muted sobbing from a huddled form under a blanket on the bed.

His heart pounded. Any minute now the general was sure to come bursting in, possibly with a pistol, certainly in a towering rage. Ten Eyke pulled the blanket off the Indian girl, who looked up at him in wild fear. He saw a child's naked form huddled into a tight ball of pain and panic. From her loins ran a trickle of blood.

"Where's her clothes?" he asked Cynthia.

"No time. Pick her up and let's get out of here."

He rolled the frightened child in the blanket and scooped up the bundle.

"Same way out," he said. "She's probably gone to warn Connor." They moved toward the door to Selena's office, but as they reached it and shot back the bolt, the door to Connor's quarters opened and there stood the general and the nurse.

"You stop right there, mister!" roared One Arm.

But Ten Eyke was through the door and into Selena's office. Cynthia slammed and bolted the door. She ran after Tenodor, who was running down the aisle between the hospital beds toward the entrance. Aroused by the commotion, the patients raised their heads to follow their flight.

371

As Ten Eyke came out into the bright April afternoon, he figured what to do. Any minute now the general and Selena would catch them. It would be best to head straight for the gates.

With Cynthia following, he ran across the parade ground. By the time he reached the gate the girl had grown heavy. She was crying again and seemed to be struggling, doubtless thinking some further evil was soon to be visited upon her.

The guards came out to see what was going on. They looked at Ten Eyke curiously.

"Open the small gate, Grimes," he ordered.

"What's going on, Captain?"

"Open the gate, soldier. Come on, Cynthia."

Without hurrying himself, Grimes opened the man-sized door set in the fort's twenty-foot-high main gate. Ten Eyke stepped through, followed by Cynthia.

He set down the girl several yards away from the gate. She looked around as if the sunlight dazzled her. Cynthia now joined him.

"Tell her to run," he urged.

Cynthia took the girl by the shoulders. "Run quickly. Don't let the one-armed demon catch you again."

The girl looked from one to the other of them. She seemed frozen there and pulled the blanket more tightly around her.

Behind them they heard shouting. As Ten Eyke turned to look back, Connor's hairy face popped through the door in the gate.

"Run!" Cynthia repeated in Sioux. "He wants to catch you again."

The sight of Connor got the girl in motion. She turned and ran off.

"Stop her!" Connor ordered.

Ten Eyke reluctantly turned to face the general as he came through the gate with eight or nine guards.

"Stop her!" Connor called again. Two of the guards lifted their Spencers.

Ten Eyke moved to block their line of fire. "Don't shoot that child!" he shouted.

"Don't fire!" Connor's voice overrode Ten Eyke's.

Puzzled, the men lowered their Spencers and turned to look at the general. "Chase her, you fools. Get going! Catch her!"

Three of the men slowly put down their rifles, thought better of it and stooped to pick them up, then started off after the girl at a dogtrot.

As the three soldiers passed him Ten Eyke chuckled. They didn't relish heading away from the fort in such a small party and plainly were prepared only to go through the motions of pursuing the girl. Then they could soon return to the safety of the fort and say she had eluded them. Better the general's wrath than that of the Sioux.

Ten Eyke took Cynthia's hand. "Let's go back. We've done all we can."

"Thank you, Tenodor."

Hand in hand they walked toward the gate, where Connor was shouting for men to get their horses and recapture his prisoner.

As Cynthia and Ten Eyke came up, he stopped his shouting to glare at them.

"What do you have to say for yourself, mister?"

"I don't know, General. What do you have to say for yourself?"

Around them the guards watched curiously, obviously pleased with the entertainment their superiors were providing. But Connor only said, "I've got ways of dealing with you, Captain. Let's call that a damn foolish thing to do."

Cynthia stepped forward. "I've been a witness to all this. If you harm my husband, General, I'll hound you till your other arm and both your legs fall off."

For a moment her fury silenced every man there. Ten Eyke put his arm around her and they faced the general, who for a change looked flustered.

"I hardly think we can call Captain Ten Eyke your husband, Mrs. Simmons," said the general after he had regained his wits. "Nor do I think army assignments are a wife's business."

She turned to speak to the dozen soldiers who had crowded around them.

"Captain Ten Eyke found a slave penned up in a room next to the general's quarters. The captain has just freed the slave. You heard the general threaten to punish the captain for obeying the law of the land. Your friends died for that law in the Great War just three years ago. Do you have anything to add, General?"

"Yes. Maybe the two of you *are* married. Birds of a feather flock together. Certainly you're both damn fools." He marched back into the fort.

Three days later Squirrel Face had moved only four miles from the fort. She was hungry and she had no idea which way to travel. Much of her day she spent looking for food—grasses, berries, insects, anything. At night she rolled up in the blanket, cried for her sister and her mother and slept. She didn't believe she would ever see her family again. On the third day she found a brook. Here she tried to catch fish with her hands, as she had seen her brothers do, but she wasn't quick enough.

She expected to die soon. Any time now a bear or a buffalo would find her and crunch her up the way she ate grasshoppers.

Crazy Horse and twenty Kit Foxes rode toward Fort Kearny. Only in the last few weeks had Crazy Horse been strong enough to ride any distance. This would be his first sortie against Fort Kearny since last year. Crazy Horse felt good. Not only had Wakan-Takan once again restored the world after it had died last winter, but Black Buffalo Woman had given him a fine boy and was pregnant again. It made a man feel full of wakan to plant children.

The war party was only a few miles from the fort when Young Hump spotted something moving along the bottom of a ravine. "A deer?"

"There aren't any grey deer." Crazy Horse pretended to punch his friend for such a foolish remark.

"Let's see what it is."

Heeding Crazy Horse's warning to be careful, for it might be a creek demon, they rode down the hill in two wide arcs, one led by Crazy Horse and the other by Young Hump. In minutes they had surrounded and caught the creature, a girl wrapped in an army blanket.

"What are you doing here?" asked Crazy Horse. "Where's your family?"

"I don't know," she answered, trembling with fear.

"Who are you?"

She gave her name and parentage and Crazy

Horse recognized her family. They lived in a band of four or five tepees and usually hunted around Stump Draw.

Some of the men thought it a great joke that she was out here dressed in only a blanket, but Crazy Horse didn't like it. "I've never seen an Indian with such a thick blanket," he remarked to Hump. "The wind runs through the blankets the whites issue us."

"Where'd you get the blanket, girl?" Hump used his sternest voice. She looked at him without speaking.

The girl bothered Crazy Horse. You never found young Sioux girls so far from their families. A mother wouldn't allow a girl of this one's age more than fifteen yards from her for fear some boy would talk her into doing something foolish. "Answer Hump, little sister." Crazy Horse put his arm around her.

At first she stiffened at his touch, but Crazy Horse had always had a way with children, horses and dogs. He stroked her as he would a frightened horse, talked to her in soothing tones and gradually worked the fear out of her.

She told them the story of her marriage to One Arm. It appalled them. For a father to accept the gift of a few horses for his daughter's hand was a custom as old as the Sioux. But for a father to give his daughter to an enemy determined to destroy the Lakota, a man who didn't have the decency to treat such a child well, was unbelievable.

Fathers who thought it gave them prestige to marry their daughters to soldiers sickened Crazy Horse. "We'll take this little sister back to her people, and talk to her father."

When they made camp that night Hump and Many Bears eyed the girl in a way that told Crazy Horse they might try to sneak her into the bushes. Crazy Horse took the position the girl's mother would have and wouldn't let her out of his sight.

He tried to learn more from her about her stay at the fort. He saw that something had happened there that had deeply shamed her. She wouldn't talk about it, though he tried to draw it from her. Whatever it was, this shame wormed beneath her surface like a mole burrowing through the earth. The planes of her face shifted darkly with grief. To look at her pained Crazy Horse. How could a father allow his own daughter to be tied to such a cruel man? He did learn from Squirrel Face that Big Mouth had paid her father with horses and rum.

The following morning brought the Kit Foxes to the girl's camp, three tepees in a clearing five miles south of Stump Draw. The first thing they saw was a grandmother sitting in the ashes of a dead campfire. As the horses approached the woman staggered to her feet and weaved back towards the safety of a tepee. The old lady's difficulty in standing amused the Foxes. She staggered like a dog in a patch of crazy berries. No sooner had the grandmother entered the tepee than three small children ran out. When they saw Squirrel Face they ran toward her, but the youngest tripped and fell. The other two shouted "Hai! Come drink too!"

Squirrel Face slid off Crazy Horse's pony and stooped to embrace them. Crazy Horse wondered what was wrong with them and how their mother could allow them to run around with so few clothes on.

"Why'd you go away?" the children asked their sister. "We missed you."

Although it was midmorning, Crazy Horse found

the girl's mother and father asleep. The grandmother too had gone to sleep. In the middle of the tent he found the reason: a keg of rum—or what was left of it, for no more than enough to wet the bottom of the keg remained. All drunk! thought Crazy Horse. No wonder no one's taking care of the children.

"Where's White Beaver Woman?" asked Squirrel Face, who had entered the tepee behind Crazy Horse.

"Who's that?"

"My sister."

"Do you know what's the matter with them?"

She pointed to the empty keg. "Too much of that drink. Maybe she's with my uncles."

"The other tepees?"

"Yes."

Crazy Horse followed her out of the tepee. In the next one they found another keg of rum, also empty, crushed into a crumpled heap of staves. The girl's sister wasn't among the stupefied occupants. They didn't find her in the last tepee either.

"But where is she?" wailed Squirrel Face. "Something's happened to her! I know it has!"

"Easy, little sister," Crazy Horse touched her arm. "Hump! Bear! Look around in the bushes. See if you can find this girl's sister. She probably drank too much whiskey and passed out somewhere like the rest."

The Kit Foxes spread out around the tiny settlement and moved through the bushes. Crazy Horse felt sick with disgust at seeing Sioux in such a condition. Whites! They touched nothing that was Sioux without spoiling it.

The others reported no luck in finding White Beaver Woman. Crazy Horse saw that the warriors were growing restless. They wanted to ride back to the fort and see if they couldn't take some mules or horses, perhaps provoke a few soldiers into a fight and count coups.

"Look some more," he insisted. "We'll go soon."

"You come and look too," Young Hump said impatiently. "We aren't dogs to go sniffing around the bushes. We're Lakota."

Crazy Horse laughed that off and joined them, taking Squirrel Face along. This time they set out on the other side of the camp and before long found some milkweed that had been crushed in what looked like a wild struggle. Further on, under some bushes, they found a steel knife covered with blood. At the sight of it Squirrel Face sent up such a wail that some of the Foxes wanted to mount their ponies and leave right then.

The trail of crushed weeds led toward a gully a hundred yards farther on. At the bottom of it they found White Beaver Woman, naked, dead, her belly slashed open as if for butchering.

They went back to camp and Crazy Horse went into each tepee. He did not find what he was looking for in the first nor the second one he searched, but in the third he knelt for a closer look at the man Squirrel Face had pointed out as her father and found blood on his hands and deerskin tunic and saw scratches on his neck.

The other Foxes were alarmed by the bad wakan of this place. Most wanted to leave at once, but Crazy Horse told them he must stay a little longer and they reluctantly agreed to wait for him.

Her face bleak with grief, Squirrel Face came up wailing from her sister's body. Her high keen had every Kit Fox shifting from foot to foot. They hated this.

That a man could kill his daughter sent shudders down their spines.

Crazy Horse, furious, got Many Bears and Hump to keep Squirrel Face from harming herself, for she had dropped the army blanket that covered her and had begun tearing out her hair, crouching naked in the cold ashes of the fire.

Going back into the tepee, Crazy Horse shook awake the father, mother and grandmother and dragged them out into the sunlight. They looked wretched. They grimaced against the light. There was dried vomit on the mother's dress.

"What you want?" asked the father. He had the crafty face of a raccoon. "Shut up that screeching child! She makes my head hurt."

"What happened to your daughter White Beaver Woman?" asked Crazy Horse.

The father shrugged, but the grandmother and the mother both started to talk then. He had attacked the girl in the middle of the night. To keep her father from raping her she had run, her father chasing her. The father had come back later and told them the girl had hidden from him.

"You killed her!" shouted Squirrel Face, struggling in the grip of Young Hump and Many Bears.

The accusation seemed to wake the father from his stupor. He lifted his hands and stared at the dried blood. He felt the scratches on his neck and face. Horror flooded his face. He looked at his wife and the grandmother and began to wail. His legs gave way and he sank to the ground, sobbing loudly. "No! Tell me it was a dream! No!"

But it was true. He had caught his daughter and

raped her several times. To keep the girl from telling her mother, he had killed her.

The combined wailing of Squirrel Face and her father woke the occupants of the other tepees, and they stumbled out to see what was going on. During this confusion the grief-stricken father flung himself on the bloody knife, which Crazy Horse had thrown into the sand in disgust. Before anyone could stop him, he drove it into his stomach and pulled it upwards as far as it would go. He died in the horrified silence that fell on the little gathering. The mother and grandmother and all the uncles and children in the camp raised their voices in grief.

Crazy Horse insisted that the Kit Foxes escort these pitiful people, now deprived of their principal hunter, back to the Bad Face village. They would leave at once because none of the warriors could stand to spend another hour in that bad place, much less the night. It would remain haunted for all time by the restless spirits of the father and daughter. Before they left, Hump rode all around the clearing and marked the trees with the sign of an inverted owl's face. This would warn any Lakota how dangerous it was here.

They reached the Bad Face camp after a two-day journey. Red Cloud led in the ceremonial giving to the poor refugees, showing what a great chief he was by presenting them with six buffalo robes, three parfleches of pemmican and two horses. Not to be outdone, others stepped forward to give generously. A few muttered that these newcomers were being treated better than families who had lived all their lives in the Bad Face camp.

That night Red Cloud invited Crazy Horse to

address the council of Big Bellies. The rumors of this tragedy disturbed him.

He wanted every chief, subchief and warrior captain to hear about it firsthand. He wanted them to know that it was the white chief One Arm who had provided the whiskey that had driven the father to murder his own daughter, who had married a Sioux child and treated her barbarously.

He wanted them to remember when next he led them into battle.

Chapter 29

General Sheridan showed his displeasure over the trouble on the Bozeman Trail by the number of messages he shot at General Connor. In one week in June of '68 he sent the commander of Fort Kearny no less than six, each one deploring the attacks by Crazy Horse and Red Cloud on civilian and military wagon trains attempting the crossing to Montana. The elections coming up that fall had put additional pressure on President Andrew Johnson, who passed it down the chain of command till it reached military headquarters in Omaha. Sheridan passed the President's displeasure westward to Connor.

Connor wasn't the kind of soldier to bottle up his frustrations. He roared for results. After Ten Eyke embarrassed him over the Indian girl, he had the captain continually on patrol and rescue missions. Several times Ten Eyke came in at five o'clock in the afternoon after being on patrol since dawn, and Connor ordered him right out again with fresh troops to rescue some group of wagons under siege. When Ten Eyke protested, Connor glared at him and said, "Ride, soldier, ride. You crossed me and now I'll cross you."

But Connor eventually grew tired of leaning on Ten Eyke. He had more interesting things on his mind. He had gathered around himself a new set of young officers, some of whom had fought with General George Armstrong Custer under a special plan of the War Department to train Indian fighters. These youngsters were eager for the battles and victories on which a man could build a career. They agreed with Connor that the proper strategy was to attack the larger Sioux villages and wipe them out in order to break the Indians' morale. One or two such victories would end all Sioux hostilities, as they had the Cheyenne. The attacks would have to be carried out in secret, of course; otherwise the peace party would stir up Congress and the Bureau of Indian Affairs would stop them. But once the deed was done, some excuse of provocation would serve as an apologia.

Connor thought this a fine strategy. During the months of May and June he and his selected officers, who had been sworn to secrecy, planned how to carry it out.

He would employ the infantry as bait and the cavalry as the teeth and jaws of the trap. Properly set up, the Sioux would run into rifle fire that would cut down their warriors as a scythe cut grass. He would turn the tables on the Sioux with one of their oldest tricks: lure them into attacking what looked like a small and weak force.

If it succeeded, there was no telling how far he could go, Connor thought. If Grant could come so far in politics by winning a war, why couldn't he? The loss of his left arm in the war would be a help, a visible reminder on the political stump that he had made a penultimate sacrifice for his country. Yes, and when this little shindig was over, he would get himself another Indian gal.

The thought of his present lack of one inevitably reminded him of Ten Eyke. Despite all his efforts, Connor couldn't seem to dent the man. His frustration over it got to bothering him so much that he finally ordered Ten Eyke to report to his office.

"I can't stand to see your face, soldier," he announced as Ten Eyke walked in. "Get out of here and pick up orders to report to Omaha. I don't want to see you before you leave. And be sure to take that whore with you."

For an instant it looked as if Ten Eyke would rise to the bait, for he stepped right up to the edge of the desk. Making it easy for the captain to take a poke at him, Connor moved around it. A poke was the sort of thing he could deal with. First he would knock Ten Eyke flat with one savage blow of his fist, and then he would have the man thrown into the hole for six months. That would teach the bastard not to mix in things that weren't his business.

But to Connor's disappointment Ten Eyke caught himself. He smiled that superior smile Connor hated. "No sir. You want me to go, I'll go. I only hope I pick up the San Francisco *Chronicle* one morning and read about the Sioux swarming into your quarters, General. They'll warm you up good for a long stay in hell."

"Get out of my office, Ten Eyke. Get off this post while the getting is still good."

"It just ain't going to work, Cap'n." Hank had been saying so for an hour and Ten Eyke had to admit

385

he was right. They had struggled to load the mule cart three times now. First they couldn't get the bed and mahogany dresser in. The second time they couldn't find room for the three tea trunks and the bed. This time they found they couldn't fit in the six dining-room chairs and the dresser. The army had allowed Clarence Simmons to use one of the large supply wagons. Ten Eyke got no such thing.

Ten Eyke was exasperated. He knew Cynthia wanted all these household things, but he would just as soon have left everything she and Clarence had accumulated and start fresh. Cynthia had argued with him not to be so foolish. They didn't have the money to indulge such feelings. Better to be practical.

In a few hours Cynthia, Ten Eyke, Jamey and Hank would head out for California with a forty-wagon train that was ready to pull out. Ten Eyke was a civilian, having convinced Omaha that for the few weeks he had left in the service it wasn't worthwhile to transfer him.

Hank would drive the cart, Ten Eyke would ride and Cynthia and Jamey would sit next to Hank, as they had coming out to Fort Kearny just two years ago. What a difference now, Ten Eyke reflected, staring at the chairs and dresser that refused to go into the cart. Two years ago he would have thought it perfect bliss to have Cynthia riding with him as his mate. Now he thought how costly it had been to win her. Despite his hatred of Connor he didn't like leaving the army under a cloud—even the Union army.

In addition to getting the cart loaded, Ten Eyke worried about Indian attacks and how Jamey would stand the arduous ride and what work he would find in San Francisco. His reverie was broken by the clash of sabers, the sound of leather slapping leather and the shouts of noncoms and officers as they marched out troops. He and Hank turned to see Captain Gallagher leading out a contingent of recruits for a practice dash through the woods against imaginary braves. Much as he didn't like the Union army, Ten Eyke was accustomed to military life and he was going to miss it.

Inside the cabin Cynthia packed away the dishes and silver flatware—another inheritance from her marriage—she and Tenodor had used for their last breakfast there. She certainly had no reservations about leaving military life. Except for Hank, the post surgeon and Tenodor, no one had spoken a civil word to her for months. Today, poised to leave Fort Kearny, she felt drained but calm. She had started as a precocious student of Latin and Greek and had married a minister. She had never expected to find herself an outcast at the age of thirty-five. What lay in store for them in San Francisco? she wondered. Tenodor worried about earning a living out West, but she had more faith in him than he seemed to have in himself, just as she had had more faith in Clarence. Would she have to prop up Tenodor too? No, he wasn't Clarence. They would be gypsies for a while, but Tenodor would find something. He had a hard-headed practicality that would serve them well. Cynthia sighed. She desperately wanted another child, but sometimes she wondered if she wanted it just to prove that she and Tenodor really belonged together.

Tenodor came into the cabin. "Come out and look at this, Cynthia. We just can't carry so much."

She sighed again. They had already discarded half her belongings.

The cart was empty once more. On the grass lay

their bedstead, the dresser, the wrapped mirrors and the boxes filled with linens, silver, cups, plates and valuable foodstuffs such as coffee, sugar and dried meat. Other trunks held Tenodor's clothes and books, her dresses and her dressmaking things.

"We packed and unpacked three times, Miss Cynthia," said Hank. "Besides being too heavy for the mules, it just don't fit."

Tenodor muttered, "Can't we get rid of some of that fancy stuff you and Clarence brought out?"

She knew he meant the large heavy bed and the antique dresser. They and the gold-patterned dishes had been wedding presents to Clarence and Cynthia and were visible reminders to Tenodor that he had, as he put it when he was in a bad mood, stolen her from another man.

"I know how you feel, Tenodor, but we have to sleep on something. What about the wagon master? Maybe he can take the bed and the dresser as freight."

"I already asked. He can't pack in another ten pounds."

For a few moments the three of them just stared at the goods spread out on the grass. They had to make a decision soon; the wagon train would be pulling out at noon sharp.

"All right," she sighed. "Let's be practical. What are the most valuable pieces?"

"I don't want to be practical," Tenodor scowled. "I want to get rid of that bed. I'm sick and tired of sleeping in another man's bed. If it takes our last cent, I want to buy our own."

"But this bed came from England! When we get to San Francisco we can sell it."

388

"I don't care if it's from Africa. I don't want it."

"Tenodor, you're not being practical."

Hank edged away.

"No, I'm not," Ten Eyke agreed. "About some things, I don't want to be."

After a few more moments of this Cynthia gave in. They could have used the money the bed would have brought, but a man needed pride too, and to tell the truth Tenodor's insistence flattered her.

One of the new officers, John Gallagher, was glad to get the bed. His wife, a bright berry of a woman, came to look it over, and even smiled warmly at Tenodor and Cynthia, as if under other circumstances they might have been friends. That smile reminded Cynthia how cut off she was from other women, how she would have to fight to make a place for herself wherever she went, how much harder she must try to make Clarence give her a divorce.

When the mule cart swung into fourth place in the long line of wagons, both Tenodor and Cynthia felt curious eyes on them. No doubt news of their outlandish behavior had already spread along the train. Would it always be like this? Cynthia supposed it could. Hugging her son to her, she raised her chin and stared defiantly ahead.

The only problem with Connor's plans to make his name fighting the Sioux was finding them. For weeks now his intelligence officers had questioned muleskinners, settlers and wagon masters who passed through on the way to Wyoming. He had listened to friendly Crow tell of Sioux strength and say where they thought the biggest camps of Sioux were, but

Connor had little hard intelligence. He needed someone to travel through Sioux country and bring back accurate details of their whereabouts.

When Nathaniel Taylor and Big Mouth arrived at Fort Kearny after one of their peace missions into the Big Horn region, Connor tried to get information from the commissioner.

"No, sir," said Taylor. "We didn't find any of the villages we were looking for, not Red Cloud's, Man Afraid's or Black Twin's. And if we had I wouldn't tell you where they were."

"And why not?" demanded Connor. "Don't you want to aid in the defense of your country?"

"I've heard disturbing rumors that you plan a military adventure against the Sioux. That's against the wishes of Congress and the policy of the War Department."

"I've no such plans," Connor denied.

"Then why press me for the location of these tribes? Don't you understand that the peace commission is striving to bring this bloodshed to an end?"

"I understand that it's the shilly-shallying of the likes of you that's got us into this mess. If it weren't for you by now we'd have whipped their tails and the whole thing would be over. That's going to happen in the long run. If you weren't so goddamn blind you'd see it."

The interview left the general's mouth with a bad taste that even a good cigar and a tumbler of whiskey did little to relieve. Besides, damnit, he still didn't know where to find the tribes.

On his way across the parade ground to the officer's mess, he spotted Big Mouth's plump figure slumped on the porch of the sutler's store. Seeing him made the general both angry and curious. He associated Big Mouth's sly moon face with the "brides" he had so enjoyed and with his loss of them. He changed direction and headed for the sutler's to pick up some extra pipe tobacco.

Big Mouth saw him coming and greeted him with his habitual grin. "You want to see me, General?" Big Mouth leered; did the general want another Indian girl?

Connor felt himself go hot and dry all over. Did he! He panted a little. Why shouldn't he have a little of what pleased him? Connor didn't like Big Mouth's sly look, but with Ten Eyke and his whore gone, why shouldn't he have what he wanted?

"As a matter of fact, I do want to see you. Why don't you come by this afternoon after I've had my nap?"

By the time Big Mouth arrived at his office, it had struck Connor that this was a golden opportunity to find out where Red Cloud's elusive tribes were.

"Same deal, Big Mouth?" he began the conversation. Big Mouth said yes, sure, he would be glad to "go hunting" again for the general. As before, could he take three horses and a couple of kegs of rum with him so he wouldn't have to make an extra trip?

"How many horses you own, Big Mouth?"

The question surprised Big Mouth. "Me, sir?"

"You, damnit."

"Three."

"How'd you like to own a dozen?"

"A dozen?"

"Stop repeating what I say!"

"Yes, sir! I'd like it, sir. You want more than one wife?"

"I want to know where Red Cloud is, Big Mouth, that's what I want."

"Red Cloud!"

"And Black Twin and Red Leaf and High Backbone, all of them who're holding out. Especially the biggest group, the one with all the warriors."

"That'd be Red Cloud."

"Yeah, it figures. I want to know where he is."

"You want him to sign the treaty like Mr. Taylor?"

"I just want to know where he is and how many warriors he's got, and how many ponies and how many guns. Also how much powder and shot. And if I can get them, his plans for the next couple of months."

He watched while Big Mouth figured out why he wanted the information. Then Connor continued, "And if you say a word about this to anybody, I'll step on you and cut off your balls and dick with my one good hand. Get me, Big Mouth?"

"Yes, sir, but I can't, sir."

"You can't what?"

"Tell you. They'd kill me."

Connor laughed. "Well, you got a choice. Me or Red Cloud, which is it to be?"

Big Mouth looked thoughtful for a moment.

"Well?"

"I could say I was looking for buffalo robes to trade for rum and ponies."

"But you'd really be looking around for a gal for me, wouldn't you?"

Big Mouth sighed. "You have a big appetite for wives, sir."

"Don't you, Big Mouth?"

"I got one wife now, sir."

"Wouldn't you like a sweet young gal, Big Mouth?"

"My wife won't let me have another, but yes, I would like one." He smiled foolishly.

"Tell you what, Big Mouth. You get me what I want this trip out and I'll give you this next gal after a couple of months. Your wife ain't going to let you refuse a gift from a general, is she?"

Big Mouth grinned at the thought. "No, sir, she can't. You mean it?"

"Sure, I mean it! If I'd known it was important to you, we could have worked out something before."

"Some of the Lakota say you shouldn't lock up your wives, sir."

"I didn't lock that girl up, Big Mouth." Connor looked hurt. "She was sick and Nurse Crawford was taking care of her. How these damn rumors get started is beyond me. You tell this one's father he can come in to see his daughter. Tell him I'll give him a gift of tobacco if he comes in. He'll see his daughter is being treated a hell of a lot nicer than he'd take care of her back in the tepee."

Chapter 30

In late June, when Big Mouth set out for the Big Horn to carry out his mission for the general, he was worried. He had not been entirely candid with One Arm about Sioux feelings regarding his young wives. True, for a father to trade a daughter for horses was normal, and what father wouldn't want his daughter married to a powerful man like the general? But One Arm hadn't quite grasped what marriage meant to the Sioux.

As long as the woman pleased you and did what you asked, didn't unreasonably nag, didn't refuse you in bed and wasn't downright lazy, the right thing to do was keep her in your lodge and provide for her. You could divorce her by declaring that you wanted to, but if all you wanted was a younger, prettier wife, the right thing to do was marry one and keep your old wife. Such a way worked fine. By the time a man reached his forties, provided he was a good enough hunter to take care of them, he had usually accumulated enough women to satisfy even the most ardent nature. Few men took more than four, and many who did found themselves regretting the demands.

Old One Arm hadn't understood that. That he had divorced his first two brides after only a few months had made their fathers angry. Now their daughters were spoiled goods and few men wanted them. Still, the fathers had only complained to Big Mouth, fearing the chiefs if word got out that they had given their daughters to One Arm. Big Mouth didn't know what had happened to the third bride except that Captain Ten Eyke had thrown her out of the fort because he was angry with General One Arm.

On this trip into Big Horn country, Big Mouth did not have the protection of Taylor's guards and he knew he would have to be very careful. He sought out small encampments and settled down with them for a night. He asked in a roundabout way about young women who might be eligible for marriage. He passed around a couple of cups of rum from what looked like a short supply. He smoked cigars and showed off the railroad watch the general had given him a couple of months back, but he couldn't get any of these hicks to understand the point of knowing what time it was. Actually, the thing was useless out there, but the children would sit for hours with the watch pressed to their ears until their mothers and fathers demanded it back so they could listen too.

Big Mouth passed out slivers of soap, which went over well, and he showed some of the men how to play cards and won ten buffalo robes. It made him smile to see how foolish these backwoods people were.

All the while, he was traveling in a big circle around the main camp of the Bad Faces, which he was told had grown to enormous size in the last months and now held some two thousand warriors. Most of the scattered bands Big Mouth met thought Red Cloud's army was stronger than General One Arm's, though the white men's bullets had much wakan to them.

By his third week out, Big Mouth knew where the Bad Face camp was heading—toward Fort C.F. Smith. Rumor had it that Red Cloud would try to burn down the fort with pitch arrows the way Young Man Afraid and his warriors had almost managed to burn the hayfield corral the year before. The huge army didn't move too fast, but it would arrive at the fort in a couple of weeks. The women and children would camp thirty miles away in Bad Bear Pass. The braves would see if they couldn't bottle up the fort and wear down or overrun the garrison.

Big Mouth marveled at the audacity of Red Cloud. He had never heard of an Indian's capturing a fort, and he was certain, being acquainted with the big guns and ample stocks of powder, that Red Cloud couldn't do it. But the boldness! And to get so many warriors to follow him! General One Arm would want to know this. It was just what Big Mouth had been sent to find out.

During his third week out a messenger caught up with Big Mouth and asked if it were true that he was looking for a wife for the soldier chief. When Big Mouth said it might be, the messenger said he represented Lone Claw, the father of a girl who might be suitable. Big Mouth questioned him and decided that she did sound like just the sort General One Arm favored—thirteen years old, slight with a pretty face and untouched.

"Where is this Lone Claw?"

"At the camp of the Bad Faces."

"Ask him to come here." The last thing Big

Mouth wanted to do was walk into the Bad Face camp.

"No, you must go to him. Lone Claw has a twisted foot. He doesn't ride or hunt and the family is poor and needs gifts to live on."

Big Mouth was reluctant, but eventually his greed won out over caution. He agreed to return with the messenger.

They arrived at the Bad Face camp the next night. Big Mouth hoped to slip in and out of camp in one evening.

But as he rode toward what the messenger said was Lone Claw's tepee, he found himself surrounded by heavily armed warriors and his four mules and stock of trade goods were taken from him.

"What is this?" he demanded.

"What are you doing here, Filthy Mouth?"

Big Mouth recognized the speaker at once. Crazy Horse! The leader of the Kit Foxes! Big Mouth's heart beat wildly, but he knew he didn't dare show fear.

"I've come to trade. See? Those braves are poking through my goods. Make them stop."

"Out buying more Sioux children?" Crazy Horse inquired.

Big Mouth's heart thumped even harder. "No, no, just trading." Had they heard about his mission? Knowing the Sioux love of gossip, he must assume they had. He thought quickly as he looked around at the cold, blank faces. Surely someone who had been around the whites as long as he had could outthink these bumpkins.

Crazy Horse eased up to Big Mouth, took his left arm and squeezed. Big Mouth gasped as pain shot across his chest. The crowd around him laughed and he was ashamed to realize that he had emptied his bowels.

Releasing him, Crazy Horse shouted, "Buffalo Woman, Senla, Merleen, take this mouse away and see if you can peel his skin off in one piece."

Big Mouth backed away in terror as the women came at him. He knew what Sioux women could do. They were incomparably cruel at torturing prisoners. They had patience, whereas a brave got bored and hacked his prisoner to death after a couple of hours.

"No, Crazy Horse!" Big Mouth howled as the women reached him. "I'll give you everything I've brought with me. No! No! I am a Sioux!"

The women lashed his hands together and carried him off, followed by an eager crowd of children, other women and youths. Whenever he saw a face he knew, Big Mouth pleaded for help. It wasn't right. He hadn't done anything wrong.

"You stole our daughters," Black Buffalo Woman accused him.

"I didn't!"

"The girls were used badly by the One Arm chief," the woman went on. "The last one lives in my lodge now. It is evil what he did to her."

Big Mouth didn't know what she was talking about. "No, she's fine. I saw her."

"What are you waiting for?" shouted a woman in the crowd.

Big Mouth tried to plead, but he was roughly thrown against a tree and lashed to it. He was gagged and his head bound to the tree. He felt his clothes being cut off and ripples of fear flickered across his fat stomach as hands touched him below.

The hands twisted his genitals and he cringed

and tried to yell, but the sound was muffled by the gag. He steeled himself, expecting to lose his genitals at any moment, but the hands let go.

He began to sweat. Oh, why had he let General One Arm talk him into this? Please God, give me a fast death. Please please please.

Big Mouth became aware of an argument among the women as to who would make the first cut. Finally it seemed to be decided. Big Mouth lunged uselessly against his bonds. He felt a sharp prick, and then the cold blade of the knife slide slowly through his rolls of fat. Big Mouth's gorge rose. He began to moan, tried to suck in his belly.

"Stop!"

Big Mouth wasn't sure what he heard because of the roaring in his ears.

"Take the knife out of him, Senla." It was the same authoritative male voice. Big Mouth felt the knife jerked out of him.

"Take off that gag," the voice commanded.

Out of the corner of his eye Big Mouth saw Red Cloud. With relief he said, "Cut me down too. This is a mistake."

"What are you doing here?" Red Cloud asked.

"He's ours," one of the women in the crowd called. She threw a stick at Big Mouth and cut him on the lip.

"Stop it!" shouted Red Cloud. He turned back to Big Mouth. "I asked what you're doing here."

Big Mouth gave his usual answer, that he had come trading.

"I don't want to trade with you," said Red Cloud. "I want to know what strength the whites have and how best to attack them."

"What?"

"How many troops does General One Arm have? Is it true he plans to attack our villages? How many howitzers does he have? Are they all on wheels? How many horses are in each fort?"

"I don't know."

"Don't you live at the fort?"

"At Laramie, you know that."

"But you visit Kearny, Reno and C.F. Smith." Red Cloud looked old and sinister in the torchlight.

"I'd gladly tell you if I knew." Big Mouth struggled to grin. "Look at me. I want to help."

Red Cloud smiled a weary smile of acknowledgment. "If I don't get what I want the women will continue."

"No! I am Lakota."

Red Cloud spit into his face. "You are not Lakota, you are a Laramie loafer. I have no respect for you. Even a white I respect more."

"You're going to let them kill me?"

"Crazy Horse and his women have a quarrel with you. I won't interfere."

"Not even if I tell you how you can beat the whites?"

"How to beat them?"

"Yes, I know how."

Big Mouth had Red Cloud's attention.

The chief asked, "Well? What is it you know?"

"First let me go. Promise you'll keep them from killing me."

"All right, but just remember, if you don't tell me the truth I'll turn you back over to them."

* * *

Amid much jeering and shouts of disappointment from the women, Big Mouth was cut down, given a blanket to hide his portly nakedness and led to Red Cloud's tepee.

Shortly thereafter a group of war chiefs met with the two. Big Mouth's ordeal with the women had taken everything out of him. He had been raised as a Lakota and as a boy had hunted and ridden with the bravest warriors, but his easy life in the shadow of Fort Laramie had softened him. All he wanted now was to get out, and the truth looked like the best way.

So he told them the story of his travels into the woods to find wives for the general, and how the general had thrown back the women when he tired of them. Most of the chiefs had heard it, but it shocked them all over again. He told them he had been sent here to find another wife and to learn where their camps were headed. He had not planned to give the general this information, he said, but that was what One Arm wanted.

"To know where we camp!" exclaimed High Backbone. "He wants to attack our villages, just like Chivington and Harney did to the Cheyenne. To kill our women and children."

"They're savages," said Two Moon. The rest shook their heads in disbelief that men could be so barbaric.

"Now, how can we beat One Arm?" asked Red Cloud. "That was what you promised to tell me when the women had you."

The wound in his belly ached, but Big Mouth paid it little attention. The faces of the chiefs sitting around Red Cloud's lodge looked menacing. These were men who had fought hand to hand for years against Pawnee, Crow and white soldiers. They were as hard as stones. No matter what he told them, he would be lucky to get away alive. Then a flash of inspiration hit him.

"I think, like you, that General One Arm wants to attack your villages. I had no choice but to come here. He said he would kill me if I didn't find him a wife and tell him where your villages are. I planned to lie."

"I don't believe you," High Backbone growled.

"Let him finish," Red Cloud grunted.

"It's true!" Big Mouth was still so frightened he believed it himself. 'I thought I'd tell him some place where you had been and when he got there you'd be gone. I could say you'd moved."

"And if he didn't find any signs of our camp?" asked Two Moon. "What would happen to you then?"

For a moment Big Mouth hesitated. "I hadn't thought that far. By then I'd be back at Fort Laramie anyway."

The chiefs jeered and called him a liar. Several suggested throwing him back to the women. Big Mouth lost hope. How did they expect him to think clearly when they all glared at him like that? It was dark in here, too, not like the lamplit houses that Big Mouth was used to at Laramie. All right, he thought, kill me and get it over with.

"You're not much of one, but you're still Sioux. Are you willing to help your brothers?" Red Cloud sounded surprisingly gentle.

The kindness lifted Big Mouth's spirits. "Help? Me? How?"

402

"Let's kill him." High Backbone's hand was on his knife. "Or let the women kill him."

"No, Big Mouth's going to help us."

"Yes, I'd like to," Big Mouth gabbled. "After all, I am a Brulé, and my grandfather rode with yours on many raids."

"Yes," said Red Cloud. "I thought you could tell General One Arm where we are, but tell him the wrong place."

"The wrong place?"

"So he attacks the wrong place."

Big Mouth saw it. "Ah! While he's out you'll attack somewhere else! Maybe the fort."

"But this one surely lies," High Backbone was filled with disgust.

"I won't lie—I mean, I'll lie only for you." Sweat trickled down Big Mouth's chest; it sought out and stung his wound.

"High Backbone is right. Suppose you don't do as we say?" asked Red Cloud. "How do we prevent that?"

Big Mouth saw the problem. Once he was back at a fort, no matter how angry the chiefs were they would have a difficult time getting hold of him. But these were a superstitious bunch. Maybe the old superstitions would work. It was worth a try.

"I could swear to you by Wakan-Takan and all my dead ancestors that I will not betray you," Big Mouth offered.

Several chiefs gasped. "I don't think we can ask more than that," said Red Cloud.

Old Hump was summoned. He was shocked by the request to administer such an oath to Big Mouth.

"This is a serious undertaking, Big Mouth," the shaman admonished him. "You don't have enough character to keep such a vow."

"All I have to do is tell the truth, isn't it? I can do that, Uncle."

So the oath, amid much pipe-smoking and chanting by Old Hump, was administered to Big Mouth. It took the better part of an hour, but Big Mouth was delighted by the length of the ceremony. Every hour they put off killing him decreased the odds that they ever would.

What he agreed to do was this: tell One Arm that Red Cloud's people were camped on North Stump, a low butte thirty miles southwest of Fort Kearny, when really they would be at South Stump, a twin butte some ten miles away. The tribes would post lookouts. When most of the general's forces set out on the campaign to wipe out the camp on North Stump, Red Cloud would move to Fort Kearny or Fort Smith and attack. Big Mouth planned to go back to Fort Laramie before any of the shooting started.

"Meanwhile our women and children will be safe," said Red Cloud. "And with most of the troops gone, we should be able to burn down the fort."

Then Two Moon frightened Big Mouth all over again. "Provided this one doesn't betray us to the whites. Red Cloud, I trust you. For two years now you've led us into battle and we've done well, but I don't see the sense of trusting this rabbit." Murmurs of agreement passed around the room.

Big Mouth heard them with a sinking heart. "I've taken the most powerful oath possible," he reminded them. "I will tell General One Arm that you plan to camp on North Stump."

"You will not betray us?" High Backbone asked harshly. "You will not go back and tell your white friends what fools we were to trust you?"

"No, I'm Sioux. I've taken an oath. Would any of you betray such an oath?"

With relief Big Mouth saw that this settled it, for of course not one of these superstitious fools would. Not that Big Mouth didn't take the oath seriously. For all his time with whites at Fort Laramie, he took Sioux religious practices seriously. He had seen too many disasters visited on men who didn't heed their relationship with Wakan-Takan.

At dawn the next day Big Mouth set out for Fort Kearny.

Chapter 31

"North Stump?" asked Connor. "You sure, Big Mouth?"

"Yes, sir." The Laramie loafer trembled as he answered.

Connor regarded him warily. While he was certain that Big Mouth was too frightened of him to take a chance on lying, he still didn't trust him. Trouble with all Injuns was none of them knew what they saw when they saw it. Half of them saw a crow and thought it was their dead grandmother. "You real sure now?"

"Yes, sir. I met with Red Cloud and High Backbone. They told me."

"You didn't," Connor scoffed. "You ain't important enough. You never sat with them in your life."

"I traded with them. I got the robes I brought in."

Can I believe him? Connor wondered. "Hawkins!" The officer of the day stepped into the office and Connor ordered him to get his staff in there on the double. When the five young officers were assembled, Connor stood before the map on the wall. "All right, Big Mouth, show us."

Big Mouth swayed. "I can't read the map, sir. North Stump, that's all I know."

With a look of disgust Connor showed him where the wavy lines marked North Stump and contrasted it with South Stump.

"By what route will they come to the fort?" asked Connor.

"I don't know, sir. All I know is that they plan to attack the fort after they've made camp there."

"What happens if we attack them first, sir?" asked Hawkins.

"They won't expect that, will they?" Connor demanded.

"No sir."

Captain John Gallager, who had taken Ten Eyke's place, suggested, "Suppose we put somebody out there to watch and see when they arrive?"

"Who?"

"A scout. Perhaps Bridger?"

"Suppose they see him?" Connor shook his head.

"That's why we send a scout. He'll know how to keep hidden."

"What do you think, Big Mouth?" Connor asked.

"Yes sir."

"Yes sir what?"

"You'll know when they get there."

"Get Bridger in here," Connor ordered.

But when the old scout looked at the map, he scowled. "Don't make sense to me. How come they're bringing the women and children so close to the fort, Big Mouth?"

Big Mouth shrugged. "I only know what they said they were going to do. They talked about making a big fight, wiping out the soldiers."

"What's these little markings here, Mr. Hawkins?" Bridger pointed.

"Those? Rocks, sir."

"And these wavy lines?"

"Cliffs."

"Don't make sense, General," Bridger concluded. "Look at this map. If you was Red Cloud, would you pick a gentle slope like North Stump to put your women and children on, or South Butte, which is more like a fortress?"

"South, of course."

Bridger turned to Big Mouth. "How about it? You sure they're going to camp on North Stump?"

"Yes, I'm sure."

Connor saw how nervous Big Mouth looked. He had been around the Indian for several months and he knew him pretty well. Something wasn't right. Without saying a word, while Big Mouth's attention was focused on Bridger, Connor picked up the poker from the fireplace and suddenly whacked Big Mouth across the buttocks as hard as he could. Big Mouth went sprawling face down on the floor. Connor walked over and put his heel on Big Mouth's hand, pinning it to the floor.

"Now talk," he snarled. "What's going on?"

"Hey, leave him alone, General," Bridger protested. "That man's a scout of ours."

"No, he's a goddamn liar." Connor bore down on Big Mouth's hand. They heard a bone crack and Big Mouth began a howl that set even Connor's teeth on edge.

"Shut him up," Bridger winced.

"Stop that bellowing and talk to me, damnit!" Connor shouted at Big Mouth. "Or so help me I'll make gooseberry jam out of your hand." He rolled his heel, ready to come down on another finger.

"No! No! Stop!" Big Mouth gasped. "I'll tell you."

"What are you going to tell?" Connor demanded. "The truth!"

"Go ahead. If it sounds like the truth I'll let up. But if it doesn't I'm going to finish this hand and start in on the other."

It took Connor five minutes to get the truth out of the creature on the floor. Red Cloud planned to move to South Stump, just as Bridger had suspected from looking at the map. He had had the gall to think he could use Big Mouth to bait a trap. North Stump indeed! What chief wouldn't put his people into a natural fortress on top of a hill? But if a modern general knew about that fortress and mapped out a way of getting in there beforehand, maybe even sneaking in at night, he could take that camp apart come dawn.

"Put him in the guardhouse." Connor indicated Big Mouth. "No, put him under it. I don't want no Injuns talking to him. I don't want anybody to know he's there. Can you do that, Gallager?"

"Yes, sir!"

"No mistakes now. This could cost a lot of lives if Red Cloud thinks we haven't fallen for his trick."

"Don't worry, sir. I'll wrap him in your office rug here and take him over to the jail personally, sir."

"Good man. And make it fast. I can't stand that whimpering."

"Sir, if anybody asks, what happened to him?"

"Tell 'em he's gone back to Laramie to report to the peace commission."

Getting the truth out of Big Mouth made Connor feel wonderful. He rubbed the stump of his arm with his good hand. "Now, let's make plans, gentlemen, for the biggest victory the United States Army has ever won from the red vermin. We're going to put Fort Kearny on the map and obliterate the shame of the Fetterman massacre."

His officers gave a little cheer of approval and in it Connor heard the first fanfare of his nascent political career. General George Connor, hero of the Civil War, greatest Indian fighter of the West, now candidate for the United States Senate and after that—the Presidency!

Taking the general's best telescope and four picked woodsmen, Jim Bridger set up camp on a cliff some four miles from South Stump. For a week the five kept watch through the telescope. Every day one of the woodsmen rode to Kearny to report that they had seen no Indians.

After ten days of such reports, Connor's spirits sagged. He had his battle plans drawn up and he had been over and over them with Gallager and the rest of the staff. They would give Red Cloud and his chiefs the day of their arrival to get settled. The next dawn two hundred infantrymen would come rushing up the south draw, the easy way to the top of the butte. Using Henrys and a howitzer, they would make as much fuss as they could. Connor figured Red Cloud would defend against the attack as he got his people off the butte the back way.

For once the red varmints would have to engage in a stand-up fight. Connor himself would be on the back side of the butte with three hundred cavalrymen. No sooner would the Indians assemble at the foot of the butte than Connor and his men would swoop down. Connor hoped they would resist. He'd mow them down with shrapnel from the howitzers he planned to emplace during the night. If they surrendered instead, Connor would emulate Colonel Chivington and pile up all their travois, tepees, hides and parfleches and burn them. That would take the spunk out of them. Some of them would resist, though, and those his men would speedily kill. The rest they would escort to the reservation on the upper Missouri. By then the degraded Sioux would be a pretty tame bunch, and he, George Connor, would have the credit.

But for ten days no sign of Indians was reported. On the eleventh day the rider reported that several Indian scouts had been seen and said Bridger told him not to go back to the outpost because he might be seen.

Connor was ecstatic. He made sure his officers and troops were ready to move out on four hours' notice.

Two nights later at midnight, the officer of the day woke him up. Bridger had sent another messenger. All day warriors and tepees of Red Cloud's band had filed up the slope of South Stump and some two thousand Sioux were there. The best time to attack would be at dawn today or tomorrow.

At once Connor realized he couldn't hit today; the butte was too far away. He planned the attack for the following dawn. Again the messenger had been told not to ride back to Bridger's camp, so he joined the men in the cavalry. Everybody wanted to be in on the turkey shoot.

By three o'clock the next morning Captain Gallager had his men in place at the foot of the draw leading to the top of South Stump. Connor by now was to have his cavalrymen on the other side of the Butte. The plan was for Gallager to rush his infantry up the slope as fast as he could, putting so much pressure on the Sioux that they would flee. The only weak feature of the plan, as far as Connor and Gallager could figure, was that they might take too much time and give the Sioux a chance to dig in. In time Connor and his troops could starve the Indians out, but nobody wanted to go through the slow ordeal of a siege. No, better to take a few losses in a rush up the slope and hit the camp directly. With any luck the Indians wouldn't be expecting an attack.

Gallager had one other reason for wanting to get to the top of the butte fast. He knew that Connor had placed himself where he could make the best captures and kills of the battle. If Gallager could get his men up that hill in a hurry, they might be able to overrun the camp before any Indians had a chance to get down the hill. In that case, John Gallager would be the hero of the Battle of South Stump, not that mangy bear Connor.

The captain's mouth felt dry. His pocket watch read four o'clock. A little grey showed in the east. Today he had the chance to boost his military career.

At four-thirty Gallager passed the word. His pistol drawn, he got to his feet. Rushing to the top meant traversing a boulder-strewn path three quarters of a mile long. The three howitzers would be pulled up at

412

the rear of the charge, ready to fire at any pockets of Indians who opposed them.

As he moved up the slope Gallager was delighted to hear almost no sound behind him. He had taken special care that his men shouldn't carry coins in their pockets or wear any clanky gear. He had had the wheels of the howitzers packed with grease, but he noted with annoyance that they still squeaked a bit.

Ten minutes later, halfway up the slope, the sky was light enough that they could clearly make out the ghostly boulders and each other. Behind him Gallager saw them spread out across the slope in a long line some four men deep. Above him a forward patrol of ten dodged from boulder to boulder looking for sentries. Somewhere along about here the Indians could announce themselves with an arrow that clinked against a rock or the slap of a bullet, and any chance of surprise would be over.

By a quarter of five Gallager could see the first tepee on the rim of the butte, but no one had spotted a single Indian. The captain could hardly believe his luck as he pressed upward. Either the Indians hadn't posted sentries or they had silently made their way up the hill wide of the soldiers' rush to warn the others. But if they had, surely the Indians would have swarmed out. No Sioux cowered in his tepee while soldiers rushed his village.

He reached the top of the butte and saw a cluster of tepees. Nothing moved in the eerie light. Soon the sun would break through the mist. Gallager turned back to the slope, where the bulk of his men were nearing the crest. He waved them forward and with his other hand motioned for quiet.

What luck! He would place his men around the

tepees. When the Sioux rushed out, the men could shoot them. He almost laughed. Old One Arm had outsmarted himself. While he sat on his nag at the bottom of the back side of the butte, Gallager would take the entire village.

Silently he waved his men into place. The three hundred crouched into firing positions, the sun at their backs so the panicked Indians would be dazzled. Still no one came out of the tepees. Gallager began to feel something was wrong; his men hadn't been *that* quiet. Then up came the howitzers, squeaking, the mules heaving and blowing. Gallager hustled them into position.

"Start firing," he whispered to the artillery gunners.

The four-inch guns had been loaded with shrapnel before they left Kearny, and it was the work of seconds to aim them, touch the fuses with lighted punk and blow holes through the six nearest tepees.

"Fire!" Gallager shouted this time and his three hundred foot soldiers opened up with their rifles. For the next ten minutes the air was filled with gunfire. The tepees shuddered as if a hailstorm were blowing through them.

But still no Sioux appeared. Increasingly worried, Gallager looked behind him. Something was wrong, dreadfully wrong. You didn't shoot at a man's house and see no one come out, not if there was someone in it. He looked around the camp, then behind at his troops, wondering if the Sioux had abandoned the village as his men made their way up the slope and were now preparing to attack from the rear. But he saw nothing but a few ghostly stunted trees.

"Cease firing!" shouted Gallager, but it took several minutes for the guns to stop.

When the men moved forward to investigate what was left of the tepees, they didn't find a single body in the wreckage. The entire village was deserted.

"Could they have escaped down the back way?" asked a sergeant.

"Maybe, maybe not." Gallager shrugged. "If they did, they've run right into One Arm."

Just then gunfire erupted from the back of the Butte.

"That's it, sergeant," said the disappointed Gallager. "That's what must have happened. Never mind. We may have missed them, but it sounds as if the general has the situation well in hand."

Down below, during the barrage at the top of the mesa, Connor had made sure his troopers were hidden on the other side of Sandman's Waterfall, out of sight of any Indian rushing down the trail. The Sioux ought to come down disorganized as hell, he figured, their goods bumping along behind them. It shouldn't be hard to wipe out the whole bunch if they tried to flee and half of them if they didn't.

When the firing had continued for many minutes and not a soul came down, Connor couldn't understand it. Strange! When the firing stopped, he decided to investigate. Taking Hawkins, he walked back toward the base of the butte, crossing the stream in front of the waterfall.

The two emerged from the shallow water and Connor still saw no one. As he turned to speak to Hawkins, the lieutenant began to gurgle and sank to the ground scrabbling to pull an arrow out of his throat.

Instantly alert, Connor pulled out his pistol and went into a crouch. Hearing a slight noise, he turned to see a pair of Indians rushing him. He raised his pistol and shot one, but the other came on.

The warrior had a tomahawk raised. As quickly as he could, Connor fired his second pistol, but he was too slow. The tomahawk hit him on the shoulder, jarring him all the way to his toes, and he went down. He pulled himself to his knees and threw himself into the stream. Wading, stumbling, crawling, he crossed the two-foot-deep creek. He turned to see behind him and recognized the war dress that Ten Eyke and Richards had described so often: red-painted face, black hands and ears, eagle feathers in the hair, yellow slashes on the arms. Red Cloud!

Eager for the kill, Connor reached for his pistols and realized that he had lost one of them in his mad scramble across the stream. He pulled the other and raised it, but before he could fire his target moved out of range.

Damn! From behind him he heard gunfire. His men! Somehow the battle had started, but where had these Indians come from? Not down the path from the top of the butte.

On the way back Connor ran into more Indians, who cut him off from his men. Connor had only the six shots in his remaining gun, and Hawkins, who reloaded for him, lay dead on the trail. Connor ran for cover among the boulders to his left. Over and over he shouted, "Grimes! Henley! Johnson!" but he got no response. All he heard from his troopers was the sound of rifles. From time to time during lulls in the firing, he thought he heard men running through the bushes, but he couldn't be certain. What was going on? Where had all these Indians come from?

Protected by three large boulders that formed natural gun ports, Connor moved from one to another, cursing the Indians and firing. In a few minutes he was down to one bullet. Damn! Damn! Damn! He knew what many men did in this situation: they shot themselves rather than let the Sioux capture them. But he didn't want to do that. By now his troops were probably polishing off the Sioux.

But somehow Connor couldn't quite convince himself of that. Red Cloud hadn't just happened to be down here ready to pounce when he was supposed to be up on the top of the butte. Red Cloud had been down here on purpose, and probably with lots of men.

Peering out between the boulders, Connor saw a shadow slide again a tree. Here comes another, he thought. He cocked the pistol. I guess I'll have to do it. But the idea made him furious.

Connor pushed himself flat against the rock to wait, hoping he was out of sight of the brave. It would give him minutes more if the savage didn't know what to expect.

He thought he heard something just on the other side of the boulder. "Grimes! Help! Henley! Help!" he shouted one last time.

No answer. Connor felt flushed and icy at the same time. Sweat ran down his armpits as cold as rain. He didn't want to shoot himself. That was a coward's way out. The bone butt of his gun felt cold and slippery in his hand. His breathing was labored, as if he had been holding his breath to see with his ears what was happening on the other side of the boulder. The tiniest noise had the effect of an explosion on his nerves.

Minutes passed. Connor put the cold gun barrel to his temple. He would sit it out. The men would sooner or later come searching for him. If they found him first, he'd live. If the Indians got to him first, he'd kill himself.

Suddenly he heard a shout and looked up. There on top of one of the boulders stood an Indian painted in violent blue, yellow, red and orange. Connor reflexively turned the pistol from his own head, aimed it at the warrior and fired. The Indian fell over backward.

Damn! thought Connor. No more bullets in the gun. He slipped to his knees and spread out the bullets from his pocket on the ground. Jamming the barrel of the pistol between his legs, with his one hand he flicked open the chamber and began to insert shells. They kept sliding out of his grasp like little balls of quicksilver.

Bits of leaf and mud clung to the shells he put into the gun. As he closed the cylinder he hoped the debris wouldn't jam the mechanism.

Just then a shrieking Sioux jumped down into the pit with him. Startled, Connor rose from his knees and swung the pistol around. Before he got it on target it went off. The Indian threw himself forward, hitting Connor and knocking him back.

Connor struggled to hold onto the gun, but his hand hit a boulder and the pistol was knocked away. With savage energy Connor pushed his opponent back; then he recognized him as the man he had seen on the other side of the stream: Red Cloud!

The chief had a knife in his hand. He scrambled

to his feet and moved toward Connor, who scooped up a stone the size of a small cannonball. As Red Cloud came closer, Connor brought up the stone and heaved it into the chief's stomach. The blow knocked him to the ground, where he sat as if the air had been kicked out of him. Connor looked around for his gun. Seeing it wedged between two boulders, he dived for it, but a firm grip on his ankle brought him down. Hard ropelike arms encircled him.

Connor rolled and managed to get a grip on Red Cloud's neck. Since he had lost his left arm his right was abnormally strong. His fingers circled his attacker's throat and squeezed. If he could get a good grip and the right purchase, Connor could break the chief's neck.

He bore down and felt Red Cloud's bear hug loosen. He bore down harder still and the two rolled over and over, bumping into the boulders. Connor raised himself slightly to get a better purchase and felt a blow to his groin that left him dizzy with pain. For a moment his fingers relaxed. It was all Red Cloud needed to slip out of Connor's grasp.

The two pulled away from each other and sat on opposite sides of the pit glaring at each other and panting with exertion. With a stirring of hope, Connor saw the butt of the pistol still sticking out between the two boulders, but Red Cloud followed his glance and was prepared to cut him off. Connor hardly trusted himself to move, but if he didn't make a play for the gun, sooner or later the Indian would.

They sprang forward at the same time and met in a bone-crushing clash. Again they rolled about the little pit. Flailing away, trying again to reach the throat, Connor's hand struck the knife Red Cloud had dropped. He brought it up blindly and stabbed, feeling it sink into the chief's flesh. Then he saw that he had hit only the shoulder.

Red Cloud grabbed Connor's hand with both of his, forced the knife out of his shoulder and turned the knife back on Connor. The blade slowly drove toward Connor's throat. He tried with all his might to resist but wasn't strong enough. Relentlessly, a fraction of an inch at a time, the blade moved down.

Everything seemed to slow then. Connor saw the corded muscles in Red Cloud's neck and the sun glistening on the blade, felt the ground slip under him as they strained against each other, heard his own harsh breathing. Slowly, slowly, death descended, and whenever Connor gathered the strength to push it back an inch or two, he reached his limit. The blade kept coming.

Finally he felt it touch his neck, just a prick. Then he felt something cold inside as the blade slid in. He wanted to shout, but his throat was full. Blood! Then he felt a bone snap under the blade and knew nothing could save him.

Chapter 32

"Sir, we just can't keep that road open." Ulysses Grant stood before President Andrew Johnson.

"We have to." The President blinked up at him from behind the desk.

"Can't. We have to face reality."

"Damn! I thought this man Connor was the best."

"He was," Grant answered. "He got his tail caught in a crack. I hated losing One Arm. Look at it practically, sir. Feeding the Indians will be cheaper than fighting them. We spend two hundred thousand dollars a year on them, and we save the five million a year we've spent on this war."

Johnson looked around his office like a man longing to escape. His voice was hoarse. "But it'll look so bad, just abandoning those forts after we fought so hard to establish them."

"With what the Congress gives me, sir, I can't keep troops garrisoned in the South as well as fight the Indians out West. Of course, we could transfer men."

"No, I'm not suggesting we pull any troops out of the South. God forbid."

"Three forts, sir. That's all. Kearny, Reno and Smith."

The President cleared his throat. "Will closing them prevent the construction of the Union Pacific in any way?"

"To the contrary, it should advance it. I'll use those troops to beef up the guard on the construction gangs."

Andrew Johnson gave a long sigh. The last three years had told on him. He looked dilapidated, like a wall crumbling under too-harsh weather.

Grant figured the President had to take his recommendation but would resist for the show of it. He had no respect for Andrew Johnson; he figured the man had brought his troubles on himself. If things went according to plan, in a few weeks Ulysses S. Grant, he who had won the Civil War, would be nominated for the Presidency. Better to get the tough decisions out of the way before he took over. The cleaner his plate after he was elected, the easier would be his job.

Johnson stood up and paced the floor.

Grant continued, "Once we have the Union Pacific running, we won't need the Bozeman Trail."

"Well, Congress is so tight with money—and there are all those do-gooders who want to make the red man happy—maybe it would be for the best," Johnson conceded. "Will the redskins sign that treaty if we pull out? Especially this chief I hear so much about, Red Cloud."

"That's a problem."

"A problem?"

"I have a report with me signed by the commission. It contains Red Cloud's exact words."

"Well?"

Grant pulled a paper from his tunic. He unfolded it and began to read. "We are on the mountains looking down on the soldiers and the forts. When we see the soldiers moving away and the forts abandoned, then I will come down and talk."

Johnson looked at him speechless, then found his voice. "An Indian sends me that? The gall of the man! We'll leave the forts *after* he's signed the treaty."

"The commission makes it clear that they've already explored it with him. We have to pull out before he'll talk."

"How's that going to look in the papers?" Johnson sounded forlorn. "I can't do that. The western papers will crucify me."

"Yes sir."

"We beat the Confederacy in the bloodiest war in history and this naked savage dares dictate terms?"

Grant sighed. How he hated civilian ninnies. Go over it with him again, he told himself. Get this thorn out of your side before next year. But Grant could see it clearly. It was just this inability to face reality that had landed Johnson in so much trouble.

"Sir, I can beat this chief, and with ease. With five thousand well-trained troops I can bring you back his head in a sack."

"I don't want his head," Johnson whined. "They'd ride me out of this town on a rail. Besides, Congress won't approve one more soldier for the army's rolls; you know that."

"Then let's get along without the forts. The Northern Pacific will be built soon and that'll provide easy access to Montana."

Johnson gave in. "All right. I'll go along. But it's going to look damn silly, going to all the trouble to build the forts only to abandon them now."

"It would look a damn sight worse to keep pouring money into a road we can't keep open," countered Grant.

"I've said all right. Good-bye."

The general turned to leave, but Johnson stopped him. "This bid of yours for the Presidency—you're serious about it, aren't you?"

"I think so."

"You're a damn fool," Johnson said sourly.

Grant raised his eyebrows.

Johnson went on, "Oh, I know what's said about me, that I'm the fool. That any idiot could have avoided getting himself impeached." Now his face looked ugly, dark with rage and grief. "But you don't know them, General, you don't know them."

"Who, sir?"

"All of them. At first they love you, all of them. Then they're querulous, wanting this and that. You find after a while that everyone wants something. Then when they see that you can't satisfy them—and you can't, General—every last one of them turns on you."

For a moment the words hung in the air. Grant felt embarrassed for the President. He was a practical man and didn't know how to answer. He didn't think he would get into such a mess. But maybe Johnson was struggling to tell him honestly what he might expect. Well, the last thing Grant wanted was Andrew Johnson's advice.

"Go on," said Johnson with a bitter look. "Go. You'll never understand till you've sat in that chair, and even then I don't think you will. The simple truth is that the job's impossible."

In late July Red Cloud made his camp in the mountains near Fort Phil Kearny. He wanted to watch the abandonment. When the white soldiers were gone he wanted to march into the fort himself.

Sometimes he still found it hard to believe that he had won. True, the wagons now came empty and went away full, a reversal of the pattern of two years before. All the men's wives, servants and children had gone and so had most of the troops. Only a handful of soldiers remained.

And to think that that fool Big Mouth had been the unwitting instrument of his victory. Red Cloud had made sure that no story Big Mouth could divulge to Connor would be the truth and then had sent Crazy Horse and the Kit Foxes to Kearny to watch. When he learned that the scout Bridger was seen on South Stump, Red Cloud knew One Arm had taken the bait. If his warriors hadn't been so eager that morning and dashed forward before he gave the command, they might have wiped out all of the horse soldiers, instead of getting only a dozen—and of course, One Arm himself.

Red Cloud knew that no Indian of any tribe had successfully driven white troopers from their own fort, much less from three. All his struggles to keep the bands together, all his battles along the road, all the deaths his people had suffered—this was his reward. The Lakota would have their hunting lands back and so would their children and their children's children.

Some of Spotted Tail's people said they wanted to live in the forts, but Red Cloud argued against the idea. Better to keep to the old ways. Better not to tempt Wakan-Takan by living the way the white man lived. We have won, let's burn the forts.

Once more he swayed the council against Spotted Tail, who seemed to lose heart toward the end of it. The Brulé chief and most of his people had begun preparations to move to the upper Missouri.

From the army's point of view the abandonment went slowly. It had tried to get the Bureau of Indian Affairs to buy the posts' supplies, but that failed. Some of the supplies were put up for public auction, but this didn't work either because the civilians wouldn't come to the sale for fear of the Sioux. Finally the freighting firm of McKinzie and Story bought some of the supplies at C.F. Smith. The rest were issued to the Crow or abandoned.

The last troops pulled out of Fort Kearny on the first of August. Red Cloud watched them go. When they had disappeared over the hill the chief waved his people forward. Some two hundred warriors and curious women moved cautiously down the hill.

The gate looked strange to Red Cloud without a guard. It was open and he walked in. Piles of abandoned goods lay in the dust of the deserted fort. No one walked about and the buildings looked like ghosts.

Red Cloud walked across the parade ground into a building, alert, cautious, not sure what wakan the whites might have left behind to spring on him. He found himself in a long room with overturned tables. Here the soldiers had eaten together. He walked on and in the rear found the room they used for cooking. A fire still burned in the stove and the remnants of the last meal were scattered about the room. They hadn't bothered to clean up. Red Cloud fished a half-burned stick out of the fire and held it to the trash on the floor. In a moment it caught. A moment more and the room began to fill with smoke. With glee he backed from the room.

The Bad Faces wandered in and out of the buildings, picking up abandoned hats, tunics, clocks, mirrors and ribbons, laughing and pointing to the strange possessions of the whites. They searched but found no guns. Then the noise of the burning mess brought everyone out to the parade ground to watch.

The fire spread to the attached buildings. Crazy Horse and the other Kit Foxes, who had sworn that they would take nothing from the fort, carried brands to the rest of the buildings. As the flames around the parade ground rose, Red Cloud saw that the fire could spread to the gates and trap them all inside. How ironic to die here in a fire! Alarmed, he ordered the Kit Foxes to make sure that everyone left the fort and led the way outside.

Climbing back up the hill, warriors, women and bright-eyed children watched the flames until the whole fort was one roaring firestorm, thundering as it struggled to detach itself to join the fire of the sun. Despite the half-mile between himself and the inferno, Red Cloud grew hotter inside as he watched. It was as if something within him, foreign and intrusive as the fort itself, had grown with the incursions of the whites and now burned with the hated structure. As usual Red Cloud's face showed nothing, but he was awed by the fury of the fire that roared through him. It seemed to rise as high as the flames of the fort, to consume everything in its path in a churning rage.

With deep chagrin, Red Cloud saw clearly that for the past two years he had lived a life of hatred.

As the fires within and without subsided, Red Cloud felt weak. For these past two years he had lived a life only *against*: against the fort, against Connor and Carrington, against any Indian who dared disagree with him. It wasn't right; life must be lived *for*. He could see that now. Tears streaming down his face, Red Cloud thanked Wakan-Takan for showing him the right path while he still had time.

All afternoon the tribe sat on the hilltop and watched. The flames ate up the fort, and sated, lay down to doze fitfully. The women prepared buffalo stew as a general air of celebration bubbled through the tribe. As night fell the site of the burned-out fort took on a different and no less dramatic aspect, a mass of flickering brands spread over acres of chirping night.

That night after the songs of victory and the feasting, Old Hump asked the younger boys to build up the bonfire again and told the Big Bellies that he wanted to address all the Lakota. The boys scurried around gathering firewood and the tribe settled itself around the fire. At Hump's directions, the drummers and flute players stopped their wild individual playing and started a series of owl and buffalo chants, introducing the shaman into the celebration.

When the bonfire was blazing Old Hump stood, looked around at the seated tribe and announced, "This victory marks a turning point for the Lakota. We have fought Pawnee, Comanche, Cheyenne, Crow and Ute, and we have beaten them all. Before, in the time of our fathers' fathers' fathers, we had no horses, only dogs to pull our travois. Today we own hundreds of horses and we are rich. We hunt the buffalo from horseback and a man may take enough meat in a day to keep his lodge for two months. But Wakan-Takan makes the Lakota strong by testing us, the way we make the wood for a bow strong by placing it in a fire. We have been tested and we have come through stronger."

He paused. The drums had stilled and only the roar of the bonfire could be heard. The Sioux stared up at Old Hump's wrinkled face, eerie in the firelight.

"Tonight we Lakota are as one," continued Hump. "We have had much disagreement about what to do with the white ghosts. Tonight the time has come to heal those wounds. I want to hear words from everyone here who has anger and resentment in his heart against another Lakota. I want him to stand and to speak to that person, to tell him what is in his heart and declare that the breach between brothers is healed."

Old Hump moved his sharp gaze around the watching circle. The people sat impassively, as they always would, but he knew that their hearts were fluttering wildly, for he had presented them with a new ceremony that they didn't understand. Old Hump foresaw that in the coming years the Lakota would need all their strength. The white ghosts were strong and determined. If what he had heard from other shamans was true, they would not easily give up their claims to Sioux land.

The drummers began to pound, but Old Hump silenced them and called on Old-Man-Afraid-of-His-Horses, knowing that if he got the oldest and most venerated warrior to speak, the others would follow.

Old Man Afraid stood up at the edge of the assembly and said yes, he had things to say. Black Buf-

falo Woman, peering up at him, saw how stooped he
was. How he had aged in the past year! At the sight
of the old man's frailness something within Buffalo
Woman spun and sank. Was this what happened to
everyone? Would this happen to Crazy Horse too? How
was it possible for the flame of a hard force like Crazy
Horse to gutter and burn out?

"I have regrets to speak about," began Old Man
Afraid. "When men get old, they should know it and
let the younger men lead. I opposed Red Cloud's leadership. I know now that I should have realized he
saw more deeply into these matters than I."

That made Black Buffalo Woman feel good toward him. She saw how his speech had strengthened
the wakan of this night.

Others must have felt the same, for half a dozen
now stood up to speak. Old Hump nodded to Red
Leaf. This chief said that he had harbored resentment
toward the leadership of Young Man Afraid and that
he hoped that Lakota would again have him for a
friend. He had come to see that Young Man Afraid
was a great chief and a brave man. Red Leaf added
that until now he had never realized how much power
Wakan-Takan had given the Lakota.

Blue Chest spoke next and admitted jealousy of
Crazy Horse; and so it went. For two hours chiefs and
warriors stood under the stern eye of Old Hump and
spoke their hearts.

It was long past midnight when Red Cloud rose
to speak. To Black Buffalo Woman he, too, seemed
to have aged overnight. He was too thin, his face gaunt,
and his eyes seemed to look inward. He stood silent
for a long time. When he finally began to speak, his
voice was so low everyone strained to hear him. It

shocked Buffalo Woman to hear her name and that of Crazy Horse.

"It grieves my heart, some of the things I have done to my brother and sister tribesmen these past months. To my own niece and Crazy Horse above all." His eyes found Buffalo Woman. "To win this war I was willing to sacrifice the marriage Black Buffalo Woman had wanted since childhood. I was wrong, niece, and I say it here before all Sioux. I say it to you, too, Crazy Horse. I was wrong."

At this point Red Cloud paused. The fire crackled, but otherwise there was silence.

"The deaths of all the young men who fought to rid our hunting grounds of the whites haunt me. They were our bravest, who left lodges full of wailing women and children and an ache in all our hearts that nothing can ease. What victory is this without them?"

Black Buffalo Woman couldn't understand this part of the speech, for how else could there have been any victory against such a powerful enemy as the white ghosts? But from the nods and mutters of the older people around her, she knew they thought what her uncle was saying was important. She was proud of him. He was obviously a great Lakota and as his niece she shared in that greatness.

To her surprise, Red Cloud said no more; to everyone else's surprise, Crazy Horse rose to speak. A little snicker ran through the crowd. Crazy Horse rarely spoke in public and no one could imagine that he would do it well. The snickering made Black Buffalo Woman angry.

"Thank you, Uncle," Crazy Horse said to Red Cloud. "I have gone into the mountains and chanted and prayed to understand, as Hump advised me, and

I do now, a little. You acted for all our people, not only for your lodge or for the Bad Faces or for your war society."

Black Buffalo Woman listened with possessive delight. But as Crazy Horse spoke she suddenly saw the face she loved twist into an older version of itself and fill with pain. And then she saw the knife stuck in his belly.

She moaned and staggered to her feet to go to him, but strong fingers closed tightly around her arm.

She turned to see Old Hump by her side, his fierce eyes burning. "He's all right," the shaman assured her.

"No!" she countered. "A knife!"

"Not yet," he told her softly.

His calm certainty made her hesitate. She turned to look back at Crazy Horse. The big knife and the terrible wound were gone. The face was twisted only with the effort it took him to speak in public.

Bewildered, she looked back at Hump.

"It may not happen," he said.

"But what is it?"

"The wakan here tonight is strong. Many strange animals and demons are flying around this camp."

She looked back at Crazy Horse and again saw the knife and the face distorted by pain. Again she started toward him and Old Hump's grip stopped her. When she looked once more, the wound had disappeared.

Shivering, Black Buffalo Woman turned to Old Hump.

"Not yet," he confirmed. "But it would be wise for you and Senla to have many children." His smile seemed as old as the mountains and as full of pain. "Boys, if possible. Lakota."

Red Cloud was off hunting buffalo when the messenger from the peace commission caught up with him. Taylor and the others wanted him to come in to Fort Laramie for the parley he had promised the White Father. Red Cloud sent back word that he must take his meat for the winter. It made all the chiefs with Red Cloud laugh to see how the whites chased after him.

After the hunt, Red Cloud called together all the chiefs who had fought with him and all the leaders of the Hunkpapa, Blackfoot, Brulé and Sans Arcs. On November 4, 1868, leading one hundred twenty-five chiefs and tribal leaders, Red Cloud rode into Fort Laramie. Two years before, Spotted Tail had spoken for the Sioux, but there was doubt that he spoke for all. This time there was no doubt about who represented the Sioux.

The chiefs again sat on the parade ground, the commissioners at the table before them. Nathaniel Taylor, looking older and more subdued, came around with the other commissioners to shake the chiefs' hand, a custom of the whites that Red Cloud saw no reason to conform to. He held up his hand, remaining seated, and briefly touched their fingers.

When Red Cloud announced that he wouldn't sign the treaty unless he understood it, Taylor seemed so glad to go over it part by part that the chief became suspicious. Come to think of it, what was he doing there? He had beaten these people; who went to the village of a defeated enemy to make agreements? They should have come to him.

When Red Cloud raised this point, they told him that they had come a long way, all the way from Washington. They spoke often like this, in riddles. Here they had intruded on his hunting grounds for years and when he allowed them to come in and talk, they behaved as if they were doing him a favor.

When Taylor read the part in the treaty about going to the reservation and farming, Red Cloud told him that he had heard all he wanted to about that from others. He knew what it said: that he was allowed to farm on special land to supplement his hunting. They would give him plows, seed corn and even mules, but what Lakota wanted such things? They also wanted him to receive annuities from Harney, but Red Cloud refused to deal with him. His uncle, Old Smoke, knew Harney and had never liked him.

The whites kept bringing up the reservation. He told them he didn't care what the treaty wanted; he didn't like that part of the country and didn't expect to spend much time there.

But he would have to stay on the reservation, they said, if he signed the treaty. He sighed and let it go. Who were they, these people he had beaten, whose forts he had burned, to say where he should camp?

They also told him they were particularly anxious to be on friendly terms with him because they regarded him as a big chief, which Red Cloud accepted as his due. He responded that he wanted powder and lead. When General Dye said he couldn't issue it without General Augur's permission, Red Cloud told him to use the talking wire to ask him. This speech bothered the commissioners, for they hadn't realized that he knew how the wire worked.

It took several more days, but finally, by making the white war chiefs admit they had given powder and lead to the Crow, and that he had to defend himself against them, Red Cloud prevailed. Of course he didn't tell them that no Sioux would waste powder on a mere Crow but would save it for further incursions by whites.

Having got what he wanted, he would touch the pen. Rubbing a little dust on his hands to keep off evil spirits, he asked for the pen.

Taylor and the other commissioners looked startled and a pen was quickly found. Red Cloud carefully made his mark, then he asked the commissioners to touch his pen. After him the other chiefs signed.

He made a speech. He was ready now to make peace as he had made war. The cause of the war had been the Bozeman road and the forts. Now that they were abandoned, he had no need for further fighting. He might have some difficulty at first controlling the younger braves, but he would live up to the treaty as long as the white man did.

He told the commissioners he wasn't sure if he would go to the reservation to accept their presents and rations. He would have to see what was offered before he made up his mind. He made sure they knew that he wanted to visit Fort Laramie from time to time to trade, and he made sure they knew he preferred John Richards to any other white trader.

When Red Cloud finished his speech, Taylor tried to tell him he must go to the reservation now, but he told Yellow Hair he was going after the buffalo.

Were these people crazy? Did they think because he went along with their custom of touching the pen that they had the strength to command him to live on

435

one small piece of ground in a worthless part of the country?

Gathering the chiefs, Red Cloud rose from his place in the center of the enclave and with a great show of dignity led the assembled Sioux tribes back out of Fort Laramie.

Afterword

The treaty of 1868 set aside for the Sioux and Cheyenne all the land in South Dakota west of the Missouri. This the Indians were to regard as "their permanent home and make no permanent home elsewhere." They would be allowed to hunt north of the North Platte River and on the Republican fork of the Smoky Hill River.

The treaty also stated that the country north of the North Platte and east of the Big Horn Mountains was unceded Indian territory. In other words, the treaty recognized Sioux title to the Powder River country but denied the tribe the use of it except to hunt buffalo. This matter remained under contention for some years.

Colonel Henry Carrington had a long hard fight to clear his name. While a commission of nine men met at his house at Fort McPherson and exonerated him for the Fetterman massacre, President Andrew Johnson ordered another strictly military investigation. This court also cleared Carrington, but the findings were suppressed for twenty years. In 1870, the widowed Carrington married Frances Grummond.

Nathaniel Taylor remained a minister. Neither he nor Clarence Simmons ever got a bishopric.

Tenodor Ten Eyke and Cynthia Simmons settled north of San Francisco and Ten Eyke went into the timber business. It was another year before Clarence Simmons agreed to a divorce and then only because he wanted to remarry. Tenodor and Cynthia were married as soon as the divorce was granted. Cynthia was expecting her second child.

Spotted Tail moved to his new reservation, close to that of Big Mouth, who was forced by the government to leave his beloved Fort Laramie. In 1870, in a drunken rage, Big Mouth attacked Spotted Tail, who killed him. In the following years Spotted Tail became an enormous force for peace, winning the respect of both red and white. In 1881, the Brulé Crow Dog, jealous of Spotted Tail's leadership, shot and killed the chief as he rode on the Rosebud reservation.

Crazy Horse didn't sign the Treaty of 1868. In 1876, Sitting Bull, Crazy Horse and thousands of Sioux wiped out General George Armstrong Custer and two hundred sixty-five men at the Battle of Little Big Horn. On May 5, 1877, sick to death of running from federal troops, Crazy Horse finally came to the Red Cloud agency to live in peace. Four months later he tried to jump the reservation and was stopped by agency Sioux and brought to Fort Laramie.

The Indian guards took Crazy Horse to the guardhouse. When he saw that he was to be imprisoned, he put up a fight. According to one story, Little Big Man accidentally turned a knife so that it stuck into Crazy Horse's stomach. According to another, a sentry bayoneted him. That night, with his father and mother by his side, the last of the fighting Sioux died. Black Buffalo Woman for a time went wild with grief, but she eventually remarried and died at ninety-one.

Red Cloud remained a great chief all through the reservation period. In 1870, along with Spotted Tail and several dozen Sioux chiefs and their wives, he rode the iron horse east to meet with the Great White Father, President Ulysses S. Grant.

For the first time he saw a train. The sight of Omaha stunned these chiefs, but it was nothing beside the shock of Chicago.

In Washington, the chiefs visited several military installations in a tour designed to impress them with the futility of opposing the government. The lesson wasn't lost on the chiefs. Shortly after his return from Washington, Red Cloud moved onto the reservation.